Kurt Austin and the NUMA team are up against perilous waters, frigid temperatures, and a terrifying superweapon as they unravel a decades-old conspiracy in the latest thrilling adventure in the *New York Times*–bestselling series.

Praise for the NUMA Files® Series

"Fantastic, edge-of-your-seat stories." —*Parade*

"[The novels] invoke the classic feel of James Bond reimagined as an oceanographer." —*Associated Press*

"A sure bet for those who crave high-concept adventure." —*Booklist*

"Fast-paced, nonstop fun." —*Kirkus Reviews*

"It's always fun to watch the NUMA guys and gals implementing their clever plans." —*Publishers Weekly*

"Breathtakingly suspenseful, wildly inventive, [and] enjoyable." —*Library Journal*

TITLES BY CLIVE CUSSLER

DIRK PITT® ADVENTURES

Clive Cussler's The Devil's Sea
  (by Dirk Cussler)
Celtic Empire
  (with Dirk Cussler)
Odessa Sea (with Dirk Cussler)
Havana Storm
  (with Dirk Cussler)
Poseidon's Arrow
  (with Dirk Cussler)
Crescent Dawn
  (with Dirk Cussler)
Arctic Drift (with Dirk Cussler)
Treasure of Khan
  (with Dirk Cussler)
Black Wind (with Dirk Cussler)
Trojan Odyssey
Valhalla Rising
Atlantis Found
Flood Tide
Shock Wave
Inca Gold
Sahara
Dragon
Treasure
Cyclops
Deep Six
Pacific Vortex!
Night Probe!
Vixen 03
Raise the Titanic!
Iceberg
The Mediterranean Caper

SAM AND REMI FARGO ADVENTURES®

Wrath of Poseidon
  (with Robin Burcell)
The Oracle (with Robin Burcell)
The Gray Ghost
  (with Robin Burcell)
The Romanov Ransom
  (with Robin Burcell)
Pirate (with Robin Burcell)
The Solomon Curse
  (with Russell Blake)
The Eye of Heaven
  (with Russell Blake)
The Mayan Secrets
  (with Thomas Perry)
The Tombs (with Thomas Perry)
The Kingdom
  (with Grant Blackwood)
Lost Empire
  (with Grant Blackwood)
Spartan Gold
  (with Grant Blackwood)

ISAAC BELL ADVENTURES®

The Saboteurs (with Jack Du Brul)
The Titanic Secret
  (with Jack Du Brul)
The Cutthroat (with Justin Scott)
The Gangster (with Justin Scott)
The Assassin (with Justin Scott)
The Bootlegger (with Justin Scott)
The Striker (with Justin Scott)
The Thief (with Justin Scott)
The Race (with Justin Scott)
The Spy (with Justin Scott)
The Wrecker (with Justin Scott)
The Chase

A NOVEL FROM THE NUMA FILES®

G. P. PUTNAM'S SONS | NEW YORK

FAST ICE

CLIVE CUSSLER

AND

GRAHAM BROWN

PUTNAM
— EST. 1838 —

G. P. PUTNAM'S SONS
Publishers Since 1838
An imprint of Penguin Random House LLC
penguinrandomhouse.com

The Library of Congress has catalogued the G. P. Putnam's Sons hardcover
edition as follows:

Names: Cussler, Clive, author. | Brown, Graham, 1969– author.
Title: Fast ice: a novel from the Numa files / Clive Cussler and Graham Brown.
Description: New York : G. P. Putnam's Sons, [2021] |
Identifiers: LCCN 2020048520 (print) | LCCN 2020048521 (ebook) |
ISBN 9780593327869 (hardcover) | ISBN 9780593327876 (ebook)
Subjects: LCSH: Austin, Kurt (Fictitious character)—Fiction. |
Marine scientists—Fiction. | GSAFD: Suspense fiction. | Adventure fiction.
Classification: LCC PS3553.U75 F37 2021 (print) |
LCC PS3553.U75 (ebook) | DDC 813/.54—dc23
LC record available at https://lccn.loc.gov/2020048520
LC ebook record available at https://lccn.loc.gov/2020048521

First G. P. Putnam's Sons hardcover edition / March 2021
First G. P. Putnam's trade paperback edition / December 2021
First G. P. Putnam's Sons premium edition / February 2022
G. P. Putnam's Sons premium edition ISBN: 9780593327883

Printed in the United States of America
1   3   5   7   9   10   8   6   4   2

BOOK DESIGN BY KRISTIN DEL ROSARIO

Title page photo: Ship among icebergs by I. Noyan Yilmaz/Shutterstock.com

CAST OF CHARACTERS

ANTARCTICA, 1939

CAPTAIN GUNTHER JURGENSON—Lufthansa pilot, expert at piloting seaplanes and flying boats, recruited for the *Bremerhaven* expedition to Antarctica

LIEUTENANT SCHMIDT—Navigator on Jurgenson's aircraft, devoted member of the Nazi Party

PRESENT DAY
Grishka *Expedition*

CORA EMMERSON—Climate expert and microbiologist, also a former member of NUMA (National Underwater and Marine Agency)

ALEC LASKEY—Captain of the *Grishka*, a forty-year-old polar research vessel

National Underwater and Marine Agency (NUMA)

KURT AUSTIN—Director of Special Projects, salvage expert, world-class diver, and boating enthusiast

JOE ZAVALA—Kurt's assistant and closest friend, helicopter pilot, and mechanical genius

RUDI GUNN—Assistant Director of NUMA, graduate of the Naval Academy, runs most of the day-to-day operations at NUMA

HIRAM YAEGER—NUMA's Director of Technology, designed and runs their most powerful computers and processing systems

PAUL TROUT—NUMA's chief geologist, graduate of Scripps Institute, married to Gamay

GAMAY TROUT—NUMA's leading marine biologist, also graduated from Scripps

ST. JULIEN PERLMUTTER—World-class historian and gourmet cook, keeps a large collection of rare nautical books and charts in his home

LEE GARLAND—Director of Remote Sensing and Communications, known as a satellite wrangler

South Africa—Limpopo Province

YVONNE LLOYD—Environmentalist and microbiologist studying ancient bacteria, part of Cora Emmerson's expedition on the *Grishka*

RYLAND LLOYD—Yvonne's older brother, CEO of Mata Petroleum, caught up in a continuing feud with his sister

ZHAO LIANG—Owner of Liang Shipping, a large tanker operation, associate of Ryland Lloyd

SERGEI NOVIKOV—Russian construction magnate, builder of ports and shipping terminals, also an associate of Ryland Lloyd

EILEEN TUNSTALL—Canadian industrialist, her company builds turbines and pipeline equipment, also an associate of Ryland Lloyd

South Africa—Johannesburg

LEANDRA NDIMI—NUMA liaison officer in South Africa and a friend of Rudi's

PROFESSOR NOAH WATSON—Microbiologist at the University of Johannesburg

LIEUTENANT CLARENCE ZAMA—Special-operations commander in the South African Navy

Europe

MATTHIAS RÄIKKÖNEN—Director of Research at the European Ice Core Depository in Helsinki

ANDREA BAUER—Lead curator at the Berlin Document Center

P-8 Poseidon Flight Crew

COMMANDER WALTER HANSEN—Commander of P-8 Poseidon aircraft code-named Hermes 51

LIEUTENANT REBECCA COLLIER—Reconnaissance Systems Operator on Hermes 51

FAST ICE

PROLOGUE

THE BOTTOM OF THE WORLD

TERRA AUSTRALIS (ANTARCTICA)
JANUARY 1939

The droning of aircraft propellers echoed across the stark winter landscape. It caromed off snowfields and along rivers of ice, a reverberating hum never heard before in this part of Antarctica.

A colony of emperor penguins nesting on the land below caught wind of the noise. They looked skyward for the cause of the disturbance, turning their heads in unison. Finding the source, they watched in rapt curiosity as a large gray "bird" lumbered across the sky.

That bird was a Dornier flying boat. An all-metal silver aircraft with a registration number painted in large block letters. It boasted a high-mounted wing and two powerful radial engines arranged sequentially along the centerline of the fuselage—one engine pulled the plane forward while the second pushed it from behind.

Those who flew this model of the Dornier called it *The Whale*, mostly because of its great size, but also because the plane's ribbed sheet metal resembled the distinctly folded blubber on the underside of many ocean-dwelling leviathans.

Inside the aircraft, a middle-aged pilot sat at the controls. He had brown eyes and graying hair, but with a thick growth of dark stubble on his face. He wore a buttonless blue jacket known as a *Fliegerbluse*. A captain's badge on the collar indicated his rank, while an eagle grasping a swastika on his breast identified him as a Luftwaffe pilot. A temporary name tag, only recently sewn onto the *Fliegerbluse*, gave his name as *Jurgenson*.

Tilting the wings and glancing down at the penguins through the heated cockpit glass, Jurgenson marveled at how the birds lined themselves up in near-perfect rows.

"Kleine Soldaten," he said in German. *Little soldiers.*

The copilot laughed and then pointed to something else. *"Blaues Wasser,"* he said. *Blue water.* "It must be another lake. That makes three in the last fifty kilometers, all along the same line."

Jurgenson turned his attention to the lake up ahead. He saw a long, narrow stretch of aquamarine water shimmering in the sun. The color was intense, standing out like a sapphire in the endless field of white snow.

"This one's larger than the others." He pressed the intercom button. "Navigator, I need a position report."

From deeper inside the plane, the navigator responded with the current latitude and longitude, adding, "We're nearing the two-hundred-kilometer waypoint. Time to perform our duty for the Reich."

Jurgenson rolled his eyes and exchanged a knowing glance with the copilot. They were officially here as explorers, photographing large swaths of the unexplored continent, but in 1939 exploring unknown lands meant claiming them for King and Country—or, in this case, for Führer and Fatherland.

To press that claim, they were required by the high command to deposit evidence of their journey every fifty kilometers. That meant dropping weighted markers through the cargo door of the plane and hoping they would land in the ice like flags.

The markers were three feet long, made of steel and shaped like arrows. They were weighted in the nose, designed to fall like spears and embed themselves in the snow and ice. If all went well, they would remain erect, proudly displaying the swastikas emblazoned on their tails.

Jurgenson found the exercise a ridiculous waste of time. As far as he could tell, the arrows either fell down upon impact or plunged so deeply that they'd vanished from sight.

Jurgenson made a quick decision and pressed the intercom button. "Our true duty to the Reich is to find things of value. Liquefied snow and ice suggest geothermal heat, which shall be of tremendous use should the high command decide to build a base here. Strap yourself in. We're turning back for a landing."

With the intercom silent, Jurgenson addressed the

copilot. "Contact the *Bremerhaven*. Tell them we're landing."

As the copilot reported back to the freighter they'd launched from, Jurgenson adjusted the controls and put the Dornier into a slow, descending turn. He passed over the lake once, eyeing it for rocks or obstructions, and then set up for the landing. On the approach, he lowered the flaps and feathered the throttle.

There was no wind to speak of, which made things easy. The Dornier touched down at one end of the narrow lake, splitting the calm water in two and carving a long, thin wake down the middle.

The drag of the water reduced the plane's speed as effectively as any brakes and the big craft was soon coasting along like a heavily laden boat. Jurgenson maneuvered the craft using the pedals at his feet that were attached to a small rudder under the plane's keel. As the speed dropped further, he added some power, turned the plane to the right and then shut the engines down.

The Dornier went quiet, drifting to a stop against the far end of the lake.

"Time to stretch our legs," Jurgenson said.

As Jurgenson released his shoulder harness, the navigator popped his head into the cockpit. "Captain," the navigator said. "I must insist that we—"

Jurgenson cut him off. "Lieutenant Schmidt," he said. "I insist that you join us. You may bring as many markers as you wish. We can even outline the lake with them, if you please. As a further honor, you shall be given the right to name this lake for the Fatherland."

Silence for a second, and then, *"Danke, Kapitän."*

The navigator disappeared back into the fuselage of the plane. The copilot grinned. "We'll make a politician out of you yet."

"Not in a million years."

Jurgenson couldn't have cared less for the National Socialist Party—in fact, he'd been an opponent of the Nazis in their early years, back when that sort of thing was still allowed. It had driven the Gestapo to put a red flag next to his name and they'd tried to keep him off the expedition. But after years working the overseas routes with Lufthansa, his level of skill in flying *The Whale* could not easily be matched. Those skills—along with a written rejection of his unionist past—had gotten him onto the expedition and out of working a coal mine in the Ruhr.

Reaching up, Jurgenson opened a hatch above his head. Most versions of the Dornier had an open cockpit, but the aircraft chosen for the Antarctic expedition had been given a glassed-in canopy for obvious reasons.

As the hatch slid back, frigid air poured into the stuffy cockpit, freshening it and making both men feel more alert. Jurgenson inhaled deeply and then pulled himself up, climbing through the hatch out onto the spine of his aircraft.

Behind him lay the Dornier's engine pod with its two inline propellers. They had come to a halt, but he could hear the hot metal parts of the engine pinging and creaking as the cold air circulated through.

Down on the side of the fuselage, a door opened. Lieutenant Schmidt and two others climbed out onto the stubby lower wing, called a sponson. This secondary airfoil had been incorporated into the flying boat's design to help with stability when the craft sat on the water, but it also made a perfect ledge to stand on when entering or leaving the plane.

Perched there, Lieutenant Schmidt fired a harpoon into the ice. A rope connected to it spooled out. Schmidt and the two crewmen pulled hard on the rope, generating just enough manpower to drag the aircraft up against the shoreline.

With the plane moored, Lieutenant Schmidt placed a long wooden board across the gap leading from the aircraft to the ice. "How much time do we have, Captain?"

Jurgenson read the temperature. Fifteen degrees below zero. Yet with the sunlight and the lack of wind, it felt quite pleasant. It reminded Jurgenson of a day he'd spent in the Alps, skiing in the morning and sitting outside at a picnic table in the afternoon drinking good Bavarian beer.

"Fifteen minutes," he said. "No longer."

The time limit wasn't for the crew—they would be fine—it was to prevent the pistons from cooling too much, which would make it harder to vaporize fuel in the pistons and, thus, harder to restart the engines.

He leaned back into the cockpit. "Keep an eye on the oil temperature. If it gets low, start the engines. I'm going ashore."

The copilot saluted and Jurgenson left him, walking along the top of the aircraft. After ducking past the propeller and underneath the wing, he hopped down onto the sponson. From there, he crossed the wooden plank to the shore.

Stepping on the solid ground, he found the snow to be packed and firm with only a thin layer of powder over the top. Walking away from the plane, he marveled at the near silence. He heard only the sound of his own breathing and the snow crunching and squeaking beneath his boots.

The landscape around him was vast, quiet and utterly stunning. The air itself was so cold it held no moisture. And though his breath seemed to freeze in his nostrils, he saw no sign of vapor when he exhaled. He found the white of the snowfield blinding, but in the distance he spied several peaks devoid of snow that looked to be dark volcanic rock. Glancing upward, he marveled at a sky that was the bluest he'd ever seen.

He walked slowly, taking it all in. He couldn't be sure, but he guessed he was standing farther south than any German in history. That had to count for something. He passed Lieutenant Schmidt, hammering his metal arrows into the ice, careful to ensure that the swastikas were prominently displayed.

Next came the obligatory photograph. As Schmidt unfurled a Nazi flag, another crewman set up a camera. They gestured to the captain, urging him to join them.

Jurgenson walked over and posed for the photo, standing lackadaisically. He kept his arms at his side as Lieutenant Schmidt and the others stuck out their arms and hands in the salute.

Official functions completed, the captain walked farther down the narrow stretch of ice, arriving beside one of the scientists who crouched at the edge of the lake.

The man was taking samples, casting a large glass bottle into the water, allowing it to sink and fill, before drawing it back to him with a length of twine.

"What do you think?" Jurgenson asked, crouching beside him. "Volcanic?"

"*Ja,*" the scientist said. "With great certainty. You can smell the sulfur from here. This lake is definitely being heated by geothermal forces."

"But aren't we on top of a glacier?"

"You are correct," the scientist added. "That's what makes this a rare discovery—geothermal heat burning through the heart of the glacier. Very unusual. And then there's this." The scientist pointed to one of the glass bottles beside him. It contained an earlier sample from the lake.

"The water is filled with contaminants. It should be pure meltwater, but it's not."

The captain looked closer, staring into the glass jar. A temperature gauge bobbing inside read thirty-eight degrees, but ice had begun forming along the top. As the scientist stirred the water to break up the ice, a swirl of green impurities could be seen in its vortex.

"Sediment?"

"Perhaps."

"Or even living material, possibly—"

"Captain," a voice shouted.

Jurgenson stood up and turned back toward the plane. One of the crewmen was standing on the aft section of the Dornier, holding on to the tail and pointing across the lake, back in the direction where they'd landed.

"The water is icing over," the crewman shouted. "We need to take off or we'll be trapped."

Jurgenson turned. He could see the aqua blue color fading to lead in the distance. Even at the shoreline beside them, a paper-thin sheen of ice had begun forming, a sheen that hadn't been there minutes before.

"Everyone back to the plane," Jurgenson ordered. He helped the scientist cap the samples and store them on a carrying tray, then left him and raced toward the plane. He reached the gangplank, bounding over it and climbing up onto the top of the aircraft.

He took a few steps toward the tail. From higher up, he could see more clearly. What he saw chilled him more than the frigid air. Ice was growing up along both shores fast enough for the naked eye to track it. At the same time, it was spreading across the lake, moving from both sides toward the middle, like frost creeping across a windowpane in a time-lapse exposure. For the moment, a channel in the center of the lake remained clear.

He bounded across the top of the plane, ducking under the wing and heading for the cockpit. "Start the engines."

"But not everyone is aboard yet," the copilot replied.

"Start them anyway," Jurgenson ordered. "Hurry."

As the copilot went to work, Jurgenson paused at the front of the plane, glancing back along the shore. The scientists were lugging their equipment and water samples toward the craft, waddling through the snow as they approached the plane. Schmidt was foolishly hammering in one last marker. "Come on," Jurgenson ordered. "Move."

The aft propeller screeched into motion, with the engine belching black smoke. The pistons fired and the propeller spun up quickly, becoming an instant blur. Down below it, the scientists clambered aboard. Lieutenant Schmidt was still coming.

The captain dropped into the cockpit and slammed the hatch above him. "Number two up and running," he said. "Start number one."

As the forward engine fired up, Jurgenson took over. He adjusted the propellers and prepared to move.

"Head count," he demanded over the intercom.

"All on board," a breathless Lieutenant Schmidt called out.

"Release the line. And shove us off. We need space to turn."

In the aft section of the aircraft, Schmidt cut the line and used the plank to push the Dornier back from the ice. It moved sluggishly, drifting a few feet out, but that was all the space Jurgenson needed.

He eased the throttles forward while stepping hard on the rudder. The effort coaxed the plane into a tight turn, the tail swinging around until the nose was pointed back down the length of the lake.

With the aircraft lined up, he set the props for takeoff and pushed the throttles to full. The engines mounted above the fuselage roared and the Dornier began to pick up speed as the power streamed through the airframe.

At first, *The Whale* moved like its namesake, plowing forward with brute force, shoving the water aside and picking up speed slowly. But as the airflow over the wing increased, the plane rode higher on its keel, reducing the drag substantially. Now *The Whale* began to fly across the water, picking up speed briskly.

Up ahead, the ice continued to grow, a crystalline pattern merging from both sides.

"How could a lake freeze so quickly?" the copilot asked.

"We must have stirred up cold water from down below," Jurgenson suggested. "Full flaps. We need lift."

The copilot deployed the flaps and the Dornier rose until it was skimming across the water, desperate to fly but not yet free.

"We're not going to make it," the copilot warned. He reached for the throttles to pull them back.

Jurgenson blocked the man's hand and kept the engines at full power. The aircraft charged into the leading edge of the rapidly forming ice. It was slush at this point, but it sprayed up against the metal skin of the aircraft, freezing instantly. The struts on the wing and the aft section of the fuselage and part of the tail were coated in seconds.

Jurgenson felt the controls grow heavy and sluggish. But the high-mounted wing and the propellers above it were still clear and dry. It was now or never.

Jurgenson pulled back on the yoke. The Dornier lifted free of the lake, climbed for a moment, then began to drop. It kissed the surface once, skipping and bouncing higher. This time, it held on and began clawing its way toward the sky.

"De-ice the wings and tail," Jurgenson called out.

His copilot flipped a pair of switches. "Heat's on."

The de-icing system channeled electrical power through heating coils in the wing and tail. The coils would melt the ice, but the process was slow. In the meantime, Jurgenson fought to keep the aircraft flying.

"We're too heavy," he said, pressing the intercom button. "Dump all excess weight or we're going to fall out of the sky."

Focused on the instruments and keeping the wings level, Jurgenson had no idea of the panic his directive had set off in the aft section of the aircraft. The cargo hatch was shoved open. Spare parts, equipment and cold-weather gear were thrown out. A sled, several pairs of skis and a fifty-pound sack of rice, provisioned to keep them alive if they ended up stranded, went next. Everything that could be thrown out was, except for Lieutenant Schmidt's weighted markers, which the navigator guarded with zealous intensity.

With the aft compartment cleared, the plane was three hundred pounds lighter. Just enough to keep it airborne.

And then the number one engine sputtered.

"Ice in the fuel line," the copilot said. "Damn those tanks on the *Bremerhaven*."

He opened a valve that let more heat from the engine into the carburetors in hopes of keeping the ice from choking off the fuel supply. It was too little too late.

The engine died and the Dornier began to shake. It

was about to stall and crash. Jurgenson had no choice. He put the nose down, picking up enough speed to control the descent. But there was no way to remain airborne.

They glided half a mile and hit the snow with jarring impact, not hard enough to destroy the plane but firm enough to damage it.

The fuselage groaned with the impact. Rivets popped and ricocheted through the interior of the Dornier. Jurgenson felt the aircraft yawing as the nose slid left and the tail swung out to the right. The plane was skidding like a car on wet pavement. He tried to control it by stepping on the rudder pedal, but it had little effect.

They slid across the hard-packed snow and then went up a slope. The speed began to drop as they climbed the hill and the plane stopped suddenly as the left wing dug into a snowbank and spun them around.

Jurgenson reached for the controls, instinctively shutting off the fuel pumps and the electrical system. Looking around, he saw no sign of fire. Inhaling deeply, he smelled no smoke or leaking fuel.

They were stopped and alive. They wouldn't burn. Beyond that, there was little to celebrate.

After sitting in stunned silence for a moment, Jurgenson stood up. He opened the hatch and popped his head out.

They'd come a thousand feet up the side of a hill before settling into deeper snow. The aircraft was turned at a forty-five-degree angle, as if it had been trying to get its nose around and head back down the hill before getting stuck.

Looking back, he saw all the damage he needed to see. The leading edge of the tail was gashed and bent badly. A rip in the side of the airframe ran from one of the sponsons all the way back to the rudder. There was no need to look further. *The Whale* wouldn't be flying again.

Dropping back into the cockpit, Jurgenson slumped into his seat. "This will not help my standing with the men in Berlin," he said. "Radio the *Bremerhaven*. Give them our position and tell them we need assistance."

As the copilot powered up the radio and made the dreaded call, Jurgenson looked through the window. He saw the lake in the distance, but the brilliant turquoise color was gone. The lake had turned a drab, solid color that made it almost indistinguishable from the ice and snow around it.

Never in his life had Jurgenson seen a body of water freeze so quickly. It didn't seem possible. Not at thirty-eight degrees Fahrenheit. Not with geothermal heat warming it from below.

He wondered if it had something to do with the sediment that the scientist had captured in the jug. Perhaps they'd found something remarkable after all.

He thumbed the intercom button. "Fritz," he said, addressing the scientist by name. "Did you manage to save the water sample?"

"*Nein, Kapitän,*" the scientist replied. "We had to throw it out to reduce the weight."

"A pity," Jurgenson said. "I would like to have known what was swimming around in that strange blue water."

1

The polar research vessel *Grishka* moved cautiously through the Southern Ocean a hundred miles from the coast of Antarctica. The ten-thousand-ton ship had a gray hull, a reinforced bow and a five-story superstructure painted a faded shade of international orange. She was three hundred feet in length but looked tiny when compared to the mountainous icebergs surrounding her.

Some of those icebergs were flat and broad, tabletop monoliths the size of cities. Others were towering peaks, their Matterhorn-like shapes sculpted by the wind and waves into arrangements as different as they were remarkable. And yet among all the giants, it was the much smaller type of iceberg that threatened the *Grishka*.

From her position on the bridge, Cora Emmerson gazed through binoculars, scanning the water for automobile-sized chunks of ice that floated low and were almost invisible.

"Growlers dead ahead," she warned.

Unlike sea ice, which the *Grishka* could plow through, or the enormous icebergs, which were easy to spot and avoid, growlers were hard to see and could be deadly. They varied in size and shape and could weigh thirty tons or more. Worse yet, they were often angular instead of smooth-sided, resulting in a tendency to puncture a ship's hull rather than glancing harmlessly off it.

"We've got another set off the port bow," Cora warned. "Five degrees to starboard and we'll clear them all."

The captain of the ship, Alec Laskey, made the turn without questioning. Cora had been at his side on the journey down to Antarctica and had barely left the bridge since they began traveling north twelve hours before.

She had remarkable stamina, he thought. And a keen eye. "I'm certain you must have been a sailor in a former life."

"I can neither confirm nor deny that rumor," Cora said, "but I've been doing Antarctic research for years now. This is my seventh trip to the continent. And, before that, I worked for the American nautical agency NUMA. It would be a shame if I hadn't picked up something along the way."

"I'd say you picked up a few things," Laskey replied. "You're vigilant."

Yes, she thought. *And I have reason to be.*

After months of searching, Cora's expedition had

discovered something both unique and dangerous. If she was right, it had the potential to alter the world. In the right hands it could be a salve for the damaged planet, but in the wrong hands it could be turned into a weapon. Regardless of its use, there were those who would prefer such a discovery had never been made at all.

Whether it was paranoia or an overactive sixth sense, Cora had felt they were being tracked even before the discovery. Getting off the ice and aboard the *Grishka* had eased that fear. Until they reached Cape Town, however, she wouldn't feel safe.

"New heading established," the captain said. "Are we clear?"

Cora swung the binoculars back toward the growlers. They rose and fell as the bow wave of the ship passed, jostling against one another. A foam of bubbles appeared as one of the miniature icebergs rolled over, disappeared briefly and then bobbed to the surface with a different side pointed skyward.

"Ice has been cleared and is falling behind us," she said.

Cora watched the growlers and then turned her attention to the path ahead. What had once looked wide open now appeared less so. A mile in front of them, a midsize iceberg—larger than the *Grishka* but smaller than the mountains of ice in the distance—was moving into their path.

The iceberg was an odd shape. But, then, no two were ever alike. It had a flat top, like the city-sized bergs that broke off from the glaciers, but its nearest end was sharply angled. Small peaks rose from various parts.

The ice itself was an odd color. Instead of pure white or a ghostly blue, this one looked jaundiced, as if it had been dusted with volcanic ash.

"Is there a current here?" Cora asked.

"West wind drift," Laskey said. "Just like everywhere else around Antarctica."

"But nothing locally?"

"Not that I know of."

"Then why is that iceberg tracking east instead of west?"

Laskey glanced toward the encroaching iceberg. "Optical illusion."

"I don't think so."

The captain seemed unconcerned but motioned toward an old cathode-ray screen. "Check the radar."

Cora moved to the ship's rudimentary radarscope. It was an ancient device, with lines burnt into the screen that remained there even when the unit was switched off. She set it to tracking mode and waited for the information to appear. After a dozen sweeps, it confirmed what her eyes were telling her. "That berg is moving southeast at a speed of four knots."

"Wind?" Laskey asked.

Cora checked the ship's anemometer. It registered five knots, coming from due north. A quick check of the pennant on the bow confirmed this. "Perhaps the back side of the iceberg is oddly shaped. It might be catching the breeze and acting like a sail."

Now the captain grew concerned. He cut the throttle and the *Grishka* settled and slowed to a crawl. "Too dangerous to try rounding it," he said. "God knows what's hidden under the surface. We'll stop here and wait for it to pass."

But the iceberg didn't pass. Whatever combination of currents and wind were moving it, the floating monolith lost its eastward momentum and began to move due southward, directly toward the *Grishka*.

Cora felt her chest tightening. "It's coming toward us."

"Impossible," Laskey said.

"Look for yourself."

He didn't bother. He cut the throttle to full stop and then placed it into the reverse position at quarter speed. The old ship responded slowly, shuddering and seeming to rest before it finally started to withdraw.

"You're taking us back into the pack ice?"

"Better than getting too close to this one," the captain said. "It could rupture our hull with the slightest impact. It could crush us if it tumbled."

The *Grishka* picked up momentum, putting some space between itself and the encroaching iceberg. But it wasn't long before a grinding reverberated through the hull.

Laskey stopped the engines. "Those would be the growlers," he said. "Must have drawn them into our wake when we passed. I need eyes at the stern if we're going to keep moving."

"I'll go," Cora said.

Picking up a handheld radio, she left the bridge. She took a ladder down five levels to the main deck and then went aft. She passed no one, as it was early morning and most of the crew were asleep.

Stopping near the aft hatchway, she grabbed a heavy

parka from a storage locker. Slipping it over her shoulders and zipping it up, she pushed out into the elements.

The bitter cold hit her instantly, the wind stinging her face and hands. She pulled the fur-fringed hood up around her face and slipped her free hand into a pocket.

With the radio in the other hand, she crossed the helicopter pad, where the expedition's EC130 was tied down. The helicopter's windows were frosted over but its rotors were covered by specially heated sleeves.

Passing the landing pad, she reached the stern, where a pair of large winch housings stood. Moving between them, she glanced over the aft rail.

To her surprise, they were already moving backward and picking up speed. Deep baritone reverberations told her they were ramming small chunks of ice with the stern's blunt end.

The nearest sections of ice were not too threatening, but larger growlers lay directly in their path.

She brought the radio to her mouth and pressed transmit. "White ice directly astern, Captain. At least three separate chunks. I wouldn't take them straight on. The last thing we need is a damaged prop or rudder."

The propellers continued churning, the ship vibrating as it picked up momentum.

Cora pressed the talk button again. "Captain, did you hear me?"

The ship's horn blared, sounding three times, to announce a collision warning. The captain's voice came over the loudspeaker. "Brace for impact. All hands, brace for impact."

With the hood surrounding her face, Cora had zero peripheral vision. She spun around, shocked to discover a shadow looming over the ship as a wall of ice approached from just off the starboard bow. It was closing rapidly despite the *Grishka*'s momentum. It hit the ship with a glancing, angled impact.

The *Grishka* rolled with the blow, heeling over fifteen degrees. The iceberg slid along the side of the hull, dumping thousands of pounds of dirty snow onto the deck.

Cora was knocked off her feet, hitting the deck beside the nearest winch housing. She dropped the radio and grasped her ribs, which had taken the brunt of the blow.

The grinding sound of ice on steel peaked and then subsided as the *Grishka* and the iceberg became locked together and moved as one until their momentum faded. The engines cut out. The ship rolled back to level and more snow and ice tumbled onto the deck.

The moment struck Cora as surreal. Instead of the ship hitting the iceberg, the iceberg had struck the ship. Then an even stranger sight followed.

All at once, a half-dozen ropes were thrown over the tip of the iceberg. They unfurled in midair, dropping and hitting the deck of the *Grishka* with dull thuds.

Before the ropes even landed, men in winter camouflage began rappelling down them. Cora saw assault rifles strapped to their backs, knives in sheaths strapped to their legs. They wore white hoods and goggles. They hit the deck in rapid succession, fanning out, while reinforcements dropped in behind them.

Cora knew instantly what was happening. She snatched the radio from the deck and tried to warn the captain, but gunfire broke out before she could make the call.

Ducking behind the winch housing in horror, she called out. "Captain, we're being boarded," she warned. "Men with guns are on the aft deck. They came from the—"

More gunfire drowned out her words. The captain's voice came next. *"They're on the bow as well,"* he replied over the radio. *"Take cover, I'm calling for—"*

The staccato sound of machine gun fire came through the radio and the transmission cut out.

Cora stifled a scream and looked around. Shouting and screams erupted. The muted thumping of small-arms fire rose from inside the ship and the decks beneath.

She considered any possible avenue of resistance. With no weapons of any consequence to fight back with, the best she could hope for was grabbing a fire ax and charging into the fray.

Before she could move, a member of the *Grishka*'s science team stumbled out of the aft hatchway. He ran toward the helicopter but never reached it. A sniper perched on the edge of the iceberg shot him down with merciless accuracy.

Another colleague came running out seconds later, fleeing whatever carnage was going on inside the ship. He ran for the stern, heading directly for the spot where Cora was hiding.

"Get down," Cora shouted.

The crack of a rifle sounded and the man's body jerked forward and tumbled to the deck ten feet from where

Cora hid. He lay prone but looked up directly at her. He saw her preparing to help and shook his head.

It was too late to hold back. Cora was acting on instinct now. She lunged forward, grabbed him by the arm and pulled with all her strength.

She dragged him halfway before the sniper fired again.

The bullet crossed the deck at three thousand feet per second. It flew on a nearly straight line, slightly affected by the wind and diverted microscopically by the rolling motion of the ship, which was still caught in the embrace of the iceberg.

The combination was enough to push the bullet a half inch off target.

It hit the back of Cora's hood, blasting goose feathers, fabric, fur and blood into the air. Cora fell like a sack of flour, landing facedown on the body of her dying friend.

She lay there not moving, her head covered with the remnants of the hood, its tattered white fabric soaked with a growing stain of crimson blood.

Up on the precipice of the iceberg, the sniper studied the results of his efforts.

A spotter beside him did the same. "Headshot," he said. "That's two kills."

The sniper nodded and scratched a pair of marks into the stock of the rifle. They joined a dozen other scratches, some old, some new.

With the deck cleared and his kills marked, the sniper

picked up a radio and sent a message to the commandos. "Aft deck clear," he told them. "What's the status inside?"

"Bridge cleared," a voice replied. *"No resistance from crew. Looks like most of them were already put down. We're down in the vault now. Be advised there's a significant amount of material here. This is going to take a while."*

The sniper nodded. He'd been told to expect as much. "Begin bringing it up. And be quick about it. We need to set the charges and send this ship to the bottom before anyone knows we're here."

2

Blinding pain filled Cora's body to every extremity. No, not pain, she realized, but the utter lack of sensation.

She opened her eyes and saw nothing but a dark, blurred image of the deck beneath her. She tried to move. It took great effort and felt tremendously clumsy, but eventually she twisted her body into a more natural position and managed to sit up.

For a moment, that seemed like a drastic mistake. Her head throbbed like a drum, her eyes went blind and she felt as if she were about to throw up.

Shutting her eyes and allowing the cold air to caress her face helped. She sat completely still as one by one her senses came back online.

First, she heard the wind whistling through the ice-covered wires and then she felt the reverberation of the ship's engines. She sensed the *Grishka* rolling gently as it moved through the swells. It dawned on her. *We're under way.*

She pulled the hood of the parka back and risked opening one eye. She saw pale skies and dark water. The day was waning. The iceberg was gone. The ship was alone.

She went to push herself up and noticed her hands were covered with blood. She saw the body she had been lying next to and partially on top of. Only now did the memory of what happened come back. The iceberg, the men with guns, the shooting.

She tried to stand, but that was too much. On her hands and knees, she crawled across the deck, reaching the aft hatchway. She pulled it open and squirmed inside.

Out of the wind and the subzero temperatures, her skin began to thaw. It felt strangely painful. Her face tingled, but her hands and feet remained numb.

Stretching her fingers, she noticed white, scaly patches and discolored lesions. The early signs of frostbite. Grimly estimating the damage, she figured she'd lose at least three digits on each hand. Better than her life, she thought.

With her strength slowly returning, Cora pulled herself up with the help of a handhold. Up on her feet, she went forward, heading for the bridge. Reminders of the tragedy appeared in the hall—splatters of blood on the wall, dead crewmen left where they'd fallen, shell casings rolling around underfoot.

She reached the bridge and pushed the door open. The captain and the ship's bosun lay still on the floor. Both of their bodies had been riddled with bullets.

She dropped beside Captain Laskey, hoping against reason that she might find a pulse, but he was cold and stiff. "What have I done?" she said, sobbing. "What have I done?"

Tears streamed down her face, while waves of guilt surged through her body. She was the cause of this brutal attack. Her discovery had made them all targets. And now, somehow, only she remained alive.

The sobbing subsided quickly. Her body was too tired to conjure more emotion. She looked up, her attention drawn to a strange beeping sound.

Standing once more, she moved to the helm. The ship was moving in a westerly direction, but there was no one to control it.

She glanced out the bridge windows. Open ocean lay ahead of them, dotted here and there with whitecaps and a few chunks of free-floating ice.

She looked to the radio shack and found it had been shot to pieces. The chirping alarm was coming from somewhere else. She scanned the damaged control console and spied a flashing indicator on its panel.

Water was coming in and the bottom deck was flooding. The bilge pumps were operating, but the watertight doors were stuck in the open position.

The *Grishka* was riding low. She could feel it wallowing in the swells. They were taking on more water than the pumps could handle.

She gave up on calling for help. If she didn't stop the water from rising, the *Grishka* would be long gone before anyone arrived to rescue her.

She stumbled from the bridge, moving as fast as her injured feet would allow. Reaching the center stairwell, she was able to drop down quickly, arriving on the lower deck near a small laboratory where she'd spent much of her time.

The place had been ransacked. Everything turned over and taken. "Of course," she muttered to herself. "That's what they came for."

It was irrelevant now, nothing mattered but saving the ship. She passed through the laboratory and reached the cold-storage vault, where her team had preserved the hundreds of ice cores taken from the glaciers over the last month.

The frigid compartment was also empty, the ice cores had been removed.

At the far end of the compartment, she came to a circular hatch. A ladder dropped through it straight down into the bilge. The sailors called it a scuttle.

She looked through the scuttle to see water swirling on the deck below. It bubbled and churned, flowing in from a hidden puncture.

She climbed down through the scuttle and stepped into it calf-high. The flooding was coming from the next compartment, spilling over the sill under the door. The door was closed but hadn't sealed properly.

That was no surprise. Not on a forty-year-old ship that had survived storms, groundings and at least two collisions. Time and work had done hidden damage to the bones of the vessel. As a result, the bulkheads were slightly warped and none of the hatches were truly watertight. If she was going to survive, Cora needed to make this one secure.

Knee-deep in the frigid water, Cora struggled to think.

She knew enough about damage control to give her a fighting chance. She grabbed a towel and a section of pipe from a workbench. Rolling the towel up, she wedged it into the curved gap, forcing it into place with the pipe. Smashing a chair to get bits of wood, she jammed those into place as well, using them like shims.

Standing up straight, she felt suddenly dizzy. She stumbled backward and nearly lost her balance. She dropped the pipe and grabbed the ladder to keep from falling.

When the vertigo passed, she looked over at her work. She'd cut the flow of water in half, yet it was still coming in. Even at this rate, it would slowly flood the ship, filling the lower deck and rising through gaps and scuttles that were no longer sealed properly.

The sinking appeared inevitable.

Physically exhausted, Cora sagged with the weight of the moment. Though her body was spent, her mind was still churning.

She wouldn't give up. Not now, not after finding what she'd been after for years and having it taken from her. Not after seeing friends and colleagues murdered for it.

She thought of her training, of her time with NUMA. There had to be a way to stop the ship from sinking. *There had to be.*

She looked around in all directions and then upward through the scuttle and into the storage vault. An idea came to her. An idea so brilliant, she couldn't help but smile.

With all the energy she had left, Cora climbed back up the ladder and found all she needed to save the dying ship.

3

Cold air whipped past Kurt Austin's face as he leaned backward, his right hand hauling on a rope, his left gripping the tiller beside him.

A triangular sail stretched taut ahead of him, filled to capacity by the brisk north wind. The strain on the sail bent a carbon fiber mast forward, pulling Kurt's small craft at breakneck speed.

Though his vessel was powered by the wind and racing along the Potomac River, it was no sailboat or schooner. Kurt was at the helm of an ice yacht, a tripod-shaped craft with a long, thin body and runners attached to the bottom of the hull. One blade was set forward, in the nose, with two others connected to a pair of outriggers stretching away from him on either side.

The stainless steel runners were shaped like samurai

swords, their sharpened edges cutting into the frozen surface of the Potomac and allowing the yacht to corner hard in the turns and run fast on the straightaways.

Gazing ahead, Kurt focused on a brightly colored pylon. He was approaching it rapidly. Too rapidly.

He loosened his grip on the rope, spilling some of the wind from the sail. At the same moment, he swung his body around, switching sides from the right to the left. Seated again, he leaned back and started the turn.

The ice yacht rounded the pylon, cutting hard. Its forward runner chattered as it scraped across the ice. The far runner took the strain and held.

Despite Kurt's effort, the runner beneath him came up in the air and the entire craft threatened to heel, riding only on the other blade. Kurt leaned farther, stretching his body and straining his muscles, to keep the yacht from tipping.

As he guided the yacht onto the straightaway, the tipping force vanished and the runner beneath Kurt dropped back on the ice. With all three blades digging into the frozen surface, the machine shot forward.

A voice on the headset Kurt wore expressed relief. *"That was close, Kurt. For a second, I thought I was going to have to call the paramedics."*

"Walk in the park," Kurt replied. "But, um, keep the number handy. I can't promise we won't wreck."

The voice on the other end of the line was that of Joe Zavala, Kurt's closest friend. Joe had helped build the ice yacht, working on the sail and the fiberglass body.

"There's no 'we' out on that yacht," Joe said with a

laugh. *"Just 'you.' And just so you know, I took out triple insurance on that machine. If you wipe out, I'll be a rich man. So pour on the speed."*

Kurt laughed and adjusted his position, getting into the most aerodynamic shape possible. He was on the straightaway, heading toward Joe, with the wind gusting from directly behind him. If he was going to break his own personal speed record, it would happen now.

"Going for one hundred," he said.

"Let it run. I'll call out the speed as you near the finish line."

Kurt pulled the sail taut once again, drawing his arms in and holding the rope in a grip of steel.

Though he'd spent half his life at sea, Kurt had never been a big fan of soft water sailing. It was too slow and ponderous, requiring too much work for such ordinary speeds and offering too much idle time between moments of activity.

Ice yachting—or hard water sailing, as some called it—was a different animal altogether. Ice yachts got their power from the wind, like a sailboat, but with almost zero drag from the sharpened blades they traveled on. They could hit triple-digit speeds, in the right hands. With the Potomac frozen solid, and a ten-day vacation on the books, Kurt had been practicing daily, getting tantalizingly close to that elusive number.

"Ninety-one," Joe told him. *"One mile to go."*

Kurt guided the tiller lightly as the yacht ran straight and true. The polished black ice stretched out in front of him like a sheet of tinted glass, the snow-covered banks of the Potomac racing by in a blur caught only by his peripheral vision.

"*Ninety-five,*" Joe said. "*Ninety-six.*"

Kurt sensed a tiny vibration through his fingertips. A buzzing that shouldn't have been there. It ran through the frame of the craft and up through the tiller.

"*Ninety-seven,*" Joe told him.

Kurt heard Joe, but he wasn't really listening. The vibration had grown rapidly worse and the sense of impending disaster had grown with it. The tiller began shaking violently. One of the runners had come loose.

Kurt spilled the wind from the sail, trying to slow down.

"*Ninety-eight,*" Joe said. "*Kurt, you—*"

There was a sharp crack as the outboard runner broke free. The right side of the hull dropped to the ice, pulling the ice yacht to the right. The nose runner dug in and snapped off, taking part of the hull with it. Sharp shards of fiberglass flew up from the nose. One piece whipped past Kurt's head, another ripped the sail.

The rest of the crash was incomprehensible chaos. The yacht spun and slid and then caught an edge, which sent it tumbling uncontrollably. The carbon fiber mast snapped, the outrigger pontoon folded underneath Kurt and the sail draped him and what was left of the machine.

The yacht slid another hundred feet before crashing into the snowy bank of the river, rebounding off it and coming to a stop in an unrecognizable heap of fiberglass and canvas.

Kurt found himself trapped inside of what remained

of the cockpit, aggravated with himself for pushing so hard but thankful for the helmet and five-point harness he wore.

Pushing some of the debris aside, Kurt sat up. He pulled off his helmet, catching sight of his own reflection, distorted and dark, in the ice. An unruly mane of silver hair covered his head. His coral blue eyes looked brown in the reflection, and the furrows in his brow made him look older than his thirty-eight years. A lifetime spent in the elements had seen to that. Not to mention a few crashes long before this one.

Putting the helmet down, he reached for the quick release on the safety harness, unbuckled it and slid out from what remained of the seat. As he pulled himself clear, he spotted Joe running toward him across the ice.

Joe had a radio in one hand and the radar gun in the other. He ran carefully, dashing several yards and then sliding along for several more in a controlled skid. He came to a stop a few feet from Kurt. "You all right?"

"I will be," Kurt said, "if you tell me we reached a hundred before the wipeout."

Joe looked at the radar gun and shook his head. "Sorry, amigo. You topped out at ninety-eight. Maybe this thing is broken."

Kurt got to his feet, metal studs on his boots giving him grip. He looked back at the yacht. "Something tells me that's the only thing *not broken* around here. Hope you were serious about that insurance."

The ice yacht was demolished, it would take weeks to repair. It might have been quicker to build a new one from scratch. Either way, the Potomac would be thawed by then and back under the control of the soft water sailors.

Before Joe could respond, his phone began to buzz. He put the radar gun down and pulled the phone from the inner pocket of his coat. "Zavala here."

Even though the phone wasn't on speaker mode, the person on the other end spoke loud enough for Kurt to hear clearly. He recognized the voice as that of Rudi Gunn, the number two man at the National Underwater and Marine Agency, where Kurt and Joe both worked.

NUMA was a U.S. government agency tasked with a wide range of nautical affairs, everything from studying ocean currents and sea life to the raising and salvaging of sunken ships, especially those of historical or strategic value.

Rudi Gunn was a logistical and operational expert. He handled most of the day-to-day affairs. He was also Kurt's and Joe's direct superior.

As Rudi spoke, Kurt waved his hands back and forth, giving Joe the international *I'm not here* signal.

Joe ignored him. "Actually, he's standing right next to me," Joe said, then added, "I have no idea why he'd be ignoring your calls. Probably a personality defect or a pathological disregard for authority figures . . . Yes, I think he likes his job at NUMA quite a bit—"

"Give me that phone," Kurt said.

Joe grinned as he handed it over.

Kurt put the phone to his ear. "Afternoon, Rudi. What can I do for you?"

"For starters," Rudi said, "you can answer when I

call. Or at least respond to one of the seven messages I left."

Rudi sounded hot under the collar, a rare occurrence for one of the calmest men Kurt knew.

With his free hand, Kurt patted down the pockets of his jacket. "Seem to have misplaced my phone," he said. He glanced over at the wreckage. "I must have left it in the yacht."

"Yacht?" Rudi said. "We're obviously paying you too much."

Kurt laughed. "It's a bit of a fixer-upper, at this point. I assume you called seven times for a reason?"

Rudi shifted gears instantly. "I need you and Joe to come into the office. I have a mission I'd like you to tackle personally."

Kurt was NUMA's Director of Special Projects. The position acted as a catchall for anything out of the ordinary that might come NUMA's way. It often meant flying off to distant parts of the world at a moment's notice. And just as often involved high-stakes scenarios of one type or another.

Based on Rudi's tone, it sounded like one of those scenarios was unfolding. "We'll be there in fifteen minutes."

Rudi acknowledged that time frame and hung up. Kurt handed Joe his phone.

"Let me guess," Joe said. "Winter break is over."

Kurt nodded, stretching and twisting until he felt three of his vertebrae pop mercifully back into their correct position. "And not a moment too soon. We're liable to hurt ourselves out here."

4

After dragging the wrecked ice yacht onto the bank—and leaving a note promising they'd be back to clean up the mess—Kurt and Joe hiked along the frozen river until they stood below the NUMA headquarters building, which overlooked the Potomac.

Climbing the riverbank and crossing the street, they entered the building and took the elevator to the seventh floor. The hallway was warm and filled with the aroma of cinnamon, as someone on the weekend staff had made hot chocolate with a liberal dosing of the spice.

Joe inhaled deeply. "If I'd known it could smell this good in here, I'd gladly come in on my day off."

"This is our day off," Kurt reminded him.

"Was," Joe replied.

Passing several empty offices, including one with

Christmas lights still twinkling on a small tree, they reached a well-lit conference room. Rudi Gunn waited inside.

Rudi was a trim man, short in stature, but fit and stern. He stood ramrod straight, staring at them, before glancing at his watch. "Sixteen minutes and forty-three seconds," he said. "You're late."

"There was a wreck on the Potomac," Kurt joked.

"On the Potomac?" Rudi said. "You mean the Beltway, don't you?"

"I mean the river," Kurt said. "We were out on the ice, testing a new sail that Joe designed for my ice yacht. Unfortunately, it worked a little too well. The rest of the machine couldn't handle the speed."

Joe disagreed. "More like pilot error."

"Or faulty construction," Kurt shot back.

Rudi smiled. He was used to Kurt and Joe building machines and wrecking them. Usually they were expensive prototypes accounted for in the NUMA development budget.

"I have no idea what an ice yacht is," Rudi said. "But at least I didn't have to pay for it. More importantly, you two don't seem to mind the cold. That'll come in handy where you're going."

Kurt unzipped his jacket and took a seat. "Sounds rather ominous."

"My thoughts exactly," Joe said. He made his way over to the coffee machine, searching unsuccessfully for the treasured cinnamon hot chocolate. "And what, exactly, are we in for?"

"Let me explain," Rudi said. He dimmed the lights and used a remote to turn on a large flat-screen. "Early this morning, one of our satellites made a pass over southern waters between South Africa and the Antarctic coast. It was a standard high-resolution, wide-scan run. The main purpose of the sweep was to study the melting of sea ice and the extent to which recently calved icebergs have moved. As you might imagine, we picked up plenty of icebergs. And then something else entirely."

Rudi clicked the remote. A wide shot appeared on the screen. It showed a large expanse of dark water speckled with flakes of white. Digital lettering in the corner revealed the time and date of the image, along with the latitude and longitude.

"I do believe you've found the Great Southern Ocean," Kurt said.

"Nothing gets past you," Rudi said. He clicked the remote again, zooming in on one speck of white in one part of the image.

At first glance, it appeared to be a small iceberg. But as Rudi continued to zoom in, the image took on the form of a ship. Closer still and the three-dimensional structure of the vessel could be seen. It had a wide bow and a tall superstructure. Every inch seemed to be covered in a thick layer of white frost, except for a square section on the top of the accommodations block and the helicopter tied down to the landing pad at the stern.

"Frozen solid," Kurt noted.

"Appears to be listing, too," Joe said.

"Doesn't look like a whaler or a fishing trawler," Kurt

said. "Not with that helicopter on the stern. It's obviously not military. Must be a research ship."

"It is," Rudi said. "We've identified it as a scientific vessel out of Cape Town. Its most recent name is *Grishka*, though the ship is forty years old and on its fifth name and seventh owner."

"Have you alerted the South African Navy?"

"Not yet," Rudi replied.

Kurt raised an eyebrow. "That would seem like the prudent thing to do."

"Under normal circumstances, yes," Rudi said. "But in this particular case, I want you and Joe to go investigate first."

"And by 'investigate,'" Kurt clarified, "you mean fly out there, climb aboard the ship and find out why it got caught in the frozen food section of the ocean?"

Rudi nodded.

Joe raised a finger to interject. "You realize that ship is about as far from Washington as it's possible to get while still remaining on the planet Earth?"

Rudi nodded. "Yes, Mr. Zavala. I do have a globe of my own."

"So why send us?" Kurt asked.

"Because Cora Emmerson was on that ship."

Once the name dropped, silence followed. Cora was a former member of NUMA and a brilliant scientist. She'd been with the organization for three years when Rudi brought her to Washington. She'd been especially close to both Kurt and Rudi, before striking out on her own. She'd also been a lot of trouble.

"Are you certain of this?"

"Not entirely," Rudi admitted, "but we know she was aboard at one point. An expedition she cobbled together chartered that ship out of Cape Town. They left four months ago. We have no track on where they went or where the ship has been since. According to the harbormaster's records, it hasn't been back to South Africa."

Kurt glanced back at the frozen ship on the screen.

"Sorry to interrupt," Joe said. "But you two are leaving me in the dark. Who, exactly, is Cora Emmerson?"

Rudi explained. "Cora was a climate expert who worked for NUMA. She'd come to us from a doctoral program at UCLA after several years working internationally. She excelled on her initial field assignments and was hungry to do more. I brought her to D.C., where I thought she would shine, but she decided government work was stifling her ability to bring about radical change in the world's climate policy. So she resigned."

"Twice, if I'm not mistaken," Kurt said, "since you shredded her first letter."

Rudi was unapologetic. "We wanted to keep her. That's what you do with good people." He turned back to Joe. "Everyone tried to convince her to stay. Everyone except for Kurt."

Kurt had no desire to open up this disagreement once more. He and Rudi were usually on the same page, but Cora's abrupt resignation had been a rare point of conflict between them three years ago.

The truth was he'd given Cora the advice he thought was best for her. "She needed freedom," Kurt said. "The kind she wasn't going to get working for a big government agency in the D.C. spotlight. I told her it was okay to reach for what she wanted. Ultimately, she made her own decision. Like all of us do."

Rudi nodded. "Unfortunately, that decision may have brought her to a cold and bitter end."

Kurt glanced at the screen again. The ship was frozen, adrift and dark. It looked dead. Obviously, Rudi figured everyone on board for a similar condition. "All right," Kurt said. "What gives here?"

Rudi narrowed his gaze. "What do you mean?"

"I mean," Kurt said, "there's zero chance you just happened to spot a frozen ship half the size of the smallest iceberg in the region with a standard weather satellite. You couldn't have found that ship unless you were looking for it. More to the point, how could you know Cora was even on board?"

Rudi's intense demeanor softened just a bit. "Because I got a message from her nine weeks ago. She said she was out on the ice shelf and that she and her team had found something incredible. Something with the power to remake the world."

"Remake the world?" Joe said. "That's a strong claim."

"There might be some exaggeration to it," Rudi explained. "You have to understand Cora. If she didn't save the planet by the time she was forty, she was going to be disappointed."

Rudi was right about that. "Did this message say anything else?" Kurt asked.

"No details about what she'd found," Rudi said. "She

promised she'd share them with us once she got back from Antarctica. Her bigger concern was making it back. She insisted there were people who didn't want this discovery to see the light of day. In her words, 'powerful, well-financed people.' She didn't know who they were but claimed her team had dealt with sabotage in the run-up to leaving South Africa and had been under surveillance at times while they were out on the ice."

"Under surveillance?"

"She said they'd picked up high-frequency radio signals that weren't coming from the camp. And on several occasions they'd seen drones in the distance. While I can't confirm any of that, I think we can all agree there's not a lot of drone traffic in remote areas of Antarctica."

Kurt nodded.

"They left camp three weeks early, in the middle of the night, hoping to shake whoever was watching them," Rudi added. "She insisted she'd contact us once she reached Cape Town. Obviously, she never made it."

Kurt set his jaw. The details only made it worse. "You might have shared that message with me. We could have offered some help, given her some protection. We could have met her down on the ice and escorted her back home."

Rudi looked across the table at Kurt. Despite the tension between them, there was still the utmost respect. "Believe me, Kurt, if I had any idea where she was—even the slightest clue—I'd have sent you out there nine weeks ago. But she didn't share that information with me."

Kurt nodded. He appreciated the words. He took

another look at the photo. "What did the infrared cameras show?"

"That the ship is cold," Rudi said. "Very cold. Engines must be off. Battery likely drained. There's a small heat plume discernible at the top of the superstructure, but the rest of the ship is at the same temperature as the background. That's part of the reason it was so hard to find. Every automated scan passed over the ship as if it were another iceberg. We had to find this the old-fashioned way."

"What's causing the heat plume?" Joe asked.

"Hard to tell," Rudi said. "Our best guess is solar panels on top of the superstructure that might still be functioning."

"So, they have electricity, but no lights, no radio calls, no distress beacon."

Rudi nodded. "Which means there's no one on board to use that electricity or there's no working equipment to do anything with it."

Kurt was less downhearted. Electricity meant heat and heat meant life. "Do we have any ships in the area?"

"The *Providence* is the nearest vessel," Rudi said. "She's a Class 1 survey ship studying deepwater currents. She's currently about fifteen hundred miles away. Close enough that she could be within helicopter range by the time you two get there."

Kurt stood up. He knew the drill. There would be a plane waiting for him and Joe at Dulles International. "We'll grab our things."

Rudi stopped him. "I know we haven't always seen eye to eye on Cora, but she was one of ours."

Kurt felt the same way. "I'll bring her home if I can."

"And if you can't," Rudi added, "then I want to know what happened to her. And who was responsible."

5

A series of small buildings lay half buried in the snow at the edge of the Holtzman Glacier. Painted a dull white, with mushroom-shaped roofs, they linked to one another and blended in with their surroundings, appearing almost invisible from overhead. The only real indication that a settlement existed in the area came from the trenches in the snow linking the habitat to structures out and away from the central hub.

The trenches hadn't always been necessary, but ten feet of snow had built up around the outpost in the months since it was set up. Ironically, the piles were not a result of storms dumping frozen precipitation from the sky. The air over Antarctica was so dry that it actually snowed very little there, no more than five inches per year at this location. But because the temperatures remained frigid year-round, what did fall never melted. Instead, it piled up, blowing about in endless drifts.

As strong winds swept across the continent, they scoured the landscape like currents in the ocean. Certain areas were laid bare, offering oasis-like spots of raw land. Others received the excess, with drifts piling higher and higher until anything on the surface was buried, entombed and forgotten.

Base Zero sat in one of those areas and would have a short lifetime on the surface. It had survived the Antarctic summer but would be lost by the end of winter, hidden by the blowing snowdrifts. The men and women who'd put the base together knew this all too well. In fact, they were counting on it.

Unlike the international scientists who had constructed their buildings on platforms that could be raised up each winter or spring, the builders of Base Zero fully intended their habitat to vanish and never be found.

And while most of them would be happy to say goodbye to the cramped little outpost, a lean figure whose subordinates called her the Ice Queen would be sad to see it go.

Where else could I find such silence? Such pristine air and calming solitude?

Leaving this place meant going back to a crowded, dusty world. One that would grow worse with every passing day unless someone altered the trajectory.

She left the main building and entered a trench that led from the habitat across to the nearby glacier. With goggles to protect her eyes, a heavy scarf wrapped around her face and a thick, multilayered cap covering her head and ears, she looked as if she belonged in Aspen or St. Moritz. All that could be seen of her were the tip of her pointed nose and a few wisps of blond hair poking out from beneath the hat.

Arriving at a Y-shaped junction, she branched to the left. The path began sloping upward until it let her out in the middle of the frozen plain.

The snow around her was glistening under the noontime sun. Scalloped drifts ran off in every direction, while mountainous terrain could be seen in the distance beyond. Twelve hundred miles past that mountain lay the southern geographic pole, the very bottom of the world. Fortunately, her destination was much closer—a small drilling rig painted white and shielded by canvas tarps to disguise it from prying eyes. She walked toward it, stopping only when her satellite phone buzzed.

Reaching under the hem of her coat, she grasped the phone with her gloved hand and slid it from its holster. A code indicated the caller's identification, but checking it was just a formality. There was only one person who would be contacting her.

Pulling the scarf away from her mouth, she answered. "Your call is early. I'm not due to report until this afternoon."

"My call is early," a male voice insisted, "because problems don't arrive on a schedule."

"You're saying we have a problem?"

"We do," he said. "Or we will. Very soon."

"What are you talking about?"

"I'm talking about your friend Cora and her old associates in NUMA," the voice said bluntly. "I warned you about her. I told you she would never become one of us."

The blond woman shook her head. "We needed Cora. She led us to what we were after. And I alerted you the moment she betrayed us by contacting NUMA. Now she's dead. And I've seen nothing to suggest NUMA tried to respond to her message."

"What you haven't seen I have," the man insisted. "One of their ships has made a sudden change of course. After weeks of leisurely operations in South African waters, it's now plowing through the sea at high speed, heading almost due south."

This was not good news. "Is it coming our way?"

"No."

"Then we have nothing to worry about."

"How I wish that were true," he said. "I've extrapolated their course and discovered their destination. They're heading for the *Grishka*."

"Impossible," she replied. "That ship is at the bottom of the sea."

"Yet again," he said. "How I wish the facts matched your confident assertions. You sent the *Grishka* on a westward course, did you not?"

"Away from us," she said. "We wanted to make sure it was farther from the bay and our area of operations when it went down. Just in case an emergency beacon we hadn't accounted for went off. That way, if anyone came looking for it, they would be out beyond the horizon."

"It certainly went beyond the horizon," he snapped.

"At least five hundred miles beyond. But it's still afloat. Drifting and collecting ice. I've seen the images with my own eyes."

She couldn't imagine how that was true, but there was no point in arguing. "What do you want us to do?"

"The Americans are obviously headed there to investigate and perhaps salvage the ship. We need to be certain they fail. Where's the tactical team?"

"They're still on the *Goliath*," she said. "Which is too slow and too far away to get there in time."

"Then you'll have to do it," he said. "Use the *Blunt Nose*."

"That vessel is being readied to bring you our genetically engineered samples," she said. "If you divert it, the samples will be delayed. Perhaps even damaged."

He was quiet for a moment. "Which is more important?" he asked finally. "Speed or stealth?"

"Secrecy above all," she replied. "But don't forget, the *Blunt Nose* is unarmed."

"I'm not expecting a running battle," he replied. "The *Grishka* is a derelict at this point. Listing and adrift. It won't take much to send it to the bottom once and for all. Since you failed the first time, I want you to finish the job. By my calculations, you should be able to beat them to the ship by several hours. Secrecy will be maintained and any clues you left behind will vanish forever."

She bit her lip and held back from firing off another salvo. "And the samples?"

"You can deliver them after you've taken care of the *Grishka*."

The call ended before she could argue the point further. The discussion was over. So be it.

She put the phone away, she would have to leave almost immediately, but she needed to check one last thing. She moved forward and ducked under the tarp. A wave of heat swept over her as she entered the operations area. Heat and humidity.

An older man with a wrench in his hand walked over to her. He was short in height but broad across the shoulders. He had hands like the paws of a bear. Even the oversize wrench looked like a toy in his powerful grip.

Scars on his face and neck stood out. They came from an explosion while working at an oil field in Venezuela years earlier. He'd been given the most basic of care, denied any financial settlement and then left for dead. Until the Ice Queen found him.

Now he was one of them. A zealot who'd had the veil lifted from his eyes. Like the rest of them, he saw the dying world for what it was—a disgusting and polluted place where humans tore one another apart and burned nature to the ground for incremental scraps of imaginary wealth. Like her and the others, he was ready to change that for good.

"Do you feel that?" he said.

Of course she felt it. "Is something wrong with the drilling rig?"

"Nothing wrong with it at all," he replied. "It's shut down because we don't need it anymore."

"Then where's all this heat coming from?"

"We've broken through and tapped the geothermal

layer," he said, offering a smile that stretched the scars painfully. "We capped the well, but it's bringing up so much superheated steam that I've had to vent some of it. Otherwise, the pressure will get too high."

"You've hit the target right in the heart," she said. "Outstanding. What's the depth?"

"Two thousand meters," he said. "Roughly six thousand feet."

There was only one pertinent question. "Will the pressure hold?"

The foreman nodded. "Trust me," he said. "There's more heat down there than your wildest estimates. You'll have all the power and steam that you could ever need."

A smile appeared on her face. Something the workers seldom saw. It made her look kind instead of harsh, attractive instead of someone to be feared. She banished it quickly. "Stay on top of this. We're two months past the solstice. The days are getting shorter. This place will be uninhabitable in a matter of weeks."

"It's going to be a long, dark winter," he said.

She nodded. "Longer and darker than anyone knows."

6

After a long flight from Washington, D.C., to Cape Town and a four-hour ride out to the *Providence*, Kurt and Joe got three hours' rest before climbing back on board the NUMA Jayhawk helicopter and flying off toward the *Grishka*.

At that point, the stricken ship was still more than five hundred miles away. Even fitted with extra fuel tanks, the helicopter would have little time to hover over the *Grishka* before it had to turn for home.

"We've got a slight tailwind," the pilot told Kurt and Joe, "but that's going to be a headwind on our way back."

"You won't have to hang around long," Kurt said. "Just get us on the deck."

The pilot nodded and Kurt sat back. He and Joe were

in the passenger section of the helicopter, their minds and bodies completing a rapid adjustment from the normal day-to-day operations back in D.C. to the intense environment of a critical field operation.

"By my calculations, we'll be there in two hours," Joe said. "Just enough time for me to pry the truth out of you."

"What truth?" Kurt said.

"The truth about Cora."

Kurt shook his head in surprise. "Sixteen hours from D.C. to Cape Town and you decide to pester me now?"

"I was plotting my strategy," Joe said.

"On the backs of your eyelids."

"Best way to make a long flight seem short," Joe said. "Besides, you know how these things go. Once we get rolling, sleep will be at a premium."

Joe wasn't wrong about that. But Kurt had found sleep hard to come by. On the flight out, he'd drifted off several times, only to be woken by memories of Cora and questions about what she'd been up to. Each string of thoughts led to the dark possibility of what they'd find on the ship.

The little they'd been able to discover regarding Cora's expedition showed it to be funded by questionable sources and steeped in mystery generally. And whatever part of Antarctica they'd eventually made landfall on, she'd gone there without getting permission from the UN or any of the national agencies that handled that sort of thing. It was a long fall from being part of NUMA.

Joe was waiting. "I can be very persistent," he said.

"The word you're looking for is *annoying*."

"That, too," Joe said. "So, give me the scoop. What's the real deal?"

Kurt gave in with a sigh. Two hours of being pestered by one's best friend was more than any man could endure.

"Cora was everything Rudi said she was. And by that I mean she was brilliant, hardworking and a handful. Rudi handpicked her to be the next member of the team. He brought her in under a mentorship program, like the one they run at Annapolis. And like that program, the duty falls to the mentor to make sure the protégée succeeds. Unfortunately, the more Cora acted out, the more Rudi came down on her. Every reprimand crushed her spirit just a little bit more. And that spirit was what made her great. The bottom line was simple. Cora was like a horse you have to whisper to. Rudi wanted to break her and build her back up his own way. I opened the barn door and set her free."

Joe nodded. He understood the tension better. "I wish I'd had a chance to meet her," he said, then, realizing how he'd phrased it, added, "I mean, um, maybe I still can."

"It's okay," Kurt said. "But for the record, you two would have gotten along famously. Together, you'd have driven Rudi to early retirement."

As Joe laughed, Kurt wondered if he should have done more to make Cora stay. It was a question without an answer. But one he'd asked himself a hundred times in the past twenty-four hours.

"Do you think she was happy after she left?"

"I think she was relieved," Kurt said. "No more structure to fit into. No more chain of command, with her at the bottom. No more fighting. She wanted to change the world. Kind of hard to do that from a desk in the basement."

"You think she reached out to Rudi to let him know she'd made good?"

"The thought crossed my mind," Kurt said.

Joe nodded and then looked off in the other direction. He'd pried enough info out of his friend.

Kurt leaned back and tried to get some rest, but sleep remained hard to come by. He wondered why Cora hadn't contacted him. He would have dropped everything to go help her if she'd reached out. *She had to have known that.* And yet the call hadn't come.

The next two hours passed slowly. Kurt tried to rest for some of it yet found himself checking his watch and counting the minutes until they'd arrive over the stricken ship.

"Coming up on the wreck," the pilot announced eventually. "Two miles out. Slowing and descending."

As the helicopter closed in on the ship, it shed altitude and speed, giving Kurt and Joe a clear view of what lay ahead. The ship looked like an ice sculpture, every surface covered in frost from the ocean's spray.

"She's low in the water," Joe said. "And definitely listing to starboard."

The pilot's voice came next. "Do you have a preference for how we approach the ship? Or where I set you down?"

Ideally, they'd have used the ship's landing pad, but the *Grishka*'s own helicopter was still on board, chained to the deck like a dragon frozen in ice.

"Circle the ship once," Kurt said. "Check the wind and then take us out over the stern. Joe and I will rappel down to the deck."

The pilot did as ordered, swinging wide and descending to a hundred feet.

As the helicopter circled, Kurt and Joe got ready for the egress. Voice-activated headsets were pulled on. Metal-studded climbing shoes, like those Kurt had worn on the frozen Potomac, were strapped to their feet. Backpacks filled with medical supplies and high-calorie liquid supplements were readied, just in case they found anyone alive down there.

With everything else set, they pulled on tight-fitting thermal coats, which NUMA called expedition jackets. Lightweight and well-insulated, they were heated by battery-powered coils and armored with rigid, puncture-resistant Kevlar panels. While the panels weren't bulletproof, they would stop a knife or the sharp point of a protruding bit of wreckage.

Built-in tracking beacons were integrated into the jackets, while twin sets of LED lights, secured where the breast pockets would have been, could be switched on with the touch of a button on the collar. The lights were angled slightly downward and designed to illuminate the darkest of problems while keeping a man or woman's hands free to work on whatever issue they found.

After checking their gear, Kurt gave the thumbs-up,

pulled a harness around his body and attached it to a cable that hung by the helicopter's door.

Joe did the same, moving carefully into position.

"You have your wetsuit on underneath those togs?" Kurt asked.

"Of course," Joe said. "Think we'll be going for a swim?"

Kurt grabbed the rappelling cable and prepared to throw it out the door behind him. "We're supposed to find out what happened to this ship. If the problem is below the waterline, one of us is going to get wet."

Joe had no doubt already predicted that. "Sounds like a job for the Director of Special Projects."

"Unless he delegates it to his trusty assistant," Kurt replied.

By now, they'd come around the far side of the *Grishka*. That brought an odd sight into view.

"Look at that," Joe said.

Kurt finished adjusting his harness and glanced at the ship. Impact damage could be seen all along the port side of the vessel, while a wedge of ice extended outward from the hull. The ice grew along the side of the vessel, sweeping back toward the stern like a wing.

"They hit something," Kurt said.

"Ten will get you twenty that iceberg is the cause of the list," Joe added.

Kurt wasn't so sure. "We're about to find out," he said. "Ready?"

As Joe nodded in the affirmative, Kurt slid the helicopter's door back, allowing a whirlwind of frigid air to sweep into the cabin. With the door locked in place, Kurt and Joe tossed out a pair of weighted ropes that were attached to anchors in the ceiling of the cabin. They eased backward toward the open door, gripping the ropes tight and leaning outward until they achieved a near-sitting position with their feet planted firmly at the edge of the doorway and their weight supported by the ropes.

After a brief glance behind them, both men pushed out and dropped toward the ship. They slid down the ropes, descending a hundred feet in a matter of seconds, much faster than it would be coming down using the winch. They slowed their descent at the last instant, hitting the deck under complete control.

Kurt felt his studded footwear dig in and hold tight. The frost was thicker than he'd expected, an inch of solid ice in some places.

He and Joe detached themselves from the lines, motioning to the crewman in the back of the helicopter to haul the ropes in.

"We're down and clear," Kurt said into the microphone attached to his headset. "What's your fuel situation?"

The pilot's response carried the whine of the engines with it, sounding as if it was electronically altered. *"Ten minutes before we have to head back to the* Providence.*"*

"No point hanging around," Kurt said. "Head back now, refuel and stand by. We'll radio the ship if we need help."

"You're putting a lot of faith in this frozen rust bucket," Joe said.

Kurt looked around. "The sea is calm, the wind is nonexistent and this ship has been drifting for weeks. No reason it should suddenly go down now."

"Unless we're the straw that breaks the camel's back," Joe pointed out.

Kurt had to laugh. "So glad you're an optimist. Let's get moving and see what we can find."

7

As the Jayhawk vanished to the north, the frozen deck of the *Grishku* grew deathly quiet. Kurt looked around. Every surface, every piece of machinery, every flat section or protrusion from the deck was covered in frost and ice.

"How many ships have you salvaged in your day?" Joe asked.

"Lost count years ago," Kurt said.

"Ever see one like this?"

Kurt shook his head. As a salvage expert since his days in the Navy, Kurt had spent countless hours on stranded, drifting or sinking vessels. He'd fought fires on burning ships, shored up ruptured hull plating and had even run a vessel aground that could be stopped from sinking no other way. He'd investigated and refloated dozens of ships of every imaginable type. Each ship had a personality, each wreck its own story.

A priceless yacht driven aground by an intoxicated owner smacked of arrogance. An overworked ferry, glued together by corrosion and the endless ingenuity of its crew, reminded him of a loyal dog that finally grew too tired to run with its master.

He saw the *Grishka* as an apparition trapped between worlds. The gray ship had been made over in white. Strangely twisted icicles hung from every wire and overhang of the superstructure. It was a ghost, but one not quite ready to pass over to the other side.

"Never seen curved icicles before," Joe said.

"They started off straight," Kurt pointed out, "curving as the list grew worse. It means the ship took on water very slowly."

"We need to be careful," Joe said. "With that much ice on the superstructure, it's going to be top-heavy."

Kurt understood. Ice-covered ships could capsize suddenly even when otherwise seaworthy. "If she weren't sitting so low in the water, I think she'd have rolled over already. The flooded compartments must be acting as ballast."

"Probably," Joe said. "And that iceberg she's attached herself to might be acting like a float. If that thing breaks free, we could be upside down in the blink of an eye."

A brief swirl of wind came up, causing the ship to creak and groan. A sound like breaking glass came from somewhere amidships as several dagger-shaped icicles broke loose and crashed to the deck.

"We should be careful when we walk under these things," Joe said.

"Or over things," Kurt said. He'd stopped at what appeared to be a mound of snow. Closer inspection revealed a body frozen to the deck. Frost and ice had covered the man's features. Brushing away revealed the gray skin of his face and a circular swath of red staining the jacket he wore.

"Blood," Joe said. "The bright color suggests it froze before it coagulated."

"He's been shot in the back," Kurt said grimly. "I wasn't expecting survivors, but this is a bad sign. Let's make our way inside."

They moved across the deck, pausing beside the *Grishka*'s helicopter.

The craft had frost on the windshield and some ice on its sheet metal, but the rotor blades and engine compartment were protected by weatherproof covers and those covers were clean and ice-free.

"Electrical lines," Joe said, pointing to cables coming from the bulkhead to the helicopter. "The covers are heated. Like our jackets."

"That explains the infrared signature that the satellite detected," Kurt replied. "As long as the solar panels haven't frozen over, there should be enough juice running through it."

"Makes you wonder why no one used it to get off the ship?"

"Probably never got the chance," Kurt said.

Joe made his way over to the helicopter and scraped

the frost off the curved windshield. The interior was dark and empty.

"Let's see how the rest of the ship looks," Kurt said. "The engine room is probably flooded and useless, but there might be an auxiliary power unit we can fire up."

Leaving the helicopter behind, they crossed the deck to the nearest hatchway. Like everything else on the ship, it was locked in position by an accumulation of frozen water.

Kurt pulled hard and, when that didn't work, slammed a shoulder into the door to break the ice free. After kicking a few stray pieces away, he pulled back using both hands. It moved halfway before jamming up again. The gap was just wide enough for them to squeeze through.

"Age before beauty," Joe, deferring to Kurt, suggested.

"You're six months younger than me," Kurt pointed out.

"But twenty-seven percent more attractive," Joe insisted.

Kurt laughed and slipped through the door. "We really need to work on your math."

The tilted corridor was cluttered and dank. Light coming through the open hatchway revealed walls coated white from moisture getting inside and freezing. Farther on, a drab avocado green paint scheme revealed itself. The dingy layer of paint was peeling in places and long overdue for a touch-up.

With his eyes slowly adjusting to the darkened corridor, Kurt reached toward a tab on his collar, clicking the button he found there. The LEDs on his jacket lit instantly to full brightness, providing a wide swath of light across the interior of the passageway.

Stepping up beside him, Joe switched his lights on as well. Between the two of them, the hallway was now lit as if by one powerful floodlight. It showed the carnage had not been limited to the outside.

They found nine bodies in the aft section of the deck. Each of them shot multiple times. A quick search of the crew quarters revealed five sailors shot in their beds at close range.

"Whoever hit this ship, they came on hard and fast," Joe said.

"This was a one-sided battle," Kurt replied. "These people never had a chance."

They continued the search without any expectation of finding survivors. They did find additional bodies in the stairwell and two more on the bridge. Heading belowdecks, they came to the science center and recognized immediately that something was amiss.

Drawers and file cabinets had been left open and emptied. A tangled web of power cords and USB cables lined one desk, but the computers and laptops they might have once linked up to were nowhere to be seen. Two keyboards and a stray mouse pad randomly tossed to one side told the rest of the story.

"This place has been ransacked," Kurt said.

Searching for anything that had been left behind, Kurt found a few random sheets of paper tucked down behind the printer.

"Anything interesting?" Joe asked.

Kurt leafed through the stack. One sheet was directions for rebooting the cooling system, several others proved to be scheduling sheets. The only thing of any interest was a black-and-white photo that had been printed on regular copy paper.

The image showed several men standing in the snow. They wore heavy boots and cold-weather gear of vintage style. Someone had drawn on the photo with red ink, adding horns on the top of one man's head. A Hitler mustache had been hastily applied to the face of another. A plaque in front of them read *Deutsche Antarktische Expedition 1938–1939*. Draped beneath it was the unmistakable banner of Nazi Germany.

Kurt handed Joe the photo.

"Well, that's unexpected," Joe said.

Kurt nodded, shuffling through the rest of the scraps. He found nothing to explain the photo or the graffiti that had been scrawled on it. Nor did he find anything to suggest what the research team had been working on. Taking the photo back from Joe, he folded it up and slid it into a pocket. "Let's see what's next."

They moved to the adjoining compartment, discovering long, empty racks that ran the length of the room. The racks were stacked like shelves all the way up to the ceiling, but they held nothing.

"Cold-storage room," Joe said. "These shelves are designed to hold ice cores. We outfitted a NUMA vessel heading to Greenland last summer with a vault like this."

Kurt touched one of the cradles. It was no colder than the rest of the room. "What happened to the ice?"

"Must have been taken," Joe said. "Even with the system off-line, that much ice would never melt. Not with the whole ship frozen solid. I think we can safely assume that whoever hit this ship was after what Cora claimed to have found."

"Speaking of Cora," Kurt said, "I haven't seen her yet. We should keep looking."

He moved forward, heading for the next compartment and stopping beside a console that housed various controls and readouts. Scraping frost off the panel, he found a row of LEDs blinking a dim orange color. "This is the control system for the cryogenic unit," he said. "It's still functioning."

"Must be getting juice from the solar array," Joe said. "Like the helicopter's de-icing system."

"Makes sense," Kurt replied. "But if the cryogenic unit is still on, why is this room the same temperature as the rest of the ship?"

Kurt looked around for an answer to his own question. His gaze settled on a bundle of insulated hoses. Instead of connecting to the storage racks, the lines ran from the side of the cooling unit, along the floor of the compartment and down a scuttle to the deck below.

Kurt pulled on the hoses. They wouldn't budge. "We need to go down there."

"That will take us below the waterline," Joe warned.

"I have a feeling we'll be skating instead of swimming."

Kurt squeezed through the circular opening and descended the ladder. Two-thirds of the way down, his foot hit something cold and wet. He pressed downward and felt his boot sliding into an icy mush.

"I was half right," he said.

"That's better than normal," Joe replied.

Kurt glanced at the slush below him and then scanned the compartment. It was flooded chest-high and the water had been turned to briny slush, with salt deposits coating the walls.

Stepping off the ladder, Kurt sank up to his thighs. The chill ran through his exploration gear but was tempered by the insulated wetsuit he wore underneath.

He moved away from the ladder, pushing through the heavy mixture and following the cryogenic hoses across the room.

It took an unbelievable amount of effort to wade through the slush, as if he were walking with a fifty-pound weight attached to each leg. The farther aft he went, the denser the slush grew, finally turning to ice near the far end of the compartment. Kurt climbed up onto the ice and crawled the rest of the way.

Arriving at the aft bulkhead, he was now up against the ceiling. This entire end of the compartment was solid ice. Ahead of him, he spied the top of a watertight door. The cryogenic lines were there as well, looping out of the solid block and back down into it.

Kurt studied the arrangement as Joe crossed the compartment and joined him. "Tell me we didn't freeze our extremities off just to find the ship's sno-cone maker."

"We've found a lot more than that," Kurt said. "Look at the hatch. It's slightly ajar. Water was coming through.

But someone stopped it by running these cryogenic tubes down here and freezing the water as it filled the compartment."

"That might explain the growth of ice attached to the hull," Joe suggested. "The cold would radiate through to the gap in it. A coating of ice would build up, eventually sealing the puncture. But since no one ever turned this off, it would continue to grow."

"That explains why the attachment of ice is smooth and swept back like a wing. It formed slowly by accretion."

"That would be my thought," Joe said. "But what happened to the people who came up with this plan? Did they get rescued before we got here?"

"I wish that were the case," Kurt said.

Using the outside of his glove, he scraped at the frost beneath them, buffing it in a circular pattern until the rough, opaque veneer turned smooth and clear. A face appeared below it. A slightly distorted vision of a woman with dark hair, fine features and eyes that were peacefully closed. Her hands remained clasped around the cryogenic lines.

"Is that who I think it is?"

"Cora Emmerson," Kurt said quietly. "Looks like she gave her life to save the ship."

"I'm sorry," Joe said.

Kurt stared for a long, silent moment. "Damn," he whispered.

He'd expected this would be the reality since they'd left Washington. That didn't make it any easier.

8

Having spent an hour chipping her from the ice, Kurt lifted Cora free and carried her to the *Grishka*'s sick bay.

Searching for anything he might be able to bring home to her family, he found a necklace, an ID card and a phone, which remained frozen solid in its protective case. He slid the items into another pocket before covering her with a blanket.

As Kurt stood up, Joe brought in the last of the dead crewmen, dragging the man on a collapsible litter. Sliding the body to a spot beside the bulkhead, Joe placed the end of the stretcher down and then picked up the manifest they'd discovered. Comparing the man's ID tag to the list, he made a check mark.

"Is that everyone?" Kurt asked.

"We're still missing one of the science team," Joe said. "A woman named Yvonne Lloyd. I've searched everywhere. She's not on the ship."

"Maybe that tells us something," Kurt said. He looked at his watch. "Let's get back to the bridge. It's time to check in with Rudi."

Broadcasting from the bridge of the ship, Kurt and Joe spoke with Rudi Gunn via a small handheld satellite phone. A grainy picture of Rudi was displayed on the phone's four-inch screen. Data lag caused the image to freeze and skip every few seconds. At times, it made Rudi's movements look robotic.

Kurt gave Rudi the bad news about the ship, the crew and Cora, explaining how she had courageously stopped the vessel from sinking. "She'd been shot," Kurt explained. "A superficial head wound. Not fatal, but between the injury and the loss of blood, it's hard to overstate the effort she made to keep the ship from going down."

Rudi took the news with notable silence, processing the sad reality with a military instinct. "I want to know who did this," he said finally.

"Whoever it was," Kurt said, "didn't leave many clues. Though there are a few things out of order."

"Such as?"

"To start with, someone's missing."

Joe explained. "Once we determined that the ship was stable, we began with a body count," Joe said. "We brought all the dead crewmen to the main deck and matched ID tags and passports against the names on the manifest. When it was all said and done, everyone on the ship was accounted for except a woman named Yvonne Lloyd. She's listed on the science team's roster as a climatologist and paleomicrobiologist . . . Whatever that is."

"Maybe she got trapped belowdecks when the water came in," Rudi suggested.

"The only flooded compartments are the bilge and the engine room," Kurt replied. "No reason for a scientist to be down there."

"Hiding is a reason," Rudi said. "That ship was under attack."

"I doubt she got the chance," Kurt said. "Looks like the ship was taken by surprise. Some of the crew were shot dead in their bunks."

"How do you take a ship by surprise in the middle of the open ocean?" Rudi asked.

Kurt shook his head. He was having trouble with that one as well.

"It's possible she was taken hostage," Joe said.

"Hostage?"

"The ship was cleaned out," Kurt explained. "The ice cores are gone. And the computers and hard drives. Basically, the science lab looks like Whoville after the Grinch came to town."

"Meaning there's no sign of what Cora found out on the ice," Rudi noted.

"None," Kurt said. "But it stands to reason that this missing scientist might have had something to do with Cora's discovery. If so, the people who attacked this ship may have wanted her knowledge, too."

Rudi scribbled something else on a notepad. "I'll have

Hiram run her name through the computer. What about the ship? Can it be salvaged? I'd like to get it back to dry dock, where authorities can go over it with a fine-tooth comb."

Kurt nodded. "Joe and I have a plan to make her seaworthy again. But the engine room is flooded beyond repair. We'll need a tow."

"The *Providence* can handle that," Rudi said. "By my calculations, she'll rendezvous with you in four hours. I want that ship ready to go when they get there."

With a great deal of work to do, Kurt and Joe prioritized what was necessary over what would merely be helpful.

Joe got the power back on by diverting fuel from the main bunker to the auxiliary power unit. That got the heat on and enabled them to restart the bilge pumps once the ice began to thaw.

The next step was to make a more permanent seal over the puncture wound.

"If we're going to get this ship moving, we'll need to cut the ice off the outside of the hull," Kurt said.

"But the ice is keeping the seawater out," Joe reminded him.

"Which is perfect," Kurt said. "As long as we're sitting still or drifting along with the current. Once we're under tow and out in rougher waters, the force of the waves will push that chunk of ice up and down, back and forth. When it breaks loose—which it will—it'll rupture the hull and all our work will be for nothing."

"You want to trim it down?" Joe asked.

Kurt shook his head. "Take it off clean and weld a plate over the breach, sealing it properly from the outside. But if that's not feasible, we'll cut the ice back as close to flush as possible. And keep the cryogenic unit on."

"I checked the ship's equipment room," Joe said. "They're well stocked. Drysuits, oxygen tanks, welding equipment. They even have spare plating handy."

"Makes sense," Kurt said. "An old rust bucket like this lives off the ingenuity of its crew."

After rounding up the appropriate equipment, Kurt donned a drysuit, insulated gloves and a full-face helmet. He strapped a single tank of air to his back and went into the water near the ship's stern.

After a minute to get adjusted to the gear, he opened a valve on the suit to release some air so that he wouldn't be bobbing around in the water like a cork.

Swimming around the side of the ship, he soon reached the icy protrusion. It was streamlined and teardrop-shaped. The only way to break it free without damaging the ship was to cut it away piece by piece. And the best tool for that job was high-temperature heat.

Kurt called out to Joe over the radio. "You in position, amigo?"

"Ready and waiting," Joe replied.

Looking up, Kurt saw Joe at the rail of the ship. "Lower the cylinders," he said. "I'm ready to begin surgery."

Up above, Joe lifted a pair of connected cylinders onto the ship's rail. Leaning forward, he began lowering them on a rope.

The cylinders contained oxyacetylene, normally used for welding. Joe had connected a pair of tanks together, wrapping them in foam and linking them through a single valve to ensure there was enough pressure to do the job.

The tanks came down slowly, one arm's length at a time, as Joe worked the line with his bare hands.

"Almost there," Kurt said. "Another ten feet."

Kurt took ahold of the tanks as they reached the water. After connecting them to his drysuit with a clip, he released the rope.

A twist of the valve got the gas flowing. A single click of the igniter brought a twelve-inch jet of blue flame to life. Kurt adjusted the flame and brought it up against the ice.

"Is it working?" Joe asked over the radio.

"Like a hot knife through butter," Kurt said.

The tip of the flame burned at six thousand degrees, enough to melt hardened steel. Kurt used it to cut a V-shaped section from the ice, which he broke off and shoved away before moving in to remove another section.

As he worked, Joe offered advice over the radio.

"I wouldn't dawdle. As the acetylene in those tanks cools down, you're going to lose pressure."

"I'm surprised it's as strong as it is," Kurt said. "How'd you manage that?"

"I warmed the tanks beside the exhaust port of the APU. Then I wrapped them in the foam."

Kurt shook his head. "Only you would place tanks containing violent explosive gases next to a high-temperature heat source. Great idea, though. Glad you didn't blow yourself up in the process. That would have made my job far more difficult."

"Don't get all sentimental," Joe said. *"How's the water?"*

"Balmy," Kurt joked. "Actually, I'm working up a sweat down here."

Kurt quickly removed sections of ice on either side and then attacked a larger section in the center. Progress was steady. In five minutes, he'd cleared half the ice. Another five and he'd be done.

While Kurt toiled, Joe watched from up on deck. With little to do but wait around, his mind wandered. He examined the damage to the side of the hull.

Some of the plating was punctured, but up high. In other spots, it was dented and gouged but still watertight. The ship's rail was bent in near the bow, part of it had been torn free and peeled back like a guardrail on a highway that had been hit hard.

The *Grishka* had clearly been involved in a collision. Nothing head-on, more of a sideswipe, by the looks of it. If the ship had been a car, Joe would have found scrapes of paint and tried to match the color to the make and model, but there was no paint to be seen, just piles of ice and snow on the deck.

Even at first glance, it struck him as odd. For one thing, there was too much of it. He could have built ten igloos from the piles littering the deck on the starboard side.

He kicked his boot through some of the snow. The surface layer was white, but it was an odd color underneath.

Joe dropped down to take a closer look. Instead of white, it was light beige and, in places, gray. "Number one rule of childhood. *Don't eat yellow snow*," he said to himself. "What about other colors?" he asked aloud.

"What are you talking about?" Kurt asked.

"Piles of snow along the rail," Joe said. "The color of portland cement. Looks a little like New York snow a week after it comes down. But not as crusty."

Turning his attention from the snow to the horizon, Joe noticed something else. He squinted against the glare of the low sun, studying a mound of water moving silently toward them.

Joe's first thought was a killer whale approaching, sinister and dangerous. The black, oily water rose in front of it and fell off behind it, just as it did over the back of an orca, but there was no sign of a dorsal fin and the disturbance was far too large to be made by a living creature.

"We have a problem," he said.

9

Joe moved to the front of the ship to get a better look at the approaching target. "It has to be a submarine," he said, considering the size and speed of the approaching disturbance. "Either that or a very large and angry whale."

"And it's headed our way," Kurt replied calmly.

"Aiming for the bow," Joe said.

Closer now, Joe could see this was no optical illusion. The submarine was at least a hundred feet in length. It showed no signs of slowing or turning. If anything, it appeared to be picking up speed.

"Get away from the ship," Joe called out. "Whatever it is, it's going to hit us."

Joe took one last look. Then, realizing that he was standing almost directly above the strike zone, he took off running. He raced back along the starboard side, heading for the stern. He was amidships when the object struck home.

The impact was jarring, but there was no detonation, no thundering wave of heat accompanied by the wrenching sound of steel plates being torn apart. Just the deck surging and tilting beneath him.

Thrown off balance midstride, Joe tumbled and sprawled in the snow, sliding to a stop as the *Grishka* rolled with the tremendous undersea punch.

Kurt's voice came through the radio. *"It's a submarine, all right. It rammed the forward section of the ship, behind the anchor."*

Getting back to his feet, Joe leaned out over the rail and looked toward the bow. He saw the top half of a streamlined craft, charcoal in color. Its nose was embedded in the *Grishku*'s side, while water churned furiously at the tail end.

"It's gone full reverse," he said. "It's trying to pull free."

"Get off," Kurt suggested. *"Once that thing breaks out, the ship's going to sink like a stone."*

Joe raced for the stern and the canisters for the inflatable lifeboat he'd seen earlier. Halfway there, he slid to a stop. He'd run right past the *Grishka*'s helicopter before an idea occurred to him.

Rushing up to the helicopter, Joe pulled the heated covers from the rotors overhead. They slid off with ease, slamming to the deck and revealing the clean black surface of the protected airfoil underneath.

He pulled a heavy plastic cover from the tail rotor

and cleared the engine intake and exhaust as well. Next, he went for the tie-down chains. He yanked one free, and then felt the deck tilting beneath him once again. "What's happening?"

"The submarine is trying to break free," Kurt said. *"It's surging forward and then pulling back."*

Joe worked quickly. With the chains released, the helicopter was a free bird. Now he just had to make it fly.

He grabbed the helicopter's door and pulled it open. Jumping into the pilot's seat, he flipped several switches. The instrument panel came to life. The gyros began to spool up.

Joe thanked his lucky stars that the helicopter had been hooked to the solar array all this time. The battery registered a full charge.

"AC power on," Joe said, running through the bare minimum of a checklist. "Fuel pumps on . . . Starter, engage."

Joe held the starter switch down as whining above him announced the rotors were turning on battery power. The rapid tick-tick-tick of the igniters joined in.

"Come on, baby," Joe said to the helicopter. "Don't let me down."

After several additional seconds, the engine roared to life. Joe released the starter as the rotors began to spin. But at almost the same time, the *Grishka* swayed once more. It rolled to port, briefly back to starboard and then back to port again.

Kurt gave him the bad news. *"The submarine has broken free. I can see a huge gash in the hull. Whatever you're planning to do, now would be a good time to do it. I'd say you've got thirty seconds, no more."*

Joe was amazed by how calmly Kurt reported this disaster.

"My plan is to hail a cab," Joe said.

"A cab?"

"Air taxi. How's that sound to you?"

"Better than treading water until the Providence *gets here."*

With the rotor blades picking up speed, Joe flexed the controls, finding all systems were operational.

As Joe counted the seconds, a bulkhead in the front part of the ship gave way. Water surged into the next compartment and the *Grishka*'s list worsened.

The helicopter, which was no longer chained down, began sliding on the ice-covered landing pad. It caught on the rail, threatening to tumble over it.

Joe pulled back on the cyclic, applying maximum take-off power. The helicopter left the deck at an angle, pulling free from the railing and peeling off to starboard like a drunken sailor stumbling in the dark.

Joe leveled the craft quickly and continued away from the ship, climbing and turning to the east.

"You're clear," Kurt told him. *"Good work."*

"What about you?" Joe asked.

As Kurt began to reply, his words were drowned out by a rumbling sound, complete with high-pitched hissing and chaotic reverberations. It was the *Grishka*'s death rattle, picked up by Kurt's microphone. The ship had capsized and gone down at the bow.

10

Knowing the *Grishka* was going to sink, Kurt had prudently swum away from the hull, putting enough space between himself and the ship to be safe from any undertow.

But as the vessel rolled and twisted, a guide wire running from the superstructure to the bow snapped. It whipped outward, cutting across the water like an eel and wrapping itself around his leg. It pulled tight as the ship went down and dragged Kurt along for the ride.

Kurt didn't bother reaching for it in some foolish attempt to pull it loose. He knew from the pressure on his calf that no human hands would have enough strength to loosen the cable. Instead, he ignited the acetylene torch and brought it toward the braided metal line.

With the blue light from the torch's flame illuminating the dark water, Kurt twisted around and made contact with the cable. The torch burned hot for several seconds but then began to dim.

The flame was dying, the victim of the icy cold and the higher pressure caused by the increasing depth. Kurt shook the tanks to stir up the liquid inside, banging them against his thigh until the blue flame grew once again.

With fire holding steady, Kurt brought it back up against the cable. The metal strands turned red and flaked away. With a twang that echoed through the water, the cable snapped, vanishing into the darkness.

The sudden release was almost painful. Kurt pulled the remaining section of the cable away from his leg. His calf throbbed, but a gash in the drysuit was letting enough frigid water in to numb the pain.

Kurt turned his attention toward the surface. While the silver light seemed a long way above him, the buoyancy of the drysuit was already lifting him. With a few strong kicks, he accelerated upward, emerging amid the churning waters where the *Grishka* had once been.

Turning from point to point, he spotted Joe in the helicopter and then the hull of the submarine. The menacing vessel was a long way off, but Kurt was a bright orange target in the middle of the sea. If they were looking, it wouldn't take long for them to spot him.

"Joe," he called out. "Do you read?"

"Ever since third grade," Joe's cheerful voice replied. *"Where've you been?"*

"Riding a metal horse to the bottom," Kurt replied. "I wouldn't recommend it. Can you pick me up?"

"As soon as I can see through this windshield," Joe said. *"It's still frosted over."*

Kurt glanced over his shoulder. The submarine was changing direction, coming back his way. As it turned head-on, Kurt noticed a pair of protruding globes sticking up above the bow. These "eyes" almost certainly were cameras and they were looking directly at him.

"I'm not sure I have time for your defroster to kick in," he said. "That mechanical shark is circling back toward me."

"Give me your bearing."

Kurt looked at the helicopter, estimating Joe's heading. "Turn left forty degrees."

The helicopter pivoted, rotating slowly.

"Too far," Kurt said. "Come back about ten degrees . . . Perfect. You're pointed right at me."

"What's the distance?"

"Half a mile," Kurt said.

Joe dipped the nose of the helicopter and began moving the craft toward Kurt.

With Joe on the way, Kurt switched his focus to the submarine that was coming from the other direction. It was going to be close.

He glanced back at Joe. "You're three hundred yards from my position. Fifty feet off the deck. Turn five degrees to the left."

Kurt admired the skill with which Joe piloted the helicopter, watching as his friend brought it within ten feet of the water while correcting his course, closing in and slowing down.

"A hundred yards," Kurt said.

The whirling blades grew louder. The water began whipping outward from Kurt in circles. Kurt swam toward the helicopter as it hovered, reaching for the right skid as Joe dipped it into the water.

He pulled himself up, suddenly feeling the weight of the acetylene torch dragging him down. He disconnected the tanks and swung a leg over the skid. "Go."

The engine roared that much louder as Joe gave it full power. The helicopter rose up, lifting Kurt free of the water. They'd climbed no more than fifty feet when the dark submersible passed underneath.

Kurt watched as it rammed the floating acetylene tanks, breaking them apart and shrugging off the minor explosion that resulted.

From directly above, Kurt got a clear look at the vessel. It was completely streamlined, shaped like a tadpole, but with a more bulbous front and a longer, narrower tail. A jagged section jutting from the bow looked to be the broken shaft of the spike it had plunged into the *Grishka*'s side.

The hull had an incredibly smooth texture, appearing part and parcel of the water it was slicing through. As it caught the light, it looked almost translucent. It passed beneath them, submerged and vanished from sight.

11

The communications suite of the *Providence* was the modern version of a ship's radio room. It sat behind the bridge in its own dedicated compartment. Instead of old-fashioned transmitters and a telegraph machine tapping out Morse code, the suite was filled with computers, flat-screen monitors and satellite communications gear.

In Kurt's mind, there was only one drawback to all the technology. Radio calls could be made while wearing pajamas, with crazy hair and three days' stubble on one's face. But if you were going to be on-screen in high definition, you had to be presentable to whoever was on the other side. In this case, that meant Rudi Gunn and NUMA's Director of Technology, Hiram Yaeger.

In his own way, Hiram was the exception to the rule Kurt had just laid down. A computer genius who'd designed and built most of NUMA's top-end technology, Hiram wore granny glasses and had his hair in a ponytail, which he'd been promising to cut for years. He was dressed in blue jeans and a long-sleeved Harley-Davidson T-shirt, which proudly identified the Cabo San Lucas dealership as its place of origin.

Despite the counterculture look, Hiram was sharp as a knife. If he ever retired from NUMA—something Rudi insisted would never be allowed—a bidding war for his services would erupt in Silicon Valley within the hour.

As Rudi questioned Kurt and Joe about the incident, Hiram sat by, tapping notes into his laptop.

"Did you get a good look at the submarine?" Rudi asked.

"Several looks," Kurt said. "A hundred feet in length, no conning tower or sail. It was fast and highly maneuverable. I'd say it was constructed of an unusual material."

"That's very descriptive," Rudi said. "Care to narrow it down for us?"

"I didn't have time to get a sample," Kurt said. "But it wasn't steel and it wasn't the type of coating we use to cover our boats. Appeared slightly translucent and non-metallic. My assumption would be a new type of sonar-absorbent material. Plastic or a synthetic polymer. Which might explain the translucent effect."

"Which suggests a very advanced operator," Rudi noted with disdain. He turned to Hiram. "See what you can find in the database about new materials being developed for submersibles. That might tell us something."

Hiram nodded and typed more notes. Rudi continued the questioning. "How about from your vantage point, Joe?"

"I saw what Kurt saw," Joe replied. "Very stealthy. Turned on a dime. From stem to stern, not the type of equipment you could buy off the shelf."

"Military?" Rudi asked.

Joe shook his head. "Unarmed. It didn't fire anything at the helicopter and it used a ram to sink the *Grishka*. Doubt they'd have chosen the giant can opener approach if they carried torpedoes or missiles."

"Well," Rudi said. "At least that tells us something."

Something but not much, Kurt thought. "Did you find anything on the missing scientist?"

"We did," Rudi said. "For one thing, she's almost famous. But I'll let Hiram explain."

Yaeger adjusted his glasses and began to speak. "Yvonne Lloyd is a thirty-four-year-old Dutch national. Though she was born in Amsterdam, she was raised in South Africa, where she attended Stellenbosch University. She majored in climatology and political science, graduating summa cum laude. After several months in Antarctica as part of a UN expedition, she went back to school and earned a doctorate in paleomicrobiology."

Joe raised his hand as if he were in class. "As a student whose most advanced degree is underwater basket weaving, I have to ask. What, exactly, is paleomicrobiology?"

"It's the study of microscopic organisms using the

fossil record," Hiram replied. "A paleobiologist performs research into bacteria, algae and viruses that lived in previous epochs before dying off or evolving into the organisms we have with us today."

"Ah," Joe said. "That's what I thought. Just wanted to be sure."

Yaeger continued. "Her earliest published work revolves around the concept of the Earth as a living organism, while comparing modern humans and our activities to a bacterial infestation. Finishing her doctoral program, she produced a dissertation on what scientists now call the Snowball Earth Theory."

"Sounds like a winter-themed amusement park," Kurt said.

Rudi jumped in. "I can promise you, there was little to be amused about during that era. If the Snowball Earth Theory is correct, the entire planet was frozen."

"Like an ice age?" Joe asked.

"Worse," Rudi said. "Consider it a super ice age. One that would bury all the major landmasses in glaciers a mile deep. It would turn the upper layer of the oceans into ice, beneath which briny slush would ooze and barely move. If the theory is to be believed, only a narrow band around the equator remained warm enough for water to remain liquefied and thus support life."

"Pretty sure my toes would have been cold," Kurt said. "How does this connect with Cora and whatever she might have been searching for in Antarctica?"

Yaeger jumped back in to explain. "Yvonne's dissertation proposed that one cause of this Snowball Earth era was microbes that no longer exist today. Her research showed that these microbes became so efficient at removing greenhouse gases from the atmosphere that they left only traces of carbon dioxide and methane behind. The result was a crystal clear atmosphere with no greenhouse blanket left to warm it."

Joe chimed in. "Like the way a desert at night is a whole lot colder than a tropical island even if the desert is much hotter during the day."

"That's the exact effect," Yaeger said. "But further compounding this effect is the reflection issue."

"Which is?" Kurt asked.

"The obvious effect of cold temperatures on water," Yaeger said. "Turning it to snow and ice. With the Earth cooling rapidly, snow fell more often and stayed a lot longer. Eventually, the continents were covered in snowpack year-round and most of the world's oceans were crusted over with ice. This coating reflected a much larger percentage of the incoming solar radiation back into space than what's reflected today. So instead of absorbing heat in the daylight hours, the planet was cooling during the day as well as cooling at night."

"A classic negative feedback loop," Kurt noted. "The colder it got, the more it cooled down. So how, precisely, did the world get out of this super ice age?"

"No one's quite sure," Yaeger said. "Some scientists disagree with the theory based on the belief that the planet could not escape such a frozen state and therefore it could never have happened. Others point to a meteor impact or a strong wave of volcanic activity as events that would impart enough energy to begin the thaw. While those ideas are still being debated, Yvonne proposed a second theory that took this idea further, applying it on a smaller scale to the regular reoccurrence of normal ice ages, which have been coming and going for the last million years with incredible consistency."

Yaeger punched up a chart, which appeared on the screen both on the *Providence* and in the conference room.

The chart compared the Earth's average temperature to the amount of glacial coverage around the world over the past million years. As would be expected, every time temperatures rose, the glaciers melted. But instead of producing runaway warmth and a tropical Earth, each spike in temperatures was immediately followed by a cooling period, with the world returning first to equilibrium and then dropping into another ice age.

Geologically speaking, the spikes and the cooling trends came at regular intervals and the resulting chart looked something like an EKG readout familiar to anyone who'd ever been in a hospital or watched a medical program on television.

"Yvonne called it the Heartbeat of Gaia," Yaeger explained. "Which is another name for Earth. She attributed this up and down pattern to the self-correcting abilities of the planet and the release of microbes from the Arctic regions during the hottest eras."

Rudi added a point. "She called this the Firewall Theory, suggesting that the Earth's stored biological history will act like a computer firewall to prevent or correct any human-created catastrophe, including climate change or global warming."

Kurt nodded. It was interesting, if far-fetched. "By what mechanism does she suggest these microbes come and go?"

"It's based on the melting of glaciers," Yaeger said. "When the Earth gets too warm, the glaciers melt. As they melt, they release viruses, bacteria and algae that haven't seen the light of day for twenty thousand years or more. These dormant microbes flood into the oceans, blooming rapidly because they have no natural enemies. They absorb the greenhouse gases, creating a lesser version of the Snowball Earth and bringing about a cooling period and another ice age. As the world ices over, these microbes are cut off from their source and slowly die."

"Did she have any proof to offer?"

"Not that I can see," Yaeger said. "But the dissertation was written years ago. A lot has changed since then. And it wouldn't surprise us if that's what she and Cora were looking for in Antarctica."

Considering what he'd heard, it wouldn't have surprised Kurt either. But looking and finding were two different things. "What are the chances of this being anything more than fantasy?"

Joe spoke up. "I remember hearing about a group of scientists who discovered strains of dormant bacteria living in the meltwater at the bottom of Antarctic lakes. And then, just last year, a research group in Tibet discovered twenty-eight previously unknown viruses dormant beneath a melting glacier."

Kurt turned to Joe. "You seem to be well versed in this stuff."

Joe grinned. "If it falls into the realm of zombie apocalypse scenarios, I make sure to stay up to date."

Kurt laughed.

"You're not the only one," Yaeger insisted. "My research has revealed similar things, including a deadly incident in Russia back in 2016, when reindeer carcasses thawed out of the permafrost and promptly released anthrax into the air. A French scientist studying the case warned that bubonic plague, Spanish flu and smallpox are lurking there as well. And that if deeper ice begins to melt, we might be facing diseases that humanity hasn't dealt with since the Neanderthals were running around. Diseases we have no immunity to."

"As if the coronavirus and swine flu weren't bad enough," Rudi said.

The communications room fell silent, everyone considering the implications of new plagues emerging from the melting ice.

"Sounds like Yvonne's theory was not out of the question," Kurt said. "And it explains why she would be on Cora's expedition. Rudi mentioned she was famous. Last I checked, publishing an academic paper or two doesn't bring the paparazzi running to your door."

"No," Yaeger admitted. "But getting into a tabloid-worthy feud with your wealthy oil baron brother does."

"Who's her brother?"

"Ryland Lloyd," Hiram said. "Owner and CEO of Mata Petroleum."

As Yaeger spoke, he tapped away at the keyboard in front of him, bringing up photos of the two siblings. Yvonne was blond and natural, her features striking, without a hint of makeup. Ryland had dark brown hair and an angular face. His skin was weathered and furrowed. In one photo he had a tuft of hair underneath his chin, in the next he sported a full beard. "Ryland must be older than her."

"Fifteen years her senior," Yaeger said. "He took care of her after their parents died. She was only eight at the time. By all indications, they were extremely close in her formative years. We found an old interview where he claimed the two of them were so similar as to be of one mind. But as he ran the oil company and she went from school to school, all of that changed. In her own words, 'My eyes were opened.' After graduating from Stellenbosch, she identified as a radical environmentalist. Radical because, in her opinion, to be anything less made one an accomplice in the Earth's destruction."

"And I thought my sister and I were different," Joe said.

Yaeger continued with more details. "By the time Yvonne was a grown woman, she was getting arrested for breaking into private research facilities and leading environmental protests that went a step too far. At the same time, her brother was buying up deepwater oil fields and mines in all parts of the world and positioning himself as a leader in the movement called climate progression."

"Which is what?" Kurt asked.

"A third side to the never-ending debate about climate change," Rudi said. "Unlike the climate change deniers, who insist global warming is not happening, and the climate change activists, who insist that it is and will soon be the end of the planet as we know it, the climate progression movement accepts the idea that climate change is occurring while insisting it will be of tremendous benefit to the Earth in the long run. They consider the idea of preventing it foolish and that, if anything, it should be encouraged and moved along at a faster clip."

"That's a new one," Joe said.

"They're a small but powerful group," Rudi explained. "Most don't like to draw attention to themselves. Ryland Lloyd being the exception."

"He certainly makes up for the quiet ones," Yaeger added. "Most famously claiming that melting the glaciers of Antarctica would open up access to eighty billion barrels of oil and countless deposits of rare earths and precious metals. When oil spiked a few years back, he floated the idea of drilling in the waters off the Antarctic coast, with plans to erect heated concrete and steel barriers to keep the area clear of ice."

"I see what you mean about them being different," Kurt said. "I'm assuming the sister wasn't a fan of his drilling proposition."

"Not one bit," Rudi replied. "She and her group attacked the idea, viciously pointing out Mata Petroleum's poor safety record, with secretly taped video of shoddy equipment and oil spills. In response, Ryland called the Antarctic continent empty and worthless in its current condition, suggesting it be strip-mined for minerals and scoured for oil. He went so far as to insist that oil is a natural product of the Earth and that a few spills would actually be good for the Antarctic environment."

"Molten lava is a natural product of the Earth, too," Joe said. "I'd rather not swim in it."

Kurt laughed. "Did Ryland ever attempt to sink a well in Antarctic waters?"

Rudi shook his head. "He spent a year pushing hard for approval, but the firestorm caused by his comments made it a nonstarter. The crash in oil prices a few years later made it a moot point. There's no way it would be profitable now."

"Fire and ice," Kurt said.

"Her two theories?" Rudi asked.

"Yvonne and her brother," Kurt said. "Two people both obsessed with Antarctica for different reasons."

"Which is why we're considering the possibility that Ryland had a hand in the attack on the *Grishka* and his sister's disappearance," Rudi said. "Obviously, a corporation involved in deepwater drilling would have all the resources and technology needed to build and operate its own submarines. Beyond that, oil companies are intimately familiar with the value of core samples and the secrets they reveal."

"It fits on a personal level as well," Yaeger added. "Assuming Ryland was willing to massacre the scientists and crew of the *Grishka* to get what Cora discovered, he still might have a soft spot for his own sister."

"Or he might want to take her hostage," Joe suggested. "Just to show her he's beaten her once and for all."

Kurt could see it. But something didn't fit. "One

problem. It's hard to imagine whatever Cora found down there being of interest to a guy who wanted to strip-mine the continent."

"Unless those core samples led to the oil or mineral bonanza he was hoping to discover," Rudi said.

That was a possibility, Kurt thought. But at this point it was all just speculation and speculation could be dangerous. It could take you down the wrong road and make you blind to other paths. "The bottom line is, we have two leads."

"Two?" Rudi asked.

"Ryland and the core samples," Kurt said.

"But we don't have the core samples," Yaeger reminded him.

"But we might be able to find something similar," Kurt said. "Or, more precisely, someone else may have already found something similar and they just don't know it yet. Off the top of my head, I can think of several large facilities around the world storing frozen ice cores for research and processing. The National Science Foundation runs a warehouse and lab in Colorado. The EU funded a similar facility in Helsinki. And there's another large storage center in Seoul, South Korea, if I'm not mistaken. Not to mention universities and national governments. If we can find core samples that were drilled in similar locations to where Cora looked, we might get an idea of what she found."

"Except that Cora's team was operating in total secrecy," Rudi said. "She went dark and stayed that way. The *Grishka* wasn't even broadcasting an AIS signal.

And the only communication we have was the coded satellite message—and that signal is impossible to trace. In other words, we have no idea where she went."

"I think she went to New Swabia," Kurt said.

Rudi looked at Kurt as if he were joking. "The new what?"

"New Swabia," Kurt repeated. "The section of Antarctica explored by the Deutsche Antarktische Expedition of 1938–1939."

As Kurt spoke, he produced the printed photograph he'd found on the *Grishka*. "Joe and I discovered this in the ship's laboratory. Unless you know something I don't, Cora and her team were the furthest thing from Nazis. Which means the only purpose for having this photograph would be a scientific one. It must be related to what they were doing or it wouldn't have been sitting around in their lab."

Kurt held the photo in front of the camera. Rudi squinted to see it.

Off to the side, Yaeger typed furiously. "German Antarctic Expedition of 1938–1939," he said, reading from the NUMA record. "It was sent out just prior to World War Two. Using a converted freighter that remained anchored off the coast while exploring the continent with flying boats. The flights covered large swaths of previously unseen territory. The crews photographed the terrain while dropping markers and other junk to establish the Nazis' privilege to control the land they'd found."

"That would be these guys," Kurt said, pointing to the men in the picture.

"No one knows what they were searching for," Yaeger continued. "Official records suggest oil or a place to set up a whaling station. Others insist they planned to build a U-boat base on the continent. They called the territory New Swabia because they were flying off a ship known as the *Schwabenland*."

Rudi nodded at Yaeger. "And where, exactly, is New Swabia?"

"About five hundred miles southeast of where the *Grishka* was discovered," Yaeger said.

"It's a fair distance," Kurt said. "But a ship could drift that far in eight or nine weeks."

The look on Rudi's face told Kurt he agreed.

"Okay," Rudi said finally. "Two leads it is. We'll look into this German expedition while you two get yourselves to Johannesburg. By the time you land, I'll have set up an audience with Ryland Lloyd."

12

Ryland Lloyd stood at the rail of a supply vessel as it crossed Cape Town Harbour. Two of his employees accompanied him, the boat's pilot and a member of his protection squad. They were headed for the outer anchorage, where a scattering of ships too large for the harbor moored.

It was night and the sky was black. The lights of the city cast an orange glow along the shore, while a darker backdrop beyond was all that could be seen of Table Mountain—the majestic, flat-topped escarpment so often seen in images of the South African city.

Ryland had spent some time on Table Mountain. A cable car ran to the top, making it easy to reach. The view from up high was spectacular both day and night, taking in all of Cape Town and miles upon miles of ocean. Yet even the sharpest eyes keeping watch from it would not see what Ryland was about to do.

The supply vessel cleared the no-wake zone and turned toward the anchorage, picking up speed in the process. It passed mothballed freighters and a carrier of crude oil off-loading its supply before zeroing in on its destination—a wide-hulled, industrial-looking vessel known as the *Colossus*.

The *Colossus* was a crane ship. It was used for off-shore construction and needed to be stable enough to move multi-thousand-ton loads without listing or toppling over. Most of these large ships were designed like catamarans, with two hulls with a deck between. Many of them were semisubmersible, meaning they could fill their pontoons with seawater, sinking lower and becoming heavier and more stable for construction operations.

The *Colossus* sported only a single hull, though it was wider than a football field and twice as long. This boxy shape gave it stability and a huge internal volume, making it possible to operate in the most distant places without the need for constant reloading. The large empty volume gave it other attributes as well, including Ryland's ability to keep his operations secret from the world.

"They're signaling for us to come aboard at the aft cargo bay," Ryland's pilot said.

"Take us in," Ryland said. "I'll step off and you two can wait for my return."

The pilot nodded. The bodyguard did likewise.

They were two of Ryland's regular employees, well

paid, vetted for trustworthiness and watched for any signs of disloyalty, but they were not capable of the leap of consciousness required to witness the truth that lay inside the *Colossus*.

The supply boat rounded the stern of the crane ship, passing by the twenty-foot letters spelling out its name and then past the blue star Mata Petroleum logo.

Moving up the far side, the pilot cut the throttle. The rumbling of the boat's engine faded and the vessel slowed. It coasted to a stop beside a cargo door that had been lowered by powerful hydraulic arms.

The open door acted as a platform. It lined up with the top deck of the supply boat.

Ryland climbed a ladder to the roof of the pilothouse and stepped nimbly from the smaller vessel onto the bigger ship.

A crewman from the *Colossus* stood guard silently. Ryland passed the sailor without acknowledgment and walked inside. He descended a flight of stairs and then walked out onto a platform overlooking the empty central section of the *Colossus*.

This vast area below him was now filled with water. Technically, the purpose of this compartment was to add ballast and stability to the *Colossus* during lifting operations. Ryland's engineers had modified it to open from the bottom, allowing submersibles to enter and leave unseen.

At the moment, a gray, tadpole-shaped vessel sat moored inside. Several of Ryland's men were working on the bow of the craft, which had been damaged during the ramming operation. There was no flash of welding torches or banging of hammers, only two machines being moved into place and a soft grinding noise.

Confident that the submarine would soon be repaired, Ryland continued down a catwalk that ran the length of the bay. At the far end, half hidden in the shadows, he found a tall, lean woman with straw blond hair.

Ryland studied her before speaking. Aside from a bruise on her cheek, she was a vision of near perfection.

"Are you hurt?" he asked.

Yvonne stepped forward. "I was injured when we rammed the *Grishka*," she said. "The *Blunt Nose* has a very stiff structure. It failed to absorb the impact the way I expected it to. The fault is my own."

He caressed her face, careful to avoid touching the discolored skin. "Taking responsibility for our own errors is an honorable trait," he said.

"It separates us from the blind," she replied.

He withdrew his hand and the two of them entered the nearest corridor together, speaking as they walked. "I'm glad to see you," he said. "We have much to discuss. Do you have the samples?"

"They survived the journey without issue," she said.

That was good news. "Have the genetic modifications been successful?"

"It appears so," she replied. "Reproduction rates have been increased five hundred percent, cycles shortened to forty-eight hours. You'll have to culture them and build a large enough seed stock before you begin full-scale production. But you should have no problem."

He nodded. That plan was already in the works. "All of that will pale in comparison to what can be released naturally from beneath the glacier. How close are we to delivering the payload from the subglacial lakes?"

"The final sluice is being carved now. We'll have direct access to the ocean within days."

"And the latest modeling?"

"Everything you could have asked for," she said. "Once the microbes reach the sea, they will spread around Antarctica. Changes in the Southern Hemisphere will become noticeable within three months."

"And then?" he asked.

"Climate change will cause increased growth of the microbes," she said, "which will cause more climate change. Significant dislocation of human activity will occur within eighteen months. And within three years a third of the world will face mass starvation due to crop failures and a reduction in fishing tonnage. The changes peak and stabilize at the ten-year time frame, at which point eighty-two percent of the world's landmass will be unsuitable for human activity. A massive reduction in human population will inevitably follow."

He nodded, imagining the peace and quiet of a world no longer teeming with people. "There will be wars, of course."

"Starving people rattle their cages," she replied, "but they lack the will to fight. At any rate, we'll be safe in our sanctuaries."

Perhaps, he thought. In the long run, it mattered little to him.

"You've done what you needed to do," he said. "You should be proud."

She shook her head. "I failed to reach the *Grishka* before it was boarded. Two operatives from NUMA were on board when we attacked."

"I assume they drowned," he said.

"Unfortunately, no," she said. "They escaped on the *Grishka*'s helicopter. But they can't have learned much. We scrubbed that ship bare."

"They must have learned something," he said. "They've asked for an audience during my party."

She went still, then asked, "What will you do?"

"Visit with them and find out what they know," he said.

"Do not trifle with these men," she advised. "Cora spoke of them often. They can be very persistent."

"Relax," he said. "Once I have learned all I need to know, I'll dispose of them. One way or another."

13

G amay Trout was in the NUMA science lab, goggles over her eyes, dark red hair tied back in a ponytail. Her gloved hands were submerged deep in a container of mud.

Pushing her fingers together and through the sediment, she scooped out a handful of slimy black sludge. She placed the sample on a glass tray, peeled off the gloves and switched on a bright halogen lamp.

Under the glare of the light, she picked through the muck with a stainless steel pointer, finding tiny shells and other clues that revealed what was living there.

"Did you lose your wedding ring again?" a voice asked from behind her. "You know, there are easier ways to get out of being married to Paul."

Gamay stood back from the mess and shot Rudi Gunn

a look that suggested she was not amused. In fact, she was fighting back laughter. She waved the steel pointer in his general direction. "You'd be wise not to antagonize a woman with a sharp object in her hand."

"I happily retract my statement," Rudi said.

Gamay allowed a smile to emerge. It was an easy smile, one that told the world she was comfortable with both being the target of a few jokes and giving as good as she got. "Retraction accepted," she said. "For now."

Safe from being impaled, Rudi stepped closer. "What *are* you doing?"

"This mud came from the bottom of San Francisco Bay," she explained. "We're comparing it with mud from 1939. Eighty years of shipping, oil spills and chemical runoff have taken their toll, but it's neither dormant nor dead. Life has adapted. We find different bacteria, different mollusks, different fish poop. A whole plethora of altered organisms are living down there now."

"Altered?"

"Adapted," she explained. "As in became far better at living in those conditions than the ones that preceded them."

"Fascinating," Rudi said, though his tone suggested he was less than enthralled. "Would you like to do something more interesting?"

"Are you suggesting my work is boring?"

"No," Rudi said. "Just that I need to pull you off this project and put you on something more urgent."

She put the pointer down and pulled off the safety goggles. "This doesn't have anything to do with Kurt and Joe's sudden disappearance, does it? They were supposed to meet Paul and me for dinner last night. Never even called to cancel."

"They were busy escaping from a sinking ship on the other side of the world," Rudi said.

"Of course they were," she replied. "It could never be just a flat tire with those two."

Rudi explained why Kurt and Joe had left so hastily, quickly filling Gamay in on what had happened with Cora and the need to know more about what she might have found in the ice cores from Antarctica.

"Sorry to hear about Cora," Gamay said. "I didn't know her very well but I thought her research was topnotch. Does this mean you're sending Paul and me to Antarctica to drill for additional samples?"

"That would be too easy," Rudi said. "And possibly dangerous at this point. I'm sending you to Finland. The European Ice Core Depository is in Helsinki. It just happens to be the largest storage facility in the world and a leading center for studying ice brought in from Antarctica."

"What makes you think we'll find what we need up there?"

"It was Kurt's idea," Rudi said, explaining the photograph and the connection to the *Schwabenland* expedition. "We counted seventeen expeditions to the geographical area that would have been New Swabia over the last two decades. Fifteen of those expeditions sent their core samples to Helsinki."

Gamay got it. "So instead of wandering around Antarctica with drill in hand, you want us to look through a million core samples stored in a frozen warehouse?"

"A few thousand should probably do the trick."

"Is that all?"

"It's going to be slow and time-consuming," Rudi told her. "But there's no other avenue to approach this."

"Level with me," Gamay asked. "What are the chances of a hit? In other words, how big is New Swabia?"

"Over three hundred thousand square miles," Rudi admitted. "The seventeen expeditions I referred to covered less than three percent of it. All told, they drilled in only one hundred and forty locations. And according to Cora's passport, she spent extended time in Helsinki in the months before her team left for Antarctica. That tells us something."

The connection was obvious. "Looks like I'm trading in my mud for ice."

"Colder but cleaner," Rudi said.

"I can live with that," she said. "When do we leave?"

Before answering, Rudi stepped forward and removed the sharpened pointer from Gamay's desk. "In an hour," he said, checking his watch. "Correction. Fifty-eight minutes."

"NUMA aircraft?"

"Not this time," Rudi said. "You and Paul are booked on a direct flight out of Dulles."

"No time to pack?"

Rudi shrugged. "You can buy clothes when you reach Finland. Just put it on the company card."

Gamay shook her head in disappointment. "Glassware and furniture," she said.

"What?"

"One buys glassware and furniture in Helsinki," she explained. "If you're going to send me somewhere with a blank check for clothes, it should be Paris or Milan."

Rudi brightened. "If you and Paul can point us in the right direction, I'll send you to both places with the card fully loaded."

14

Paul Trout stood on the snow-covered sidewalk outside a clothing store in the center of Helsinki. He wore a long winter overcoat, fur-lined boots, a heavy scarf and a knit cap. His gloved hands were shoved deep into his pockets and he'd whirled the scarf around his face three times, covering everything except his eyes. Somehow, he was still chilled to the bone.

As he attempted to keep his chin tucked in under the scarf, Gamay laughed at him. "You look like a turtle."

"A frozen turtle," he replied.

"A giant frozen turtle," she corrected.

Paul was six foot seven. With the boots on, he stood nearly six foot nine. Frankly, he'd been amazed to find clothes that fit. On average, it turned out, Nordic people were among the tallest in the world. That played to his advantage.

"I know why they put the ice core facility in Helsinki," he said. "Because if the power fails, the ice still wouldn't melt."

The outside temperature was seventeen degrees Fahrenheit, only ten degrees colder than Washington had been, but Helsinki was known for the cold, damp wind blowing in off the Gulf of Finland and that wind lived up to its reputation. To make matters worse, it was already dark, the sun having set around four in the afternoon.

"You might be right about that," Gamay said, fiddling in her pockets as if she was looking for lost change.

"What are you doing?" Paul asked.

"Activating my hand-warming packets," she said. She'd shoved two of them into each pocket and was massaging them to get the chemical reaction going. That done, she adjusted her pair of furry earmuffs. "If this doesn't work, I'm getting one of those giant Russian hats. I hear they keep your whole body warm."

"Communist propaganda," Paul insisted. "Which way to the facility?"

Gamay looked at the signs. They were written in two languages, Finnish and Swedish, neither of which she could read. But the letters *EICD* were also stamped on the sign. "This way," she told him. "Eight blocks. We could take a cab, but walking will do us good."

"More Communist propaganda," Paul replied. "But lead on. I shall gladly follow."

Despite Paul's complaint, he found the walk enjoyable and scenic. Lampposts on both sides of the street were wrapped in garlands and holiday lights. An enticing glow spilled from the windows of shops, while the center of each roundabout displayed ice sculptures lit up by colorful pastel floodlights.

"Assuming we don't freeze to death," he said, "this might be a grand place to explore."

"In July or August," Gamay insisted.

Paul thought that sounded reasonable.

They soon arrived at a sprawling three-story structure. Light streaming through large windows of triple-pane glass made it look warm and inviting inside while the steeply sloped copper roof and exposed steel beams gave it a modernistic style. The illuminated letters shone from a sign by the door.

"This is it," Gamay said.

Entering the building and signing in, they were met by a man named Matthias Räikkönen. He was tall and thin, with wispy gray hair and hazel eyes. He had peaked eyebrows and a long, narrow nose. The features gave him a hawk-like appearance.

After shaking the man's hand, Paul stood back and allowed Gamay to do the talking. She was the charming one, after all.

"Thanks for meeting us on such short notice," Gamay said.

"It is the first time I've been honored with a call from NUMA," he replied, speaking English. "The reputation of your organization precedes you. How may I be of service?"

Gamay had spent time on the phone with him as they flew across the Atlantic. But she hadn't given him the details of what they were after.

"We're planning an Antarctic expedition," she said. "To an area near the Fimbul Ice Shelf and deeper into Queen Maud Land. We're building on the work of a former colleague of ours. You might know her. Cora Emmerson?"

"Oh, yes," Räikkönen said. "Cora was a fixture around here for a while. Always bringing us biscuits or cakes when she came in."

Gamay had been thinking they'd have to beat around the bush asking about Cora's work but now sensed an opportunity to cut to the chase. "Would you be able to show us what she studied when she was here?"

"Of course," the man told her. "Have a seat. And take off those heavy coats. All our data is recorded and digitized. We can look at everything from right here in my warm and cozy office."

Paul and Gamay shed their winter layers, feeling several pounds lighter by the time they were finished. As they made themselves comfortable, Räikkönen sat at his desk, tapping away on a keyboard. "Are you certain that you want to look at *all* the cores Cora studied? If so, you may be here through spring."

Gamay glanced over at Paul and then turned back to their host. "We're most interested in the data from her later studies. The last cores she looked at before she left for South Africa."

"That should narrow things down," Räikkönen promised, tapping away. "Let me check the dates. Ah . . . Here's the list."

Gamay slid closer, glancing at the monitor as Räikkönen explained the notations. "These ice cores were recovered in 1996 by a Swedish expedition. The samples run from a depth of three hundred meters—pardon me, you're American—from one thousand feet to approximately six thousand four hundred feet below the surface." He pointed to a notation on the file. "Here you can see the location on the glacier in latitude and longitude. And if I click here, I can you show the chemical breakdown based on depth."

"This might be easier than we expected," Paul offered.

Gamay shot Paul the look that said *Don't jinx us.*

She turned back to Räikkönen. "Would you start with the deepest sections first?"

Räikkönen set a depth range on the screen before hitting enter on the keyboard. An icon appeared and cycled several times. Finally, a pair of words appeared. Gamay couldn't read the Finnish, but a diagonal red line through the icon suggested something had gone wrong.

"How odd," Räikkönen said. "The file has been corrupted. Let me check a different depth."

Räikkönen pulled up several different depths at random and received the same notice in angry red letters. "The entire folder must be corrupt," he said. "Perhaps it happened when we migrated from the old computer system to the new."

As he went back to work, Gamay glanced at Paul, then back to their host. "Try a different sample," she suggested. "Maybe one of the cores she looked at earlier in her visits."

"Of course," Räikkönen replied. He pulled up a second core by its identification number, double-checked that it was on the list of samples Cora had studied and requested the data. "Cora did the actual lab work on this one," he said. "It had never been tested before."

"Even though it was recovered in 1996?" Gamay asked.

"Oh yes," Räikkönen said. "We have nearly two million core samples stored here. Each of them a meter in length. For proper examination, they need to be sliced into very thin sections and studied one millimeter at a time. In some ways, the EICD is like a library. There are books that get checked out on a regular basis and there are books that gather dust for years before someone takes a peek. But all of them sit and wait. The samples Cora studied hadn't drawn much interest because they are from a less active part of the continent."

As Räikkönen explained the process, Gamay watched the computer screen. The search icon appeared once again, cycling for what seemed like an eternity before finally giving way to the familiar notice in its angry red. "Another corrupted file."

Räikkönen's cheeks flushed. Without any prodding from Gamay, he pulled up three additional files, getting the same admonition each time. "I don't understand."

"I do," Paul whispered, low enough that only Gamay heard him.

"What about the cores themselves?" Gamay asked. "Are they kept on-site?"

"The sections that haven't been processed are."

"Can we look at them?" Gamay asked. "I mean, physically look at them?"

Räikkönen nodded and went to work, studying the screen for the data. "We have two hundred cores from the '96 expedition still in storage. Half of them from a depth below five thousand feet. They're kept in the older building."

"On-site?" Gamay said, standing up.

Räikkönen nodded. "You might want to put your coats back on."

"Do we have to go outside?" Paul asked.

"No," Räikkönen said. "But it's thirty-five below in the warehouse. Fifty degrees colder than it is on the street."

Paul grabbed his coat while Gamay grabbed hers and pulled on her earmuffs. "Should have bought that Russian hat."

15

To reach the storage facility, Paul, Gamay and Räik-könen walked through a tube-like bridge that spanned the access road between the two build-ings. It was enclosed but neither heated nor insulated. A chill could be felt as soon as they stepped inside.

Gamay looked out the half-frosted windows as they moved along. A small van with yellow fog lights was pull-ing in on the snowy road beneath them. "More deliveries?"

"They come in constantly," Räikkönen replied. "Par-don the pun, but global warming research is heating up. That makes the EICD a hot spot. We now take ice cores from all around the world. We have some from Greenland and Antarctica, others from glaciers in South America, Eurasia and the Himalayas. We even have ice from Africa taken off the slopes of Mt. Kilimanjaro."

They reached the far side of the bridge, arriving at a sealed door.

Räikkönen typed a code into a keypad and a hiss of air could be heard as the door opened. As cold as it was on the bridge, the air escaping from the storage chamber cut into them like the wind. They stepped inside and went down to ground level again, entering the locker room.

All around lay cold-weather gear. Fur-lined hats with earflaps. Racks of gloves. Coveralls on pegs along the walls.

"Let me see your gloves," Räikkönen said.

Paul and Gamay held out their gloved hands.

"I'm afraid those will never do," he said. "Find a pair of the heavy gloves and pull a pair of coveralls over your clothes. You'll both want to drink a bottle of water as well. It's exceedingly dry in the storage chamber, drier than any desert. You'll never feel yourself sweating, but your bodies will lose moisture rapidly."

Paul and Gamay did as they were told. Then, dressed appropriately, they passed through another door into an examination room.

Here they found a worktable with a precision saw waiting to carve ultrathin slices from the cores. Microscopes, gas chronometers and other high-tech equipment lined the far wall.

A woman dressed in cold-weather gear of her own stood over one of the microscopes.

"Good evening, Helen," Räikkönen said.

She looked up from her work. "Matthias," she said warmly. "I wasn't expecting you tonight. What brings you down here?"

"Visitors," Räikkönen replied. "These are the Americans I told you about. They've come all the way from Washington to see our work. As it turns out, they're old friends of Cora Emmerson."

"Cora," Helen said. "How delightful. Where is she these days?"

Gamay answered quickly. "Antarctica."

"Excellent," the woman replied. "What can I do for you?"

"We've had a little problem," Räikkönen said. "Several of the computer files seem to be corrupted."

"I could retrieve the physical files for you," Helen said, "but they're stored at another site. It will take a few days."

"That would be helpful," Gamay said. "Out of sheer curiosity, we'd love to see some of the core samples Cora studied while she was here."

"Of course," Helen said. "Matthias, why don't you show them? Assuming you can still find your way around the warehouse."

"Very funny," he said. "I've already got the bin numbers. We'll go retrieve them. If you'd set up the exam table while we're gone, that would speed things up."

They left Helen behind and entered the storage facility itself. Astonishingly, this room was ten degrees colder than the exam room and dressing area. At this point, the difference in temperature really couldn't be felt. What could be sensed was the dryness.

Each time Gamay inhaled, the air scratched her throat and windpipe. Her eyes felt as if they had been drained of all liquid. Either that or the tears were crystallizing in place.

"I see why we needed the water," Gamay said.

Now out in the warehouse itself, they were dwarfed by three-story racks that reached to the ceiling, aisles of them, like a gigantic shopping center. On each of the racks were bundles of shimmering silver tubes. Thousands upon thousands of them stacked in cradles.

"This is incredible," Paul said.

"Each of these tubes contains a meter of ice," Räikkönen said. "The warehouse itself is larger than a city block."

As he spoke, Räikkönen led them to the right and deeper into the warehouse. They passed a dozen seemingly identical aisles before he found what he was looking for.

"21-B," he said, entering the aisle and taking them down it. Halfway down, they cut over to another aisle and, farther on, they made another turn.

"I feel like a rat in a maze," Paul said. "I'm not sure I could find my way out."

"If we are the mice," Räikkönen said, "we are about to reach the cheese."

Checking the small numbers on the racks as he passed them, Räikkönen finally stopped. "Here it is. These are the core samples from the 1996 expedition. The ones Cora studied are up top."

Gamay craned her neck to look upward. The highest level was at least thirty feet above her head. "Even you won't be able to reach that," she said to Paul.

"Very funny," Paul said. "I assume you have a ladder."

"Even better," Räikkönen said.

He stepped to a keypad that had been installed on the rack in front of them and pressed a green button. The pad lit up, allowing him to enter the number of the tube that was needed. A whirring, mechanical sound reached them from a far part of the warehouse.

Gamay and Paul turned in unison to see a vehicle coming around the corner. It was the size of golf cart but only half as wide. It had no driver and was electrically powered. It pulled up to the rack in front of them and stopped.

Räikkönen reached out, unlocked a small gate and stepped onto the platform. "Cherry picker," he said. "Would you care to join me?"

Paul shook his head. "I'll pass. As odd as this might sound, I'm afraid of heights."

"I'll be brave," Gamay said.

She stepped onto the platform. Räikkönen touched another button. As the entry gate shut behind her, the electric motors began whirring once again. Instead of moving forward or backward, the platform began to rise upward.

Gamay looked over the edge, seeing that a pair of scissors-like supports were unfolding. She held on to the waist-high railing as the platform climbed past the first level and then the second. While it was a smooth ride, the platform was so small it felt precarious to be perched on it.

Reaching the third level, the platform stopped. Gamay looked around. She could see over the tops of the racks to the aisles beyond. Row after row spread out before her. They reminded her of bookshelves in a library.

"This makes no sense," Räikkönen said.

She turned to find him examining the writing on the end of a tube he had pulled out. He slid the tube back in and checked another tube and then a third. He grew more frustrated with each discovery.

Gamay's grin melted away. She didn't need to ask what he'd discovered. She'd half expected it since the moment they'd found the computer files had been corrupted. "The cores are missing, aren't they?"

"I'm . . . I'm not sure . . ." he said. "But these are the wrong numbers. It's as if someone had filed them in the wrong place."

Gamay glanced at the end of the tube. A sticker placed on the curved surface displayed a bar code and a long string of numbers and letters. Gamay could see that the tubes in the nearest bin all ended in *08* or *09*. She figured that was the year.

She allowed her eyes to wander, spotting a tube in the adjacent section that ended in *DG-96*. "What about that one?"

Räikkönen squinted and then nudged the control, sliding the cherry picker sideways.

The sudden movement startled Gamay and she grabbed the rail with both hands. "Warn me next time you do that."

"Sorry," Räikkönen said, reaching for the tube. "Get so used to being on these things that I don't even think about the possibility of falling."

"I'll do enough of that for both of us," Gamay said. "Is that the right sample?"

Räikkönen nodded. "This is one of the '96 cores, but it's been placed back in the wrong spot. But where are the others? There should be three compartments filled with them."

Räikkönen tapped the intercom button. "Helen, this is Matthias. I'm going to need your help. Someone has been misfiling the cores."

He waited a moment but got no response. Pressing the intercom button again, he called her name several times. "Helen? Helen? Are you listening? Helen?"

There was no response on the intercom. Then a hissing sound wafted through the warehouse.

"What was that?" Gamay asked.

"Air lock doors opening," Räikkönen said.

The sound of the air lock sealing itself shut came next, followed by muffled voices and heavy footsteps.

Räikkönen was about to press the intercom button again when Gamay stopped him. A sixth sense told her there was too much urgency to the footfalls she was hearing. And too many of them altogether.

"She's not going to answer," Gamay said. "And we have a bigger problem to worry about."

16

Down on the floor of the warehouse, Paul heard the air lock open and close. The sound of men running along the concrete floor followed. He moved to the end of the aisle and glanced around the corner.

A group of men had come in. They wore jackets and gloves, but not the type designed for the frigid air of the warehouse. They were also armed and fanning out in the classic spread-out-and-search grid.

Paul raced back to where Gamay and Räikkönen had begun descending. Waving his hands back and forth, he got their attention, warning them not to come down.

Paul was still signaling when one of the armed men came around the corner.

The man raised his weapon and shouted to his friends. Paul took off running and dove to the ground as muted shots rang out. The gunman had a suppressor on his short-barreled rifle to muffle the sound when fired.

Paul landed on the ground and rolled to the side as bullets skipped off the floor around him. He was too far from the end of the aisle to escape and too big of a target to expect he'd be able to run between the lead raindrops for long. He raised his hands and stood up slowly.

The gunman rushed forward, his eyes on the target, his weapon aimed at Paul's chest. He made it halfway down the aisle before getting hit from above by an avalanche of the silver ice-filled tubes.

They hit him in several places at once—his shoulder, his knee, his foot. One of the core samples hit the barrel of the rifle, jarring it from his hands and onto the concrete floor.

The bombardment was effective. Each tube weighed thirty pounds and their combined weight was a heavy beating. As he tried to get up, another cylinder of ice hit him, this one finding the back of his head, flattening him for good. The man slumped, face-first, out cold.

Paul knew this was his chance. He charged forward and pulled the man's rifle out from under him.

"Look out," Gamay shouted.

The gunman's associates had arrived at the end of the aisle. Paul snapped off a shot in their direction but was quickly driven back as the men took cover around the endcaps of the aisle and returned fire.

Additional missiles of ice were lobbed from up above. They fell short, serving only to draw the attention of the men to where Gamay and Räikkönen perched on the cherry picker. The attackers quickly refocused and opened fire.

Paul watched as bullets tore into the frozen core samples stored around Gamay. Chips of ice and fragments of the silver tubing were blasted in all directions, catching the light and creating a snow globe effect.

Knowing Gamay and Räikkönen had nowhere to hide, Paul dropped to one knee and began firing down the aisle. The targets ducked out of sight as his own shots went wide or into the ice.

Realizing the tubes of ice made for half-decent sandbags, Paul slid a group of the core samples from their bin, stacking them in front of him in a small pyramid. He dropped down behind the stack, lying prone on the floor and looking over it and using it as a gunsight. Flat like this, he would be hard to hit and would be in a good position to shoot anyone who came his way.

When the men at the end of the aisle reappeared, Paul fired, missing wildly but forcing them back into hiding.

"I'm a better shot than this," he said to himself.

Checking the rifle, he realized the problem. One of the core samples had hit the weapon as it fell, slamming it into the hard floor. The result was an almost imperceptible bend in the barrel, causing every shot to peel off high and wide to the left.

Guessing at a correction, he fired a third salvo of shells. Still, the weapon proved hard to dial in.

Watching Paul from above, Gamay and Räikkönen could see a new problem developing. After a brief exchange among the men, one of them sprinted away, backtracking and vanishing down the next aisle.

"They're flanking him," Gamay said.

"Hang on," Räikkönen warned. "I'm moving us into the action. We can swing around and intercept."

Räikkönen pushed the cherry picker's joystick forward while Gamay pulled additional ice cores from the stack beside them, loading them into the basket of the picker.

The cherry picker began to move, accelerating in a jerky motion. It quickly reached the end of the aisle, at which point Räikkönen pushed the stick to the side.

Gamay was sure they'd go over. When Räikkönen leaned in the opposite direction, the vehicle somehow remained upright.

"This thing is not very stable," Gamay said.

"Don't worry," Räikkönen said. "We do this every day. Too time-consuming to descend back down to the ground, reposition and then raise the platform back up."

Räikkönen released the stick and the cherry picker stopped.

"Is he coming?" Räikkönen asked.

They were parked at the endcap of the aisle. Gamay leaned out and peeked around the corner. The man who was attempting to outflank Paul was racing down the aisle toward them.

"Yes."

"Tell me when."

She waited. "Now."

Räikkönen pushed the joystick once more and the

mobile platform surged into the adjacent aisle just as the fleet-footed pedestrian reached the corner.

The impact sent him flying. To Gamay, at least, the man seemed to be airborne for several seconds before slamming into the ground and sliding into the next rack of ice cores.

She hoped he was knocked out, but he rolled to the side, got his bearings and then looked directly up at them.

"Trouble," Gamay said.

Räikkönen moved the joystick back. As the cherry picker reversed course, it bumped into the corner of the storage rack. The platform swayed precariously, stabilizing just as the gunman below found the trigger.

The soft popping sound of a rifle was cut off by Räikkönen shouting in pain as a spread of shells punched holes in the floor of the platform. Gamay pulled back, lucky to avoid being hit, but Räikkönen crumpled to the floor, two shots having pierced the same leg.

Gamay went for the ice cores, heaving the tubes over the side one after the other. She tossed them without looking, hoping to make up for it with sheer volume.

When the shooting ceased for a moment, Gamay reached over and pushed the joystick that controlled the platform.

The cherry picker surged across the aisle, heading in a diagonal path, until it slammed against the storage rack on the far side.

More shots came their way.

"We've got to get off this thing," Gamay said, throwing the last of the frozen missiles toward the shooter. "We're birds on a wire here."

"Up," Räikkönen said. "Take us up."

Gamay pressed the button and the platform rose another six feet before stopping. It was now even with the top of the rack.

Gamay gave Räikkönen a boost, pushing him up and out. He climbed onto the top of the storage rack and turned around to reach for her.

As Gamay pulled herself up, another spread of bullets tore into the cherry picker. She leapt for safety, her foot shoving the picker over and toppling it like a tree.

She crawled forward, glad to be off the unstable machine.

"We're safe up here," Räikkönen said. "No bullet can go through thirty feet of ice. But what about your husband? He'll be surrounded."

Paul wasn't oblivious to the danger of being surrounded, but there was little he could do about it. He kept his eyes on the men down at the end of the aisle, trying to track their movements.

He ducked for cover as one of them opened fire. His small pyramid of ice took a few hits and then began to crumble.

Paul fired back and rolled to safety under the nearby stack of shelves. Pressing as far into the space as he could, he felt as if he were about to make his last stand. He gripped the weapon and peeked out into the aisle. To his surprise, the attackers were running away.

Paul looked around, baffled. He heard no alarms. He saw no police or security teams coming to their rescue. Why their tormentors would suddenly depart in what seemed likely to be a moment of triumph made no sense to him.

At least until a series of explosions erupted.

A half-dozen grenades and incendiary charges went off in rapid succession. Flames shot through the stack of shelves that Gamay and Räikkönen had been searching only minutes before. Magnesium and thermite burning at temperatures of several thousand degrees.

What wasn't blasted to shreds in the initial series of explosions would melt in the ensuing fire. Worse yet, the detonations had bent the support columns and the heat was weakening and deforming them.

The multistory rack of ice began to sag. It leaned in Paul's direction. Dozens and then hundreds of the silver tubes slid free just as the entire unit toppled over.

The rack fell like classic steel shelves in the stacks of a library, collapsing sideways, slamming against the next storage rack and then sliding halfway down. It wedged itself tight and held ten feet above Paul's position on the ground.

Paul crawled out from under the debris and stared in silence at the devastation. He scanned the aisle, peering through the smoke, looking for any sign of their attackers.

The men were long gone, even the man who'd been knocked unconscious. In fact, the only thing that remained were the shattered remnants of a thousand tubes of ice spread across the floor.

17

Kurt and Joe were back on solid ground.

After catching up on sleep while the *Providence* sailed north, they'd boarded the ship's Jayhawk once more, this time for a long flight back to Cape Town. From there, they'd taken a commercial jet to Johannesburg, arriving midafternoon to glorious sunshine and eighty-degree temperatures.

"That's more like it," Joe said, stepping through the airport's exit doors and out to the curb. "Who's picking us up?"

"A friend of Rudi's," Kurt said. "Her name's Leandra Ndimi. She's a NUMA liaison officer."

"Great," Joe said. "Any word from Paul and Gamay?"

Kurt was in the process of checking his phone. "They report Helsinki to be both freezing and dangerous. They were attacked inside the ice core facility. At least four men with guns. Authorities are checking surveillance footage, but the cameras inside the facility were turned off."

"Are they all right?" Joe asked.

"No injuries to report. But the attackers used incendiary charges and grenades to destroy the cores they were looking for. Computer records had already been tampered with, but there's some reason to believe that was Cora's doing."

"So back to square one," Joe said. "The last time I heard of anyone getting this aggressive over ice, it was the compressed carbon kind that gets divided up in Antwerp."

Kurt had to agree. He put the phone away. "Let's hope we have more luck with Mr. Lloyd."

Joe pointed to an approaching car. "Looks like our ride is here."

A beige minivan was flashing its lights at them. It pulled to the curb and the front passenger's window slid down, revealing the smiling face of a young woman in the driver's seat. She had jade green eyes, a smooth brown complexion and her hair pulled back.

"You two look like the wandering souls Rudi asked me to collect," she said. "I must say, you're not half as forlorn as he described you."

Kurt laughed and shouldered his bag. He noticed Joe staring. "Rudi likes to keep expectations low," he said.

"That way, people aren't disappointed," Joe added.

Leandra smiled warmly. "Not disappointed at all," she said. "And for the record, I've been looking forward to meeting the men who helped unravel the mystery of the *Waratah*. You have no idea how much joy the discovery of that ship brought to people in this country."

The *Waratah* was an ocean liner that vanished off the South African coast in 1909. Kurt and Joe had helped unravel the century-old mystery behind its disappearance. And NUMA had recovered the ship and sailed it back to Cape Town.

"We had nothing to do with it," Kurt insisted, as he opened the passenger's door. "And don't let Joe tell you any different."

Kurt climbed into the seat while Joe tossed his gear in back and took a seat of his own.

"While my friend is technically correct," Joe said, "we did have our hands full with the madman whose ancestors hijacked the ship in the first place."

As Joe slid the door shut, she put the van in drive and pulled out, merging with traffic. "I'd love to hear all about it. But you two have dossiers to read and a party to attend."

"What party?" Joe asked.

"Ryland Lloyd's annual fund-raiser," she said. "It benefits his favorite politicians and his game park. Which is to say, it benefits him in the form of connections and favors."

Kurt had been informed of the party, but initial information suggested it was a closed guest list. "Did Rudi get us invites? Or are we sneaking in with the catering crew?"

"Three invitations," Leandra said.

"Three?"

"Rudi suggested I keep an eye on you."

Kurt laughed. "Sounds about right. Do we have time to shave and shower?"

"Afraid not," she told them. "Ryland's place is three hours from here. Out in the bush."

"This is my best T-shirt," Joe said. "But it's not going to get me into a luxury ball."

Leandra laughed. "Tuxedos are hanging in the back."

Kurt looked over his shoulder, spotting a trio of garment bags neatly clipped to a hook. "Let's hope Rudi got our sizes right. Now, what about the files he sent you?"

While navigating the traffic with one hand, Leandra reached down beside her with the other and retrieved a pair of manila envelopes from a pocket file on the back of the door. She handed them to Kurt, who kept one and passed the other on to Joe.

The files contained new information on Ryland and Mata Petroleum. The long drive to Ryland's estate gave them plenty of time to go through them and discuss the contents.

"Have you read this?" Kurt asked Leandra.

"Maybe," she said with a smile.

"What do you think?"

"I think our friend Ryland is an odd duck. Brilliant and driven enough to build up a multi-billion-dollar conglomerate and foolish enough to be teetering on the verge of bankruptcy. It's as if he became a bad business-man overnight."

Kurt read through the financial reports. Ryland was in negotiations with his creditors for extensions for various lines of credit. At the same time, he'd been buying up huge tracts of land for his mining ventures. "By the look of this, the oil company borrows the money and the mining concern spends it."

"They don't spend it well," Leandra said. "According to the geological reports, the land he's bought is all but worthless."

Kurt leafed through the file, discovering the reports Leandra referenced. The sites Ryland had bought were massive and remote. They were so far off the beaten track that no boots on the ground surveys had ever been performed. The best analysis came from a U.S. government study that used the basic landform and similar geological structures to calculate a grade. It came back as universally poor.

"Maybe he knows something the rest of us don't," Joe suggested.

That was always possible. The best way to get rich in mining was to find land others didn't value and literally strike gold—or platinum or rhodium or any number of rare earths or metals. But based on the meager output of his existing mines, Ryland didn't seem to be a natural at it.

"He's certainly swinging for the fences," Kurt said. "He's bought land in Uganda, Kenya and the Congo. Not to mention New Guinea, Ecuador and a swath the size of Oklahoma in northern Brazil."

Joe had found more. "He also bought a bunch of islands in the Indian Ocean and several others scattered throughout the Pacific. Most of them appear to be uninhabited. One is a former guano island that played out thirty years ago."

"Guano island?" Leandra asked.

"Bird poop," Joe said. "Perfect fertilizer. Built up into mountains on certain islands that have millions of birds and limited rain. As disgusting as it sounds, the stuff is more valuable than gold per ton of earth moved."

"Not once it's all gone," Kurt said. "And thirty years isn't enough time for it to build back up. You need centuries to make it worth it."

Leandra shrugged. "Like I said, suddenly he's a bad businessman."

Kurt studied a raft of satellite photos depicting the newly acquired holdings. The land appeared untouched, aside from small developments here and there. There was no evidence of mining, just trees and green fields and mile upon mile of untouched terrain. The islands were in a similar state. Breakwaters had been built on a few of them, metal roofs of storage facilities sprouted here and there, but there was little sign of industrial activity.

The closer he looked, the less it made sense. Realizing he couldn't tell anything from the small details, Kurt pulled back and tried to envision the bigger picture.

The newly acquired holdings weren't concentrated in any one country or region and it didn't seem as if there was anything political in play. As far as Kurt could tell, Ryland had bought in democracies and dictatorships, in stable countries and unstable ones. Nor was he focused on one kind of terrain or geology. He'd bought up mountainous areas and open valleys. He'd bought a hundred thousand acres of rain forest and twice as much desert.

About the only pattern Kurt could discern was

geographical. All Ryland's new holdings lay within several degrees of the equator. All had single-degree latitudes. Nothing too far north, nothing too far south.

The islands were more widely spaced and each sat in hot, humid areas like the Indian Ocean and the tropical zone of the South Pacific.

"Most rich guys are happy to own one island," Joe said. "This guy has twenty and counting."

The choice of islands was odd as well, mostly low-lying atolls, including one island that had recently become uninhabited after a storm hit during high tide. Realizing the island was unsafe, its five hundred inhabitants were relocated to Australia. Ryland had purchased it a year later, lock, stock and rusting barrel.

Kurt pointed it out to Joe, who was just as baffled. "Makes no sense," he said. "A few more years of rising seas and that island will be gone."

Kurt nodded. There had to be a reason for Ryland's actions, but at the moment he couldn't see it.

By now, they'd left the suburbs around Johannesburg and traveled out through the farmland beyond. A hundred miles later, they crossed into Limpopo Province, the northernmost part of South Africa, where they stopped briefly to change into their evening wear.

The countryside resembled a postcard from a bygone era, with grassy meadows divided by meandering streams. Exotic trees and animals spotted the rolling hillsides. Water buffalo could be seen roaming in one valley while several dozen crocodiles lay on the banks of a stream.

Returning to the car, they drove the rest of the way, turning onto a red dirt track as the sun began to set behind them.

"This is Ryland's property," Leandra said.

The new road ran beside a twelve-foot wrought iron fence with angled barbs at the top. Five miles later, they turned once more, passing between two huge stone lions and traveling down a thousand-yard driveway toward a sprawling villa constructed to resemble a nineteenth-century hunting lodge.

The exterior was rustic, with a thatched roof supported by beams of yellow pine. The lobby was spacious and open, its charm enhanced by period furniture and waiters wearing pith helmets and Victorian-style uniforms. Up above, ceiling fans turned slowly, their blades made of decorative local woods carved into the shape of acacia leaves and palm fronds.

"Nice place," Kurt said.

"Is this a home or a hotel?" Joe asked.

"A little bit of both," Leandra told him. "Ryland spends a fair amount of time here, but guests are welcome to rent it for lodging or events."

"Sounds like you looked into it," Kurt joked.

"I did," Leandra replied. "If I ever get married, this would be a great place for the reception. A little out of my price range, unfortunately."

"Depends who you marry," Kurt said.

Leandra smiled. "I go for poor and self-reliant, I'm afraid."

Kurt glanced back at Joe. "You may have a chance after all."

Joe got momentarily flustered. "He doesn't know what he's . . . I mean, I'd be flattered, but I haven't said . . ." He paused to collect himself, then looked out the window. "Thank God, the valet is here."

One of the runners dressed in safari gear had reached them and was opening Leandra's door. He looked at their invitations and pointed them toward the main entrance, where a short line of people waited to go through a security checkpoint.

All the guests were dressed to the nines and the three of them were no exception. Kurt and Joe wore tuxedos with French-cuffed shirts, crisp bow ties and polished Italian shoes. Leandra wore a black dress with embroidered details on the body and sheer sleeves. Stiletto heels completed her look.

After they stepped through a metal detector, a hostess offered flutes of champagne. "Please enjoy the run of the lodge," she said. "The main bar is one floor down while the items on silent auction are on the lowest level. Dinner will be served on the veranda in one hour."

With champagne glass in hand, Kurt took the lead. "Let's explore."

They stepped into the lodge, discovering a spacious, terraced interior. They were on the top floor, standing on a balcony that overlooked the rest of the lobby. The luxurious lower floors spread out before them, all three levels linked by a pair of curving staircases and framed by a transparent wall at the back of the lodge. The wall was made from sixty-foot panels of translucent acrylic, as clear as any glass and stretching the entire length of the lodge. It framed a view that was nothing short of spectacular.

Out in the distance, the mountains were turning red and brown as the setting sun painted them in glorious bands of color. The valley before them was a mixture of green and yellow, the dry grasses waving in the breeze acting like a shag carpet beneath the bushes and small trees. Wildlife flocked around a large pond in the center of the valley. Kurt saw elephants drinking along one shore, while giraffes stood on the far side, stretching their necks to soak in the last rays of the setting sun.

"Now, that's what I call a million-dollar view," Joe said.

"A million wouldn't cover the interest," Leandra said. "Ryland spent fifty million on the land alone."

Taking a sip of champagne, Kurt turned to the steps. He could have gone either direction, since the marvelous staircase divided and swept off toward both sides of the room before curving back and meeting again on the second level, where a luxurious bar was manned by a trio of bartenders.

Descending the stairway, Kurt had to admire the setup. The bar top itself was made of thin granite and lit from beneath, creating a warm yellowish light. Behind it, a huge fish tank, one that would have been at home in any major aquarium around the world, added a hue of aqua to the scene.

Reaching the bar, Kurt placed his champagne glass down and requested a tumbler of whiskey. As the bartender poured the drink, exotic fish swam in endless circles behind them.

"Interesting collection," Kurt said, recognizing several rare species, including a European eel and a small group of pinkish fish near the bottom of the tank that Kurt knew to be a type of rockfish.

"They're pretty," Leandra said.

"They're also critically endangered," Kurt pointed out. "Interesting."

The bartender poured Kurt's whiskey over a single globe-shaped ball of ice and then handed him the glass. Kurt thanked the man and turned away, taking in the scene.

Guests were still streaming in, with each level of the lodge slowly filling up. "It's going to be a full house before too long."

"That should help us keep a low profile," Leandra said.

"Helps the other guests do the same," Kurt said.

After scanning a few dozen faces he didn't recognize, his attention was drawn to a video screen playing an informational piece about the game park. The sound was off, but, from what Kurt gathered, the animals were allowed to roam free, kept away from the main buildings and the roads by electrified fences carrying a pain-inducing one hundred and forty volts.

A second set of graphics told him the park had forty-nine elephants, three hundred critically endangered black rhino, five hundred zebra and unknown numbers of water buffalo, crocodiles and hyenas. A recent addition was fifteen lions, purchased from zoos and parks around the world. Ryland's stated plan was to turn this mixture of males and females into a free-roaming pride.

"Quite a collection," Kurt said, taking a sip of his drink.

"Animals and people," Leandra said. "I have some intel, if you want it."

"Absolutely," Kurt said.

She nodded toward the stairs. "The Russian we passed was Sergei Novikov. He's a big name in the construction world. His company builds ports and shipping terminals."

"I knew I'd seen him somewhere," Joe said.

"He's on record insisting that climate change will be good for world trade and that it will be *great* for Russia in particular," Leandra said. "Once all the Arctic sea ice melts, he has plans on drilling for oil above the Arctic Circle."

"Which makes him a natural ally of Ryland," Kurt noted.

"I noticed him talking with a group speaking Mandarin," Joe said. "I could be wrong, but the leader of the group looked a lot like Zhao Liang."

"Of Liang Shipping?" Leandra asked.

Joe nodded. "Tanker group. Have over a hundred oceangoing vessels in all sizes."

"Ports and shipping," Leandra said. "Could be Ryland is getting into a new business."

"Doubt he has enough money left," Joe said.

Kurt joined the conversation. "I've been looking at the animals while you two have been studying the real wildlife. I need to up my game."

"I've been telling him that for years," Joe said.

"I'm a slow learner," Kurt said. "Let's mingle and see who else we can find."

They left the bar and moved out among the other guests. Despite many striking faces, they recognized no one else and soon found themselves on the bottom floor studying the items up for bid at the silent auction. Among the usual items—rare collectables, dinners at Michelin-starred restaurants, antique jewelry—they found something more.

"Look at this," Joe said. "Guided safari and big game hunt. Winning bidder provided with the use of the lodge and the option to shoot and take a trophy from a bull elephant, a horned white rhino or a male or female lion. Guess the safari theme is not just for show."

Suddenly, the rescuing of lions from around the world seemed far less noble.

Before Kurt could comment, a tall, elegantly dressed man appeared at the top of the stairs. He tapped the side of his champagne flute with a sterling silver knife, ringing it like a bell, until all eyes turned his way.

"The man of the hour," Leandra said. "Ryland Lloyd."

Ryland had a long, thin face and finely brushed hair that hung straight, lacking in any sort of style. He reminded Kurt of the king on a playing card, with down-turned eyes and a trimmed beard that jutted out from his chin.

"Thank you for coming," he said. "I trust you're having a wonderful evening at my lodge. Enjoy it to the fullest. And remember, the election will be upon us before we know it. Which means we don't have time for checks and would prefer donations to be made in cash."

The crowd roared with laughter.

"I expect you're salivating over the braised shanks of wild boar currently being prepared for you," he said. "I know I am. But before I lose you to that epicurean delight, I'd like to say a few words about the new wave of industrialization and the dawning of a new day in South Africa."

He went on to sound more like a politician than a businessman, skillfully building a picture of South Africa as the economic engine of the continent. Insisting it was South Africa's destiny to bring good fortune to those who would be part of the transformation.

Cheers erupted as Ryland finished and he bowed with exaggerated humility before leaving the balcony.

As Kurt watched, the man walked down the stairs, shook a few hands and then stepped briskly toward a hallway that led to a distant wing of the building.

Kurt put his glass down. "This is my chance to talk to him."

"What if he's just run off to the bathroom?" Joe asked.

"In that case, I'll have a captive audience," Kurt said. "And total privacy."

18

Kurt cut across the room heading for the stairs and then went up. After circumnavigating a tightly packed group of guests, he spotted Ryland down the hall. He was standing in front of a door, focused on the lock.

Ryland produced a key, unlocked the latch and pushed the door open. Stepping inside, he released the door behind him.

Kurt raced the last thirty feet down the corridor and stuck his foot in the gap just in time to stop the door from latching again.

Allowing a few seconds to pass, he put his hand on the door and pushed it open, expecting to come face-to-face with a security guard, a pushy executive assistant or Ryland himself. When he did move forward, he was surprised to find himself in Ryland's office . . . alone.

Looking around for the owner, Kurt studied the décor. It kept to the hunting lodge theme, with dark paneling on the walls, the pelt of a lion on the floor and two overstuffed chairs sitting before a curved desk of polished mahogany.

The heads of several animals adorned the room, including a zebra with perfect stripes and the largest warthog Kurt had ever seen. Another section of the wall displayed the head and shoulders of a deer-like animal, its long, curved horns twisting artistically as they ran up over the head and back toward the animal's body.

It wasn't all nature and hunting trophies. Framed on the wall was a blueprint of a refinery. Below it sat a model of a seagoing oil rig, presented as if it were drilling through a platform of ice and into seafloor down below. A placard on the side of the case read *Habakkuk 51:5.*

Name and model number of the platform, Kurt assumed. He finished his study of the room by focusing on a quotation carved in a wooden sign hanging on the wall behind Ryland's desk.

> *The reasonable man adapts himself to the world: the unreasonable man persists in trying to adapt the world to himself. Therefore all progress depends on the unreasonable man.*
>
> —GEORGE BERNARD SHAW

As Kurt finished reading, Ryland appeared, returning to the room through a side door. He had a bottle of cognac in one hand and a knife in the other.

He paused at the sight of Kurt, thrown off by the

presence of someone in his private office, though he did not seem alarmed. "You appear to be lost," he said.. "The party is down the hall."

"I just came from it," Kurt said. "My compliments to your staff."

"I'll be sure to pass them along," Ryland said. "And whom should I say lavished them with such tepid praise?"

Kurt didn't offer his hand, as Ryland was holding the bottle and the knife, and, beyond that, there was nothing to suggest the meeting had become a friendly one. "Kurt Austin," he announced. "I'm with the National Underwater and Marine Agency. Out of Washington, D.C."

"Ah," Ryland said, recognition appearing on his face. "Late additions to the party. You and your two associates, Mr. Zavala and Miss Ndimi."

Diverting his attention from Kurt, Ryland took the knife to the neck of the bottle, cutting away the wax seal and then working the stopper free. He pulled it clear, allowing the aroma of the liquor to waft toward him. Inhaling slowly, Ryland appeared deeply satisfied.

"Cognac," he said. "This is a twenty-year-old bottle. XO. Or Napoléon Reserve, as some call it."

"The good stuff," Kurt said.

"Undoubtedly," Ryland said. From a tray beside the model of the oil rig, he plucked a pair of tulip-shaped glasses, placing them on his desk side by side. "Since you're here, Mr. Austin, we might as well share a drink."

Ryland poured a sample of the golden liquid into each one. He put the bottle aside and sat down. "As you probably know," he said, "cognac has to breathe before you drink it. The proper way is to allow a full minute for every two years of its age. It will be ready to drink in no less than ten minutes. You have that long to tell me why you're here, assuming you can keep my interest."

This was not the reception Kurt had expected. He'd encountered plenty of powerful men and women in his life, few of them liked intrusions, especially not from mystery guests who were members of an American government agency. Ryland seemed to welcome it as a challenge.

Kurt gestured to a chair.

"By all means," Ryland said.

Taking a seat, Kurt assumed a relaxed posture as if he owned the place. "Quite a collection," he said, glancing around. "Your decorator should be commended for assembling such an impressive array of specimens."

"I'm the decorator," Ryland replied.

Of course, Kurt thought. And by pointing it out, Ryland proved he was the type who had to boast of his accomplishments. That could work in Kurt's favor.

"I took each of these magnificent animals myself," Ryland continued. "And not with a modern rifle, mind you, but a bolt-action Springfield manufactured in 1909."

Ryland sat, leaning back in his desk chair farther than Kurt possibly could in the rigid guest chair. "Each of them was a challenge," he insisted. "That warthog, for instance. It took four shots and almost killed me before I hit it with a fifth at close range. Very dangerous, warthogs. And the ibex . . . That beauty was standing on a rock face nearly a thousand yards' distance when I felled it with a single bullet. I had to hit the poor beast in a way that it would be thrown back and not tumble down into the canyon. Otherwise, its value would have been ruined by the fall. Quite incredible, if I do say so myself."

"What about the lion?" Kurt asked.

"It had me treed and had already slashed and wounded my loader. He was bleeding to death when it ran me up into the branches. It raked my leg with its claws and came for me with its jaws wide open. I put the barrel of the rifle down its throat and pulled the trigger."

"If it only had a brain," Kurt said.

Ryland stared at him, looking as if he didn't know whether to laugh or be insulted by the quip. "I assure you, they're very cunning. And anything but cowardly."

"Certainly," Kurt said. "Although I'd be more impressed if the animals had guns of their own."

Ryland's eyes narrowed. "Not a fan of hunting?"

Kurt held up his hands. "Nothing against it in general. I eat meat. I understand the circle of life. What I'm against is the irrational act of hunting species to extinction, especially those that are threatened with dying out. Something that's happening at an accelerating pace here in Africa."

"It's the poachers who will force the world's species to extinction," Ryland said. "Not game hunters. A poacher kills a hundred times what any game hunter takes. Just to provide a gift of ivory to some big shot in a smog-choked city."

"And yet you've sanctioned hunting on your preserve," Kurt noted. "You're auctioning off big game safaris. Wouldn't it be better to keep those animals alive and breeding rather than kill them off?"

Ryland cocked his head as Kurt spoke. It almost looked as if he was listening with an open mind. "The animals I've cleared for the hunt here are past breeding age," he explained. "And each animal that is shot here means one less to be shot out in the wild. It means funds to expand this game park, revenue to hire guards who keep the poachers at bay."

Kurt didn't argue. He'd only brought up the issue in hopes of throwing Ryland off his game. Clearly, it hadn't worked.

Kurt glanced at the clock behind Ryland. Only three minutes had gone by. The spiced aroma of the liquor had begun to fill the room but the rules meant tasting would have to wait. He decided to take another stab at Ryland. "I understand that your sister didn't appreciate the hunting either. Did she?"

"My sister?"

"Yvonne."

Ryland paused, his brows converging. "What does she have to do with this?"

"She's always been a thorn in your side," Kurt said. "Bitterly opposed to your vision of the future. She attacked your projects in the press and rallied the opposition against your idea to drill for oil in Antarctica." Kurt gestured toward the model as he spoke.

Ryland leaned back farther, a genuine smile appearing on his face. For reasons beyond understanding, the more Kurt pressed him, the more pleased he seemed. "I suppose you consider such an endeavor irrational as well?"

"A scheme like that is expensive *and* reckless. There is

no need to go into pristine environments and drill when thousands of existing wells already sit dormant."

Ryland tilted his head as if he could come up with a few reasons but ultimately let it pass. "A great pipe dream of mine," he said. "But with the world awash in oil, no one wants to spend the money to drill on the frozen continent. The oil is there, I assure you of that. And when the price climbs enough, the UN treaty banning exploration and drilling in Antarctica will be conveniently forgotten."

"And you'll lead the way, I assume?"

"Not only will I lead," Ryland said, "I will make it happen."

"Of course you will," Kurt said. "You're the 'unreasonable man.'"

Instead of appearing insulted, Ryland beamed with pride. He even returned the compliment.

"As are you," he said. "Who else would invite himself to my home, barge into my private office and challenge me on the manner in which I run my business, spend my wealth or conduct my life?"

Kurt offered a slight nod. Ryland had him with his own words. "Perhaps I've been too harsh."

"Not at all," Ryland said. "You've been exactly as I expected you to be. You see, I've read about you, Kurt Austin, Director of Special Projects for the National Underwater and Marine Agency. If the reports I've seen are true, the world has bent to your will more times than even you might have hoped it would. The very definition of an unreasonable man."

This time, it was Ryland who turned his gaze toward the glasses of cognac. But as Kurt had realized a few minutes before, it was not yet time. He went back to speaking.

"So why are you here? What part of the world are you attempting to bend to your will today? Are you here to change the future? Or maybe the past? Both, perhaps? Before we share a drink, I think I deserve to know what made it necessary for you to demand my attention."

"I wanted to speak with you privately," Kurt said. "About your sister."

"Ah," Ryland said. "Back to my sister. What has she done this time? Gone running to the American government to tell them of my secret plan to pollute the Arctic, destroy the environment and kill all the baby seals? It's a fantastic scheme, I assure you. And we're well along with it."

"She's missing," Kurt said calmly. "And, unfortunately, she's almost certainly dead. I figured you'd rather hear that in private."

Ryland stared at him blankly. As if an internal logic program was running slowly as it tried to figure out the correct response. "Well," he said finally. "That is . . . terrible news . . . I appreciate you telling me before it hit the press. How did it happen?"

"We don't have all the details," Kurt admitted. "But as you may know, she was on a science expedition to Antarctica. Her ship must have run into trouble on the way home."

"Go on."

"The strange part is, no one seemed to be looking for it. We only found it because a NUMA survey plane flew over it while dropping remote sonar buoys. We went to investigate and render assistance. The ship was frozen solid. It must have been adrift for weeks, if not months. Worse yet, everyone on board had been shot. Unfortunately, the ship was in bad condition. It sank before we could collect any evidence or retrieve any of the bodies."

Ryland's expression began to resolve, as if some mystery were clearing in his mind. "An expedition to Antarctica," he said, sounding dismayed. "Of course that's what she does with the money I give her. I suppose it makes sense. At least to her. In my sister's mind, I'm the evil industrialist polluting the world. She's the white knight saving it. What better way to use my support than to study snowflakes or penguins, just like all her useless friends?"

Kurt assumed he was talking about Cora. But the lack of emotion was astonishing. "I'm not sure you heard me correctly. This was no accident. The ship's crew had been gunned down."

"I heard you quite clearly," Ryland insisted. "And it doesn't surprise me at all. If you only knew how radical she truly was. My sister had many enemies. She collected them like trophies. It wasn't just my company she attacked, there were others. She and her friends detonated explosives in a mine in Lesotho, collapsing the main gallery and the entry shafts. Several employees were killed. And the damage to the mine was so extensive, repairing it put the company out of business. They used computer hacking to damage pipelines, causing them to overload and destroying pumping stations in the process. Just last year they blew a hole in a Japanese whaling ship that had come to port to make repairs. It sank in Cape Town Harbour. Leaking oil and toxic chemicals, I might add. And six months ago, one of my seagoing rigs was sabotaged. She and her friends beat two security guards half to death in the process. I feel anger, but it's my sister, so I let it go. Some of the others whom she's attacked are run by more ruthless men who might have wanted a pound of flesh in return for their pain."

Ryland had suddenly become worked up. He settled quickly. "I'm sorry to hear of her demise, but, trust me, my sister is not some pacifist environmental warrior. She's a terrorist."

"Was a terrorist," Kurt said.

"Yes. Of course. Was."

"And an unreasonable woman, by the sound of it."

Ryland glared at Kurt before conceding the point. "She was that as well. The only thing we had in common."

Kurt found the whole exchange curious, especially Ryland blaming his sister for her own death. "Do you have any idea what she and her friends were studying in the Antarctic?"

"What do you mean?"

"You describe them as saboteurs," Kurt said. "So why go out on the glaciers? Not much in the way of mining or drilling for oil down there. Unless, that is, you know something I don't."

"I know a great many things you don't," Ryland insisted. "But what drove my sister to act as she did will baffle me to the end of my days."

Kurt nodded politely and said nothing more.

Ryland sighed and looked over to the waiting glasses. "Let us drink to her," he said. "And to your brave efforts to save her ship."

He slid one of the glasses toward Kurt, moving it along the polished desk with care and ease. As Kurt lifted it, Ryland took the other glass in his hand. After briefly waving it under his nose to sample the aroma, he raised the glass high. "To my wayward sister. May she find peace wherever the afterlife takes her."

Kurt raised his glass respectfully, then took a sip of the cognac. The hint of nutmeg and dried apricots came through. Ryland had chosen an excellent bottle. As he savored the taste, he glanced at the clock behind Ryland. To his surprise, only seven minutes had passed. The unreasonable man had reached for the glasses three minutes early.

19

While Kurt shared a drink with Ryland, Joe and Leandra watched the foreign guests whom they'd spotted.

"The 'internationals' are doing their best to remain wallflowers," Joe noted.

"Which in a strange way makes them stick out," Leandra said. "Considering how far they've traveled to be here, they haven't done any mixing or mingling. Not exactly social butterflies."

"More like birds of a feather," Joe said. "They haven't moved from that spot or spoken with anyone but each other all night. I noticed the Russian guy keeps checking his watch. They're clearly waiting on someone. And not all that patiently."

"My money is on that someone being held up, entertaining your partner," Leandra added. "They've been in there awhile. What do you suppose they're talking about?"

"Knowing Kurt, something boring and humdrum. Run-of-the-mill small talk is his specialty. Trust me. You wouldn't want to spend your free time with him. You'd be bored to tears."

Leandra smiled. "Whereas you're charming and interesting, I assume."

Joe raised his glass. "So glad you noticed."

Despite the banter, they kept their eyes on Ryland's international visitors. Novikov checked his watch for the third time, venting his frustration to the others. In response, Liang, the Chinese shipping magnate, turned to one of his assistants and whispered a few words.

The man left, returning shortly with a member of Ryland's staff. The woman spoke with each of them, trying to reassure them. Having done that, she relayed a message via her radio.

A response must have come quickly. The radio went back into the woman's jacket pocket and she turned and led the group from the middle level down the stairs and toward the veranda that lay beyond the wall of glass.

"The birds of a feather are flocking together," Leandra noted. "Should we follow?"

Joe glanced down the hall. Kurt was nowhere to be seen, but he could take care of himself. Joe offered his arm. "Let's go for a walk."

Leandra looped her arm through his and they took the stairs to the ground floor. The international group continued toward the glass wall and then through a doorway and out into the garden.

"Let's follow them," Joe said. "But without it looking like we're following them."

"Those are not very precise instructions," Leandra said.

"Just keep it loose," Joe said. "Improvise as the moment strikes you."

With Leandra no less foggy on what to do, the two of them walked out into the garden, moving along a pebble path. They kept the international group in sight, even as they passed shoulder-high rosebushes and a fountain with an elephant sculpture in the middle spraying water from its trunk.

"They're clearly not out here to admire the scenery," Leandra noted.

"They're heading for that building," he said, nodding toward a maintenance shed with walls of corrugated metal and several garage-style doors. Bales of hay sat out front, feed for the animals. Oil drums stood stacked nearby, two of them with hand pumps attached. An old pickup truck was parked behind the hay.

"Must be the motor pool," Joe said. "Which means our guests are about to go for a ride."

The international group followed Ryland's assistant to a door cut into the side of the building. The Russian entered first, followed by his security team and then Liang's small group.

"Let's go," Joe said.

They took the same path around the fountain, arriving at the door and pausing. Joe put his hand to the knob and turned it slowly. It opened without resistance.

Joe looked inside. He saw no one in the immediate vicinity, just equipment, tractors and supplies.

"Hey," a voice called out from behind them. "What are you doing here?"

Joe turned to see one of Ryland's men. An earpiece with a coil cord looping to a radio on his belt suggested he was part of the security team.

"Sorry," Joe said. "We were—"

"Just looking for some privacy," Leandra said, batting her eyes at the man while curling up to Joe.

"In the work shed?"

He wasn't buying it. His left hand went to the radio while his right slipped into the inside pocket of his jacket.

"Have you ever heard of 'a roll in the hay'?" Leandra asked.

The man hesitated. Joe considered rushing him, but officially they were still guests. He doubted they were about to get shot. Most likely they'd be ordered back into the main building or, at worst, they'd get kicked out of the party. That made a fight seem unnecessary. A second man coming up behind the security guard suggested it was a losing proposition anyhow.

"Base, this is two-eight," the man said into the radio. "We have a problem out by the work shed. Two of the guests have—"

Before the man could finish his sentence, the figure approaching him from behind reached out and pulled the cord from the radio.

The guard turned in surprise. "What the—"

He didn't finish that sentence either. A punch to the gut followed, doubling him over. A right cross finished him off in record time.

Joe raced forward and helped subdue the man. "About time you showed up," he said, recognizing Kurt. "Where have you been?"

"Sharing a drink with Ryland," Kurt said. "Interesting guy. I was coming to tell you all about it when I saw you guys following some of the guests out the door. And then I saw that guy following you. So I followed him."

"A whole lot of following going on," Joe said, pulling off the guard's tie and using it to bind his hands. As Joe did that, Kurt found a cloth nearby, creating a makeshift gag so the man wouldn't be able to shout for help when he woke up.

As Kurt and Joe finished securing the security guard, Leandra found a place to hide him, opening the door of the old truck. "Put him in here. We can cover him with this blanket."

Kurt and Joe lifted the man and slid him onto the bench seat of the truck. Joe used the seat belt to bind his feet and Leandra threw an old blanket over the top of him.

She closed the door quietly, but another sound was heard.

"Say again, two-eight, you were cut off."

The security guard's radio lay on the ground demanding a response. Joe cleared his throat and pressed the talk button. "This is two-eight," he said, doing his best to sound like the South African. "Disregard. Just a guest who can't hold his liquor. Helping him to the washroom."

"Better you than me," the voice from base said. *"Update us when you're back on patrol."*

"Wilco," Joe said.

"That was quick thinking," Kurt said. "But no one says 'wilco' anymore."

"Let's hope you're wrong about that," Joe said.

With nothing more coming from the radio, Joe turned toward the work shed. "They went in there. I think we should find out why."

"Lead the way," Kurt said.

Joe went for the shed's door and eased it open. As he peeked inside, the sound of a finely tuned engine coming to life reverberated off the metal walls.

"Sounds like the safari tour is about to begin," Leandra said.

Joe saw lights near the front of the building but nothing nearby except silent machinery and farm equipment. He moved inside. Leandra and Kurt followed.

Picking his way through, Joe led them to a spot beside a front-end loader. The hulking piece of construction equipment was half covered with mud, but it made for a good hiding spot. Crouching behind it, they could see most of the room, including the taillights of a rugged but modern-looking vehicle.

"Mercedes G63," Joe whispered.

The G63 was an extended version of the topflight Mercedes SUV. The six-wheeled chassis added a third axle and a short pickup-style bed on the back. Joe noticed the wheels had been shod with large off-road tires. This was a workhorse of a machine, one that could drive over the roughest terrain while keeping its passengers comfortable in the luxury of its spacious cabin.

As the garage door in front of it rattled up and out of the way, the driver revved the engine. The twin-turbo V-8 made a throaty sound and the gleaming vehicle drove through the open bay and out into the park.

"We'll never keep up with that on foot," Leandra said.

Joe pointed to a small dump truck being loaded and attended to by a pair of Ryland's game wardens. "We could steal that one."

"Stealing it would cause more trouble than it's worth," Kurt said. "If it's going anywhere near where they went, however, it couldn't hurt to hitch a ride."

"While I'm not against getting dirty," Leandra said, "don't you think one of us should stay behind? In case that truck isn't going where you think it is? Or in case the guests come back and go somewhere else?"

Kurt nodded.

"Good idea," Joe said. He handed Leandra the radio.

"I was thinking one of you two would hang back," she said. "But if you insist . . ."

"Rudi would kill us if anything happened to you," Joe said.

"So I'm going to miss all the fun?"

"What follows will be less than fun," Joe said. "Of that I have no doubt."

Kurt nodded. "Keep your ears open," he said, pointing to the radio. "If they discover us, you'll hear about it. And if that happens, get out of here and away from the danger. We'll link up with you back in Johannesburg."

Leandra gave the thumbs-up and Kurt and Joe turned and crept within spitting distance of the truck.

Taking cover behind a support girder, they watched as Ryland's workers pushed a wheelbarrow up a ramp for at least the tenth time and dumped its contents into the back of the truck.

"That'll do it," one of the men said, sounding exhausted. "Let's move. Ryland doesn't like to be kept waiting."

One man made his way toward the cab of the truck and climbed in on the driver's side. The second man shoved the wheelbarrow to the side and then walked around the truck and climbed in on the passenger's side.

"We can ride in the back," Kurt suggested.

"You realize it's probably filled with manure," Joe said.

"Good thing these tuxes are rentals."

The diesel engine rumbled to life, with black smoke pouring from the stack behind the cab.

"Go," Kurt said.

Joe took off running, with Kurt right behind him. They cut in directly behind the truck, raced up onto the loading ramp and leapt in the air just as the dump truck lurched forward.

Joe landed on its bed and slid awkwardly. Kurt dropped in behind him with more grace, but he just about lost his balance as the truck lurched again when the driver shifted gears.

Joe remained still despite the awkward position. He heard the men in the cab speaking.

"Where'd you learn to drive?" the passenger joked. "You'll strip the ruddy gearbox like that."

"This truck has had it," the driver replied. "One of these days it's going to strand someone out in the bush with those bloody lions. You know they almost killed Vance the other day. Rushed him in a blink as soon as he turned his back."

Even with the windows open, the men hadn't heard Kurt and Joe. Nor had they felt the impact of their awkward landings. The roaring engine, straining to pull the heavy load, combined with the creaks and groans of the truck's suspension as it bounced along the dirt track, had drowned out every sound.

Relieved that they were safely aboard, Joe turned his attention to the contents of the truck's bed. His hands were going numb where they rested, a cold aura soaked his body.

He moved to a more comfortable position and studied the material below him. It wasn't manure after all.

He looked over at Kurt and whispered a single word. "Ice."

20

The dump truck was filled with ice, from large blocks that might have been good for building igloos to piles of cubes and crushed ice good for drinks.

Timing his movements with the next shift of gears, Kurt moved nearer to Joe. "It seems we can't get away from the stuff."

Joe was busy getting in a more comfortable position than the one he'd landed in. "Now I know what it feels like to be a shrimp cocktail."

There was little chance they'd be discovered. There was no rear view into the dump truck's bed from the cab and the roar of the engine and constant jostling along the bumpy dirt track they were on made it impossible for the driver or passenger to hear them.

"What do you suppose they're doing with all this?"

Joe offered a thought. "When I was a kid, I worked on a ranch in New Mexico during the summer. They used to dump blocks of ice into the drinking troughs so all the water wouldn't evaporate. This is a game park. It's hot out there. They might be doing something similar."

"Meaning we could be on our way to a watering hole surrounded by lions," Kurt asked.

"Or a crocodile pond in need of a temperature reduction."

"Hard pass on either experience," Kurt said. He moved to the front, where the lip of the dumping bed extended out over the top of the cab.

Popping up over the top, he found they were traveling on a dirt road, with wild grasses lining both sides. The main lodge and the maintenance shed were now far behind them. "We're out in the bush and heading deeper."

"Any sign of our guests?" Joe asked.

Kurt could see the taillights of another vehicle out in front. "That's got to be them. They're heading for a small building."

Thankfully, the dump truck followed. Heading for the same destination.

"Probably the reptile house," Joe said. "Remember the Komodo dragons in Japan?"

"How could I forget," Kurt said. "You had so much fun playing in the sand with them."

"Once was enough," Joe said. "I'm sure you've thought of this, but we probably shouldn't be in the truck when it comes to a full stop. Even though they loaded this thing by hand, they're not going to unload it that way."

Joe had a point. Given the opportunity, Kurt would have ridden the truck into the shed and taken his chances, but lights coming on outside of the building and a man positioning a conveyer belt told him the truck wasn't going inside.

He left the front of the truck and moved toward the end of the bed. Climbing over the tailgate, he stood on a rusted metal bumper. Fortunately, the big truck wasn't moving all that fast. "Hit the ground and stay directly behind the truck."

Joe gave a thumbs-up.

Kurt took one last look at the dirt speeding by and leapt into the air.

He hit the ground, tucked and rolled, tumbling a couple times before coming to a stop in the red dirt.

Joe landed a few yards away, grunting with the final impact and lying flat in the darkness, as the truck rumbled on toward its destination.

When it was clear no one had seen them, Joe propped himself up and looked over at Kurt. "I give you eight-point-five on the dismount," Joe said.

"I give you a ten for not landing on me," Kurt replied.

They watched the truck pull up to the building. It stopped, made a three-point turn and backed toward the loading dock.

As Joe had predicted, the ice was dumped onto the dock. Two men shoveled it onto a moving conveyor belt, which hauled it up and into the building through an opening at the upper level.

"That's our way in," Kurt said.

They moved closer, remaining outside the radius of the lights until the unloading was finished and the dump truck drove off. As the last of the ice was loaded on the belt, Ryland's men moved inside.

"Looks clear," Joe said. "Let's go."

They sprinted through the dark toward the conveyor belt. It was wet with meltwater and no longer active, but its rubberized surface made it easy to climb.

Kurt went up first, climbing up quickly and ducking through the opening. Joe followed a few paces behind.

Now inside, they found themselves in the rafters where the conveyor split into three separate tracks. Two of them were dry. Kurt followed the trail of water. It led to the far side of the building, where a large hopper made of stainless steel had collected the delivery.

A metal chute was connected to the far side of the hopper. It was in the upright and locked position at the moment, but there could be no doubt it was designed to empty ice into a long, rectangular pool down below.

"If someone starts swimming laps," Joe said, "I'm going to be terribly embarrassed at all the conclusions *you* jumped to."

Kurt pointed to an electronic board at the far end of the pool. It resembled the scoreboard on a playing field or a temporary highway sign telling drivers the ramp up ahead was closed. Glowing digital numbers recorded the time and temperature. The pool water was 32.1 degrees

Fahrenheit. "No swimming tonight, unless someone's training for the Polar Bear Plunge."

The sound of voices became audible, accompanied by footsteps on the concrete below. A group of five walked out to a spot on the far side of the pool.

Ryland, Liang and Novikov were in the lead. A woman whom neither Kurt nor Joe had seen before was with them. A fifth member of the party, one of Ryland's technicians, followed. He left the group, taking up a position behind a control panel near the lighted information board. He stood with his hands behind him, waiting for orders.

"No dragons or crocodiles," Joe said. "But I think we're about to get a show."

21

Ryland strode around the pool, leading the party to the proper viewing area while fielding questions from his guests. Pointed, accusatory questions. He steeled himself to remain on the offensive, firing back with queries of his own.

"I'll start with you, Ms. Tunstall," he said. "When will the turbines be delivered to my technicians?"

The woman stared back at him. Eileen Tunstall was the matriarch of a wealthy Canadian family that owned three separate industrial companies. Her father had started them and she'd built them up after wresting control from her brothers. Fighting against the regulators and competitors every step of the way. She was the type who backed down from no one.

"The turbines have already been shipped," she said.

"But they won't be delivered until you convince me this scheme is more than a pipe dream. And that you're more than a second-rate con man."

"I assure you," Ryland said, "I'm second-rate at nothing. As for your demands, will you commit if I meet them?"

"Yes," she said plainly. "But at this point the bar is very high."

Ryland was fine with that. "And what about the rest of you," he said. "Are you also committed?"

"We have demonstrated our commitment many times over," Liang replied. "Six months ago, I provided this venture with thirty million dollars. That should be enough to prove my intentions."

"Thirty million is a drop in the bucket," Ryland said. "It buys a single oceangoing vessel. And a small one at that."

Liang was not impressed. "The thirty million I speak of was only the latest transfer. I have made others beforehand. All told, you've received one hundred and fifty million dollars from my company."

"And nearly as much from mine," Novikov chimed in. His deep Russian accent came off as gruff and gravelly, a great contrast to Liang's sharp, scolding voice.

"These were not gifts," Ryland insisted. "They're investments. Do you think I would include you in this venture without making sure you had skin in the game? There are plenty of others who would choose to be the first movers of the revolution, which I'm about to provide."

The Russian cleared his throat. "My company has

purchased vast tracts of land above the Arctic Circle. Land for drilling and mining. Not to mention rights of way for pipelines, railbeds and roads. We have optioned the prime coastal areas in which to build the new ports at great expense. We've had 'skin in the game,' as you call it, for two years now. At this moment, that investment is frozen, literally and figuratively. It's buried under snow and locked up by permafrost, which sinks ten meters into the earth. It also sits on my balance sheet as a massive liability. One that requires monthly interest payments. You've been promising to turn that liability into an asset for some time, but, so far, we've seen nothing."

"We've made similar purchases in Canada and Greenland," Ms. Tunstall said. "None of us will give you another penny until we verify your claims. You insist you've made a breakthrough. Now prove it."

"I intend to do just that," Ryland said calmly. "You see the pool before you. It's been cooled to a temperature of thirty-two degrees Fahrenheit. It represents the water above the Arctic Circle."

"It's not frozen," Liang said.

"The depths are not frozen," Ryland said, "but there is a layer of ice on the surface."

Novikov dropped down beside it, dipping his hand in the pool. The ice, clear as glass, cracked with the slightest touch, allowing his hand to sink in.

Novikov pulled back, annoyed that the cuff of his shirt had been soaked. "It's as he says," he announced, while flicking the water from his hand.

"Surely you don't expect to convince us by melting a paper-thin layer of ice?" Liang asked.

Ryland grinned. "Of course not." He turned to his technician. "Open the slide."

The technician manipulated a lever on the control panel, guiding the stainless steel chute out over the pool. At the touch of a button, it tilted downward and the doors of the hopper opened.

Ice began to pour down the chute, arriving in a rush, splashing and spreading out as it hit the water.

Tunstall and Liang stepped back to avoid being doused. Novikov got his feet wet and cursed, while the technician moved the chute from side to side, spreading the ice evenly.

When the last of the ice had fallen, a frozen layer covered the entire pool. In some places, it was jumbled up in small ridges, in others it had frozen together in blocks shaped like miniature icebergs.

"Five thousand pounds of frozen water," Ryland said. "If taken to scale, this would represent a shelf of sea ice thirty feet thick—far thicker than what we actually find in either the Arctic or the Antarctic. But I will account for that."

Some of the ice had missed the pool. Novikov and Tunstall kicked the chunks back into the water, picking up a few stray cubes and examining them before tossing them in.

The pool had become a pond with a frozen layer on top. The lighted board showed the overall temperature dropping until it read 26.4 degrees.

"Now what?" Tunstall asked. "Do we chant the magic words together?"

Ryland was growing annoyed at her flippancy, but he needed her contributions more than the others at this point. The high-pressure turbines her company built were the key to his plan.

He turned to his assistant. "Release the catalyst."

The technician pressed an illuminated button, holding it down until it turned from red to green. A pair of doors in the side of the pool opened and a dark liquid began pumping into the water beneath the ice.

The liquid swirled into the pool, twirling out and bending back as it spread.

"Switch to black light," Ryland said. "I want them to see this clearly."

The technician turned off the regular pool lights and powered up a bank of purple bulbs. Under black light, the ice took on a whiter hue, looking more like the snow-colored sea version than it had before. The pool itself was like a dark glass, but the injections from either side glowed brilliantly in neon green.

Thirty seconds into the demonstration, the pumps shut down and the doors in the side of the pool closed back up. For several minutes, nothing happened. The guests watched and waited, growing bored and then restless.

"I don't know whether to laugh or cry," Ms. Tunstall said.

"There had better be more than this," Liang warned.

Ryland glanced at his watch. "Give it time," he said.

Finally, a crack appeared in one section of the frozen surface. The glowing green liquid rose through the fissure and filled it in, widening the break with each passing second. Additional fissures appeared in other parts of the pool and the ice began to move.

Ryland's guests looked closer.

To their left, a pile of loose ice broke apart and then bobbed to the surface. It quickly separated into a dozen small pieces, which melted rapidly. To the right, a large circular gap opened, spreading quickly in all directions.

"It's eating the ice," Tunstall said.

"Astounding," Liang added.

Ryland stood quietly, reveling in the moment, as the green liquid spread and the ice dissolved before their eyes.

"As you can see—and feel—the ice is melting despite the temperature remaining below the freezing point," Ryland said.

"What is the temperature?" Novikov asked, looking up from the glowing waters.

"Twenty-six-point-five," the technician replied.

The digital board indicated the same.

"The water has not been warmed?" Tunstall asked.

"Test it yourself," Ryland said, "if you don't believe me."

She dipped her hand into the water at the edge of the pool, made a fist as she pulled it from the supercooled liquid.

Her fingers were bright red. "It is very, *very* cold."

Ryland offered her a towel to dry her hand. "Colder than it was before."

"How is that possible?" Novikov asked.

"The miracle of heat transfer," Ryland said. "The catalyst absorbs heat from the water while it breaks the bonds between the ice crystals. The colder the water, the faster it works. Up to a point, of course."

"And what is the catalyst?" Tunstall asked.

"It's a type of microbe, a species of algae that lives under the glaciers," Ryland explained. "We've genetically altered it to be more effective and to reproduce much faster. All we have to do is spread it near the poles and the sea ice will melt away, never to freeze again."

"Surely it won't act this rapidly?" Tunstall said.

"Of course not," Ryland replied. "This is a vastly more concentrated demonstration. But over time the algae will multiply and spread. Within a year, the so-called Northwest Passage will be wide open for navigation. Within two years, there will be no summer ice in the Arctic at all. And the increased heat absorbed by the dark water will warm the frozen tundra of Russia and Canada. The two of you, with all of your new real estate holdings, will become the wealthiest landowners in the world, having bought what was worthless only to see it opened for mining, farming and oil exploration in the blink of an eye."

He walked around the pool as he spoke. "Ports will be built on the extremities of all northern nations, ships will be needed to carry the new bonanza of trade. Each of you will be in the position of first mover. Each of you will double and triple your wealth and status."

"And you?" Tunstall asked. "What do you get out of all this?"

"A portion of the wealth you generate will flow to me," Ryland said proudly. "I'm invested in each of your companies at this point, am I not?"

"You are a minority investor," Liang reminded him. "A very minor one at that. A long list of others will make much more. Now that I see what you can do, I'm surprised you've demanded so little."

"I have other incentives," Ryland insisted.

Novikov laughed deeply. He turned to his associates. "He's working a different game. With a kingdom of his own there for the taking. Isn't that right?"

Ryland offered a slight bow, as if to say, *You have me.*

Novikov continued, "We have the north between us. He has the south alone."

The Russian turned to Ryland, a smile on his face suggesting he felt a great deal of pride for having figured Ryland out. "The Antarctic will be yours. Isn't that the way you see it?"

"The oil is there," Ryland said, sounding much as he had when speaking to Kurt. "Oil, minerals, gemstones. All the diamonds that used to be so plentiful here in South Africa. With the ice gone, we'll walk around and pluck them off the surface, find them in every shovelful of soil. Not to mention rare earths and precious metals, like platinum, gold and tungsten. That is my desire, yes."

Ms. Tunstall laughed. "They will never let you have it," she insisted. "They will never let you mar their pristine little paradise."

Ryland offered a shrug. "When we're finished, Antarctica will be a gray and barren land. What little animal life exists today will quickly die off. With no wildlife or 'pristine' snowscapes to protect and nothing but broken-down glaciers retreating by the day, they will quit caring what happens to it. Mark my words, the prevailing wisdom will change as soon as dollar signs appear."

The look on Tunstall's face said she doubted him, but she shrugged instead. Her tracts in northern Canada would be worth billions. "I trust you have scientific proof to back up what you've shown us?"

"A data transfer is being sent to each of you as we speak," Ryland said. "It's twenty gigabytes of genetic information, climate studies and thermodynamic data. I'm sure each of you have people to summarize it for you."

Novikov nodded. "So be it," he said. "You will have the last transfer of funds."

"And your turbines," Ms. Tunstall added.

"And your tankers for transporting the catalyst," Liang insisted.

Ryland nodded to each of them in gratitude, then stood tall and proud. "And each of us will have our own end of the Earth."

22

From his spot up in the rafters, Kurt listened intently. He kept his breathing shallow and steady and his body completely still.

By the sound of it, Ryland hadn't given up on his fantasy. Instead, he'd found a way to remove the snow and ice that made it so difficult to get at.

Down below, Novikov found a chunk of ice on the pool deck. He kicked it back into the water. It bobbed up and down before breaking in half and shrinking away like the rest of the ice had.

After staring at this last chunk for a moment, Ryland motioned to his technician. "Drain the pool."

The technician opened several valves and a pair of circular grates appeared in the bottom of the pool. The water began to flow out, pouring through the drains so quickly that small whirlpools could be seen extending down from the surface into the opening.

As it swirled away to an unknown end, Ryland gathered up his guests, led them out of the pool house and back toward the waiting Mercedes.

"We need to get a sample of that algae," Kurt said.

"You better act fast," Joe said. "At the rate that water is going down the drain, the pool will be empty in a matter of minutes."

Kurt looked for a way down, preferably one that would make it easy to remain unnoticed by the technician. He settled on using one of the girders that supported the roof. It had the advantage of being sturdy and located behind the man and his control panel.

Kurt moved toward it, stretching from one truss to the next. He twisted his body to climb around a bundle of electrical cables and reached the girder without being noticed.

Putting his hands and feet on either side of the I beam, Kurt began to descend. He'd made it halfway down when Joe held up a clenched fist, signaling him to stop.

Footsteps on the concrete told Kurt the technician was moving, but he couldn't see around the beam. He looked back at Joe. The fist remained clenched, but Joe's eyes were on the target below, turning and tracking until . . .

Joe looked at Kurt, released his fist and pointed downward repeatedly and rapidly. *Go now.*

Kurt all but slid the rest of the way down, landing solidly and bending his knees to absorb the shock.

The touchdown was surprisingly quiet. He glanced around. The technician had vanished down the hall. Kurt let him go and moved toward the pool.

By now, the water had drained appreciably. No more than a foot of liquid was left at the bottom—and that would be gone in another minute.

Kurt needed a container to collect a sample. He opened a cabinet beside the control console and found tools, work lights and extension cords. A second cabinet stored paint cans and sealant. None of which helped.

A bottle of chlorine sat nearby, but even if Kurt dumped the contents the residual bleach inside would kill the algae and make the sample worthless. He needed something else, something sterile.

His eyes darted around the room, spotting a plastic water bottle that someone had placed on a shelf and forgotten about. Kurt grabbed it, dumped the water remaining in it and hopped down into the rapidly emptying pool.

The pool was four feet deep at the shallow end, with a six-foot depth at the other end where the twin drains were sucking the water down. The shallow end was dry, with only a thin film of water clinging to the surface under Kurt's feet.

Kurt sprinted to the deep end, dropping to one knee and submerging the bottle under the last few inches of water. Bubbles streamed from the opening as the greenish fluid filled it.

A sound from above got Kurt's attention. Joe had banged his fist on the hopper and was gesturing madly.

He looked like an NFL quarterback trying to change the play at the last second. He pointed to a spot behind Kurt, following that with a walking motion using two fingers. *The technician was coming back.*

Kurt pulled the bottle from the water, capped it and tucked it into his jacket pocket. He threw himself against the wall and crouched low as the sound of footsteps and something being dragged along the concrete floor approached from behind him.

Kurt looked up as a shadow fell over him. He saw the toe of a boot sticking out over the edge. A jet of water appeared, firing across the pool and blasting the far wall with a high-pressure stream of liquid.

Kurt noticed a hand attached to the brass nozzle and the pressurized curve of a narrow-gauge fire hose. The technician was using it to wash down the last of the residue, directing the spray in a side-to-side motion. He couldn't see Kurt unless he looked straight down and Kurt couldn't move without revealing himself.

As the technician finished washing down one section, he shuffled a few inches to the left. Once the next section had been rinsed, he moved again.

Each time the technician repositioned himself, Kurt moved along with him. But this maneuver had its limits.

Still pressed flat against the wall, Kurt glanced up at Joe, thinking now would be a good time to do something.

Joe stared for a moment, held up a finger . . . and then promptly disappeared.

Kurt shook his head. Retreat was not what he had in mind.

Up in the rafters, Joe was planning anything but a retreat. He'd been watching and calculating. By his own rough estimate, he had a sixty percent chance of success.

Climbing into the ice hopper, he crawled toward the stainless steel chute, which remained pointed toward the pool.

Inching forward, Joe lay down on his stomach. To make this plan work, he would need to time his slide just right.

He saw the jet of water come into view as the technician continued to move in side steps.

"Just a little farther," Joe whispered.

The technician took another step to the right. Joe released his grip and slid forward, picking up speed as he raced down the chute. The technician stepped directly in front of him as Joe flew off the end.

Joe crashed into the man waist-high, taking him to ground in a crunching tackle.

Kurt heard the crash and saw the water jet veer off target. He knew Joe had sprung into action. Popping up, he climbed out of the pool, ready to lend his assistance.

He found Joe pinning the technician down, but the man wasn't fighting. He looked groggy, like he didn't know what hit him.

"Nice trick," Kurt said.

"Chutes and ladders," Joe said. "You took the slow way down. I took the express."

"There are advantages to that," Kurt admitted.

At that exact moment, the far door opened and one of the men who'd shoveled the ice onto the ramp appeared. "What's all the noise about?"

"And disadvantages," Joe said.

The new arrival was big and burly. At six foot five, with a substantial gut and arms like pythons, he looked like the type who might wade into a bar fight with a grin on his face. But instead of attacking with his fists, he reached for a pistol on his belt.

Kurt and Joe dove in opposite directions. A gunshot rang out, followed by its ricochet.

Kurt found himself by the nozzle of the fire hose. He turned it toward the big guy, blinding him with a blast of high-pressure water and then yanking the hose to the side, twisting his body as hard as he could in the effort.

The armed man had ducked out of the surging stream, bringing an arm up to shield his face. He never saw the second hit coming, as Kurt's strenuous effort brought the length of the hose up off the ground and whipped it forward.

It snapped taut and caught the man in the backs of the knees. His legs folded and he went over backward. He hit the ground, rolled to the side and turned back toward Kurt. Just in time to get hit in the face by another blast.

He raised the pistol, firing blindly and attempting to block the water with his free hand. Before he managed to get a clear view, Joe came in from the side and kicked the pistol from his grasp and dropped down on him with a flying elbow.

The impact slammed the burly man into the pool deck. His face hit the concrete and his nose shattered. He rolled over, his face bloody, his eyes filled with rage.

Joe threw a right cross, but the man caught it in his big paw and stopped the punch cold.

He stood up, pulling Joe toward him and then grabbing him by the tuxedo lapels.

Joe kicked the man in his substantial gut, but it had no effect. The man lifted him up and heaved him across the room like he was a small child.

Joe flew uncontrollably, crashing into the cabinets and bringing them down on top of him.

Rushing into action, Kurt charged around the far side of the pool, dragging the hose with him and hooking it around the brute's body.

Kurt heaved on the line, but the big man was stout. He absorbed the force, taking a single step back but otherwise holding his ground. Turning the tables on Kurt, he locked onto the hose with both hands and ripped it from Kurt's grasp.

To avoid being toppled into the pool, Kurt let go. As the big man stumbled backward in victory, Kurt raced to Joe's side and helped him to his feet. "Let's get out of here."

They rushed for the door as the big man punched a large red button on the far wall. Alarms began to sound. Automatic doors began to close.

Sprinting for all they were worth, Kurt and Joe made it through the exit just before a steel-barred gate slammed shut.

"Now what?" Joe said.

"Keep running."

23

Leandra was still in the maintenance shed when she heard the alarm go off. Red lights began flashing inside and sections of the fencing between the shed and the main compound slid shut. "So much for making a quick getaway."

She crouched in her hiding spot, listening to the dull whoop-whoop-whoop of the alarm and watching as the Mercedes carrying Ryland and his guests pulled in and parked.

Stepping from the car, Ryland was met by two of his employees—an older man who was his primary gamekeeper and a younger ranch hand.

"What's the alarm about?" Ryland asked calmly.

"Animal escape," the gamekeeper said.

"Where?" Ryland demanded.

"Back at building four."

To Leandra, Ryland looked preternaturally calm. "We've just come from building four," he said.

The gamekeeper raised his hands. "All I can tell you is someone activated the high danger alert. It's probably those damned lions again. They were raised in zoos and circuses. They were mistreated badly and they're dangerous. At this point they associate humans with food."

"So you've told me," Ryland said. "I doubt they're the problem this time. Give me your radio."

The gamekeeper produced his radio and handed it over. Ryland held it to his face and pressed the talk button. "Building four, come in, this is Ryland. What's your status?"

Leandra had the volume on her radio turned down to the bare minimum, but the scratchy sound of a human voice came through. She pressed the speaker to her ear to listen.

"*. . . spotted two intruders after you left. I don't know how they got in here, but they beat up one of my men and took a sample of the pool water. I hit the emergency animal alarm to lock down the building but they got out before the doors shut.*"

The details made little sense to Leandra, but Ryland's guests looked instantly concerned.

"Sample?" the Russian said. "Of your catalytic algae?"

"Relax," Ryland said.

"With a sample, someone could develop a counteragent."

"Unlikely," Ryland said. "Besides, they'll never have the chance. They're in the middle of a game park teeming with wild animals and surrounded by electric fences."

Remaining unflappable, he brought the radio back up and pressed talk once more. "Were these intruders two men in tuxedos, one of average height with short dark hair and a taller one with silver hair and an irritating smirk on his face?"

"That's them for sure."

"I thought so," Ryland said.

Liang seemed agitated by this news. "You know these men?"

Ryland nodded. "Two Americans from an organization called NUMA. I was suspicious of them from the moment they requested an invitation."

"Then you should have refused them entry," Liang snapped.

Ryland shook his head. "Refusing them entry would have raised their suspicions and I wanted to learn their intentions. Now that I know their goal, I will deal with them appropriately."

"How?" Tunstall asked.

"In a way that looks like an explainable tragedy." He turned back to the gamekeeper.

"Those lions were brought here to be hunted," he said. "It seems only fair to let them have a little fun of their own. Take a few of your men and release them. Bring the night vision scopes and find the Americans. Once you spot them, keep the lions moving in their direction."

"Those lions are overdue for a feeding," the gamekeeper said.

"Yes," Ryland said, grinning. "That should make them even more keen to do the job for us."

24

Kurt and Joe were running in a southerly direction when they heard the first sound for the lions behind them. The roar of a male could travel for miles, but this call was much closer. Other roars followed and it sounded as if a skirmish had broken out between several of the beasts.

"That's not a sound I wanted to hear," Joe said, continuing to move.

Whatever caused the disturbance, it soon died down.

"I'd prefer if they kept roaring," Kurt said. "If they stay quiet, we'll never know where they are."

"At that point I think you can assume they're sneaking up on us."

Kurt and Joe had no way of knowing that the gamekeeper and his assistant were using cattle prods to force the maladjusted lions out of their cramped pens. Or that the big cats, now agitated, had balked, swatting at the prods and roaring with each painful jab.

Running at a pace they could maintain, Kurt kept moving south, bending their course wide of the main building and its inviting lights.

"What about Leandra?" Joe asked.

"Let's hope she's heard the commotion and got out," Kurt said.

Coming upon a tree with a Y-shaped trunk, Kurt climbed up and gazed off into the distance.

"What do you see?" Joe said, breathing deeply to re-supply his muscles with oxygen.

"Headlights and dust," Kurt said. "They've got a couple vehicles out there, weaving back and forth."

"Sounds like a modern cattle drive," Joe said. "Or, in this case, a lion drive."

Kurt had no doubt they were using the vehicles to spur the lions forward. He wondered about doubling back, then realized it would be too slow on foot to get around the lions and the men in the vehicles.

He looked the other way. There wasn't much light, but based on the glow from the lodge, he estimated the fence was no more than half a mile off. "Let's run for it."

Kurt hopped down and the two of them took off once again. Picking up the pace and running in silence.

A glance back told Kurt their pursuers were coming closer. He saw four vehicles spread out in a V formation, headlights glaring like the eyes of some infernal beast. He had to assume the lions were somewhere in the front of that beast.

"Remember Satchel Paige's advice," Joe said. "Never look back. Someone might be gaining on you."

"He wasn't wrong," Kurt said, picking up the pace even further.

The vehicles were moving slowly, no more than fifteen or twenty miles an hour, but it was twice the speed a man could run for any appreciable length of time.

Kurt changed direction and veered to the right. Joe matched him.

It didn't take long for the approaching formation to change its path as well, swinging around with remarkable precision, until the yawing V was lined up directly with their new course.

"Who knew lions were related to bloodhounds," Joe said.

"The men in the trucks are doing the tracking," Kurt said. "Must be using thermal or night vision scopes."

Joe pointed to a looming rock formation ahead and to their left. It rose fifty feet from the ground, sloping on all sides like the back of a giant tortoise. "Night vision can't see through rock. Let's put that mound of granite between us and them."

"Great idea," Kurt said.

They cut to the left, running at a reckless pace, one that couldn't be sustained.

The vehicles trailing them swung around to follow, slowed by the maneuver but still closing in. The sound of engines and tires on the rough ground was growing louder, shouts could be heard as the men yelled to one another and cursed at the lions they were relentlessly driving forward.

Kurt reached the edge of the rocks with Joe a few paces behind. He cut around the corner and then turned toward the fence, careful to keep the rocks between them and the headlights.

He'd gone no more than twenty yards when he had to put his heels into the ground and come to a sudden stop. Joe pulled up beside him, dropping into a crouch and freezing in position.

In front of them, shimmering in the dark, loomed a pair of luminescent eyes. A second pair rose out of the grass beside the first, with several additional pairs soon appearing beyond them.

"Looks like the lions outflanked us," Kurt said.

"I don't think so," Joe replied. He heard a yipping sound.

"Jackals?" Kurt suggested.

"Hyenas."

Whatever they were, the pack of animals grew to at least a dozen. At the same time, light from the pursuing vehicles had begun to creep around the rocks, stretching across the grass and bringing light out onto the open plain.

"Talk about being caught between a rock and a hard place," Joe said.

"I choose the rocks," Kurt said. "Let's get back—and quickly."

They backed up, keeping their eyes on the hyenas until they neared the rocks, at which point they turned and sprinted up onto the dark stone. Kurt climbed as quickly as he could, taking cover halfway up where he found a gap in the rock. Joe pressed into the fissure beside him.

Out on the grass, the hyenas stood tall, sniffing the air. Their ears pricked up and their nostrils twitched. The sound of vehicles didn't bother them—they were used to the presence of men and machines in the park—but they smelled something else. Another animal invading their turf.

Kurt inched forward as the lions made their first appearance. The big cats were illuminated by the lights of the vehicles following them. They loped into view and slowed to a walk and then came to a stop altogether.

"They smell the hyenas," Joe said.

Kurt counted seven animals, four females and three males. They looked a little mangy, no doubt from their treatment in places they'd been rescued from. He saw scars on their hides and noticed one of the males moved with a limp.

Out in the grass, Ryland's men pulled their vehicles to a halt near the edge of the granite outcropping. The lead vehicle was an open-top jeep sporting a roll bar and no doors. The other vehicles pulled up beside it, two SUVs and a flatbed truck.

A man in the passenger's seat of the jeep stood up, poking his head and shoulders above the roll bar. He surveyed the terrain with a night vision scope, scanning back and forth.

Kurt whispered to Joe. "This might be our chance to get some wheels."

"Sounds a lot safer than running through the Wild Kingdom on foot."

Kurt climbed from his spot and went up, reaching the crest of the rock pile. From there, he moved in the direction of the parked vehicles, hoping they'd stay where they were until he got to the edge.

As Kurt and Joe moved in silence, the lions began to roar. Out on the grass, the dominant male made a false charge, his huge maned head tilting back and up as he bellowed at the hyenas. The other males followed suit.

The hyenas looked hesitant, but they didn't retreat. They were not small animals themselves and they outnumbered the encroaching lions almost two to one. They gathered themselves together in a defensive pack, answering back in a series of barks and yips that sounded like mocking laughter.

"Don't they know this isn't a laughing matter?" Joe whispered as he crawled up beside Kurt.

"Apparently, they can't read the room," Kurt said. He eased forward, soon reaching the precipice of the rocks. Stopping there, he studied their options.

The rock formation descended in distinct steps—a six-foot drop from the top to an intermediate ledge that would take them closer to the stopped vehicles, then a ten-foot drop to the ground.

The four vehicles were parked close together. One of two Toyotas was tucked in close to the ledge, beyond which was the flatbed, then the jeep, then the second Toyota.

"We should go for the jeep," Joe suggested.

The jeep would be easy to get into, with no doors and an open top. But there was a problem. It was the third in the line of four vehicles.

"We could loop around," Kurt said. "Or—"

Before Kurt could finish his sentence, a pack of hyenas charged forward, four in the middle, two more on the right flank. They raced toward the dominant lion, swarming toward him from both sides.

The big animal reared back and knocked two of them down with a single swipe of his great paw. As those animals tumbled away, the lion lunged toward a third. At the same moment, one of the hyenas snapped at the lion's hind legs. As teeth caught skin, the lion jumped and spun, chasing the hyena that had bitten him.

The smaller animals were quicker and healthier. They raced off cackling as if they'd played a trick on the big cat. Even as they left, other hyenas raced in.

The lion was suddenly on the defensive, spinning, roaring defiantly and snapping his jaws at anything in range as he tried to defend himself from all quarters.

For a moment, it looked like a game, with the hyenas racing around the lion and the larger beast swatting at them, always a step too slow or a split second too late. But the rest of the pride came on suddenly, six more lions charging forward at once, and what had been a playful and interesting encounter took on the look of a vicious brawl.

Some of the hyenas ran, others returned to the fight.

In seconds, it became a confused, dust-obscured melee. All of it caught in the glare of the headlights.

"This is our chance," Kurt said.

He dropped to the intermediate ledge and ran forward. Instead of jumping to the ground, he leapt off the precipice and landed square on the roof of the first Toyota, denting it and dropping to one knee. Standing up, stepping forward and leaping, he landed in the flatbed, which gave him the perfect runway on which to gather speed and launch himself toward the jeep.

Leaping high enough, he was able to grab the roll bar, vault over it like a gymnast and swing his legs forward.

His feet connected with the surprised gamekeeper, who took a boot to the face and went flying out onto the grass.

The driver flinched, looked back at Kurt and instinctively stomped on the gas.

The tires dug in and the vehicle surged forward. Kurt fell backward, grabbing the bar to keep himself from falling out. Collecting himself, he sprang forward and put the driver in a headlock.

The driver struggled and clawed at Kurt with one hand while jerking the steering wheel from side to side with the other. Stretching to get leverage, the man kept the accelerator pedal pinned to the floor.

The jeep raced off into the night, swerving and threatening to tip over. From the corner of his eye, Kurt saw one of the lions flash past them. He then saw a pair of hyenas scattering in opposite directions.

Needing to end the ride quickly, Kurt reached for the gearshift and jammed it down into low.

The jeep slowed instantly. Between Kurt's weight and the sudden decrease in speed, the driver was thrown forward. Kurt slammed the man's head against the steering wheel. It whiplashed back, the driver looking dazed and confused.

Kurt grabbed the wheel, turned hard to the right and pushed the man the opposite way. The jeep whipped into another turn and the driver went out the opening where the door should have been.

Straightening up, Kurt hopped into the front seat, put the jeep back into drive and got the ride under control. He swerved around a small tree and dodged a piano-sized boulder before turning back in the direction he'd come.

"Now," he said to himself, "time to find out what happened to Joe."

25

Joe had been left behind. He'd watched Kurt from the ledge and saw him hopscotch his way across the parked vehicles like they were stepping-stones. Joe figured if Kurt could do it, he could make it look easy.

He jumped from the ledge, landing deftly on the roof of the nearby Toyota. He leapt from there to the flatbed and raced forward, just as Kurt had, launching himself into a perfect jump, high and long, with a soft landing envisioned. But the jeep surged forward just as Joe took to the air. He fell short, managing to grasp only the tailgate as the vehicle sped off.

He held tight and tried to pull himself up, but as the jeep swerved and bounced over the uneven terrain he was thrown loose.

Ending up in the tall grass, in the dark, Joe held still.

The flatbed and the Toyotas were heading his way. One of them stopped to pick up the fallen gamekeeper while the others continued on. They passed Joe without pause, swerving off to the left and chasing after Kurt and the stolen jeep.

Joe emerged as the red taillights grew more distant and the dust cleared. Staying low, he looked around, painfully aware of the lions and hyenas circling and fighting a short distance away.

"All things considered, I'd rather be on a frozen, sinking ship," he muttered.

His only hope now was to make a run for the fence. He moved cautiously at first, so as not to attract attention. Once he'd put some distance between himself and the animals, he chose a direction that would take him away from the lions, the hyenas and the vehicles chasing Kurt. Satisfied with his choice, he took off at a sprint once again.

Joe took his own advice and didn't look back. He raced away from the commotion, heading toward a darker and quieter section of the park. He passed a row of scrub bushes, hopped over a small pipeline and continued on.

He saw the fence up ahead—it was no more than a hundred yards away—but the lights of another vehicle had come onto the scene. It was moving down a frontage road this side of the fence.

Forced to stop, Joe crouched in the bushes. "There's an awful lot of car traffic in this so-called wildlife preserve."

The approaching vehicle continued down the access road, passing him. He recognized it as Ryland's six-wheeled Mercedes. It looked like the head man had come out to lead the hunt in person.

As Joe watched, the Mercedes slowed and began a wide turn back in his direction.

Not wanting to be spotted, Joe took a step. He froze at the sound of a hyena coming up behind him.

Turning slowly, Joe saw the animal was injured and favoring one leg. A second animal trotted along beside it. They stopped, having picked up Joe's scent. A low growl issued from one of the animals.

Out on the frontage road, the Mercedes had finished its turn and was coming back his way. The swath of its headlights covered Joe and the hyenas.

"If I didn't have bad luck, I wouldn't have any luck at all."

With the animals squinting against the blinding light, Joe figured this was his chance. He took off, dashing toward the fence, without looking back.

The hyenas hesitated, bothered by the light, but the driver of the Mercedes didn't wait. The engine roared and big machine surged toward Joe, attempting to cut him off at the access road.

With the lights no longer blinding them, the hyenas' instincts took over. They broke into a chase, the healthy one closing the gap with astonishing speed.

Joe ran with every ounce of energy his body could muster. His feet were flying, the rest of his body trying to keep up. It was not enough.

The faster of the two animals caught him at the verge of the road. It leapt toward his back, taking him to the ground.

They separated as they tumbled, with the hyena ripping Joe's tuxedo jacket from his shoulders and mauling it for several seconds before realizing Joe wasn't inside.

Joe was already up and running. He raced across the access road, leapt onto the iron bars of the fence, making sure not to make contact with the ground at the same time.

He'd jumped high enough to escape the shock and pulled himself up. He was grasping the spiked barbs on the top of the twelve-footer when the hyena lunged, hitting him awkwardly and knocking him free.

Joe landed on the ground, rolling away from the snarling creature. He saw the animal get back to its feet. He knew he was about to get mauled and there was only one way he could think of stopping it. He jumped for the fence, wrapping both hands around it as the hyena lunged for his legs.

The animal got its mouth on Joe's right calf with two claws on his other leg.

The circuit closed between Joe, the hyena and the ground. Electricity surged through his body and into the animal. Joe felt his muscles convulse and twist. He heard a howl of pain from the beast. And he felt himself tumbling.

Landing in the dirt, Joe rolled over defensively and covered his head. He looked up to see the hyena racing off, yelping and barking as it scampered back toward the trees.

Joe's hands tingled, his ears buzzed and his nostrils were filled with the aroma of burnt fur. He put a hand to the ground, intending to get back on his feet, but it was too late. Freed from one foe, he was now at the mercy of another.

Lights had found him and the big Mercedes was pulling to a stop beside him.

Joe sat back down, waiting for the inevitable.

The door opened. A face appeared. An attractive face, with olive green eyes.

"Don't just sit there," a female called out. "Get in."

"Leandra?"

"Are you disappointed?" she asked.

He peeled himself off the ground, suddenly gifted with new energy. "Not in the least."

Lumbering over to the vehicle, Joe climbed inside and slammed the door. "Didn't we tell you to get out of here if things went haywire?"

"You did," she replied. "But you never specified how. If we must go, I figured we might as well travel in style."

Joe grinned. "You're going to fit in just fine around here," he said. "Now all we have to do is find Kurt."

"Where is he?"

Joe pointed into the distance, where several pairs of headlights and taillights were chasing one another around in a whirling cloud of dust. "Somewhere down there."

26

After making three loops and trying to confuse his pursuers, Kurt had doubled back in a wide, sweeping turn. This took him away from the lions and hyenas and back toward the bluff. He had yet to see any sign of Joe.

If he wasn't on the grass, maybe he was still hiding in the rocks.

Kurt made another half circle, churning up a new cloud of dust, and headed for the outcropping of rock they'd used as a refuge.

The radio attached to the dashboard squawked. Kurt turned it up, catching the back end of the message. *". . . He's alone in the jeep,"* a bitter voice said. *"If you can't catch him, light him up."*

A couple garbled responses were unintelligible, but the sound of rifles discharging was perfectly clear.

The men were shooting at him from the backs of the Toyotas. He took evasive action and didn't hear or feel anything hitting the jeep. Not a surprise, considering the darkness, dust and the uneven terrain they were bouncing over.

Still, it took only one lucky shot to put the jeep or him out of action. Kurt chose to make himself harder to hit.

Cutting one way and then back the other, he raced past the outcropping of granite with the high beams on. The lights swept the ledge, but there was no sign of Joe.

"Come on, Joe," Kurt said. "This is no time to play hide-and-seek."

He was forced to swing wide as bullets ricocheted off the weathered stone, but once he'd gone wide he cut back in the other direction and drove behind the bluff, putting the rock formation between him and the men with the guns.

"Keep him away from the fence," another voice said over the radio. *"If he breaks through, there's nothing but open road out there."*

Kurt found the radio call odd. For one thing, he was nowhere near the fence. For another, the voice sounded awfully familiar.

"He's gone behind the bluff," a harsher voice snapped. *"Cut him off on the far side."*

The Toyotas were still following, while the flatbed raced around the far side, attempting to catch Kurt in a pincer move.

Kurt slammed on the brakes, sliding the tires and stirring up a billowing cloud of dust. Killing the headlights, he spun the wheel and mashed the accelerator to the floor once again, turning away from the rocks and out into the dark.

Driving blind was dangerous, but it made him almost invisible. Kurt squinted through the coated windshield, trying to avoid crashing. He clipped a small tree and then swerved to avoid a boulder, barreling through some low bushes in the process.

The two vehicles attempting to trap him fared worse. They converged in the cloud, each thinking they'd found him, shooting first and then nearly colliding.

"Look out."

"Stop shooting. You're firing at us."

"Where the hell did he go?"

Kurt took great pleasure at being the cause of their frustration.

"Well, he's not heading for the fence," the more familiar voice said. *"Clearly, he's too dumb to try that."*

Kurt grinned as he heard the last radio call. It was Joe. The sarcasm only drove the point home.

He couldn't fathom how Joe had gotten a radio. But Joe was clearly telling him to run for the fence.

Keeping his foot off the brake so the taillights wouldn't give him away, Kurt circled around one more time, clearing the bluff and heading for freedom.

The jeep picked up speed on this straightaway, its wheels rumbling across the dry terrain. Spotting the silhouette of the Mercedes parked on the access road, he grabbed the microphone from the cradle and pressed the talk button. "What happened to the other American?"

"You mean the good-looking one?" Joe replied. *"He probably met up with a beautiful woman and drove off into the sunset."*

"Correction," a female voice said. *"He was rescued by a beautiful woman and they drove off into the moonrise."*

Even better, Kurt thought. "I'll ram the fence," he replied, done with the pretense. "You guys get ready to pull through behind me."

Knowing it would best to hit a weak spot, Kurt aimed for a joint where two sections of the cast iron fence had been welded together. He kept the accelerator down and barreled forward, pulling the seat belt on with one hand and driving with the other.

The jeep bounced across the access road and surged toward the barrier. It hit the fence at forty miles an hour, acting like a three-thousand-pound battering ram.

The impact was sudden and jarring. Kurt felt the belt tighten and yank him hard. His head snapped forward and his hands flew off the steering wheel. The jeep tilted and went over on the passenger's side, sliding to a stop.

Kurt looked up. The jeep was on its side, partially caught in the fence, but only after breaking through to the long driveway.

The Mercedes turned on its lights and rumbled through the gap and stopped next to him.

Joe leaned out the window. "Careful, the fence might be hot even though it's down."

Kurt noticed Joe's hair was standing straight up. "What happened to you?"

"Electroshock therapy," Joe said.

"I've been recommending you try that for years," Kurt said.

Unlatching his seat belt, Kurt freed himself and used the roll bar to pull himself up. Standing on the side of the jeep, he leapt over the downed fence and into the bed of the Mercedes.

Securely down, he tapped the roof twice and Leandra hit the accelerator.

The Mercedes roared off, heading down the road. The turbocharged, 500-horsepower engine propelled it at a pace that neither the workman-like Toyotas nor the diesel-powered flatbed could possibly hope to match.

Watching the road behind them, Kurt saw the vehicles pull up to the fence and stop.

A sliding window in the back of the cab opened and Kurt came face-to-face with Joe. His hair looked even more amusing up close, like a punk rock musician's. "That's a good look for you. I'd keep it like that."

"Very funny," Joe said. "Speaking of keeping things. Tell me you didn't drop that water sample in all your antics out there."

Kurt reached into his jacket pocket. The bottle was there, tucked down deep inside. He pulled it out to make sure the cap was still screwed on tight.

"Safe and sound," Kurt said. "Now all we have to do is find out what we risked our lives for."

27

The Auckland Park Kingsway campus of the University of Johannesburg sported a collection of futuristic buildings arranged around a manicured lawn. Bountiful trees here and there offered shade for the students and professors, while curving paths branched out from one building to the next.

Kurt, Joe and Leandra made their way down one of those paths and into the science building, where they entered a lab run by Noah Watson.

Watson was the ranking professor in the microbiology department. He and Leandra knew each other well. Like her, the professor had worked with NUMA before, primarily as part of their effort to save the world's reefs from the effects of pollution and ocean acidification.

"Professor," Leandra said warmly as they came through the door.

Watson was in front of a computer when they arrived, an intense look firmly in place. Seeing Leandra, his face softened considerably. "Ah, you're here," he said, standing and greeting her. "At last I can stop reading the endless footnotes in this student's paper."

The professor stepped forward, hugging Leandra and offering a hand to Kurt. He was a bit taller than Kurt, a bit rounder, too. He wore a polo shirt with the Springboks logo on it, the South African rugby team. He seemed quite pleased to meet Kurt and Joe in person.

"I've heard so much about you," he said, his voice filling the room. "Too much, perhaps. When Leandra called and asked that I assist you, I was very skeptical. Considering the stories I've heard, I assumed you were imaginary figures, mere figments of some publicity department's creative minds."

Kurt shook Watson's hand with a firm grip. "I'm sure the tales have grown in the telling," he said. "We just do our jobs. Sometimes that leads us into a scrape or two."

Watson laughed. "I'm told you had a scrape or two last night."

"They were on foot," Leandra said. "Trapped in a game park surrounded by lions and hyenas."

Watson shook his head. "Lions *and* hyenas? You found yourself caught between the two greatest enemies on the savannah and came out alive. That's a rare thing."

"Don't forget the men with guns," Joe added.

The professor laughed deeply. "I see you prefer maximum level of difficulty."

Kurt stretched and felt the aches and pains of the night's efforts. "In all honesty, I prefer to sit on a sunny beach with a cold beer in my hand. But it never seems to work out that way."

"Well, considering all you've been through," Watson said, "the least I can do is examine the sample for you. You say these men were using algae to melt the ice?"

Kurt handed over the water bottle, which the professor studied through the clear plastic. "That's what we overheard. Ryland claimed it was genetically modified algae. And the water changed to a dark green tint during the demonstration."

"Looks rather clear to me," Watson said. "But many golden brown diatoms and yellow algae appear invisible unless they're present in high concentrations. I suppose we shall see."

The professor shook the bottle gently to stir up anything that had settled and then poured small samples into a pair of test tubes. He put one in a machine that would check the mineral qualities of the water. The other was subject to a chemical dye test that should have brought out the presence of algae in the liquid. Yet again, the water appeared clear.

"Most interesting," Watson said.

"I don't see anything," said Joe.

The professor cocked an eyebrow. "That's what makes it interesting."

Using an eyedropper, the professor took another sample and placed several beads of the water onto a glass slide, covered the sample with another slide and then placed it under the lens of a high-powered compound microscope.

The compound microscope had two eyepieces instead of one. This allowed it to focus more precisely and enabled the viewer to detect minute, three-dimensional structures.

"This model is designed for medical use," the professor told them. "It magnifies images up to twenty-five hundred times. If there are any bacteria or algae in the water, we'll find them."

After adjusting the settings, Professor Watson took a look. He began with the 100 power setting before quickly switching to a more powerful lens. "Most types of algae will be visible at less than a thousand times magnification," he said. "So far, I'm not seeing anything."

Kurt stood back, letting the man do his job and passing the time by glancing at the machine that was analyzing the chemical content of the water. It churned and hummed as a few LEDs blinked but offered nothing to suggest any discovery.

The professor switched lenses again. "There are a few stray bacteria visible at a magnification of eight hundred. Probably left over from the mouth of whoever drank from this bottle before you used it as a collection vessel."

"Will that skew the results?" Kurt asked.

"No," the professor said. "To have any hope of performing the task you described, we would have to find something at a high level of concentration. A few bacteria would not affect that."

Satisfied that there was nothing to see at eight hundred times normal size, the professor increased the magnification to a thousand times normal and then to fifteen hundred. He looked away from the eyepiece, scribbled a note and then looked back into the microscope.

Finally, he raised the magnification level to the full power of twenty-five hundred times normal. Kurt noticed a slight nod of the head and a change in the professor's posture.

Pulling back from the microscope, Watson appeared satisfied. "Well," he said. "See for yourself."

As Professor Watson stood back from the microscope, Kurt moved in. He adjusted the eyepieces and pressed against them, squinting until his eyes became accustomed to the bright field of view.

Focusing intently, he looked for any sign of bacteria or algae. "I don't see anything."

"Because there's nothing down there to see," the professor replied. "No algae. Very little in the way of bacteria. Nothing organic of any consequence. This water is surprisingly sterile. Are you sure this is the right sample?"

"It came straight out of the pool," Kurt said. "I collected it myself."

The professor nodded politely and scratched at a spot below his ear. "It seems you've risked your lives to recover a bottle of purified water."

"That's impossible," Joe said. "We saw Lloyd use this to melt the ice."

"Perhaps it was heated," the professor said. "Or perhaps the ice wasn't really ice to begin with."

"Trust me," Joe said. "We sat on that ice, it was real and it was freezing. My glutes have only just thawed out."

"The pool water was still frigid when I collected the sample," Kurt said. "At most, it could have been just above freezing. That would have left the ice there for hours, if not days. It couldn't have accounted for what we witnessed."

The professor didn't argue. "I don't know what to tell you. If the ice was real and the water was cold, then something else must be at work."

The machine behind them emitted a subtle beep. "Ah," the professor said. "The chemical analysis is complete."

He tapped a button on the face of the machine and an old dot matrix printer began spitting out the results of the test. When it was complete, Professor Watson grabbed the sheet of paper and tore it off.

"Well," Kurt said, grinning. "Don't keep us in suspense."

The professor cleared his throat. "Your water sample contains elevated levels of calcium chloride. Along with even higher levels of potassium chloride, sodium chloride and a strong concentration of sodium acetate and glycol."

"Rock salts," Kurt noted.

"And aircraft de-icer," Joe said, referring to the glycol.

"So Ryland pumped de-icing fluid into the pool once he dimmed the lights," Kurt said.

"The de-icer would float to the surface," Joe said. "It would separate the ice from the water, eating away the frozen stuff at warp speed. Especially if it was heated before entry."

Kurt understood now. "The rock salts would spread through the pool, changing the melting point of the water and keeping it from freezing once the glycol and sodium acetate had done their job."

"He tricked them," Leandra said.

Kurt nodded.

"But why?" Joe asked. "Why fool your own allies? Especially when they're the kind of people who might react violently to being misled?"

Kurt fell silent, considering the question from a couple different angles. In the end, there were only a few possibilities that made any sense. "Either he doesn't have the algae or it doesn't work the way he says it does. Or . . ."

"Or what?" Joe asked.

"Or Ryland's playing a different game," Kurt said. "A longer, more complicated one. And we're only seeing a small part of the big picture."

28

Rudi was in his office, sitting behind his laptop, reading the latest baffling news from Kurt with a scowl on his face. He scanned the page twice to make sure he hadn't missed anything, then closed the laptop screen with a deliberate excess of force.

"Easy, now," a voice said from the doorway. "Computers are people, too. Or they soon will be."

Rudi looked up to see Hiram Yaeger leaning against the doorjamb, arms folded across his chest.

"A revolution you will no doubt be at the forefront of," Rudi said.

"Maybe," Hiram said. "Although, realistically, we're years away from the robot takeover."

"Good," Rudi said. "That'll give me time to erase the computer's memory, so it won't hold my crimes against me. We have more immediate problems anyway. Kurt came up empty in South Africa."

"He didn't find anything?"

"He found something," Rudi said. "But it was a whole lot of nothing."

Yaeger furrowed his brow. "A lot of that going around. Kurt asked me to study the historical record from the *Schwabenland* expedition to see if we could match that photo to a particular flight and landing location."

"Sounds like a good idea," Rudi said. "But from the look on your face, I'm guessing it didn't work out."

Yaeger came in and sat down. "I've had our computers look through every known source of information about the *Schwabenland* expedition. Public, private, even classified records from an old OSS file. There's no match for that picture anywhere in the existing photographic record."

"Could you have missed something?"

"Doubtful," Yaeger said. "I even had the photo digitized and put each of the characters in the picture through a facial recognition program. The system compared the images to photos of the known explorers and crew members on the ship."

"How'd that work out?"

"More nothing," Yaeger said. He held up a hand to prevent Rudi from interrupting. "Now, I'll admit we don't have photos of every deckhand and third-class enlisted sailor that worked on the ship, but there are multiple, high-quality images of all the officers, air crew and scientists who participated."

"And?" Rudi asked, already knowing the answer.

"Not a single person in that photograph was part of the *Schwabenland* expedition. The men in that picture simply weren't on the ship."

Rudi drummed his fingers on the desk. Some information was better than none. Maybe this told them they were looking in the wrong direction. "Could the photo be a hoax?"

Yaeger shook his head. "Not a computer-generated one. I've run our deep fake analysis a couple different ways. The pixels, the light angles, the shade and the photographic depth are all legitimate. There are no artifacts to suggest the photo was manipulated or subject to editing. Whatever else it is, that picture is not computer generated or photoshopped."

"What about a real photograph but staged?" Rudi suggested.

"Possibly," Hiram said. "But you'd have to find an old Dornier flying boat, restore it to flying condition, take it out to a frozen lake and snap the photo. You'd also need a vintage camera with authentic glass lenses and film with the exact ratio of silver and chemical levels to match what was produced in Germany in the late 1930s. Which would have to be made from scratch, I might add, because that type of film isn't produced anymore."

"That's a lot of trouble to go through for a single picture covered in graffiti," Rudi admitted. "If it's not a hoax and it isn't from the *Schwabenland* expedition, who and what is it a photo of?"

Yaeger shrugged. "The only way to figure that out

would be determine where Cora got the picture from. And I think I have an idea how we can do that."

Rudi perked up. "That's what I like to hear. Just tell me it doesn't involve a psychic or a soothsayer."

"Neither," Hiram said. "Just a special blue light and the actual printed copy of the photograph. The one in Kurt's possession. Assuming he hasn't lost it."

"The printed copy?" Rudi said. "Not the original picture?"

"Correct."

Rudi was baffled. "How will that solve the problem?"

"Well," Yaeger said. "Few people know this, but the vast majority of modern printers embed microdots in every single page they print."

"Microdots?"

"Tiny dots of ink," Hiram said. "Offset from the color of the actual printed page. Usually it's done using a shade of yellow. Each dot is so small and light that it's invisible to the naked eye. And with thirty or forty spread throughout the page, it doesn't alter what's printed either. But the end result is a pattern, readable like a QR code. This pattern records the time and date of printing and includes a unit identification code that reveals the make, model and serial number of the printer that produced this particular page. Once we have that information, all we have to do is check with the manufacturer and find out who they sold that printer to and we can find out where Cora printed the photo, helping us to track down the original."

Rudi eyed Hiram suspiciously. "Which printers did you say are doing this?"

"Almost all of them," Yaeger said. "Anything manufactured in the last ten to fifteen years or so."

"Ours, too?"

"Of course."

"You've got to be kidding me."

Hiram shook his head. "It's ubiquitous," he said. "You could pluck any piece of paper, from any random garbage can, from anywhere in the world, and within minutes I could tell you precisely where and when it was printed and on what machine. We've used this method to catch people who leaked documents to the public or who stole corporate secrets. We've even caught counterfeiters who were printing their own money using this method."

"Sounds like the robot takeover is closer than you think," Rudi said. "With my phone listening to every word I say and my computer keeping a record of everything I do, and now my printer ratting me out if I use it for any non-approved purpose, it feels like Big Brother is watching."

"Oh, he is," Hiram said. "Big Sister, too. And the entire extended family. But in this case, we can use it to our advantage."

29

Back in Professor Watson's laboratory, Kurt, Joe and Leandra listened to Yaeger's instructions over a speakerphone.

"Sounds pretty simple," Kurt said. "Stand by."

With great care, Kurt pulled out the printed sheet of paper with the old Nazi photograph on it. The page had spent the better part of a week folded up into a pocket-sized square and would need to be smoothed out before they scanned it.

While Kurt worked to ease the creases out, Joe, Leandra and Professor Watson modified a scanner to emit the wavelength of blue light that the test required.

"The new LEDs are in," Joe said, putting the machine down.

Leandra switched it on while the professor used a

photometer to check the wavelength. "We're within the parameters."

Kurt looked over. "I won't make any jokes about how many of you it takes to change a lightbulb."

"Good," Joe said. "Because that sheet of paper was getting the best of you for a while."

Kurt laughed. "I'll have you know my job requires precision workmanship."

On the speaker, Yaeger cleared his throat to let them know he was still there, waiting.

Kurt handed the delicately flattened sheet of paper over to Leandra, who inspected his effort before placing the paper down on the scanner and closing the lid.

"Ready," she said.

Joe pressed the button.

They took four scans, each at maximum resolution. The scans were run through a program that melded all four together and then performed a digital search for the microdots.

Kurt sat with the others watching the computer screen for the results. For several seconds, there was nothing. Then a pattern appeared.

"Looks like a random distribution," Leandra said.

"Or the beginnings of a Jackson Pollock painting," Joe said.

To Kurt, it looked more like an arrangement of stars—a few here, a few there. With a bit of imagination, he could have connected the dots and made his own constellations. To the computer, it was like a punch card from the 1950s. And it contained information that could be used to access the database of printer manufacturers.

With an electronic chirp, the answer appeared on the screen.

Joe leaned close and read it aloud. "Laser Jet Pro," he said. "Euroline PLC Model 9117, serial number 783-692 D-19."

"We're seeing that, too," Yaeger announced over the phone. "Stand by while we try to get a fix on where the Euroline printer with that serial number might be located."

"This all seems a little far-fetched to me," Leandra said.

Kurt thought so, too, until he considered that most modern printers were connected to the internet and that everything on the internet used IP addresses and "handshakes" and other technical ways of identifying itself to every other bit of electronic machinery on the network. For whatever it was worth, Hiram seemed to think it would be a slam dunk.

It didn't take long for him to be proven correct. "Here's your answer," he told them. "This page was printed at the Berlin Document Center in Germany."

"Please tell us that's not a FedEx or Kinko's or random internet café," Kurt said.

"Not at all," Hiram said. "In fact, it's exactly what we've been looking for."

30

Paul and Gamay arrived in Berlin, finding it warmer and wetter than Finland but just as gloomy. The overcast sky was heavy and low. A spitting rain drifted in the air like mist.

"I'm sure we'll see the sun again," Paul mused. "One of these days."

"Not any time soon," Gamay said. "By the description Rudi gave, we'll be going underground soon."

Traveling by car, they crossed Berlin, passing the Brandenburg Gate and then the famous Reichstag, which housed the German parliament before World War II, only to be abandoned and left to rot until the reunification of East and West Germany.

The Reichstag was an impressive structure, old in style and designed with unrepentant grandeur but updated with modern touches, including a glass-domed roof that was lit boldly at night.

Berlin was filled with many such buildings, along with plenty of modern architectural wonders offering eye-pleasing lines. The Berlin Document Center was not one of them.

As they pulled onto the property, Paul summed it up succinctly. "This is a depressing-looking place."

"It was once the secret headquarters of Hermann Göring and the SS," Gamay replied. "Surely you weren't expecting rainbows and unicorns."

The name itself was part of the problem. Calling it the Berlin Document Center conjured up images of a modern government building, something big and square, with glass walls and open plazas. But the BDC was made up of smaller buildings constructed in the 1940s. The structures aboveground had once accommodated loyal SS members, while the bunkers down below served as a domestic spying operation in which hundreds of trained eavesdroppers tapped phone lines throughout the city. Nearby lay barracks that had once housed squads of vicious commandos and brutal interrogators waiting for their next victim.

In stark contrast to the drab site, Paul and Gamay were greeted by a stylish woman named Andrea Bauer. She was attractive but stern, wearing rimless glasses and a navy blue pantsuit. Ms. Bauer was the lead historian at the center.

"*Guten Morgen,*" Gamay said. "*Vielen Dank, dass Sie uns so kurzfristig getroffen haben.*" She'd been learning

German for several months and was attempting to say *Good morning. Thank you for meeting us on such short notice.*

"You're most welcome," Ms. Bauer replied. Her accented English was better than Gamay's attempt at German. "Your office in Washington alerted me to your needs. We have everything prepared. Please come this way."

They followed her past the small buildings and through a heavy iron gate to a larger concrete structure. On the far side, they took a stairway down to one of the bunkers.

After passing through a bombproof door installed in 1943, they emerged into a large open room. What had once been the heart of the wiretapping operation now was a research center. Staff members stood at tables around the room, busily working on various documents.

Ms. Bauer explained. "Millions of files from the Nazi Party were recovered after the war. And millions more have been rounded up over the past fifty years. They have been meticulously stored and catalogued here. A microfilm record was made in 1994, but microfilm has been proven to be inadequate to capture all the details of the files, like colors or faded notations. Nor does the film last forever. As a result, we are in the process of making a new and more detailed record with high-definition cameras."

Gamay had a feeling she'd given that speech before.

Speech completed, Ms. Bauer led them through the main room and into a smaller, secondary annex. Modern lighting, sleek office furniture and new computers resting on clean desks helped brighten appearances, but the heavy architecture remained. The walls were unadorned concrete, solid steel doors with exposed hinges hung at the far end of the room. A row of cast iron safes lined the wall.

"What are those for?" Gamay asked.

"We don't use them anymore," Ms. Bauer said. "They once held the personnel files of high-ranking Nazi leaders. In truth, they're too heavy to move. But we also have no desire to forget what this place was truly used for."

Paul and Gamay took a moment to appreciate where they were. Paul imagined the treachery that had been plotted in these rooms, the terror once devised there. Gamay felt the darkness of the place. Yet also a sense of triumph, that the Allies vanquished the Nazis and rebuilt a society in which the truth had not been wiped away and hidden.

Ms. Bauer seemed to read her mind. "When the Allies swarmed in, the Nazis were already in the act of destroying what they could, but they'd waited too long and had wildly underestimated the task. The German war machine had kept such vast and meticulous records that the truth could not be burned or destroyed even with several days' notice to get the job done. That attention to detail convicted many of the gestapo and SS murderers during the postwar trials."

"We're looking for something earlier than that," Paul mentioned. "And far less violent or controversial."

"Yes," Ms. Bauer replied. "The files Ms. Emmerson viewed. They have been pulled and collated for you there."

Gamay turned to see two small stacks of paper, each about a foot high. Many folders and documents were covered in protective plastic, others were not.

"We may need help with the translations," Gamay said. "I've learned some German, but not enough to read through pages of text at any sort of speed."

"You won't need any help at all," Ms. Bauer promised. "At least, not human help. The terminals are equipped with instant scan translators. You place the paper under the scanner and a virtual document is created. Using the keyboard, you can get an instantaneous translation into any language you wish. All we ask is that you use the gloves while handling the files."

She pointed to a box of white gloves that would keep the oil on their fingers from damaging the documents.

Paul slid on a pair of gloves and plucked the first sheet of paper from the stack. It was a Hamburg weather report, circa 1938. Placing it under the scanner and looking at the screen, he saw a perfectly reproduced image. Tapping on the keyboard, he found a menu. He clicked on the tab marked with the English flag.

Paul expected a text box to pop up, indicating what had been written and where, but instead the image blurred and then refocused. Overall, it looked identical to the original image. Every crease, smudge and stray ink mark remained where it had been before, only the words had changed from German to English. But even this was not accomplished in a clumsy, computer graphics style. It looked as if the ink on the page had magically rearranged its molecules into a new language. Even the handwriting looked the same.

Paul looked from the screen to the paper and then back to the screen. "Remarkable."

Ms. Bauer beamed with pride. "It uses an artificial intelligence system and is accurate ninety-nine-point-seven percent of the time. It has even learned and translated many of the unique forms of shorthand and symbols some SS officers used. I believe you'll find it quite helpful."

Paul was impressed. "If we had this back at NUMA, it might be able to read Kurt's chicken scratch."

Gamay laughed. "What if it finds something it can't translate?"

"In that case, the system will flag it," Ms. Bauer told them. "We have human interpreters on staff who can help you. Or you can simply ask the system to guess."

"Impressive," Gamay said, pulling on a pair of gloves and settling in at a second terminal across from Paul.

Ms. Bauer waved a short good-bye. "I'll leave you two alone. Contact me on the white phone if you need anything."

The pile of folders waited. "I suggest we read through everything and then make a list of documents that might be helpful," Paul said.

"Look at you," Gamay said. "Choosing logic over going at this willy-nilly."

"When have I ever done anything willy-nilly?"

Gamay laughed but said nothing. She was already

pulling out her first document and sliding it under the scanner.

At first, she found herself mesmerized by the virtual translation. After a short while, she grew so used to the technology that it seemed totally natural.

Despite the advanced system, progress was slow. After an hour of work, they'd gone through only a quarter of the stacked folders, most of which related to ship movements and aircraft assignments.

The second hour brought them records from various vessels. This included more weather reports and bills of lading. The first sign they were getting anywhere came with the appearance of a familiar name.

"I've found some records related to the *Schwabenland* expedition," Gamay announced.

"That must be where Cora started," Paul said. "But I may have found something even more interesting. Look at this. It's a photo of a second freighter that was originally supposed to join the expedition. There's a communiqué here indicating it was left behind in Hamburg after a damaged boiler had to be replaced. It finally sailed"—he was looking for a date—"two weeks later."

Gamay looked over the photo of the ship. It was an old freighter, similar to the *Schwabenland*, right down to the catapult and a pair of Dornier flying boats secured on deck.

"Hiram's analysis of the photo ruled out any members of the *Schwabenland* air crew as being part of the photograph," Gamay said. "But what if the people in Cora's photo were on the other ship?"

"My thought as well," Paul said.

"What's the name of the ship?"

"The *Bremerhaven*."

Gamay began looking through the documents in her pile for anything related to the *Bremerhaven*. She found nothing from the *Schwabenland*'s captain or crew referencing the ship. "See if you can find the ship's log?"

Paul searched but found only a harbor document indicating its departure date and a return date of May 7. "That's roughly five months, the same length of time the *Schwabenland* spent at sea."

Gamay nodded. "It could have easily made it to the South Atlantic and back by then. But why haven't we ever heard of it?"

Paul continued plucking through the pile. "Maybe this is why. According to this directive, the ship was operating under special orders from Admiral Doenitz, head of the Kriegsmarine. While the official trip was being undertaken to claim a section of Antarctica for Germany, the *Bremerhaven* was used to look for suitable places where the German Navy might operate a remote fueling facility. They stopped at Bouvet Island and then continued on down to Antarctica to perform their official duties."

"A secret attachment to an already secret mission," Gamay noted. "How clandestine of them."

"Apparently, that wasn't enough," Paul said. "There's another directive here classifying the entire mission as 'Highest State Secret' under the orders of the Schutzstaffel in 1942."

Gamay tilted her head slightly. "Two questions. First, why would anyone feel the need to reclassify a mission that happened three years before? And, second, why would the SS be the one classifying it? I thought it was a naval mission, under Doenitz."

Paul looked back through what he'd found earlier. "It was."

"See if you can find anything about the aircraft that were carried on that ship," Gamay said. "Logbooks or flight paths."

Paul divided the stack of documents related to the *Bremerhaven* and each of them looked through half in search of answers.

Gamay made the first strike this time when she came across the very image Cora had copied. "Here's the photo."

Paul looked over as Gamay held up the black-and-white image of the men out on the ice with the Nazi flag. "Are there any notes attached?"

"It's connected to a personnel record of this man," Gamay said.

The file was annotated with the service photo of a middle-aged pilot. Gamay compared the photo in the file with the photo of the men out on the ice. Aside from a growth of stubble on his face and a few pounds added to his body, the images were identical. "This is the pilot," she said. "This is our man."

Paul looked over, studying the picture. "That's him, all right. What's his name?"

"Jurgenson," Gamay said. "Captain Gunther Jurgenson, aircraft commander of Dornier Do J Wal flying boat D-AGRB, nicknamed Thrace. According to his personnel file, he was originally a Lufthansa pilot, trained in operating amphibious aircraft on the South American run."

Gamay continued reading from the translated page. "His induction date into the Nazi Party is only a month before the ship sailed from Hamburg. Some handwritten notes reveal he wasn't quite a shoo-in for the position."

"Really?"

Gamay nodded and read the text. *"The subject's loyalty has not been adequately verified. Trade union affiliations have been discovered. However, they are not currently active. Expedition approval conditional."*

"Conditional upon what?"

"Probably had to renounce his past," Gamay said. "Unions were considered fronts for the Communist Party in 1930s Germany."

Gamay looked back into Captain Jurgenson's personnel file, reading aloud when she found anything of interest. "Assigned to the *Bremerhaven*, November fifth, 1938. Suspended from duty due to a crash, January twenty-eighth, 1939. Cleared of responsibility and returned to duty, May twenty-first that same year."

"January twenty-eighth would have been during the time they were in Antarctic waters," Paul pointed out. "Which makes sense, because I have this from the *Bremerhaven*."

He held up a plastic-encased document. "It's the catapult log from the *Bremerhaven*. The officer of the deck kept it and recorded each flight launch and who commanded it. According to the list, Jurgenson launched in his Dornier each of the first two days. The second aircraft was launched on day three, and both aircraft sortied on day four, with Jurgenson launching first and the backup aircraft launching several hours later. Five additional flights took place on the following days, but all of them were undertaken by the second aircraft. Jurgenson never flew again. Nor did the aircraft he'd been given command of."

Gamay looked through the personnel file for anything relating to the crash. Eventually, she found an "action verdict" that reappointed him to flight status. The report had been signed by a Luftwaffe Colonel in Hamburg. It read:

> Captain Jurgenson could not have been expected to know the peril of the rapid icing agent present in the lake upon which he landed. His exemplary flight skills not only saved himself but his entire crew. Reinstatement to active flight status is effective immediately.

"He did crash," Gamay said.

Paul had discovered a map, drawn by the *Bremerhaven*'s commanding officer. Long, thin sections were marked in red and numbered. They looked like flight plans to Paul, out and back from the *Bremerhaven*'s position.

"*Eins, zwei, drei, vier, fünf,*" Paul said, doing his best

to pronounce the German numbers. "If Jurgenson's plane crashed on flight number four, this would have been his planned flight path."

The long outbound flight covered five hundred miles of territory. A thirty-mile crosswind turn took them east, before another long leg brought them back to ship's position. "That's still fifteen thousand square miles," Paul said.

"Better than half a million," Gamay replied. "Which is what the *Schwabenland* expedition covered."

"It's not a bull's-eye," Paul said. "But it's a start. All thanks to our friend Jurgenson. Whatever happened to him anyway?"

Gamay returned to his personnel file, summarizing aloud as she went. "He was discharged prior to the start of the war. He was then reactivated for duty in December of 1942."

"Total war," Paul said. "On two fronts at the same time. At some point, the Nazis began running low on pilots, soldiers and everything else."

"Except he wasn't assigned to fly," Gamay said. "When I look at his personnel record, he was assigned directly to the SS itself."

Paul's eyebrows knitted together. "You're kidding me?"

She read the orders. "Captain Jurgenson reinstated to military service and promoted to rank of Major, concurrent with responsibilities required by Alpine Unit, Schutzstaffel."

"Drafted and promoted," Paul said. "Interesting."

Gamay continued. "His initial post was to the Norsk Hydro plant in Norway."

"Norsk Hydro was the Nazi heavy water manufacturing facility," Paul said. "The British blew it up, concerned that the Nazis were on track to building an atomic bomb."

"He was there only a few weeks," Gamay said. "His later assignment took him farther up the peninsula, to the top of Norway, above the Arctic Circle. That was his last posting. He was killed during an attack by Norwegian resistance members two months after arriving."

Paul frowned. "A sad end for a man who clearly never wanted to be a Nazi. What was he working on?"

Gamay paused. There was a code name connected to his assignment, but the computer program hadn't come up with a direct English translation. She clicked on the menu and then tapped the option that asked the computer to guess.

A little hourglass appeared on the screen. It flipped over several times before vanishing just as the answer appeared.

"He was assigned to a project known as . . . Fast Ice."

31

Rudi Gunn found himself in NUMA's latest tele-conference room. Arranged in a triangular shape, it had a table at the back wall and a pair of jumbo-sized screens along the other two sides.

Sitting at the conference table, Rudi could converse with NUMA personnel all around the world and it would feel as if they were sitting in the same room.

After initially dismissing the idea as a waste of money, Rudi had come to embrace the setup. Seeing his teams live and up close gave him a chance to make eye contact, a chance to study their body language and read the expressions on their faces.

At the current moment, Kurt and Joe graced one screen while the Trouts appeared in high definition on the other.

Paul and Gamay were easy to read. A sense of quiet triumph came from their screen. On the other side, Joe was like the kid who couldn't wait to get out of class, fidgeting in his seat, and building a structure with Post-its and paper clips just to pass the time.

Kurt was the outlier and a study in quiet intensity. He was calm and relaxed, but the set of his jaw told Rudi he was coiled like a steel spring, ready to get back into the fight, a fight that was a long way from over.

Gamay proudly summed up what she and Paul had learned in Berlin, finishing on a down note. "Unfortunately, there's no information on the nature of the Fast Ice project."

"That's not quite true," Rudi said.

On-screen, Kurt leaned forward as if he hadn't heard right. "I thought you said Hiram's computers had come up empty?"

"They did," Rudi insisted. "But someone else has succeeded where all our technology failed."

Rudi turned in his chair and pointed to the man sitting beside him.

St. Julien Perlmutter was immense in size and nattily dressed. Weighing in at almost four hundred pounds, Perlmutter was an unapologetic fan of fine dining and a connoisseur of the best wines, bourbons and cognacs. More importantly, he was a superb historian and a collector of all things nautical, with a near-photographic memory.

Perlmutter had an extensive library in his home. Or, more accurately, had turned his sprawling home into a storehouse of old books. Thousands of rare volumes filled the structure, stored here and there in every possible nook and cranny. They competed for space with old charts, hand-drawn maps, nautical diaries and stack upon stack of ships' logs. The vast majority remained where he placed them, arranged in an order only he could ever recall or understand.

Many of his volumes were one-offs or the last-known versions of their kind. If a fire ever took down St. Julien's house, the world would lose a treasure trove it never knew it had.

"St. Julien," Kurt announced. "Good to see you. Forget what they say about the cameras, this one hasn't added a single pound to your svelte frame."

St. Julien grinned. "Nor has it darkened your overgrown and graying hair. Shouldn't you be applying for Social Security by now?"

"I'd take it if they offered," Kurt said.

St. Julien loved to joke and he appreciated getting it back in return, especially from his closest friends, of whom Kurt was one.

Rudi intervened to prevent the two of them from trying to one-up each other. "If you would, St. Julien."

"Without delay," Perlmutter said. He began to speak, enunciating his words in the jovial voice of a man who enjoyed the spotlight. "Hiram's computers couldn't find any record of the Fast Ice project for the same reason you've never heard of it, my boy. Because almost no one knows of its existence."

"Aside from you," Kurt said.

"And very few others," Perlmutter said. "We can assume the Nazis destroyed all record of it. Or perhaps there were few made in the first place. I only know of it by chance as I have in my collection the unpublished diary of a Nazi U-boat captain who was assigned to the venture. I won't be specific about his written description—it would be impolite, considering the choice words he used—but I will say this. The Germans can swear with the best of them."

On the wall-sized screens, Paul and Gamay laughed.

Joe broke into a broad smile. "A skipper who didn't like the orders from the high command. Who ever heard of such a thing?"

"Even the Nazis thought their superiors were *Dummkopfs*," Perlmutter announced.

"What was this U-boat captain so all fired up about?" Kurt asked.

"The impossible task," Perlmutter said. "Fast Ice was a long-shot Nazi project. Much like the atomic bomb, or the cannon designed to shell London from the shores of France. Only, in scale it was much more audacious."

"More audacious than the atomic bomb?" Kurt asked.

"In terms of feasibility, yes," Perlmutter said.

Rudi interrupted. "We all love a good story, St. Julien, but this time we should probably cut to the chase. Tell them what you found."

"Of course," Perlmutter said. "Fast Ice was a desperate attempt to save the Third Reich from fighting a two-front war. It was initiated by the high command, probably by Admiral Doenitz or even by Hitler himself. The timeline is a little unclear, but it was given the green light sometime in 1942."

"After the invasion of Russia bogged down," Paul noted.

"Precisely," St. Julien replied. "As you know, Hitler launched his invasion of Russia in the summer of 1941. His armies had reached the gates of Moscow by that winter, at which point a stalemate set in. The Nazis weren't winning and the Russians were bleeding them dry.

"Hoping to keep the Soviets in the war, the Allies began sending convoys filled with supplies to Russia. But the only feasible route was through the Arctic Sea, traveling up over the top of Norway and east to the Russian ports. The convoys made for Archangel in the summer and were forced to take the more dangerous route to Murmansk in the winter."

"Why Murmansk?" Joe asked.

"It was the only Russian port not frozen solid during the winter months," Perlmutter explained.

"Ah," Joe said. "Makes sense."

"The Nazis had some early success in attacking these convoys," Perlmutter continued. "Particularly the disaster of convoy PQ-17. That convoy was lightly defended and, fearing a mass attack, the ships scattered. U-boats and German aircraft sank twenty-four of the thirty-five vessels. That only prodded the Allies into providing stronger escorts for the convoys, deploying the type of naval power the Nazis could not hope to match."

Perlmutter cleared his throat and continued. "Knowing that adequate supplies would allow Russia to continue fighting and killing Germans, Hitler and Doenitz grew desperate. They came up with a different plan. If they couldn't stop the Allies' ships from sailing, perhaps he could stop them from entering the ports and unloading their cargo."

This was Rudi's cue. After a nod from St. Julien, he tapped the keyboard in front of him, bringing up a map of the Arctic Sea and the Russian coastline. "As St. Julien mentioned, Archangel and Murmansk were the only Russian ports the Allies could reach. With Archangel ice-locked in the winter months, Hitler knew that shutting down Murmansk would starve the Russians of food, fuel and ammunition, forcing them to sue for peace. The Fast Ice project was born from this thinking."

Perlmutter took back the conversation. "The idea, as bold as it was, depended on the use of freighters, ocean-going tugs and submarines equipped with battering rams to push, pull and otherwise maneuver icebergs into choke points in the narrow channel leading to the harbor. If this could be accomplished, Hitler reasoned, the icebergs would create an impenetrable barrier through which the convoys could not pass."

"Couldn't the Russians just use icebreakers to clear the way?" Paul asked.

"Icebreakers ride up on relatively thin sections of sea ice," Perlmutter explained. "Breaking the ice by crushing it down with their great weight. Such ships are useless against a million-ton iceberg."

"As are submarines and tugboats," Kurt pointed out.

Perlmutter laughed. "Quite right," he said. "It was a ridiculous notion. Though, I must point out, moving the ice would not have been impossible. The Germans had already identified favorable ocean currents and winds they could use to their advantage. Indeed, part of the plan entailed men going aboard and rigging giant sails across the tops of the bergs to take advantage of these winds. By the Germans' estimate, a speed of three knots could be attained and kept up throughout most of the process."

"Faster than Washington traffic at rush hour," Joe noted. "What the heck was supposed to happen when these icebergs reached port?"

"They were never actually supposed to reach the port," Perlmutter said. "The facilities at Murmansk are twenty miles upriver from the sea. The icebergs needed only to reach the channels leading in from the ocean. Once lodged there, they would become immovable."

Rudi clarified. "The idea was to run the icebergs up the channel, timing the entry with the incoming tide. They would hope to run aground precisely at the high-water mark. When the tide went out, their great weight would drive the underside of the iceberg down into the sediment. At that point, there would be no force on Earth that could move them."

"Yes," Perlmutter said. "In addition, the Nazis hoped that the outer sections of the icebergs would collapse once their massive weight was no longer supported by the seawater. The idea being that once the tide went out, and buoyancy was lost, large sections of the iceberg would fracture along existing lines of stress. In one or two cycles, these fractures would give way. The unsupported parts of the iceberg breaking off and crashing into the area around them. The rest of the channel would be sealed, preventing inbound ships from skirting the edges of the obstruction. As an added bonus, they expected this to cause massive flooding due to both the calving effect of the iceberg and the backing up and diversion of river water caused by the frozen plug in the heart of the river."

"Before you tell yourself this couldn't happen," Rudi said, "recall that Alaska, North Dakota and Minnesota have all experienced massive flooding caused by ice-jammed rivers. This would be far worse."

"Flooding from a collapsing iceberg would be no picnic either," Joe said. "I've seen a few glaciers calve up close. The waves are second only to those of a tsunami."

Rudi noticed Kurt nodding almost imperceptibly.

"I can see why this idea would be attractive to the Nazis," Kurt said. "But towing an iceberg is a monumental task. Even with a dozen submarines and as many tugs to do the job."

"Quite right," Perlmutter said. "It would also be incredibly dangerous. Even if the ships avoided structural damage from the ice, they would be vulnerable to attacks from the Russian aircraft and vessels when they neared their objective."

"Did this ever get beyond the planning stage?"

Perlmutter shook his head. "A few minor tests were carried out. Some by our U-boat captain with a flair for profanity, others by the tugboat fleet. It was decided that more power would be needed. When they drew up a plan to modify the battleship *Tirpitz* for the job, Hitler vetoed that idea because the *Bismarck* had recently been sunk and he didn't want to lose any more capital ships.

That put it back to the submarines and it pretty much just sat there."

"Why call the plan Fast Ice?" Gamay asked. "Sounds like the process is pretty slow to me."

Rudi answered this one. "Fast ice is the version that is secured—and made fast to—the shoreline. Its properties are similar in nature to free-floating sea ice, except that it grows thicker and sticks around longer because the land it's attached to is colder than the seawater. That's why you can walk on the ice near shore in the early winter even when the middle of a lake is still liquid."

St. Julien jumped back in to finish things up. "Part of the German plan, vague as it was, intended that the presence of the icebergs would chill the stagnant water that remained behind in the harbor. This chilling effect would cause everything to freeze solid well into the spring."

"What would happen when the ice melted?" Joe asked.

"It would have taken years for an iceberg of any size to melt down completely," Perlmutter said. "By then, the war would be over. One way or another."

"It's bold," Kurt said, "I'll give them that. But how does the former Lufthansa pilot fit into all this? He wasn't a submarine commander or part of the German Navy. He was barely even a Nazi, by the sound of things."

"We're not sure," Perlmutter said. "There's no reference to him in the diary. But there is a cryptic note in the commander's final entry before the U-boats were released from the project. It reads, '*Will this ludicrous dream never end? Now we're told of a new plan—to freeze Murmansk solid by use of a "magic liquid" from under the glacier. Save us from these fools and let us go fight properly, as men of the Kriegsmarine are supposed to.'"*

"Magic liquid?" Joe said.

"That's the translation," Perlmutter replied. "There is nothing more about it."

Paul offered a knowing look. "Sounds a lot like Yvonne Lloyd's theory suggesting there's living material under the glaciers that would cause the Earth to freeze over."

"And Jurgenson's explanation of his crash," Gamay added. "The report said it was caused by rapid icing on the aircraft due to an agent in the lake water."

Rudi saw the connection as well. It lined up perfectly. "It's possible he crashed because the aircraft and the lake had become covered with this magic liquid that made the water freeze more quickly."

Gamay nodded. "That would explain why the SS snatched him out of retirement, promoted him to major and sent him north to study the glaciers. They wanted him to look for lakes like the one he'd landed on in hopes of finding a similar catalyst that would allow them to freeze the Russian ports the way it froze his plane."

Rudi nodded. He and Perlmutter had come to that same conclusion before the conference began. He was encouraged that his team was reaching the same answer. He summed up the idea. "The way I see it," he said, "Cora and Yvonne must have discovered the German records from the *Bremerhaven* expedition while they were searching for proof of this Snowball Earth Theory. Recognizing that the rapid icing of Jurgenson's plane was a clue pointing directly at what they were looking for, they ran off to Antarctica, following in Jurgenson's footsteps and drilling their own ice cores.

"After finding something promising, Cora sent her message, telling us she'd made a discovery that would change the world. They made their way back to the *Grishka* and that's when Ryland attacked them. Taking the ship, the computers and the ice cores to stop them from sharing what they'd discovered."

"Adversaries to the end," Gamay suggested of Ryland and Yvonne. "One trying to melt the Antarctic, the other trying to keep it frozen."

Rudi nodded, looking at his team in all their high-definition glory. Paul and Gamay were convinced and content. Joe wore his regular grin, enhanced by having answers to some of the questions they'd been asking. Only Kurt's appearance struck Rudi as suspicious.

Kurt's eyes had a thousand-mile stare. As if he were looking right through Rudi, on through the wall and all the way off to infinity. Rudi had seen that look before. It meant Kurt was considering the question from a different angle than everyone else. Flipping it around in his head, looking at it sideways, backward and forward, upside down. Laser-focused on some detail the rest of them had missed.

Rudi saw the color return to Kurt's face, watched his clenched jawline relax. And even saw him nod slightly. Kurt had found what he was looking for.

"You're absolutely right," Kurt said, firmly back in the here and now. "And completely wrong."

32

I assure you, Kurt," Perlmutter said, "we've gone through the data from top to bottom and back again. Odd as it might be, this is the only conclusion that makes any logical sense."

Kurt stood up, accepting the challenge. "I have no doubts about your research, St. Julien. In fact, I'd just as soon question the firmness of the Earth as I would question your knowledge of obscure nautical history. I also accept the fact that Jurgenson found something on the ice when he crash-landed down there. And the idea of a Nazi plan to seal the Russians in their icehouse of a country by freezing the ports solid seems par for the course when talking about that particular regime."

"If you agree with me," St. Julien said, "how can I also be wrong?"

"Not you," Kurt said. "Rudi."

"Well," Perlmutter said, grinning. "In that case, go on."

Perlmutter might have been happy, but Rudi was less so. He folded his arms across his chest. "What, exactly, have I gotten wrong?"

"Not much," Kurt said. "You have most of it correct. Cora's movements, her connection with Yvonne, the two of them becoming friends and fellow idealists and traveling to Helsinki and Berlin and then to Antarctica together. And your conclusion that Cora found what she was looking for on the glacier is the epitome of hitting the nail on the head. It's the final piece of the puzzle that you've placed wrong."

It sounded to Rudi as if Kurt was playing games. "I thought Cora's discovery was the final piece of the puzzle."

"No," Kurt said. "The final piece is what happened afterward. That is, Ryland attacking the *Grishka*, taking the ice cores and kidnapping his sister."

"I hate to remind you," Rudi said. "But that's the only thing we're sure of."

"We may be sure of it, but that doesn't mean we're right," Kurt replied. "Look at it this way. If Ryland wanted to prevent Yvonne and Cora from thwarting his plan to melt the ice, then he should have blown the *Grishka* to scrap metal or sent her to the bottom."

"He did send her to the bottom," Rudi noted.

"Only after he took everything off the ship," Kurt pointed out. "Including his sister, whom he supposedly has a blood feud with."

Rudi uncrossed his arms. He sensed his Special Projects Director was onto something. "Keep going."

"Ryland tells the world he wants the ice to melt. That he wants to open the seas to navigation and unfreeze the permafrost for farming and mining. His official and oft repeated line is that it's going to happen anyway, so we might as well get on with it. That's the very scheme he's been selling to his partners. The entire thrust of the climate progression movement. But he doesn't need Yvonne and Cora for that. He doesn't need their data, or the ice cores, or the 'magic liquid' hidden in the glacial lake. In fact, the continued existence of those things threatens his entire plan. It's literally the one thing that might overturn his dream. And yet instead of destroying the data and the ice cores, he took possession of all those things, keeping them safe, even though they might destroy him. Does anyone really buy that?"

Rudi glanced at St. Julien, who raised his brows.

"You make a good point," Rudi said. "But we know he did take the materials. And you're the one who convinced us he took Yvonne. I assume you're about to tell us why."

"Because he's not who he claims to be," Kurt said.

Rudi leaned back. "Surely you're not suggesting an impersonator."

"I am," Kurt said boldly. "Ryland is impersonating himself. He's playing the part of Ryland the industrialist. The man who doesn't give a damn about the planet and puts profit before anything. I'm telling you, it's an act. It's a put-on."

"But he wanted to drill in the Antarctic," Rudi pointed out.

"Did he?" Kurt asked. "I know that's what he said, look at the way he said it. He claimed Antarctica was 'a worthless wasteland' and that an oil spill would be 'good for the environment.' All that did was raise the volume of the conversation up to eleven. It invited attacks not only on his company but on every other corporation that ever dreamed of industrializing Antarctica. Effectively ending any possibility of it ever happening."

"You think he doth protest too much," St. Julien said, vaguely quoting *Hamlet*.

"I do," Kurt replied. "No CEO talks like that. They promise to drill cleanly. They insist they'll use best environmental practices and blah blah-blah . . . Even if they don't mean it, they say it. And that's because they want the world to relax and let them go about their business. Yet Ryland doesn't play that game. He invites the firestorm, he stirs it up, stoking it, pouring fuel on it, making it impossible for anyone listening to forget what drilling and fracking and mining do to the planet."

"There are plenty of powerful people who think they can say whatever they want and the rest of us should just deal with it," Rudi said.

"True," Kurt said. "But ignore what he says and look at what he does. He claims to value profits above all else, yet according to Wall Street he never manages to make one. His mines don't produce much, his oil wells are old and declining. Instead of sinking more wells or turning to methods like fracking or high-pressure injections, he just lives with a dwindling income and borrows more money."

Kurt took a breath and then continued. "His personal actions are even more of a giveaway. His game lodge had a large aquarium on the main floor. I noticed a pair of endangered species tucked safely inside. His preserve is home to lions and tigers and elephants rescued from zoos and circuses. According to what Leandra told us, there are three hundred black rhino on his property. These are rare, nearly extinct creatures numbering only a few thousand left in the rest of the world."

"As I understand it, those animals are there to be hunted for sport."

"One or two, perhaps," Kurt admitted. "Not the younger animals or the breeding pairs. And even that's all just part of the show."

Perlmutter spoke up. "So, if he's not this base industrialist, who is he?"

"An ally of Yvonne's," Kurt said. "A partner instead of an enemy. He once told a reporter he and his sister were 'of one mind and purpose.' I'm suggesting they still are."

Rudi nodded. "That would explain why he took her off the ship after they shot everyone else."

"It would also explain how he knew about the ship in the first place," Kurt said. "It would explain how he knew what it was carrying and where to find it and how to intercept it. It would explain why a half dozen of the crew were shot dead in their bunks."

"Because Yvonne shot them while they were sleeping," Rudi said.

Kurt nodded.

St. Julien shook his head sadly. "Poor Cora."

"Poor Cora indeed," Rudi added. "She thought they were being followed and tracked, she thought they were in danger. She never guessed the mole was her partner in crime."

Kurt wondered if Cora had an inkling who it was that had betrayed her. The secret message she'd sent to Rudi suggested she was worried it might be someone close to her. "The bottom line is, once Yvonne knew that Cora was going to share what she'd found with NUMA, Ryland had no choice, he had to take action. He couldn't wait for the ship to reach Cape Town because there was always a chance that a NUMA vessel would meet them before they got home. Or that Cora would send more information."

"If they're all on the same side, why turn on Cora?" Gamay asked.

"Because in the end," Kurt said, "Cora was one of us and not one of them. And what they're planning to do is not something a reasonable person would come up with."

"Which is what?" Rudi asked.

Kurt could only guess at this point, but he had a fairly good idea. "They're going to use what Cora discovered to cause a new ice age, maybe even turn the world back into Snowball Earth."

33

Rudi considered Kurt's theory. "Bury the world in ice," he said. "What would be the point? Where's the profit in that?"

"There isn't one," Kurt said. "Not in dollars. But Ryland is an unreasonable man. He measures himself by how successfully he bends the world to his will. For a person like that, altering the course of humanity would be the ultimate victory. The ultimate act of vainglory."

Perlmutter raised another objection. "I must point out, my boy, that if Ryland is truly an environmentalist, he'd be aware of the damage an ice age would cause. It would wipe out as many species as any level of global warming. If not significantly more."

Gamay, a biologist, chimed in next. "An ice age would

be devastating. Anything close to a Snowball Earth would qualify as a mass extinction."

"Ryland has spent billions on large tracts of land in multiple countries along the equator," Kurt said. "This makes absolutely no sense if he's expecting a radically hotter world. If he's expecting an ice age, it makes all the sense in the world. These holdings are isolated and remote. In most cases, they're hundreds of miles from the nearest population center. And if we look close enough, we'll see that they are self-sufficient and easily defendable. These holdings are his ships made of gopher wood. His Noah's arks. He can fill them with whatever animals he chooses. He can breed different species, keep them in captivity or let them roam free. But as the rest of the world slowly freezes, his sanctuaries along the equator will be largely unaffected."

"That works for the islands as well," Joe pointed out. "He's bought at least two dozen islands. They're dotted throughout the tropical seas. If the ice age happens and the glaciers rebuild themselves, the seas will drop, we know that. Depending on the severity of the ice growth, sea level could fall a hundred feet. At that point, his low-lying islands would look more like a Tahitian paradise than atolls just barely poking up above the surface."

Kurt nodded. "And just like the landlocked preserves he's set up, these islands are all a long way from civilization."

"Safe zones," Gamay suggested.

Rudi shook his head. "He'd have to be deranged. And

we've encountered enough madmen to know this type of God complex exists. As a friend of mine used to say, when a lunatic is shooting at you, you don't stop and wonder what made the man go crazy. You get a rifle and fire back. So, assuming you're right, and that Ryland and his sister are hell-bent on causing a new ice age, how do you propose we stop him?"

"We beat him to the punch and cut him off at the pass."

"Which is?"

"The glacier. And the lake that Captain Jurgenson landed on," Kurt said. "For Ryland's plan to work, he needs to transport large quantities of the algae from the lake to the sea. The most efficient way to do that is by pumping them. Considering that Eileen Tunstall's company makes turbines for pipeline systems, I'd bet that Ryland's building a conduit, one that runs directly from glacial lake to ocean."

"That should be easy enough to spot," Rudi pointed out. "And to destroy."

"Not this one," Kurt said. "It won't be made of iron and steel. It'll be a tunnel through the ice, right through the heart of the glacier and out to the ocean. It might be hundreds of feet beneath the surface, which will make it impervious to whatever type of bomb you throw at it."

"That's one hell of a tunneling job," Rudi said.

"Actually, it's easier than building a pipeline on the surface," Kurt said. "All he'd need is an adequate supply of hot water. A geothermal strike would give him plenty."

Paul nodded. He was the geologist. "Hate to add to the bad news, but that area of Antarctica is riddled with volcanic activity."

Rudi rubbed his temples. "Which means we're back to square one. Figuring out where Cora went and where Jorgensen landed ninety years earlier."

"Gamay and I have narrowed it down for you," Paul insisted.

"Twelve thousand square miles is not exactly a bull's eye," Rudi replied.

"Then you'd better start narrowing it down further," Kurt replied.

"And how do you propose we do that?"

Kurt shrugged. "I'm sure you can pull a rabbit out of your hat. In the meantime, Paul and Gamay can fly south for the winter and Joe can plan the expedition."

"South?" Paul said. "I hope you're suggesting Miami or the French Riviera."

"Farther south," Kurt said. "About as far as you can go."

"Figures," Paul sighed. "I guess it can't be any colder than the ice core facility."

"Oh, I'm sure it will be," Gamay added. "With the added bonus of wind and driving snow."

Kurt laughed. "I promise you one day of sun in Cape Town before we set off. But we need you down here."

"We'll be on the first flight," Gamay said.

Rudi raised his hand. "Just one question," he said. "While the Trouts are flying, and Joe is planning, and I'm searching for a hat and a rabbit of the correct size and shape, what will you be doing?"

"Talking to a man about a horse," Kurt said. "And by that I mean a boat."

"We are a nautical agency, after all," Rudi said. "I believe we have a few of those sitting around. Planes and helicopters, too."

"I know that," Kurt said. "So does Ryland. He's probably been tracking NUMA's movements since the moment Cora sent you that message. That's how his submarine managed to appear within hours of Joe and me setting foot on the *Grishka*. That's why he knew everything about us when we showed up at his party."

Rudi sat back and looked at Kurt. "You're looking for a horse of a different color, I assume."

Kurt nodded. "One that doesn't look quite so American."

34

Ryland and Yvonne sat in the passenger compartment of a Kamov Ka-62 helicopter as it crossed the sparkling waters off the coast of Angola. The Ka-62 was the civilian version of a military helicopter used extensively by the Russian Federation. It was fast, rugged and reliable. Ryland's company owned three such helicopters, using them to ferry men and equipment to his offshore oil platforms.

"Do you think we have enough seed material?" Yvonne asked.

Pressure-sealed fifty-five-gallon drums lined the compartment around them, twenty-six in all. Eight additional drums were carried in the cargo compartment behind a thin bulkhead.

Each of the drums contained a highly concentrated batch of the genetically modified ice-forming algae. Had anyone opened the drums, he'd have discovered a pungent green mush with the consistency of paste. Enough to cover no more than a few hundred acres of water once it had spread into a thin layer. As Yvonne mentioned, this was seed stock, not meant to do anything except get the process started.

"This should be plenty," Ryland said. "The tankers will have a long, slow journey north. By the time they reach the Arctic Sea, their storage tanks will be full of growth."

"Then why do you look so concerned?"

"Austin and NUMA concern me," he said.

"You should have shot them."

"In the middle of my party? In our home? And how would I explain that to their government?"

She shook her head. "Being mauled by lions was preferable?"

"Eminently," he said. "An explainable accident, caused by their wandering off. Which their government would expect them to do, given the situation."

"Austin and his friend are very"—she struggled to find the right word—"resilient. I heard stories about them from Cora. You would not believe where they've been or what they've done. They were on the *Grishka* when we sank it. They survived that also. I just hope their presence didn't spook our partners. We need those turbines and tankers."

"Don't be concerned about Liang and Tunstall," Ryland said. "You should have seen them react to word of American agents prowling around. Any doubts about our scheme flew right out the window, replaced by a gripping fear that the Americans might stop us from melting the permafrost." He laughed at the thought. "If anything, NUMA showing up was all the proof we needed. We couldn't pay for that sort of validation."

She cocked her head at him. "Then why are you worried?"

Ryland turned toward his sister. "Because Austin— in addition to being resilient, as you so aptly described him—is the epitome of an unreasonable man. I worry that he will not stop pursuing us."

Yvonne nodded. "It must be in their DNA," she said. "Cora was the same. At first, that was to our advantage because she led us to something no one else believed existed. Once we found it, she wouldn't listen to me or be persuaded to keep the discovery secret. Even after I sabotaged our radio and satellite gear, she still found a way to send a message to NUMA."

"You should have killed her while you were out on the ice," Ryland said.

"In front of our crew?" she replied, turning the same logic back on him that he had used earlier. "They were loyal to her. She'd found and hired most of them personally. If I hadn't shot them in their sleep, they'd have fought to the end and we might never have taken the materials from the *Grishka*." Yvonne shook her head in frustration. "Truth is, I would have shot Cora if she'd left that captain's side for one minute. But she was on the bridge from the moment we left the glacier until the *Goliath* found us."

"Understandable," he said.

"If only that damned ship had gone down," Yvonne said, "NUMA would never have discovered us and we'd have nothing to worry about. I still don't know how it remained afloat. We blew a hole in the side and sent it charging through a sea filled with icebergs and growlers."

Ryland waved a hand dismissively. "In a week or so, none of that will matter," he said. "What we do over the next seven days will tell the outcome. We can't have any more interference. Not now. Not this close to the finish line."

"How do you propose to stop it?"

"I'm sending High Point and the tactical squad with you to the pumping station," he said. "You and he are to defend the station at all costs. And if Austin and his friends show up, you make sure they die there in the cold and the snow."

A smile creased her face. "With pleasure."

Ryland turned to the window. A towering oil rig loomed in the distance. An even more massive vessel held station several hundred yards from the structure. The ship was a VLCC, which stood for "very large crude carrier." It displaced two hundred thousand tons—twice the weight of an American aircraft carrier. At over a thousand feet in length with a wide beam, the ship was a certified monster that could carry two million barrels of crude oil.

Her hull was painted navy blue, her flat deck a pale

green. A stylish blue on the side of her superstructure identified her as one of Liang's tankers. One look told Ryland the ship was empty as she rode high in the water, a large red swath on the lower half of the hull exposed for all to see.

He checked his watch. The ship should have been almost full and low in the water by now. In fact, had things gone according to schedule it should have cleared the artificial island and begun its journey north.

Ryland gave the pilot a new order. "Get me on the platform as soon as possible."

The pilot brought the helicopter down on the helipad with authority, planting its landing gear firmly on the deck. As the ground crew rushed to secure the craft, Ryland and Yvonne left the helicopter in search of the platform's Chief of Operations, a man named Ober.

They found him on the north side of the rig, standing near the rail with a radio in his hand. He was overseeing the tanker operation personally, barking orders and marking the progress on a clipboard.

"What's the holdup?" Ryland demanded. "That ship was supposed to be on its way by now."

Ober understood the stakes. He was one of Ryland's oldest hands. He'd been part of the inner circle from the beginning. "The wind made the initial docking cumbersome. Getting the tanker in position took a while. Hooking up the pipes was another issue. She's secured and loading now."

"Any problems with the crew?"

"Not really," Ober said. "And as far as they know,

we're pumping light sweet crude directly from the well. They probably think it's a black market deal," he added. "I'm sure it wouldn't be the first time. I'm not sure what happens if they inspect the tanks and find a mix of seawater and slurry. But I'm assuming they have orders not to."

"They won't question the cargo," Ryland insisted.

"Happy to hear it," Ober said. "What about Liang?"

"He knows what he's getting," Ryland said. "Up to a point, at least. It's been explained to him that the slurry is food for the algae. He just doesn't know what the algae is going to do when these tankers dump it in the sea."

Ober nodded and allowed a look of pride to come over his face. For eight years, he'd been part of Ryland's long-term plan. He'd worked on oil rigs and ramrodded efforts at various mines, earning a reputation as a ruthless taskmaster—all while waiting for the moment that Ryland had promised would come, when they would emerge from hiding and change the world. "So, this is it? It's finally time?"

Ryland nodded. "It's time. And the sooner we get these ships loaded and sent on their way, the better. The next tanker is due here in three hours. Can you get this one filled by then?"

Ober shook his head. "I'll need five hours at least," Ober said. "Unless you want me to send her out a little light."

"No," Ryland said. "Top her off. I'll contact Liang and have him delay the other vessel."

Ober nodded and got on the radio, giving a new order to the tug that was helping keep the huge tanker in position.

"Have the turbines arrived?" Yvonne asked.

"They were delivered this morning," Ober said. "We hoisted them aboard and kept them on the cable. The crane operator is standing by to load them whenever your transport arrives."

"It's already here," Yvonne said.

Ober looked at her oddly. "Where?"

She pointed to the water beneath the platform. Ober leaned over the rail for a better look. A long, tubular shape rested in the shadows of the oil platform. The vessel was grayish white in color, like an old koi swimming in a murky pond.

"Would you like me to assist?"

"No," Ryland said. "We'll take care of the turbines. You just get that tanker loaded and on its way. I want it off the platform and heading for the open sea as soon as possible."

35

Rudi stared at the list of equipment Joe Zavala was requesting. He didn't recognize half of what was written there. "Are you planning an expedition to Antarctica or a trip to the moon?"

No longer in the high-tech conference room, he was talking with Joe on an old-fashioned speakerphone. It felt positively antiquated.

"Antarctica is more treacherous than the moon," Joe insisted. "No storms on the moon. No snow or hidden crevasses waiting to swallow up men and equipment. No hundred-mile-an-hour winds or killer penguins."

"Except for the last part," Rudi said, "you have a point. About the only things I recognize on this list are the electrically powered snow machines. I assume that's a type of snowmobile?"

"One that doesn't make a lot of noise," Joe said. "Or give off much heat. Helpful if the bad guys are looking for us with infrared cameras."

Rudi could see where this was going. "Understandable. But what on earth is a 'haptic feedback suit with remote linkup'?"

"It's a suit with a virtual reality system built into it," Joe said. "Allows the person wearing it to control vehicles, drones and automated scouting systems."

"Automated scouting systems?"

"Robots," Joe said.

"Are we sending you any robots?"

"We have a few on the list. Don't worry, you won't need to pay for seats in first class. They're relatively compact and stored in small boxes. We'll put them together on-site if we need them."

"At least you've got standard cold-weather gear and high-calorie food supplements on the list. There's also something called a snow racer? Tell me that's not a car with studded tires."

"It's a lightweight craft that flies over the snow with only a couple skis touching the ground. Like the drones, it's portable and can be put together on location. And because it's sail-powered, it's fast and silent and creates no heat signature."

"Sounds like Kurt's ice yacht," Rudi said.

"Very similar."

"Let's hope Kurt's better at driving this contraption than he was piloting that."

"He could hardly be worse," Joe said with a laugh.

Rudi checked a box next to the snow racer, to confirm his approval, and then quickly checked the rest of the boxes. "I've approved everything," Rudi said. "It'll be airlifted to you overnight. But then what? Has Kurt found a suitable boat yet?"

Joe hesitated, which Rudi took to mean he was choosing his words carefully.

"As I understand it, he's kicked the tires on a few things and is close to making a decision."

"Why does that sentence fill me with dread?"

"Because you know Kurt too well," Joe replied. "How close are we to figuring out a location? This equipment isn't going to do us much good if we still have to wander around half the continent hoping to bump into Ryland and his sister."

Rudi glanced at the clock on the wall. He'd been waiting to place a phone call until he could be sure it would be answered in person. "I'll let you know when I have something. Hopefully, pretty soon."

As Joe signed off, Rudi sat quietly. He waited for the numbers on his digital clock to read 5:01. As soon as the last digit changed, he picked up the phone and dialed the private line of an old friend at the Pentagon.

The line rang three times before a gruff voice answered. "This is Whitaker."

Rudi leaned back in his chair. "Good evening, Nate. This is Rudi Gunn."

Silence for a second, then, "That's Rear Admiral Nate to you, Gunn. I've got an anchor and a star on my shoulder these days."

Rudi laughed. "Sorry about that, Admiral. I guess I still remember you as a fourth-class plebe at Annapolis. A scrawny kid whom I had to rescue from trouble and mold into a successful midshipman."

Nathanial Whitaker and Rudi Gunn had been students at the Naval Academy together. Whitaker was in the class behind Rudi, who was charged with mentoring the younger man. Over the years, they formed a strong bond. When Rudi graduated first in his class, Whitaker arranged a party that went nonstop for two days. A year later, when Whitaker graduated second in his class, Rudi returned the favor. He threw his friend an equally epic soirée and began a lifelong habit of needling Whitaker about his lowly class ranking.

Whitaker spoke again. "I'd be a full admiral by now if you'd have done your job right. My nefarious association with you has done nothing but hold my career back all these years."

"Wouldn't surprise me," Rudi said with a laugh. "All the same, I need a favor."

"What kind of favor?"

"I understand you're in the reconnaissance business these days."

"Vicious rumor," Whitaker insisted. "I might know someone who is, however. This better be important."

"I wouldn't have called you if it wasn't," Rudi said. "I need a recon pass over a long, narrow strip of the Antarctic."

"Just use one of your satellites," Whitaker said. "At this point, you have more birds than we do."

"I need more detail than I can get from a satellite. And I need to see beneath the snow. I'm hoping you have something that can perform that task?"

Whitaker remained silent for a moment. "We might. But why Antarctica? What on earth are you looking for down there?"

Rudi sighed. "Admiral," he said. "You wouldn't believe me if I told you."

36

K urt stood on the deck of a South African patrol boat as it cruised in tight formation with a black-hulled container ship. He wore South African Navy fatigues, a flak jacket and a helmet. Seven men of the South African Navy stood beside him in similar gear.

The patrol boat had pulled in tight beside the larger vessel and was now riding on the very cusp of the ship's bow wave.

"You've got a good pilot at the wheel," Kurt said, addressing the boat's commanding officer, a South African by the name of Clarence Zama.

"He's showing off," Zama replied. "He knows who you are."

"You mean an old friend who shows up out of the blue and asks for an impossible favor?" Kurt said.

"Yes," Zama replied, laughing. "That's exactly what I mean."

Kurt and Zama had worked together on an anti-smuggling operation years ago. They'd tracked down and captured a group of poachers who were smuggling ivory and endangered species out of Cape Town.

Rather than give up, the poachers had set off explosives, attempting to scuttle their ship. Zama had been trapped belowdecks, Kurt managed to save him by ramming a hole in the side of the poacher's vessel and giving him a way to get out.

"I doubt we'll see any explosions today," Zama said. "But these illegal China trawlers don't give up so easily either."

"How often do you deal with them?"

"All the time," Zama said. "They sail in groups. Sometimes ten or more. The moment they see us coming, they scatter and run in all directions. Obviously, we can only go after one boat at a time. So even if we catch it, nine fully loaded trawlers get away. And usually the captain of the vessel we catch has dumped his catch before we get aboard. When that happens, our efforts are all for nothing. And if they make it to international waters, then we aren't even allowed to board them."

A trio of seagulls flew overhead, calling out loudly and riding the wind off the container ship's hull.

"You expect this time to be different," Kurt noted.

"I do," Zama said. "Because the trawler you picked is a larger vessel and working alone. And because this time they won't know we're coming."

"Hiding behind the container ship was a great idea," Kurt said.

With a broad smile, Zama thanked him for the compliment. "The illegal trawlers use radar and lookouts, but behind this wall of steel we can't be seen. Not with human eyes or electronic beams. While I've wanted to try this tactic for years, the big wigs in my government have refused to allow it. Now, thanks to you we've finally been granted permission."

"Glad I could help," he said.

"Don't be too happy," Zama said. "If something goes wrong it's going to be blamed on you."

"It usually is," Kurt said. "My only concern is the container ship. What's to stop someone on board from giving us away?"

"Two of my men," Zama said. "One on the bridge and one in the radio room. Add to that the fact this is an Indonesian vessel and we should be okay. The Chinese fish their waters mercilessly. There is no love lost between them. Also . . ." he added. "I may have mentioned a cash reward."

"How much of a reward?"

"How much do you have on you?"

Kurt laughed. "Get me on that ship and I'll see what I can come up with."

Zama checked his watch. They'd been traveling in formation with the container ship for two hours. "We're almost abeam the trawler. Once we get there, you'll feel the full power of our engines. I suggest you hold on."

Kurt locked one hand on the rail and placed his

other hand on the inner collar of the flak jacket as Zama checked his watch. The seconds counted down, with Zama raising his arm for the helmsman to see. When the clock hit zero, he brought his arm down with a flourish, like the starter at a drag race sending the cars off down the track.

The surge from the vessel's gas turbine engines hit almost instantly. A powerful vibration coursed through the hull and the patrol boat jumped forward.

It nosed over the edge of the bow wave, riding down it and picking up speed. By the time it shot out ahead of the container ship, the patrol boat was traveling at thirty knots.

Kurt, both hands now on the rail, looked to his right. Just over a mile away, he spied the Chinese trawler. A two-hundred-foot vessel with a pea green hull, fishing booms out on either side and a large net trailing from the stern.

The patrol boat cut to the right, the g-force of the turn forcing everyone on deck to brace against the acceleration. Now on an intercept course, the boat straightened, heading for the trawler and jump-crash-jump-crashing across the waves. Each jump offering a full second of zero gravity, each crash enough to buckle a man's legs if he wasn't ready for it.

Zama got on the radio, broadcasting to the Chinese ship, ordering them to cut engines to full stop and await boarding.

The repeated warnings went unheeded and it became clear that the Chinese had no intention of obeying. A flurry of activity began in earnest. Kurt saw them cutting away the nets and dropping the lines from the booms. Other men were running about the deck, while black smoke began to billow from the funnel and the trawler turned away.

"She's pouring on the coal," Kurt said, shouting above the wind.

"Making for international waters," Lieutenant Zama replied. "But she'll never get across the line before we reach her."

The enthusiasm in his voice was that of a man who'd been held back from doing his duty by bureaucrats for far too long. Now, finally given a chance, he was acting.

Kurt felt the enthusiasm of the group around him. And while he had his own reasons for wanting to capture the illegal fishing trawler, he couldn't help but feel a camaraderie with the men on the patrol boat. "Where do you plan to go aboard?"

"It depends if they come to their senses or not," Zama replied. "Should they heave to and cut their engines, we'll board at the stern. If they continue to run, we'll pull up on their port beam and fire a few lines across."

A quick glance told Kurt the trawler wasn't slowing. In fact, it continued to pick up speed, appearing surprisingly quick for such an ungainly looking ship. "Better get those lines ready," Kurt said. "Something tells me they're not pulling over."

"They want to make it interesting," Zama said. "So be it." He shouted to his men. "Get ready to show them what we can do."

The men reacted quickly, securing braided nylon lines to rocket-propelled anchors, which they loaded into weapons that resembled World War II bazookas.

Kurt stayed out of the way, keeping his eye on the trawler. Spotting a man on deck with a machine gun, he shouted a warning. "Get down."

The crew heard Kurt shout and dropped behind the patrol boat's steel wave blocker just in time to hear small-arms fire pinging off the outside of it. Another spread of bullets raked the superstructure above, denting the armor and blasting chips from one of the windows.

"Do they always fight this hard?" Kurt asked.

"Only when they have something to hide," Zama said. "Last year, one of their ships rammed one of ours. Turned out they had a cargo hold full of very expensive tuna."

The lieutenant addressed the men around him, half of whom were armed with rifles. "Return fire. Keep them pinned down. And ready the fifty-caliber, in case they don't want to play nice."

Working in synchronized precision, Zama's men popped up above the rail in separate places. They peppered the bow of the trawler with shots, then the stern and then amidships. Their gunfire drove the machine-gun-wielding man back into the hull.

They pulled up beside the trawler, swinging close and slowing until they were in a position abeam the midship section of the Chinese ship.

"Now," Lieutenant Zama ordered.

His men fired three rocket-propelled harpoons at the

trawler. The first plunged into the side of the ship's superstructure and held fast. The second harpoon hit the metal plating surrounding the base of one of the fishing booms. It also held fast. The third harpoon glanced off some equipment, skittered to the right and failed to secure itself.

The man who'd fired it began hauling on the line.

"Leave it," Zama said. "Two lines will do."

While that man put the launcher aside, the South African sailors hooked themselves onto the ropes and shimmied across the gap between two ships.

Kurt moved up behind them, but Lieutenant Zama kept him back. "I'm afraid you'll have to stay behind until we've secured the ship. I did not expect this type of resistance."

"I'd really hate to sit this out," Kurt said.

"I insist," Zama said. "You're my guest."

Kurt nodded. He was in no position to argue, even if Zama and his men were endangering themselves on his account. He stood down as the men moved across the rope. It was a dangerous way to go from ship to ship.

At one point the trawler came toward them again, trying to sideswipe the patrol boat. When the South African helmsman reacted by turning away to keep them at a safe distance, the trawler swung abruptly in the other direction.

"Back to starboard," Zama ordered.

The patrol boat leaned into the turn, but one of the lines had become stretched. It pulled free before pressure could be relieved and two of the commandos were dumped in the sea.

They swept out behind the speeding ships, bobbing to the surface thanks to the buoyancy of their life jackets.

"They'll be okay," Zama said. "Keep us in tight."

By now the other two commandos had reached the trawler and dropped onto the deck. They were immediately outnumbered and pinned down.

"Let's go," Zama said to the last of his men.

The two of them hooked into the line and began pulling themselves across the churning waves. As they went over, Kurt watched the trawler like a hawk, looking for any sign that it was about to turn.

With the South Africans halfway across, the Chinese ship began to roll to the outside, a sure sign that it was turning toward the patrol boat again. This time, the line sagged. Kurt grabbed it and pulled, taking up some of the slack.

"She's turning in," he shouted to the helmsman. "Pull away, but not too hard. Be ready to turn back as soon as she rolls level."

The pilot did as Kurt suggested. Between the course change and Kurt's effort, they managed to keep the line from dipping in the water.

Kurt cut his eyes to the stern of the trawler. A change in the rudder position would cause an instant change in the eddies swirling around the stern of the ship. It would be visible crucial seconds before the two-hundred-foot vessel began to swing away from them.

Leaning back with the line hooked tight around his arm, Kurt saw the water change from frothing white to dark sea green. The rudder had swung opposite.

"Back to starboard," he shouted.

The trawler was turning away. The rope connecting the two ships rose as the gap widened. It began to pull taut. Kurt released the slack and the patrol boat responded to the helm, easing back toward the trawler and narrowing the gap once more.

With the line remaining anchored, Zama reached the trawler and dropped onto the deck. The commando behind him was not as lucky.

The Chinese man with the machine gun had reappeared, this time accompanied by several friends. They took up positions around the superstructure, sniping at the boarders down below them.

As the gunfire rained down, another crewman took a fire ax to the remaining line. It broke loose with a single chop and a third South African went into the water.

At almost the same time, a separate group of Chinese sailors appeared near the aft section of the fishing boat. They lit and hurled Molotov cocktails toward Zama and his men. One of the makeshift grenades exploded on the deck. A second fell amid a stack of nets that quickly burst into flames.

The South Africans had no choice but to open fire, cutting down two of the attackers and causing a third to take cover, but the act had turned the tables. Kurt could see more crewmen on the tail end of the ship gathering up fishing gaffs. It had the look of a mob ready to charge. And with smoke from the fire obscuring this new threat, Zama and his men were in trouble.

"Pull in closer," Kurt shouted to the helmsman.

"My orders are to maintain station," the helmsman shouted back.

"Closer and forward," Kurt demanded, "or you're going to lose your commanding officer and the rest of the team."

The helmsman was no fool. He could see the situation was getting out of control. He did as Kurt requested, though he had no idea what this American had in mind.

Kurt wasn't exactly sure either, he was making it up as he went along, but it dawned on him that outflanking the Chinese would make it possible to beat them at their own game. He grabbed the last of the rocket-propelled harpoon canisters, disconnected the line and slung it over his back using the shoulder strap.

As he readied himself, the patrol boat picked up speed, drawing even with the outstretched fishing boom. "Get in front of the boom and drop back."

The helmsman didn't question Kurt this time and the patrol boat pulled wide, surged forward and then tucked itself back in close. Kurt raced to the stern as the patrol boat lost a few knots of speed and drifted into the boom.

Kurt didn't even have to jump. He just grabbed the boom, pulled himself up and crawled the rest of the way. In a few seconds, he'd dropped neatly onto the trawler's deck.

He took cover as the dull and rapid hammering of the machine guns continued, broken occasionally by the sharp crack of the assault team's carbines and shouts on both sides. Smoke billowed out from the gunfire, making it impossible to see the stern, but Kurt knew the mob was back there.

He needed a quick way to end this and there was only one person on board who could make that happen. The trawler's captain.

Moving with surprising speed considering the bazooka he was carrying, Kurt ducked around the front bulkhead of the superstructure, reaching the far side of the ship. With all eyes focused to port, where the South African patrol boat and the commandos were, Kurt found it easy to race up the starboard ladder and push his way onto the bridge.

He found three men inside, one of them at the wheel, the other two squinting through the port windows, looking out into the smoke.

All three turned with a start. One of them charged at Kurt, but Kurt swung the launch tube around, catching the man in the side of the head. The sailor tumbled to the deck and lay still.

The remaining two stared at Kurt in shock. Their attention went from his face to the pointed end of the harpoon that was aimed directly at them.

Kurt targeted the man with the more impressive uniform. "Tell your men to surrender."

For effect, he switched the safety off, causing several lights to illuminate on the trigger housing.

The helmsman raised his hands and stood back from the wheel. Kurt nodded, making sure to look pleased. The captain stood stubbornly, so Kurt reached toward the panel, grabbed the microphone that connected to the ship's PA system and tossed it to him.

The captain got the picture. He took the microphone,

switched the selector to shipwide and gave the order to stop fighting.

Kurt stood there, keeping the captain under guard, as Zama and his men disarmed and secured the Chinese crew. It took several minutes. Once it was done, Lieutenant Zama made his way to the bridge.

He pulled the door open and stopped. He stood there in shock, staring at Kurt, then glancing back toward the patrol boat and then turning to Kurt again.

"What . . ." he began. "When . . . How . . ." Shaking his head in disbelief, the lieutenant got ahold of himself. "You're supposed to be on the patrol boat."

Kurt shrugged. "I got caught up in the excitement," he said. "And I figured you and your men could use a hand."

"How did you even get over here?"

"Pirate-style," Kurt said. "I came over on the outstretched boom."

Zama laughed heartily. "Of course you did." He laughed again. "Okay," he said. "Very good. Next time, you can go first."

Kurt found that offer acceptable. "Now," he said. "Let's find out what these men were hiding."

37

With the South African crew in control of the Chinese trawler, the patrol boat circled back and recovered the commandos who'd fallen into the sea. One of the men had a dislocated shoulder. The other two were uninjured and happy to rejoin the boarding party.

As the tactical team kept the trawler's crew under guard, Kurt and Zama searched the ship from top to bottom. Making their way to the hold, the smell of fish became overpowering.

"This is why they ran," Zama said.

They'd come to the trawler's processing deck. Heaps of recently captured tuna filled the deck, some as large as ten feet long from nose to tail. "Each one of these bluefin is worth a hundred thousand dollars."

Kurt nodded. He knew the price of tuna had soared in recent years. Especially for the larger fish. But tuna wasn't all the ship held. In addition, they found dolphin carcasses and hundreds of fins cut from captured sharks, the bodies of which had been tossed overboard after the de-finning.

"What a waste," Kurt said. It was one thing to fish, even for sharks and dolphins, but shark finning was decimating the world's shark population. And taking out apex predators was known to cause disastrous effects on the food chains on land and in the sea.

To Kurt, it was no different from the killing of rhino and elephants for their horns and tusks, no different from the wholesale slaughter of the world's tigers so their claws could be ground into powder for superstitious people to use in all manner of ridiculous ways.

"So much of humanity is foolish and shortsighted," Zama said.

Kurt stood there quietly, looking at all that was left from a hundred dead sharks. More certainly needed to be done to protect the world's ecological balance and save threatened species. But there was no call for cataclysmic plans like those of Ryland and his sister, which would destroy half the planet or more in the process.

He turned away. "Let's finish checking the ship."

"And then what?"

"Can you spare a skeleton crew?" Kurt asked.

"Prize crew for this ship? Of course. But what are you going to do with it?"

"I'm going to point the bow south and let her run."

38

The sun flared through glass panels of the cockpit as the P-8 Poseidon banked into a turn at thirty-seven thousand feet. Commander Walter Hansen squinted and glanced down at the instrument panel so as not to take the full brunt of the sunlight.

"Turning right to a heading of one-eight-zero," he called out.

"Roger that," a voice replied over the intercom. "Continue on heading one-eight-zero, until I call out the mark."

From a distance the Poseidon looked like a modified Boeing 737, which it was. But that was the exterior. Inside, the aircraft was packed with advanced electronic equipment, sensors and various types of detectors, which the tactical systems operators used to track hostile submarines.

These operators occupied a section in the center of the aircraft, where comfortable, padded seats were bolted to the floor in front of an expanse of computer terminals, with multiple screens, keyboards, joysticks and mouses.

The aft section of the Poseidon was normally taken up by wine racks, which were cradles with slots in the side where sonobuoys were stored. These buoys were free-floating sensors that could be dropped from the aircraft into the sea, where they would listen for the sounds made by hidden submarines.

But the wine racks had been removed from this particular aircraft. Replacing them was a high-intensity, millimeter-wave radar unit known as an SPS, or a surface-penetrating system.

Hansen and his crew were the first to fly this model and had been testing it for months.

"Please climb to new altitude of four-one-thousand," the voice over the intercom said.

The request came not from air traffic control but from Lieutenant Rebecca Collier, the recon systems operator who occupied the first row of the seats in the back of the aircraft.

Though Hansen was the pilot and commanding officer, it was Collier who would call the shots during the data-gathering leg of the flight.

When Hansen didn't reply, Collier seemed to grow nervous, adding, "If that's okay with you, sir."

Hansen grinned. Collier was green. She had a master's

degree in electronic something or other and was fresh out of OCS and two separate radar schools. She was a young high-tech expert stuck in a unit filled with crusty fifteen-year vets.

So far, she'd held her own. But she hadn't yet grown comfortable enough to crack a joke. Hansen was fine with that. He'd tell the lieutenant when it was her time to be funny. "Roger that, Lieutenant, climbing to flight level four-one-thousand."

Hansen pulled back on the control column and brought the nose up. With the aircraft climbing smoothly, Hansen glanced out at the ocean and the frozen continent beyond. "We'll be over the ice in five minutes."

"Which begs the question," Collier said. "What, exactly, are we doing here, sir? Aren't we supposed to be hunting submarines?"

Hansen had been wondering that himself. Since the end of World War II, the American surface fleet had reigned supreme, leading opponents to concentrate their efforts on building submarines.

The Soviet Union had built a massive underwater fleet during the Cold War. Their designs included the largest, the fastest and the deepest-diving subs ever to prowl the depths.

In the last decade, the Chinese had taken a similar path, constructing entire fleets of modern submarines, not to mention underwater drones, hyper-range torpedoes and submarine-launched cruise missiles that had one solitary purpose. To destroy American aircraft carriers.

While the Russian subs had been loud and easy to track, the Chinese ones were smoother, quieter and covered in sonar-absorbing layers of exotic materials. In some cases, they were made of nonferrous metals that made magnetic detection impossible.

The Navy's response was the radar in the back of Hansen's P-8. Its beam looked down through the water. It couldn't detect a submarine directly, but it was so precise it could pick up minute pressure variations caused by a submarine moving through the water, even if that submarine was operating at depths of several hundred feet.

Like surface ships, submarines displaced water as they moved. Only they did so in three dimensions. And while the ocean currents and waves dampened the effect, some of that pressure still reached the surface, forming a barely detectible bulge similar to a ship's wake that stretched and widened behind the submarine along the path it had just traveled.

The SPS could track the wake, which was like a giant arrow pointing directly to the hidden vessel. And while the system was still being fine-tuned, it had already proven itself in calm weather over moderate seas.

Hansen had been advised to expect more intense trials over the storm-tossed ocean, but no one had said anything about testing it over ice and snow. He couldn't imagine what the brass was thinking.

"It's top-level stuff," he told Collier. "You're not meant to know. But considering we've had to refuel twice just to get here, someone must think it's worth it."

"If you say so," Collier replied. "As far as I'm concerned, some desk jockey at the Pentagon has lost his mind. Either that or he thinks there's a submarine buried under the snow."

Hansen laughed at the idea. He did suppose there could be something else of interest down there. "Would the radar find it?" he asked. "If it was there? Can SPS look through snow and ice?"

"Possibly," Collier replied. "Unlike most materials, water actually becomes less dense as it solidifies. And snow is mostly air gaps. But I doubt we'll spot anything. The system is dependent upon movement. A submarine keeping station or drifting cannot be detected. So, unless there's something burrowing under the ice, we probably won't find . . . um . . . squat, sir."

Hansen nodded, continued his scan of the instruments and watched as the sun disappeared over the horizon. It was already dark in the frozen land below. Dark and empty. He wondered once more what the Navy was really looking for, then decided he didn't even want to know.

39

Twelve hours later, in a room populated by computers and large screens, Hiram Yaeger and Rudi Gunn were wrestling with the information from the flight.

Studying the screen showing the Great Southern Continent, Rudi saw no sign of a discovery. "Any progress?"

Yaeger adjusted his wire-rimmed glasses and looked up. "We finished downloading the raw data from the Navy. But it's just that. Raw data. We had to figure out how to work with it, so I ran it through an intense algorithm and assigned values to each of the signal responses."

"Normally, I'd ask you to spare me the technical mumbo jumbo," Rudi said. "Since I sense you're stalling, please do continue."

"I'm only stalling because even my computers have to manipulate the data before they make something useful out of it," Yaeger insisted. "Just so you understand, we're talking billions upon billions of data points here."

"How long before we see the results?"

"The answer is coming," Yaeger said, nodding toward tiny red and blue marks appearing in various places on the screen in front of them. "Decision time will soon follow."

Rudi focused on the screen. At first the tiny marks were scattered, dotting the image here and there like the first drops of rain hitting a dry sidewalk. But as the seconds passed, the minuscule dots began to create a shape, filling in a thin band over which the Poseidon had flown.

"Zoom in," Rudi said.

Hiram adjusted the resolution and cropped the contours of the map. He continued to adjust the scale until it displayed only the section of land underneath the path of the reconnaissance flight and a small area around the perimeter.

The region in question was thirty miles wide and almost five hundred miles in length. It covered the last-known flight path of Jurgenson's Dornier. The increased level of magnification revealed thousands of additional marks. Had Hiram continued to zoom in, it would have revealed millions and eventually billions more, each one covering only inches of the Antarctic surface.

As the seconds passed, many of the red and blue indicators changed to gray.

"Are we losing something?" Rudi asked.

"No," Hiram said. "The computer is normalizing the data. It's determined that those marks are in tune with the surrounding landform, taking into account snow-drifts, hills and crevasses the way the Navy's program accounts for waves, currents and tides."

By the five-minute mark, the search grid was ninety percent gray. Only a mountainous area devoid of snow and a series of thin blue lines, running in haphazard directions, remained colored. "Is that a signal or just noise?"

Hiram leaned forward and studied the data on a laptop directly in front of him. "Hidden depressions in the snow," Hiram said. "Fault lines in the ice and cracks in the glaciers. Basically, you're looking at a map of fissures and crevasses. Most of which are probably covered with snow."

"Make sure you save that data," Rudi said. "Might come in handy once Kurt and his team are on the ground."

Hiram nodded and typed an instruction into the computer.

"If the blue dots indicate unaccounted-for microde-pressions, what do the red dots tell us?" Rudi asked. "I notice there are fewer and fewer of them as the picture fills in."

"Red indicates a surface feature out of place with its surroundings," Hiram said. "There are so few of them because the software blends the surface together and finds a consistent landform. When the Navy uses this, the red points indicate an inconsistent rise in the water level. That's the signature of the submarine moving toward the sensor. Blue indicates it's moving away."

Rudi nodded. If Ryland had built a steel pipeline and buried it under the snow, a long red line would soon appear on the screen. And if he'd used geothermal water to melt a tunnel through the glacier as Kurt suggested, the microscopic settling of the ice above it would become noticeable as a thin blue streak.

The truth finally appeared. A long blue line that led directly to the sea. With only a single red area at its origination point.

"Nothing in nature draws a perfectly straight line," Rudi insisted.

"There are two small detours," Hiram pointed out, "but they're consistent with a canal or a pipeline dodging around mountainous terrain."

"The line stops about twenty miles from the ocean," Rudi said. "If it is Ryland, does that mean he's not finished?"

"Impossible to tell," Hiram admitted. "The line terminates near a glacial fault zone. Might mean they ran into problems. Or they might have found a meltwater route directly to the bay."

"Meaning they could already be pumping the algae."

Yaeger nodded.

"Worst-case scenario," Rudi said. "Antarctic glaciers in the twilight of the southern summer would be at maximum melt-off."

"He's thought this through," Hiram said. "I'll give him that."

"We're going to stop him. Stop him at the source," Rudi said. "Precisely as Kurt envisioned in the first place."

"Which source?"

"That red spot. That's got to be a control unit or a pumping station. If we take it out, the rest of the pipeline is irrelevant."

"You might be guessing here," Yaeger warned.

"Now that we know where to look, I can easily get confirmation." Rudi picked up the phone and dialed an internal extension. A voice answered on the first ring.

"Remote Sensing," the voice said. "This is Lee."

Lee Garland oversaw NUMA's remote sensing and communications wing. Garland called himself a satellite wrangler because he was constantly repositioning any number of NUMA's satellites, most of which were designed to scan the oceans or to act as secure communication relays.

"Lee, this is Rudi. How long would it take you to get a high-resolution pass of the Holtzman Glacier and the Fimbul Ice Shelf?"

"Fimbul?" Lee said.

"Correct," Rudi said. "It's a remote glacial area in Antarctica, not very well known. It's on the opposite side of the continent from McMurdo and the Ross Ice Shelf."

"Yeah," Garland said with a strange tone to his voice. "I know where it is. Shouldn't take long at all. We have a weather sat transitioning to a south polar orbit right now."

"Weather sat?" Rudi repeated. "Why would you be moving one of those over the pole?"

"Haven't you heard?" Garland replied. "There's a huge storm brewing down there. They're calling it Superstorm Jack. It's going to sweep into the Southern Ocean tomorrow and bury half of Antarctica in a weeklong blizzard."

"Which half?" Rudi asked.

"The half with the Holtzman Glacier and the Fimbul Ice Shelf on it."

"Of course," Rudi said. "Get that satellite pass done before the storm hits. I know those weather sats aren't designed to pick up small targets on the ground. I need you to remedy that. Fine-tune the optics. Change the software. Give the damn thing a pair of glasses, if you have to. I need a clear image."

"There are a few tricks I can use," Garland told him.

"Good. Hiram will be sending you the coordinates we need scanned."

"I'll watch for them," Garland said.

Rudi acknowledged and hung up, then offered Yaeger a grim look. "If Ryland's plan is operational, or close to it, a week is an awful long time for him to be pumping microbes into the sea."

Yaeger offered a counterpoint. "And if his plan isn't up and running yet, the storm might delay him long enough for us to put more resources into play."

Rudi shook his head. "Ryland's operation is mostly underground. That storm isn't going to have much effect on his plans."

"Which makes this situation even more precarious," Yaeger said.

Rudi agreed. "After you get those coordinates over to Lee, I'll need you to build me a computer model simulating Ryland's plan, his chances of success and the effect of us getting there a week late. Put everything we've learned in it."

"To what end?"

"Superstorm Jack just made putting boots on the ground a lot more dangerous," Rudi said. "If I'm going to order Kurt and his team to take the risk, I need to be sure it's worth it."

40

Kurt stood on the aft deck of the Chinese trawler, squinting into the spitting rain. Overcast skies and mist had cut the visibility to less than five miles, while heavy swells rolled in one after another.

Because of their size, the waves appeared to be moving in slow motion, building as they approached, lifting the trawler upward and then letting it down gently as they passed on by. Waves weren't a concern at the moment. Kurt didn't need a weather report to tell him things were going to get worse.

Hearing an approaching helicopter and then spotting its landing lights through gloom, Kurt stepped from his sheltered spot and moved out into the rain. He had a radio in one hand and a powerful flashlight in the other. He wore yellow rain gear from head to toe.

He called Joe on the radio. "Have you in sight, amigo. Hope you can see me. I'm waving a light and dressed up like the Gorton's Fisherman."

A scratchy transmission delivered Joe's response. *"Don't worry, Kurt, we've got you on the FLIR and the UV channel. I can see you plain as day. What I don't see is a helipad to land on. I'm assuming you have something up your sleeve. But you might want to share it because I have a couple nervous passengers up here."*

The Chinese trawler was a processing ship, which meant it was longer and larger than a standard trawler. But Joe was right, it didn't come with a helipad.

"I've taken a blowtorch to the midships booms," Kurt said. "We tossed all that gear over the side so you would have plenty of space to land. We've welded a few plates to the deck to keep things level."

The helicopter descended through the clouds, closing in on the trawler and then easing up beside it in formation.

To the consternation of the Chinese captain, who remained aboard, Kurt, along with Zama and a few of his men, had cut away anything that might have interfered with the helicopter's approach and landing. The result was a clean-looking ship, lighter and more stable, but with a few metal stumps sticking up here and there.

Flat steel plates and several layers of plywood had been welded to and hammered into the deck where the Jayhawk was supposed to touch down.

As Kurt stood by, waving the flashlight back and forth, the Jayhawk hovered beside the ship, riding the wind like a seagull.

Joe's voice returned over the radio. He sounded more irritated than pleased. *"Under normal conditions, I'd say no problem. But these are far from normal conditions."*

"I figured you might need a little help," Kurt said. "I rigged up a bear trap for you. Drop the centerline down and I'll reel you in."

"Now you're talking."

In the pilot's seat of the helicopter, Joe worked the controls like a virtuoso. His hands moved independently, seeming to do three or four things at once. He eased the helicopter sideways, fighting the swirling air currents and keeping the craft level as the trawler dropped and then rose back toward them.

In position over the ship, he looked downward through the clear footwells.

One moment the helicopter appeared to be steady and hovering eighty feet above the ship with its landing gear aligned evenly with the flat deck. Seconds later the trawler would be rolling into a trough, the deck tilting twenty degrees to horizon and the ship itself dropping away. Thirty seconds after that, the trawler would come rising back up, looking as if it were going to hit the Jayhawk and knock it out of the sky.

And while Joe was cool and calm, his passengers—who had no control over the situation—were close to terrified.

"I can't watch," Gamay said, looking around the cabin and then out into the distance.

"We'll be all right," Paul said. "Though I'm going to need a field dressing if you keep digging your nails into my arm like that."

"Sorry," she said, releasing him.

With Kurt flashing the light at him, Joe flipped a switch and dropped the Jayhawk's centerline cable. It was weighted at the end and reeled outward with the force of gravity.

Down on the trawler, Kurt used a boat hook to grab the cable and then hauled it back toward the center of the landing zone. He threaded the cable underneath a steel bar and then dragged it toward a winch and hooked it in.

Pulling the radio out of his pocket, he notified Joe. "I have you locked in. Maintain a hover and I'll pull you down."

"Roger," Joe said. *"Get us close and I'll cut the power when you come up to the top of the next swell."*

Kurt activated the winch and the cable began to drag the helicopter downward. All Joe had to do was maintain side-to-side control and avoid a rotor strike if the ship tilted more than expected.

They rode one swell down and then up. By the time they began dropping into the next trough, the helicopter was only thirty feet above the deck. Kurt paused the winch as they dropped down, engaging it again as they came up the face of the next wave.

The helicopter moved closer . . . ten feet . . . five . . . three . . . Joe throttled back and the wheels of the Jayhawk touched down firmly, denting the temporary plating beneath them.

Kurt immediately pulled up the slack, pinning the helicopter tight to the deck. With the bear trap locked, he ran to the Jayhawk. He slid the side door open as Joe shut down the engine. "Make sure you set the parking brake," he shouted.

"We're going to need more than that if this storm gets worse," Joe said.

"I have some straps to tie it down with," Kurt said.

As Joe acknowledged Kurt with a wave, Paul and Gamay made for the exit. Gamay reached the door first. Kurt had never seen her look so green.

"You arranged this," she said to Kurt. "I ought to throw up all over you."

Kurt grinned and helped her step down. "I'm wearing rain gear that's spent years being used in a fish processing bay. It couldn't possibly smell any worse."

Gamay's nose wrinkled. "Oh, God," she said, picking up the aroma. "That's awful."

She headed toward the bulkhead with a hand over her mouth.

Paul came down next. "At least you've gotten her mind off the terrible flight," he said. "That's something."

With Paul and Gamay out of the aircraft, Joe flipped up the visor of his helmet. "You have no idea what I've been dealing with. While you've been out here on a pleasure cruise, I've been fighting against a passenger-led rebellion."

"That's not going to be the last storm-tossed flight for any of us," Kurt said.

"How bad is it going to get?" Joe asked.

"Let me put it to you this way," Kurt said. "There's never been a hurricane over Antarctica. You and I might get to see the first."

41

Rudi walked down a quiet hallway, passing empty offices and heading for the elevator. It was after midnight in Washington. Only a skeleton crew remained in the building, most of whom were camped out in the communications department, which ran twenty-four hours a day.

Taking the elevator up several floors, Rudi found Hiram Yaeger sitting behind a computer terminal with three separate screens in front of him. The first displayed lines of code, the second showed a number of graphs, while the third displayed a live satellite view over the South Pole.

"Glad to see I'm not the only one pulling an all-nighter," Rudi said. "How's it coming?"

"Depends what you're referring to," Yaeger replied.

He turned in his seat. "If you mean the storm, it's going swimmingly."

"I have the forecast," Rudi said, waving sheets of paper. "The storm is intensifying and continuing south. It's being pushed by a ridge of high pressure right into Kurt's lap."

Yaeger nodded. "They're not exactly sailing in a Class 5 cutter. You sure that rust bucket of a trawler will hold together?"

"I'm not sure at all," Rudi said. "Which is why I need to make a go/no go decision rather soon. Is your ice age model ready to spit out a few answers?"

"More answers than you're going to want," Yaeger said.

Rudi got comfortable as Hiram checked through a few more lines of code and then initiated the program.

"We're guessing at some of the parameters," Yaeger said. "But based on Yvonne's Snowball Earth dissertation and the claims Ryland made to his associates—which were, basically, mirrors of the truth—this is what it looks like."

Hiram hit enter and the program started to run. On one screen a world map showed temperatures decreasing sequentially as sea ice increased and snow cover lingered. Hiram narrated the effects. "One year out, it's nothing more than a harsh winter and a cool summer. But by year two the winter is bitter and months too long in both hemispheres and the summer heat never materializes. By year three, the summer ice pack stretches south of Greenland."

Rudi saw the visual representation on the screen. The planet turning whiter from both poles toward the middle.

"By year five, a third of the world's agriculture is being impacted by a shortened growing season. Hard frosts keep people from planting and seeds from germinating. All the fresh water locked up in snow and ice. That, along with less evaporation because of colder temperatures, makes for less rain and lower growth rates once the short growing season does arrive."

Rudi studied the graphic representation of what Yaeger was telling him. He noted the three lines running close together through the first five years of the chart and then diverging at year five and widening substantially thereafter. "What are these lines?"

"Best-, average- and worst-case scenarios."

"Give me the best case," Rudi said.

"Worldwide temperature drops averaging twenty-four to thirty-nine degrees," Yaeger said. "Canada, the northern U.S. and half of Europe end up in a frozen state akin to Siberia today. Much of Russia and northern China will become uninhabitable. A one-third drop in land-based food production by year ten, accompanied by a staggering eighty percent drop in catch rates and tonnage for sea-based food sources, caused mostly by overfishing as countries around the world attempt to make up the food deficit."

"Mass starvation," Rudi said. "That's our best-case scenario?"

Yaeger nodded. "Even if we all stay in our frozen homelands, pile on the insulation and turn up the heat."

As grim as that was, it was probably too good an outcome to hope for. "What's the midline simulation looking like?"

"See for yourself," Yaeger said. He tapped a button on the keyboard and the simulation resumed following the central plotline.

As Rudi watched, the permafrost crept down the map, slowly covering the United States until it reached south of Atlanta, Nashville and Dallas.

"Only Florida, southern Arizona and a thin sliver along the coasts will remain ice-free," Yaeger explained. "Europe looks even worse. Everything north of Rome will be frozen tundra year-round. Only Portugal, parts of Spain and the southeast corners of the British Isles will escape and that's only while what's left of the Gulf Stream remains intact. It could easily die out."

Rudi studied the map to see how other parts of the world would be affected. Most of China would be frozen solid, buried in rapidly accumulating snowfall and advancing glaciers. By year ten, Japan was connected to the mainland by ice sheets. By year twenty, those sheets extended halfway to the Aleutians.

South America would fare no better. Everything below Rio would look like Norway in winter. Only Africa was largely spared, though the southern third of the continent would have to endure long, harsh winters more like the climate in Alberta.

"I'm guessing snowdrifts will be quite a surprise to all the elephants, lions and crocodiles. No wonder Ryland bought all his land around the equator."

Yaeger nodded. "He's obviously run the simulation himself. His islands also remain in the liquid zone, even under this scenario. But even he can't account for all the variables. Let me show you the third line. I call it the Doomsday Scenario."

"Wonderful title," Rudi said.

"And accurate," Yaeger insisted. "You see, the farther out we go, the more we encounter feedback effects and inputs that are not directly related to the algae itself. For instance, as the atmosphere cools, it also thins and loses its ability to retain moisture. Both impacts cause it to be less effective at insulating the planet, allowing even more heat to radiate out into space. By chance, fallen snow and ice are white and reflective. As the snowfall spreads and lingers longer on the ground, we end up essentially coating the Earth in a reflective blanket, causing the sunlight to be bounced back into space instead of absorbed by the dark ground and the equally dark sea. These things all result in feedback loops, meaning the colder it gets, the colder it will continue to get."

"Snowball Earth," Rudi noted. "Yvonne's original theory. Doomsday for humanity. Or close to it. I'm assuming we'd build underground shelters, tap geothermal sources and scratch out a method of survival. But it wouldn't exactly be a party."

Yaeger nodded. "In the worst-case scenario, the Earth slowly enters a frozen state, one from which it cannot emerge without a jolt from something large. Either massive volcanoes or some type of surface-heating system reflecting extra sunlight and heat onto the planet or even nuclear weapons and purposeful release of more greenhouse gases."

"Could you imagine the irony?" Rudi said.

Yaeger shook his head.

"Why is it so quick to take hold?" Rudi asked. "Ice ages normally take thousands of years to get going."

Yaeger swiveled in his seat to face Rudi more directly. "Under normal circumstances, the glaciers would melt slowly and the algae would start flowing into the sea at a trickle, only becoming a rush over decades or centuries. The algae's own ice-forming activity would trap it in a mix of slush and brine in the coves and bays that it initially flowed into. New ice would only grow at the margins with the algae itself caught behind that."

Rudi could visualize that. "Go on."

"At that pace, it would take hundreds of years for the algae to encircle Antarctica in large enough numbers to have any effect. And based on global ocean currents, it would be centuries more before it reached the northern polar seas, where it could perform the same trick. Ryland is intending to use high-pressure turbines to pump the algae from the glacial lake directly into the ocean at incredible volumes. Instead of a trickle, we're looking at thousands of gallons a minute. He's got tankers full of the stuff headed toward the Northern Hemisphere, where they'll seed the Arctic and the seas above Russia and Canada. And considering his boast, and Yvonne's background as a biological engineer, it becomes easy to imagine him genetically engineering the algae to grow and spread faster. All which compresses a thousand years of ice formation into a decade or less."

"What about our ability to destroy it?" Rudi asked.

"First we have to find it," Yaeger said. "Then we have to figure out how to kill it in massive amounts without poisoning the entire ocean at the same time. On top of that, we have to make sure we got all of it, every single flake, because anything we missed will simply regrow. Realistically, it's impossible to imagine we could eliminate the algae once it escaped a confined area. It's like trying to eradicate that damned COVID virus. If you quarantine nine million people who have it and leave one of them out and walking around, all you've done is buy yourself time before it flares up again."

Rudi understood the difficulty. NUMA had recently spent millions of dollars working with the Coast Guard and the state of Florida trying to mitigate the red tides that flowed into Tampa Bay. That was a speck on the map, compared to the Arctic or Antarctic oceans, with calm waters and bases nearby. And even they hadn't been particularly successful.

There was no point in further conversation. The facts were clear. It would be impossible to put the genie back in the bottle once Ryland let it out. In this case, an ounce of prevention would be worth ten million tons of cure. "We have no choice," Rudi said. "We have to send Kurt and his team in. My only question is, how do we get them through the storm?"

42

Kurt and Joe stood over a chart in the navigator's compartment on the Chinese trawler. As the trawler rolled to port, Joe grabbed the edge of the table to hold himself in place.

Kurt pinned the chart down with one hand and then threw the other against the bulkhead to keep himself balanced. When his coffee mug began sliding toward the edge of the table, he released the chart and snatched the mug out of midair before it could throw itself to the deck.

"Nice catch," Joe said.

"They should make these things with magnets on the bottom," Kurt joked.

"We're going to need more than magnets," Joe replied. "We're going to need a miracle."

The chart they'd found was ten years old, annotated in Chinese and not all that detailed. Joe had a straightedge and pencil. Kurt was getting condition reports off a National Weather Service radio bulletin. It was a far cry from the high-tech, real-time system NUMA used, yet the basic question was the same. How do we get there from here?

With Paul and Gamay looking on, Kurt marked the landing zone. "If we're right, Ryland's pumping station is here. The last satellite pass before the storm showed two heat plumes. One large and one negligible. We have to assume the large flare is a result of the turbines and the geothermal layer they've tapped into."

Joe measured once, scribbled some numbers and then measured again. Shaking his head, he looked up. "We're still too far out. Even with the extra fuel we loaded on the Jayhawk and a one-way trip in mind."

At that moment Zama came in. "How goes it, my friends?"

"Up and down," Kurt said. "How's the ship?"

"About the same. My men and the Chinese crew who stayed aboard have shored up all the hatches using two-by-fours and other materials. But they're nervous. And they don't know what we're getting into. Do you?"

As Zama spoke, the trawler rolled with another swell. Kurt switched the coffee mug to the other hand and braced against the opposite bulkhead. "It's going to get worse overnight."

Zama didn't look happy. "Then we're going to be shipping water," Zama told him. "It only takes one hatch or port to fail and we'll have flooding inside."

Kurt wasn't about to put Zama and his men in danger. "You've done more than enough already. I promise you we'll get off this boat so you turn back north before the bad stuff hits. We just need to get a little closer first." He pointed to the map and Joe's measuring stick. "We're at least two hundred miles out of range. Can you coax any more speed out of this tub?"

"The diesel is old and running hot," Zama said. "I can't risk calling for more power. Losing the engine in this storm will be fatal for all of us."

"Actually," Joe said, looking up from the chart, "I was wrong. We have to leave now or abort the whole mission."

Kurt turned back to Joe. "You just said we're too far away."

"We are," Joe said. "But we're going to get farther away the longer we wait."

Kurt knew better than to fence with Joe on something mathematical. He had an engineer's mind and did numbers like a computer. "Care to explain?"

Joe held out a hand. "Coffee mug."

Kurt handed it over, and Joe placed it down on the chart on a specific spot. "This is the center of the storm."

Kurt nodded, looking on with everyone else.

"We're in the Southern Hemisphere," Joe added. "Storms spin clockwise down here, not counterclockwise like they do up north." As he spoke, Joe drew circles around the mug. "That means if we leave now and track west for about thirty minutes, we'll get ourselves a tailwind for the rest of the journey."

He reached down and moved the mug. "If we wait and the storm gets to here, we'll be fighting a crosswind. Not fun to fly in and not helpful to get us where we're going."

Reaching down, Joe moved the mug again. "Six hours from now, when the storm gets to this point, it will be blowing across the continent and back toward the coast. That's a hundred-knot headwind at our altitude. Meaning six hours from now, we'll actually be farther out of range than we are now, even with the distance we gain by continuing to sail south."

Kurt looked the chart over. It made sense. "Ride the wind and hope it holds. That's your plan?"

Joe tossed the pen onto the chart. "You got a better idea?"

Kurt did not. He glanced around the room as the ship pitched forward once more. "And what if the storm doesn't follow the expected track?"

Joe hesitated. "Then we might still make the ice shelf."

Kurt had a sense that was wishful thinking. He turned to Paul and Gamay. "We can save weight by leaving you two behind."

Gamay and Paul shared a look. Gamay spoke for both of them. "Much as I love the aroma of fish guts," she said, "you're not leaving us on this rusting tub. If we do get there, you're going to need my help identifying the algae."

"And my help with figuring out their geothermal setup," Paul said. "You blow up the wrong thing, you might just make it worse."

Kurt appreciated their bravery almost as much as the thin attempt to make it seem as if they were doing anything but volunteering. Truth was, they would need all the help they could get.

43

Unshackling the Jayhawk's chains proved to be the most dangerous task so far. They were driving through twenty-foot seas now, with the occasional thirty-foot swell every five or ten minutes.

With Joe and the Trouts secured inside the helicopter, Kurt and Zama worked in the wind and the rain. The deck was rising and falling like a slow-motion roller coaster. Spray was blasting up over the bow of the ship and pelting them with each passing wave.

Once Kurt released the bear trap, only two straps remained. They were anchored to a single point. The safest way to launch was to allow the Jayhawk to build up to full power and then cut both straps loose.

Kurt turned to Zama, shouting to be heard over the wind. "These last two have to stay hooked until we're lifting off. Otherwise we might go over the side before we can get airborne."

"Understood," Zama said.

Another wave rolled under the ship. The trawler rose up, balanced on the crest for a moment and then slid back down the far side.

"We'll launch at the top of a swell," Kurt said. "That will give us a boost." He handed Zama a fire ax. "When you see the straps pulled tight, cut them at the base. One chop. Hit it hard and strong."

Zama took the ax and gripped it. "Are we close enough for you?" he asked. "Does this plan of yours stand a chance of getting you to your destination?"

"If Joe says we can get there, we'll get there," Kurt replied. "We have to try. I'm just hoping you and the crew can get safely out of the storm."

"We'll head east once you launch," Zama said. "With the waves behind us, it'll be an easy ride. In a few hours we'll begin a turn back to the north. That will keep us clear of the worst problems."

"Good to hear." Kurt extended a hand.

Zama grasped it firmly. "Things always seem to get interesting when you are around, my friend. I wish you good fortune. And a safe return."

"You as well," Kurt said. "Thanks for your help. Drinks are on me when I get back to Cape Town."

"That I will not allow," Zama said. "But we can argue about it at the bar."

"Fair enough," Kurt said.

He released Zama's hand and turned toward the helicopter. The rotors were spinning now, the navigation lights were on, while the rotating red beacon beneath the fuselage flashed every few seconds.

Climbing into the Jayhawk, Kurt pulled the door shut. Only now, out of the driving rain and spray, did the feeling of being soaking wet sink in.

"Strap yourself in," Joe said. "This is gonna be a wild one."

Kurt dried his face with a hand towel and buckled the harness as Joe brought the helicopter up to full power.

With the rotors howling above them, the ship bottomed in the trough of a wave and began to rise. Joe angled the cyclic so the helicopter would lean into the wind and pulled back on the collective. The Jayhawk strained against the last of the straps, the engine running at full takeoff power.

Outside on the deck, Zama felt the ship begin rising toward the top of the swell. He saw the helicopter pulling on its leash. He stepped forward, leaning into the wind as he brought the ax up. He felt the trawler begin to level off. *Now*, he thought.

With a twist of his torso and the leverage of his powerful arms, Zama brought the ax down on the target. The blade severed the straps and bit into the steel deck beneath. The taut nylon snapped like a rubber band, vanishing in both directions, and the helicopter broke free, rising as the ship fell in the back of the wave.

Zama watched it climb and turn off toward the west, wondering if he would ever see the men and woman aboard it again.

44

The first part of the flight went smoothly—if being slammed around inside a metal box was one's definition of smooth. Joe controlled the helicopter with great skill, his focus so intense that he didn't seem to notice the constant jolts that felt as if they'd hit something midair.

The passengers were not so lucky. With less to focus on, they felt every bump, twist and turn. The Trouts had gone stone silent in the back of the Jayhawk. Even Kurt, who wasn't prone to motion sickness, found himself looking forward to the moment they would turn and ride with the wind instead of fighting across it.

"Are we there yet?" he joked.

"I'm not sure," Joe said.

"Do not tell me we're lost," Gamay warned from the backseat.

The Jayhawk had a moving map display on a touch screen. It linked to the precision military version of the GPS system, accurate to within sixteen inches. They weren't lost.

The Jayhawk continued to barrel through the storm. The hardy little helicopter had been designed for all weather conditions and upgraded per NUMA's specific requirements. Kurt wondered if the designers had something like this in mind.

Finally, Joe detected what he was looking for and altered course. He made a fifteen-degree turn initially and several minutes later turned almost due south, on course to the target zone.

Kurt noticed the fuel computer estimating a range of four hundred and ninety miles. He said nothing. They had over six hundred miles to go.

Much like the trawler with the following sea, the helicopter had a smoother flight with the wind pushing them. And while the buffeting continued, the severity was greatly reduced.

"You two okay back there?" Kurt asked.

"Feeling better now," Paul said.

"Gamay?"

No response.

"She'd rather not talk right now," Paul advised. "For fear she might say something that would be used against her later."

An hour went by, one that started in a heavy rain squall and ended with them flying though a swirl of snow.

Joe had every de-icing system on the aircraft set to full power and the Jayhawk never missed a beat. After another hour, he made an announcement. "You can take off those life jackets. We're over the ice shelf. We can always skate from there."

They still had eighty miles to go. The computer, though, calculated a maximum range of about sixty. While the tailwind had helped tremendously, they were still looking at landing a little short.

"Think we can stretch it?" Kurt asked.

"It's going to be close. May have to put us down a few miles from our hotel."

Kurt picked up a tablet computer that was connected to the aircraft's navigation system. "I'll look for a nice flat spot, should we need it."

Zooming in on the final target zone, Kurt scanned for flat terrain. The standard database had only limited elevation measurements. Rudi and Hiram had downloaded the information from the Navy flyover, which was hyperdetailed.

"Bless you, Rudi," Kurt said.

Working in five-mile increments, Kurt earmarked three different spots that would be promising landing zones for the helicopter when it ran out of gas.

"Don't suppose this thing is like my old Mazda?" Kurt asked. "Where empty means you can still go thirty miles?"

"Doubt it," Joe said. "Never took the chance to find out, though. The wind has helped us a lot but it's fading as we get farther away from the center of the storm."

As Joe finished speaking, the Jayhawk began to talk. *"Low fuel,"* the computer announced. *"Low fuel."*

The message repeated itself over and over until Joe found the button to silence the alarm. Even then, the warning lights continued to flash on the panel.

Fifteen minutes later, the computer began to talk again. *"Fuel critical . . . Fuel critical . . . Fuel critical . . ."*

As Joe silenced the new alarm, Kurt glanced at the estimated range. It was ten miles. Less than five minutes of flight time.

"We need an off-ramp," Joe said calmly. "What have you got?"

"Exit 101 coming up," Kurt said.

He tapped the location on his touch screen and Joe entered it into his navigation computer.

Joe took a quick look and changed course. He cut the power and began to descend. Lower and slower, they experienced less turbulence, but the tension rose.

"We're getting a local headwind here," Joe said. "Air currents getting deflected off the peaks to the east of us."

"Is that going to be a problem?"

"Definitely," Joe said. "We're going to run out of fuel fast."

Kurt could see from the GPS indicator that their ground speed had fallen substantially while the fuel consumption was the same.

Joe was forced to add power. The moment he did,

a whole panel of warning lights came on one after the other. An audible alarm began overhead. The engines were cutting out, rpm dropping.

"Definitely not like your Mazda," Joe said.

He aimed the nose of the helicopter downward, adjusting the pitch of the blades to keep them spinning, the helicopter's method for gliding called autorotation.

Kurt was thankful that they weren't dropping out of the sky like a brick, yet they seemed at the mercy of the wind. He gazed at the needle on the altimeter. It crossed below five thousand feet and then, after another quick lap, dropped below four thousand.

Kurt looked at the computer tablet with the ground information. The elevation was listed as 2,134.

Joe banked the helicopter just as a furious gust hit. It threatened to roll them over, but Joe countered it.

"Terrain, pull up," the computer warned. *"Terrain, pull up."*

Kurt noticed they were below three thousand feet now.

"Do me a favor," Joe said. "When we go below twenty-five hundred feet, turn on the landing lights so we can see what's below us."

"What if it doesn't look good?" Kurt asked.

"Then you turn the lights off again."

Kurt put his finger on the switch. They'd been flying in blackout mode with all the exterior lights off, but Joe would need a brief glimpse of the ground to land them safely. It offered a minuscule risk of detection, but Kurt doubted anyone would be watching the sky in the middle of a blizzard. Not ten miles from the pumping station.

The altimeter dropped below twenty-five hundred. Kurt flipped the switch.

A pair of high-intensity lights came on underneath the nose. They blazed into the night, but all that could be seen was storm-driven snow whipping past the helicopter. Joe slowed the craft further and turned directly into the flow of the wind.

According to the computer, the ground was coming up fast. Kurt could see nothing. "Two hundred feet to the ground," he called out. "One hundred and fifty."

It felt like a sped-up version of feeling for the bottom on a deep-sea dive. Where you could see nothing yet knew it was coming up fast.

The helicopter continued to drop, swinging wildly in the gusts.

"One hundred feet," Kurt said.

A field of volcanic rock emerged from the gloom, dark brown against the white background. It helped with the depth perception. Joe still had to change course to avoid hitting the upward-thrusting formations.

He dodged them and aimed the helicopter toward a field of snow. The ground seemed to rush up at them. Joe flared the helicopter at the last moment, bringing the nose up like a regular airplane just above the runway.

Kurt noticed that Joe hadn't put the landing gear down. He kept that to himself.

The ground turned blindingly bright as they approached. It darkened suddenly as the Jayhawk plowed into the snow and the lights were buried beneath it. The impact was jarring but not disastrous. The flat bottom of the helicopter took the shock and spread it out like the underside of a boat. They slid forward, losing speed quickly and coming to a stop.

Kurt was leaning forward, his shoulders held tight in the straps of the safety harness. The only sound he heard was the wind whipping past and a strange ticking that came from somewhere above them as the rotors continued churning with built-up inertia.

Incredibly, the landing lights under the nose of the helicopter continued to function. Though they were now buried, they managed to spread a soft glow through the translucent snow around its base.

Joe shut everything down except the lights. That done, he removed his helmet. "You're now free to move about Antarctica."

"Thank God, we're on the ground," Gamay said. Her first words in three hours. "I am never flying with you again."

"Great landing," Kurt said. "Now all we have to do is cross ten miles of forbidding terrain while fighting through a blizzard."

From the back of the helicopter, Paul laughed. "At least the hard part is over."

After pulling on their cold-weather gear, including insulated versions of the expedition jackets, they stepped from the helicopter and unloaded the snowmobiles.

Kurt, Joe and Gamay donned heated gloves, triple-insulated ski caps, neck gaiters that pulled up and covered their faces and insulated goggles to protect their eyes.

Paul had chosen a balaclava, ski goggles and an oversize fur hat with earflaps. He pulled it down tight and secured it with a strap under his chin.

Gamay shook her head at his fashion choice. "I thought you said those hats were Communist propaganda?"

"This one is Canadian," Paul said. "And it's incredibly warm."

Kurt glanced at Paul, who looked ridiculous. But considering the cold was already biting at Kurt's ears despite the modern material of his own hat, he guessed Paul would have the last laugh on that one. "Let's get the explosives loaded and get moving."

45

Yvonne Lloyd sat on a folding canvas chair in the dimly lit control dome of Base Zero. A pair of ruggedized laptop computers sat on a table in front of her. They were field units, with protective rubber cases, waterproof keyboards and heavy battery packs that could power them for several days if need be.

Low levels of red light streamed through the keys, illuminating each letter, while screens set to minimum brightness showed the condition of the high-pressure turbine her team had recently installed.

Everything in front of Yvonne suggested the turbine was operating flawlessly, but she preferred a hands-on report to the opinion of a computer. She picked a radio off the charger and spoke into it.

"All markers showing nominal," she said. "What do your eyes and ears tell you?"

Yvonne's foreman was three hundred yards away and a hundred feet beneath the surface. A relay system connected his radio to the world aboveground. "No signs of vibration," he said. "Pressure holding. We can begin drawing the lake water whenever you're ready."

She was more than ready. Eleven weeks of constructing an underground tunnel to the sea had felt like torture. Cora's betrayal and the sudden interference of NUMA had become a major last-minute threat. All that was about to become irrelevant.

She tapped a key on the control computer. "Valves opening . . . Water flowing . . . Keep an eye on everything and let me know if you spot any problems. If everything continues looking good, make your way back to the compound."

The foreman didn't hesitate long before replying. "If it's all the same with you, I'd rather stay put," he replied. "Just in case something goes wrong, I'd rather be here where I might be able to do something about it."

Yvonne understood. Her foreman wanted to remain at his post, like a master chief in the engine room of a great vessel. That didn't surprise her. All of them knew that the crucial moment had arrived and each seemed to deal with it in a different way.

For some, it would mean celebration. For others, a deeply spiritual moment of communion with the environment that they were trying to save.

Yvonne didn't know what to feel. At least the work

would be done. The future course altered. Years of struggle at last paying its dividend. Instead of euphoria, she found exhaustion creeping in.

She glanced around the room. In addition to herself and the foreman, nine others remained at Base Zero, eight of them members of the tactical team, the same team that had stormed the *Grishka* almost three months before.

Ryland had insisted they transfer to the base to protect the turbine that would pump the lake water through the ice tunnel.

After helping deliver and install the high-pressure turbine, these men had had little to do. To Yvonne's surprise, this level of inactivity had affected the group, particularly a man they called High Point. He was the team leader and the man who'd shot Cora and the others on the deck of the *Grishka*.

Perhaps his unease made sense. As a sniper, he was used to being camouflaged in a hiding place where he could watch over large swaths of territory. Being cooped up inside a target as obvious as a building made him feel vulnerable.

At the moment, he sat nearby, tapping away at another laptop, cycling through the views from a bank of cameras he'd deployed. Some of them visual wavelength, most operating on infrared.

With little to see but darkness, he got up and walked over to the windows. They were covered on the inside with condensation. He wiped the window down only to find the outside caked with snow and ice.

"We're too passive here," he said, turning to Yvonne. "We're easy targets, should anyone attack."

Yvonne was not concerned. "The only people who even know about us are those fools from NUMA. My brother has an eye on them. Their nearest ship is a thousand miles away, struggling in the storm and heading directly back to where the *Grishka* sank. They're lost and grasping at straws."

"We should have set up a portable radar," he said.

Yvonne shook her head. "A radar beam would lead them right to us. They could follow it down like a homing beacon."

"Lookouts, then."

She motioned toward the window and the blowing snow. "Be my guest."

He glanced toward the window, said nothing.

"It's twenty below out there," she pointed out. "That storm is going to get worse before it gets better. Until then, we don't have anything to worry about."

He turned without a word and went back to his desk. Slumping into his own canvas chair, he began cycling through the cameras once again.

He'd placed a ring of them around the habitat and others farther out on the rocky ridge above the valley. The most distant unit was three miles off and its signal had been lost in the storm. While closer cameras were still downloading images, half their lenses were now covered over in snow.

And yet, one of them had picked up something that wasn't cold and dark.

He leaned closer, froze the image and then called Yvonne over. "Look at this."

She got up and walked to his side. Studying the screen, she saw a thermal image that was blurred and flickering. It looked like a blob of orange and blue on a field of black but became more distinct as High Point tapped at the keyboard.

"It's moving," he said.

"Track it," she ordered, suddenly concerned. "Zoom in."

High Point locked the thermal camera and tightened the focus. It resolved into a discernible picture. Four human-shaped targets riding on a pair of machines.

"Snowmobiles?"

"Hard to tell," he said. "They're not making a lot of heat. Based on the speed, though, I'd say yes."

Her heart began to pound. A sense of embarrassment at her earlier bravado hit, combined with the fury of dealing with more outside interference. "Where are they?"

"They're on the high side of the valley," he said. "Must be trying to stay out of the wind by hugging the ridgeline. But they're headed right for us."

The images began to fade as they pulled out of range.

"We're losing them."

"They should show up on the next camera any moment."

He tapped a key and the image switched. It was dark at first, and then the glowing shapes emerged out of the darkness.

"Send three of your men out to the drilling rig," she ordered. "You and the rest of them come with me. We're going to spring a trap and deal with this annoyance once and for all."

46

Kurt was at the controls of one snowmobile, with Joe seated behind him and two backpacks filled with explosive charges strapped to the sides. Paul and Gamay rode an identically loaded machine a few feet to their right and ten feet back.

The trip from the helicopter had been strenuous, as they fought the wind, the snowdrifts and the darkness. Of the three, the dark was the worst.

The snowmobiles had a night vision system built in. It linked to a heads-up display projected on the windshield in front of the driver. So far, it had proven itself to be almost useless.

Like most night vision systems, it worked by amplifying visible light. Yet amid a storm, in the middle of the Antarctic night, almost no light at all was reaching the ground. What it did pick up were millions of chaotically swirling snowflakes.

Switching to infrared mode proved slightly more effective. Kurt was able to see a difference between the landforms and the sky, the difference between rocks and snow. Ironically, the snow was warmer. But deep drifts and drop-offs were hard to spot. And despite riding at a reduced speed, they still had occasion to take urgent evasive action.

With little choice in the matter, they'd been forced to turn on the headlight that was tucked underneath each snowmobile's chin. Like fog lights on a sports car, it was supposed to illuminate the ground but not the falling snow. They offered, at best, fifty feet of visibility. Even that was an improvement.

Because Kurt had to concentrate so intently on the actual driving, he was relying on Joe for directions. Joe had the GPS tablet locked in a stand. He was using the map that Rudi and Hiram had created from the reconnaissance flight to help them avoid areas of rough terrain or fissures in the ice waiting to swallow them up.

"We're getting a little low on the slope," Joe said. "Bear right five degrees. And try to keep us in tight to the ridge, there's a boulder field approaching on the left."

Kurt eased to the right and rode up the slope, continuing forward and fighting against gravity like a car on a banked racetrack. He slowed a little as a series of volcanic outcroppings appeared in the dim light.

The rocks were covered in piles of snow on one side but stripped bare by the wind on the other. Their reddish brown color was a stark contrast to the achromatic black sky and white ground.

They passed through a gap between two of the larger boulders and the track widened once again. As they reached the other side, a flare shot off into the sky.

It curled upward and then tailed off into the storm, vanishing as it was carried away on the wind. Kurt knew they'd tripped some type of alarm.

He cut the throttle and killed the headlight, but it was already too late. As the machine slid to a halt, the snow-field came alive with the glare of high-intensity halogens. Four lights blinded them from directly ahead, a warm, incandescent hue suggesting older bulbs.

At the same time, a pair of stark white lights shone in from the left, with additional illumination from behind.

Before they could back up or turn, Kurt, Joe, Paul and Gamay were surrounded.

47

Shielding his eyes from the glare, Kurt saw that the vehicle ahead of them was a snowcat, while off to the side and behind was a trio of snowmobiles. He counted four automatic weapons pointed their way, led by a man with a long rifle who stood in front of the snowcat.

The man stepped forward, never once taking his rifle off Kurt. He stopped a few yards out of reach. "You blink and I'll kill you."

Kurt was honestly surprised he hadn't pulled the trigger already. He raised his hands and nodded to Paul and Gamay to do the same.

The door of the snowcat opened. A thinner, sleeker person stepped out. Kurt could tell this was a woman, he saw the blond hair streaming from under her wool cap. She stepped forward and walked right up to Kurt.

"NUMA," she said, pointing at the logo on the snow-mobiles. "I might have guessed."

Kurt nodded.

"Take off your balaclava," she ordered.

Slowly, so as not to provoke her, Kurt slid it down.

"Goggles," she demanded.

Kurt propped them up on his helmet.

"Of course," she said. "Kurt Austin. It would have to be you."

"Yvonne Lloyd," Kurt said.

"However did you guess?"

"We figured out your double life a while ago," he said. "Or, should I say, your brother's double life. You might as well lay down your weapons. There are squads of Arctic-trained soldiers no more than a mile behind us."

She didn't seem impressed. She turned to the man with the long rifle. He adjusted his stance for a second to look at an electronic tablet strapped to his arm. As he did, Kurt noticed the notches in the wooden stock of his rifle. Each group of four lines was crossed through with a fifth mark, like a prisoner counting off the days on the wall of his jail cell. If the marks were what Kurt assumed them to be, the man claimed at least sixteen victims.

The man looked up from the tablet and shook his head. "He's lying. They're alone."

Yvonne turned back to Kurt. "Lies won't help you at this point. You've snared yourself in my web. You'll soon be buried here and never heard from again."

Kurt held her stare. He noticed her words were clear and precise, as were the words of the man with the rifle.

His own speech was muffled and dull, the effect of lips too numb to form proper syllables.

He studied their machines, starting with the snowmobiles to his left and then looking over to the snowcat directly ahead. They were coated, as the fluffy white flakes stuck to the metal skin, where they melted slightly and then created a perfect surface for more snow to adhere to. The wipers on the snowcat ran back and forth, clearing a wide enough area to see through, leaving the rest of the windshield caked over.

They'd come from the warm out into the cold. And now they were standing in the swirling snow.

A thought arose in Kurt's mind. A way he might turn certain death into a chance of survival. He decided to keep them talking. The longer, the better.

"Killing us won't help you," Kurt said. "We know about the algae and the pipeline and the tankers you're using to spread the destruction north. Liang's ships will be stopped before they cross the equator and the business end of your pipeline will be obliterated by cruise missiles before it can pump anything into the sea."

She smiled and tilted her head to one side. "You do try so hard," she said, mocking him. "I'll give you that. Trust me, Kurt Austin, we have considered these possibilities. We have saboteurs on board each of the tankers. They'll blow the hulls apart from the inside at the first sign of a hostile boarding. As for the pipeline . . . . Well, broken pipes still leak. We don't care how the algae gets to the sea just as long as it gets there. So, pin your hopes on these moves, if you must. You'll only be disappointed. By attacking Liang's ships and smashing the end of our pipeline, you gain nothing but a bit of time. The algae will still fill the ocean. It will spread on the currents, growing, multiplying, as it makes its way to the polar regions. The ice age and the Earth's destruction will only be delayed, not stopped. And when it does come, it will hit all the more vengefully."

She smiled again, obviously enjoying the cat-and-mouse game and the position of power from which she could dictate and dominate. "But then," she added, "I think you know that already. You wouldn't be here, throwing your lives away, in a desperate effort to stop me. Just like your naïve little friend Cora."

Kurt bristled at the mention of Cora's name, but kept it from showing.

"Four dead troublemakers," she finished. "Remembered only as notches on the stock of High Point's gun."

Kurt squinted against the glare, looking straight at Yvonne and then past her to where one of her men was wiping the snow off the barrel of his weapon. It was time.

With his hands still up, Kurt glanced at Paul and Gamay, then turned back to Yvonne. The snow had begun to coat her hair, an adornment of frost.

"Cora didn't throw her life away," Kurt said. "Your friend over there missed. And what's more, he's about to miss again."

Kurt dropped onto the snowmobile, ducking behind the handlebars and twisting the throttle to full as he threw all his weight forward. The powerful electric motor provided instant torque, the tracks dug into the snow and the machine leapt forward as if it had been launched from a spring.

High Point reacted quickly, lowering the barrel of his rifle. As he pulled the trigger, the mechanism jammed. Snow had coated the weapon, melting because it was warm from being inside and then refreezing to solid ice as everything cooled off out in the frigid night air.

High Point moved to clear the weapon, banging his hand against the stock and pulling back the slide. But Kurt clipped him with the snowmobile as he raced by.

High Point was thrown backward. He slammed against the bumper of the snowcat and his body whiplashed around it like a wet rag. The back of his head smashed against the glass, leaving a circular indentation in the windshield, and he dropped face-first in the snow.

Paul and Gamay had known Kurt long enough to learn his patterns and to trust him. His sudden change from surrender to attack was not a surprise and Paul twisted the throttle of their snowmobile no more than a second after Kurt had.

They raced forward, shooting across the same gap and speeding along the trail. A smattering of gunshots followed, but they were late and inaccurate.

For her part, Yvonne hadn't expected the sudden attack, yet her reflexes were quick enough that she was able to dive out of the way. She got up and waved her people on, sending her own snowmobiles after the NUMA instigators.

As they sped by, she jumped into the snowcat and shouted at the driver. "Go."

The man put the big rig in gear and stepped on the accelerator. The machine surged forward, turning and driving over her former sharpshooter before swinging back in the direction of the NUMA team.

48

Kurt kept the speed up, much faster than was safe or reasonable.

"Their camp is a mile ahead," Joe said from behind him. "But the pumping station is out on the glacier."

"Glad you held on this time," Kurt said.

"Learned my lesson at the game park," Joe replied.

Kurt nodded, glancing in the mirror as Paul and Gamay caught up to them.

Riding side by side, Paul shouted to Kurt. "How'd you know their guns were going to jam like that?"

"Snow was sticking to everything they had," Kurt said. "I figured they'd gone from warm to cold. And that they hadn't left their guns outside to keep them cold."

"Great call," Paul shouted, "but they won't make that mistake again."

Gamay shouted next. "Hate to break up the chitchat, boys, but they're coming after us."

Kurt looked in the mirror again. He saw the intense white lights from the snowmobiles closing in on them and the warmer-colored lights of the snowcat farther back.

"Time to split up," Kurt said. "Go dark and head down into the valley. Joe and I will keep our lights blazing and try to lead them astray. Swing wide and make your way to the pumping station from the back side. That's your best chance. If we can shake them, we'll meet you down there. If not, we'll keep them busy."

"All right," Paul said. "Good luck."

Paul and Gamay left the trail and headed downslope while Kurt and Joe continued straight ahead. With nothing left to lose, Kurt switched on the high beams, hoping to make themselves a more obvious target.

The bright lights cut a hole through the darkness. The sensation the white ground and blowing snow created was like driving through a tunnel.

A soft pop-pop-pop of suppressed gunshots sounded, barely audible over the wind. Kurt heard a metallic clink as a shell hit the frame of the machine somewhere and watched as one of the mirrors shattered from the impact of another bullet.

"This trail is too straight," he said. "Going to go off-road." He cut to the right and sped up the slope, climbing at an easy angle. "How many are following us?"

Joe turned around and looked back over his shoulder. "All of them."

"That's good," Kurt said.

"They're gaining."

"Not so good. Aren't these sleds supposed to be fast?"

"They're carrying less weight and using gas-powered machines," Joe said. "The longer we run, the nearer they're going to get."

Needing more speed, Kurt turned parallel to the ridge once again and ran straight for a moment. Coming upon a slope with an easier grade, he cut all the way back, reversing direction and heading higher like he was taking a switchback road up into the mountains.

Yvonne's men skidded around the turn, three sleds trying to navigate a hairpin at the same time. Two of them crashed together, the third swung wide and raced forward like a rock hurled from a slingshot. The others quickly regained their composure and rejoined the chase.

"They're still gaining," Joe said. "And it looks like the snowcat has taken the more direct approach."

The heavy machine, with its low center of gravity and giant caterpillar tracks, had turned straight up the hill, climbing it with ease.

"I forgot they could do that. Any thoughts?"

"Only the one," Joe said.

Kurt could guess what he had in mind. "This ridge is wind-loaded with tons of snow."

"And the higher we go, the deeper it gets," Joe added.

Kurt straightened up once again, picking up some speed. "I'll try to get above them, you get the charges ready."

As Kurt turned up the slope again, Joe gripped the

frame of his seat with his knees and twisted around to reach one of the backpacks filled with explosive charges. He pulled the first charge out. It was the size and shape of a coffee can and contained twelve pounds of a dense explosive more powerful than C-4. Arming the device, Joe tossed it as far as he could in the snow above them. Grabbing a second charge, he did the same.

The third charge slipped out of his hand, bounced off the back side of the snowmobile and flew off into the darkness on the low side of the machine. "Don't worry, it's armed," he said, gripping the fourth charge more firmly. "Take us up, if you can."

Kurt turned slightly downhill, to pick up some speed, and then swung wide and turned uphill. He went up as steeply as he could, climbing and leaning forward, until the snowmobile's treads began to slip.

Releasing and adding power in an on/off fashion, he kept going for another twenty feet. But the snow was too soft and too deep. The snowmobile lost speed and sank in, burrowing forward until its tracks began spinning uselessly.

"It's no good," Kurt said. "This is as far as we go."

Joe tumbled off the back of the machine and into the snow. Kurt turned to see what awaited them.

The snowmobiles were cautiously following Kurt and Joe's tracks, coming higher and getting closer. The snowcat was grinding up toward them from below.

Joe emerged from the snow, stood tall and hurled the last charge. It landed no more than fifty feet away.

"We need to work on your arm strength," Kurt said.

Joe had another device in his hand and it wasn't for throwing. "As long as my button pushing skills are satisfactory, we should be fine."

The lights were on them now, converging from all directions. Kurt stared into the cab of the snowcat and saw Yvonne looking right at him.

He smiled. "Now."

Joe pressed the switch and a signal went out to the explosive charges. They detonated simultaneously, causing an instant and powerful shock wave.

The wind-loaded ridge shook with the blast and a thousand-foot-wide sheet of snow broke loose. It was only loosely attached to the ridge, having built up over recent weeks and during the last twenty-four hours of the storm. The ice beneath it was thick and firm yet brittle. It all gave way at once.

The initial break seemed to occur in slow motion. And then, suddenly, everything was moving and the avalanche began.

49

From inside the snowcat, Yvonne saw Kurt and his friend stuck in the deep snow. They'd gone for the top of the ridge and gotten caught trying desperately to climb over it.

"Run them down," she urged her driver. "Before they get free."

The snowcat climbed straight up the slope like cars clinking toward the top of a roller coaster track. The lights of the machine brightened the view, spreading across the snow and painting the trapped Americans in a warm glow. She saw Austin staring down at her, his frozen face looking concerned.

And then . . . he smiled.

The look chilled her to the core. *What did I miss?*

The charges went off a second later, four powerful

flashes erupting simultaneously. Three to the left, one almost directly in front of her.

The explosion threw a wave of snow into the windshield and the snowcat rocked backward and stopped. A deep and ominous resonance came next. It echoed around them, like a heavy wave crashing onto a beach. But instead of first increasing in volume and then fading, it grew louder and more intense with every passing second.

The snowcat began to slide backward as if it were on ice. It was sinking and turning even as a wall of snow surged toward them.

"Move," Yvonne shouted.

The driver was trying. When he mashed the gas pedal to the floor and moved the controls to the right, the ground beneath them was disintegrating and becoming part of the avalanche, the machine powerless to escape it.

She braced herself with both arms. The wall of snow hit, sending the big machine tumbling down the slope. Yvonne felt herself being thrown into the ceiling and then slammed to the door.

The windshield exploded inward in a shower of glass. Snow and ice poured through. The roof was crushed. Three of the four exterior lights blew out, though miraculously one remained operational even as its housing was bent downward and in.

Up and down lost all meaning, as they tumbled for another thirty seconds before slamming into some jutting volcanic rock.

The impact was like a head-on collision. It stopped

the tumbling instantly, but the avalanche wasn't over. Snow and ice poured into the cab, filling the space in a matter of seconds and trapping them.

Battered and bruised, Yvonne tried to climb free. She realized the machine was on its side, so she crawled upward, attempting to squirm through her side window.

She got her head and arms out the opening but found her legs and torso trapped by the packed snow that had forced its way into the cab.

She twisted and strained and with each passing second the pressure on her lower half increased. It felt as if her body was encased in wet concrete. She managed to get one arm through the window and to pull herself up a few more inches. There, she was stuck.

The snow continued to pour down the slope. A chunk of ice hit her in the shoulder, cracking something. Another hit her in the head. A final surge moved the snow-cat a few feet, twisting it to one side. And then suddenly it was over.

The avalanche had passed on by, its thundering call still audible downslope.

Yvonne's face and one arm were free, but she couldn't move. The pain in her shoulder was intense yet rapidly numbing. The wind continued to howl, cutting at her face and eyes. Snow was trickling here and there, the air was filled with a diamond dust of pulverized ice and snow.

She looked around and saw nor heard any sign of anyone else. No headlights. No engines. No cries for help. Nothing but wind and snow and darkness.

A choice flicked into her mind. Given the option of her own rescue or Austin's death in the same avalanche, she chose to hope that he'd died in the madness he'd caused.

While Kurt had been ready for the explosion, even he'd been surprised at how quickly the ground fell out from beneath them.

The snowmobile vanished from sight, as if sucked down into a vortex. Joe jumped to one side and began to run uphill, trying to get above and around the trouble.

Kurt did the same, turning and struggling up, but it was like running against the powerful undertow of outgoing waves at the beach. His legs just didn't seem to move. He made it four or five steps before his feet were pulled from beneath him and he was being dragged backward by a force more powerful than any riptide.

As he slid, the snow churned around him like foam. It washed over him, swept him along and pulled him under.

He moved his arms as if swimming, because he'd heard that advice given for people caught in an avalanche. Whether it did a bit of good or not, Kurt didn't know. He did the breaststroke with his arms anyway and kept his legs moving.

In the middle of the turmoil, his feet hit something firm. He pushed off, launching himself upward. He emerged above the snow and was soon tossed aside.

Now outside the avalanche, Kurt tumbled and slid,

coming to a stop on the hard-packed snow. He ended up sprawled out, watching as the avalanche continued down the hill. It moved with the sound of a freight train, roaring through the night.

He noticed one of the snowmobiles tumbling like a child's toy. He saw the lights of the other machines being dragged away. They dimmed as a fog of atomized snow spread across the slope and then vanished as the avalanche swallowed up the machines and buried them deep.

Eventually the sound and fury began to fade. The moving snow was now slowing, spreading out and settling in the valley below. In its wake, a kind of quiet returned. To Kurt's surprise, it seemed almost peaceful.

He stood up wearily, studying a landscape remade. A huge swath had been gouged out from the mountain. A bed of rock had been exposed and a long tongue of debris revealed. Downslope from him, the land was featureless and white. A single amber light burned at an odd angle, pointed down into the drifts. He recognized it as belonging to the snowcat.

Looking around, Kurt saw nothing of the snowmobiles, but something else loomed out of the dark.

At first, it appeared to be an outcropping of volcanic rock, like those they'd passed in the valley, but as Kurt stepped closer, he saw it was actually a large gray fin. It resembled the dorsal fin of a giant shark but was made of metal.

The fin was canted over at an angle but connected at the base to a wide metal hull. A few feet ahead of it the blades of an old-fashioned propeller broke the surface. They were still attached to the bulky engine that powered them. Thirty feet to one side a wingtip reached through the snow like an outstretched arm.

Kurt stepped closer to the fin, which he recognized now as the tail and rudder of an aircraft. He brushed the snow from the frozen metal, revealing weathered but still readable letters. The word *Thrace* was painted in curving script. Next to it was the unmistakable image of a Nazi flag.

"The German expedition," Kurt whispered.

Kurt could barely believe what he was seeing. Only then did it dawn on him that he was seeing it alone. He turned, looking for any sign of his partner.

"Joe!"

There was no answer.

"Joe! Can you hear me?"

Kurt turned from point to point. There was no answer to his calls. That could mean only one thing: Joe was buried somewhere under the snow.

50

Kurt's mind cleared as a surge of adrenaline raced through his body. He put aside the discovery of the old plane and gazed through the dark looking for any sign of his friend.

Time was now the enemy. A person could survive being buried in the snow for a while, but the maximum duration was around eighteen minutes. In the end, it wasn't lack of oxygen that killed him but carbon dioxide. Even hard-packed snow contained plenty of oxygen in between the ice crystals, but as a person trapped within it exhaled, the carbon dioxide built up in the snow around the person's face. Eventually it became so concentrated that the person lost consciousness. Death followed within minutes.

Kurt glanced at the oversize watch strapped to the outside of his expedition jacket. It read 3:12 a.m. If he didn't find Joe and dig him out by 3:30, Joe would almost certainly suffer brain damage or die.

Before he began a search, Kurt needed a way to keep his bearings. Otherwise he'd be wandering around in all directions. He dug into a pocket and pulled out a rescue flare. He lit it and stuck it in the snow near the exposed tail of the old aircraft. It burned and crackled, giving off an uneven red glow.

With the flare and the dim light from the snowcat acting as reference points, Kurt began a search, zigzagging back and forth, covering a hundred feet on either side of the line.

He switched the heating unit in his coat on, knowing he needed to stay warm or he'd lose speed. Tapping a second button by the collar, he switched on the lights embedded in the front of the jacket. It made him an obvious target, but he doubted anyone from Yvonne's crew remained alive to shoot at him. And at this point, he didn't much care if there was.

Higher up, the ground was hard and icy. The fresh snow from this part of the ridge had been swept away. Joe had to be farther down.

Kurt moved lower until he came to an area where his boots sank halfway to his calves. Here he widened his search and picked up the pace. He soon found a glove, and then a hat, but neither item was NUMA issue. A minute later he came upon a section of tread that had been torn off the snowcat. Broken bits of plastic lay nearby, but still there was no sign of Joe.

He swung back the other way, trudging through the

snow and burying his chin in the collar of his jacket to keep it out of the wind.

He looked and looked and then stopped. How many yards had he gone? He turned around to find he'd wandered farther this time. The cold and the exhaustion had started to affect him.

He dropped down a few more yards and started back toward his centerline. His watch read 3:21. "Come on, Joe," he muttered through numb lips. "Give me a sign."

Catching his foot on something, Kurt fell to his knees. Turning with a start, he reached for the offending object and brushed the snow away. A handlebar appeared, and then the stub of a shattered mirror. It was the NUMA snowmobile.

Common sense told him Joe should have ended up near the machine, but common sense didn't always hold in the chaos of an avalanche. Kurt stood up, looking around in all directions. He had to start digging soon, but where?

An idea came to mind, and Kurt began digging right where he stood. He jammed his hands into the snow and scooped out large heaps of the frozen and crystallized water. He worked with absolute intensity, his heart pounding against the wall of his chest, his head throbbing.

With the snowmobile over on its side, Kurt was able to clear the area around the seat and soon found what he was looking for: the tablet computer that Joe had used to navigate.

The screen was cracked and the stand it was locked into had been bent to one side, but the device lit up when Kurt touched it.

Unlocking the clamp that held it, Kurt pulled it free and opened a program. Thankfully, NUMA gloves were designed to work with iPads and other touch screens.

After launching the tracking program, Kurt tapped the search icon. The expedition jackets contained tracking beacons. If Joe was lying in the snow somewhere, the warmth from his body and the heated clothing would melt enough ice to make the sensor think he'd fallen overboard. Or if Joe's hand was in the right place, he could activate the beacon himself.

After Kurt waited for what seemed like an eternity, the GPS localized and a signal appeared.

Kurt estimated the bearing and charged downhill. As he closed in on the spot, the snow grew deeper and softer. Soon he was sinking halfway to his knees.

He stopped directly on top of the marker. There was no sign of Joe at the surface, but considering the GPS was accurate to within eighteen inches, Joe had to be right beneath him.

Kurt put the tablet down and started digging, excavating the first foot of snow in a few quick scoops. The second foot was removed just as easily but the deeper Kurt went, the harder it was to dig.

He widened the hole, dropped down into it, and kept digging until his hand hit something metal. Scraping the snow away, he discovered a long narrow shaft. One end had a spear-like tip while the other was wide and flat.

Kurt pulled it free and began using it as a shovel, digging with the flat end and heaving the snow over his shoulder as he went. His pace quickened. He'd soon created a pit almost as wide as it was deep. He stopped when he noticed something in the dark.

Turning his own lights off, he waited a second for his eyes to adjust. A soft glow was rising through the crystalline snow. He could see the outline of a man.

Using the pointed end of the shaft, Kurt drilled carefully downward toward the figure. Pulling the shaft out, he drilled a second hole and then a third, all of them within inches of what he hoped was Joe's face. The idea was to vent the carbon dioxide and allow oxygen to replace it. If he was close, it would give Joe more time.

After punching a half dozen holes as deeply as he dared, Kurt got back to digging. With two more feet of snow removed, he found Joe's arm and then his shoulder.

Tossing the improvised shovel aside, Kurt dropped to his knees and began digging with his hands once again.

A swatch of dark hair appeared. Kurt grasped it and pulled.

"Joe," he shouted. "Can you hear me? Tell me you're alive."

Joe's eyes opened just a sliver and he coughed as if he were choking on something.

Kurt began brushing the snow from Joe's eyes, clearing it roughly from his nose and mouth. "Are you all right?"

Joe blinked and squinted. "I will be," he said. "When you stop scraping my face with your gloves like that."

Kurt pulled his hand back and laughed. He went back to digging, clearing Joe's arms and then his torso. Joe was soon squirming back and forth, trying to free his legs.

Kurt offered a hand, and with a powerful heave, he pulled Joe free.

Climbing out of the pit, both men collapsed against the pile of snow Kurt had excavated.

While Kurt allowed his muscles a well-deserved rest, Joe breathed deep and slow, replenishing the oxygen in his blood. He stretched every muscle, testing his limbs one by one. Incredibly, nothing was broken. "Next time," he said, eyeing Kurt, "you push the button."

Kurt nodded and laughed but said nothing. He noticed Joe looking past him, out across the slope to where the exposed tail of the old German flying boat was lit up by the flare.

"When did that get here?" Joe asked, sounding puzzled.

"About eighty years ago," Kurt said. "It's Jurgenson's plane."

"You're kidding me?"

"Nope."

"I suppose that explains your shovel," Joe said, pointing to the makeshift tool that Kurt had used to dig him free.

Kurt turned toward it, examining it in detail for the first time. It was a three-foot shaft of metal with a weighted point at one end and broad fins at the other. Only now did Kurt see the slightly raised swastikas on each of its tail fins.

Kurt shook his head at the discovery, wryly amused. "Well," he said. "At least we know we've come to the right place."

51

With no one on their tails, Paul and Gamay cruised safely across the surface of the glacier. They rode on a foot of soft powder that cushioned the ride and muffled all sound.

With the lights off, Paul was driving almost blind, but Gamay kept up a steady stream of directions, vectoring him around obstacles and toward the target.

"Wish I could see more than fifty feet ahead," Paul announced.

"Just keep your eyes on the road and do everything I tell you," Gamay said.

"You must be loving this," Paul joked. "It's every backseat driver's fantasy."

She laughed. "Bear to the left fifteen degrees. And

pick up the speed, you're driving like my ninety-year-old nana."

Paul smiled and did as directed. They swung out wide and then back to the pumping station. Once he turned toward it, there was no mistaking the target. In a sea of gray and black, the station appeared on the infrared screen like an inferno. Heat poured from several individual vents, trailing away on the wind, while a few dim lights illuminated the area around it.

As they closed in on the target, Paul slowed their approach. What appeared to be blazing fires on the infrared screen were actually plumes of superheated steam blasting out of several pipes.

The steam rose into the air, streaming on the breeze and condensing into snow. It fell in huge piles, creating a small hill downwind of the station.

Paul came in behind one of them, using it to shield them from any lookouts or cameras. With the motor disengaged, the snowmobile stopped directly behind the artificial ski slope.

"A real blizzard wasn't enough for you?" Gamay said, admiring the ice crystals falling all around them. "You had to park under a snowmaking machine, too?"

"Maybe I just want to test my hat in extreme conditions."

Gamay laughed. "Couldn't get much more extreme than this."

They climbed off the snowmobile and scanned the area for trouble. "No sign of guards," Paul said, "but that doesn't mean there aren't any. They could be hiding or underground."

Paul grabbed a backpack and slung it over one shoulder. It held four of the explosive charges. Gamay grabbed a second pack, but Paul put out a hand. "I'll take that."

"This is no time for chivalry."

"I'm not trying to be gallant," he said. "Just being smart. One of us should be armed and you're the better shot, the more agile person and the smaller target. I'll be the pack mule. You keep me safe."

Gamay hesitated for a second and then handed the pack over. "Paul Trout," she said. "You never cease to amaze me."

Without another word, she pulled a short-barreled MP5 machine pistol from the back of the snowmobile. Having seen what happened to Yvonne's gunmen, she checked the action and cycled it twice to make sure it wouldn't jam.

With the weapon in her hands and the safety off, she began a careful march toward the nearest exhaust stacks.

The first thing they came across was a huge machine. It was covered in frost and partially wrapped in tattered canvas from tarps that had been ripped free by the wind before getting caught in the machinery.

"Drilling rig," Paul said. Beside it were stacks of pipe, all covered in snow.

"They don't seem to be using it," Gamay replied.

"They'd use this to drill through the rock and tap into the geothermal layer," he said. "Then they use the hot water and high-pressure steam to bore a tunnel through the glacier. We did a similar thing in Greenland last year."

As Paul finished speaking, a sound like thunder echoed across the valley. It was muffled and distorted by the storm, but it was unmistakable.

Both he and Gamay looked up and gazed into the distance. They saw nothing but a few dim lights on the ridge, half hidden by the storm. While the lights went out quickly, the thunder continued to roll.

"Avalanche," Paul said. "Could be Kurt and Joe."

"Could be anything," Gamay said. "Let's not dawdle."

They moved past the drilling rig, arriving beside the nearest of the exhaust ports and ducking under the high-pressure blast of steam coming out of it. They found the port to be a steel tube four inches in diameter. It stuck out of the ground a couple feet and was surrounded by a pool of water and slush where the heat from the pipe continuously melted the snow and ice.

Paul dropped the packs and pulled out the first charge. He compared it to the pipe. "I'd like to dump these down the chimney and be done with it," he said. "But we have a problem."

"What's that?"

"Four-inch pipe, six-inch explosive."

"Even if we could drop them into the pipes," Gamay said, "the pressure of that steam might just launch them into the sky like mortars. We're going to have to go inside."

"How? I don't see any door or hatch."

"There were lines on Rudi's map," she said. "The system labeled them as fissures because they were depressions, but when I zoomed in I could see that they were all dead straight. Short and geometrical. They're either tunnels or trenches. One of them led directly here from what we suspected was the habitat. Something tells me that's where we'll find the front door."

She pointed to a spot past the other exhaust pipes.

Paul stood up, took a couple steps and then fell as gunfire rang out and searing pain cut through his right thigh.

Gamay dove to the ground and returned fire, her shots cutting through the wind and hitting the edge of the very trench she and Paul had been looking for. A pair of men hidden there ducked down as the bullets from the MP5 blasted the snow and ice around them.

Wounded in the leg but not interested in standing anyway, Paul crawled on his stomach back to Gamay.

"You're hit," she said.

He nodded. "I'd like to say it's only a scratch but I think it's more than that." He reached down to feel for the hole. He found an entry wound on the front of his thigh and an exit wound on the back. "Think it went through the muscle and out. That's both good and bad. At least the bullet didn't hit the bone and shatter it."

As Gamay unleashed another barrage from the MP5, Paul dug down into the snow, scooping out handfuls and packing the wound. That would help the blood coagulate and would reduce the searing pain.

"How many gunmen do you see out there?" he asked.

"Two or three," Gamay said. "But they're down in that trench."

That didn't sound promising. "Please tell me those trenches don't circumnavigate our current position?"

"Not that I saw," she said. "And I can keep them pinned down, so they won't be too much of a threat, but we're not going to be able to get to them either."

"Stalemate," Paul said, "which means they win."

"We can't allow that," she said.

Gamay triggered off another couple shots. "We could use the snowmobile as an assault craft," she said. "Charge them at high speed while keeping our heads down."

"That might work," Paul said. "But even if we could cross the open ground between here and the trench, we still have to get into the trench and fight those men without getting shot. Considering I'm already limping, I don't love our chances."

"We could hurl the explosives at them."

"What's your best shot put distance?" Paul asked.

Gamay looked up. "Not seventy yards into the wind. We'll have to get closer. Unless you have another plan?"

Paul thought almost anything sounded better than trying to charge armed men in a trench. "You said something about mortars earlier."

She looked puzzled. "You can't fit the explosives into the pipe."

"Not that pipe," Paul said. "The other ones will do just fine."

Gamay was lying prone in the snow, looking through

her sight at the trench. She scanned it back and forth to make sure she wasn't focusing on only one spot. Every time she saw movement, she fired. "I have ten shots left and a spare magazine. I can pin them down while you do whatever it is you're going to do."

Paul crushed some more snow into his wound and began to crawl away. "Stay here," he said, before switching into his best impersonation of the Terminator. "I'll be baaack."

With Gamay laying down sporadic shots of harassing fire, Paul made his way to the snow-covered stacked pipe. It was unused equipment meant for the original drilling rig. The long sections, called pipe string, were not going to help him. They were forty feet in length and too heavy for a person to move. Shorter sections, called couplers, designed to link lengths of pipe string together, would do the trick.

He dug the snow away from a stack of couplers and pulled a six-foot length free. Using another pipe to support it, he wedged it into the snow at a shallow angle, twisting and shoving and leaning all his weight against it until at least a foot of the pipe was buried in the snow.

Now came the tricky part—setting the elevation. This was pure guesswork, since he had no idea about the wind and the force that his homemade weapon would produce, but he kept it low, reasoning that a bouncing and rolling explosive would be more effective than a bomb that flew well past the trench.

With the pipe wedged in and roughly aimed, Paul slipped the backpack off his shoulders. He pulled out the first explosive, set a switch on the face of it to 1. He slid that charge into the end of the pipe. It fit, with an inch to spare on either side.

With the first charge at the bottom of the pipe, he pulled out the other explosive charges, lined them up and set all their detonation selectors to 2.

If everything went as planned, the first explosive would act as the powder of a cannon, launching the other three charges as projectiles.

Now all he needed was some wadding, something to prevent the explosive force from bypassing the projectiles or ripping them apart. He emptied the backpack and stuffed it in the pipe, pushing it down as far as his long arm would allow.

Shining a light into the pipe, he could see he needed more. He looked around him, considered what he might find back on the snowmobile and then made a quick decision.

Pulling off his oversize Canadian hat, he reluctantly stuffed it into the tube. After packing it down, he slotted the other explosives into the barrel, one on top of the other.

In the distance he could hear Gamay trading fire with the men in the trench. He hoped he was about to give them a big surprise. With the detonator in hand, he crawled to a safe distance, dropped flat to the snow and selected 1 on the detonator.

Covering his head, he pressed the button. A hollow boom sounded, and the pipe itself blew apart, with fragments flying in all directions.

In the flash of light, Paul saw the charges being hurtled through the air. He watched with great pride as they flew toward their adversaries, landed and skidded through the snow in the general direction of the trench.

Seeing this, Paul switched the detonator to 2 and pressed the button again. Three explosions went off in rapid order. One in front of the trench, one behind the trench and the third from inside it.

Fire, snow and smoke blasted upward in a long, straight line. The walls of the trench were blasted outward before collapsing in. The detonation seemed to calm the wind for a second. By the time it returned, Gamay was up and running, charging toward the target like a soldier storming the beach.

Paul followed the best he could. When he arrived, Gamay had taken the trench without firing a shot.

There were three men in the trench. Two of them appeared dead. The third was bleeding and burnt in places. He raised his hands before lapsing into shock and losing consciousness.

Gamay took their guns just in case.

"Well, we've secured the area," Paul said. "Now what?"

Gamay shone a light toward the end of the trench. A heavy steel door stood there. It resembled a watertight hatch on a ship. "Now we find out if we have enough explosives left to get through that."

52

When Joe had recovered enough from his time under the snow, he and Kurt backtracked to the snowmobile. They dug it out and righted it. The machine was damaged, but still operational, and the hardy electric motors sprang to life the instant Kurt twisted the accelerator on the bent handlebar.

While the motor was fine, the battery pack was not. It registered twenty percent and the icon on the dash was flashing yellow.

"Let's go find Paul and Gamay," Joe said. "Before we end up walking."

"One stop first."

Kurt eased the machine down the slope, conserving power and allowing gravity to do most of the work. They slid to a stop several feet from where the snowcat had come to rest. The last surviving light was growing dim, but it still cast an amber circle across a few feet of the snow.

Kurt got off and walked toward it. He found Yvonne stuck in the snow, buried up to her chin. Her face was frozen white, covered in frost.

Joe came up beside him. "She might still be alive. Should we dig her out?"

Kurt glanced at his watch. They'd lost too much time already. "Leave her," he said, turning back toward the snowmobile.

"But Kurt . . ."

"She killed half a dozen crewmen on the *Grishka*," Kurt said. "Shot them in their sleep. This is a better end than she deserves."

Joe didn't argue the point. He climbed back on the snowmobile and grabbed the handholds as Kurt twisted the throttle. They drove around the buried snowcat and down toward the glacier.

T hree . . . two . . . one . . ."

As Paul and Gamay crouched fifty yards away from the steel door, Paul pressed the button on the detonator. They'd decided the best plan was to use a pair of the charges on the door and save the second pair for the turbine once they got inside.

The detonation sent a column of fire upward and back, blasting a ten-foot crater in the snow around the door. When the smoke cleared, the door, blackened and dented but unbroken, still stood.

"Well, that didn't work," Paul said.

They examined the blast's pattern and discovered the problem. While the door had been singed and bent in slightly, the force of the blast had merely rebounded, surged outward, making the V-shaped crater and sending a fireball down it.

"We're going to need something heavy to direct the explosion into the door," Paul said.

"If we use these last explosives, we might not be able to destroy the turbine once we get inside," Gamay replied.

"We won't be able to do anything if we don't get in there," Paul countered.

"Maybe we could knock the door down with our snowmobile," she said. "This trench makes for a perfect alleyway."

Paul nodded. "Worth a shot."

Gamay climbed on the machine while Paul packed the snow down in front of the door and then limped out of the way. She backed the snowmobile down into the trench, using the slope created by the initial mortar explosion.

Once she was inside the trench, she lined the snowmobile up and started her run.

Moving slow at first, she opened the throttle wide and secured it in place with the thumb lock. As the machine sped up, Gamay slipped off the back and slid in the snow, covering her head until she came to a stop.

She looked up in time to see the snowmobile careening down the trench. It sideswiped one wall, bounced off the other side and straightened up just before slamming into the steel door.

The fiberglass nose of the snowmobile shattered. The door on the receiving end of the blow buckled and flew off its hinges. The machine came to a stop on its side with the tracks still spinning. The door lay on the ground a few feet away.

Standing up, Gamay stared proudly at the destruction. "That was oddly satisfying," she said, rubbing her shoulder, which had taken the brunt of her landing.

"I'll be sure to enter you in a demolition derby," Paul replied.

As the two of them admired their work, they kept their eyes on the door, which was lit up brightly by the lights on the front of their jackets.

What they didn't see was the injured member of Yvonne's tactical team stirring. He'd been knocked out cold by the original explosion and felt like a rag doll when Paul and Gamay laid him in the snow beside his comrades. Burns on his face and blood oozing from several shrapnel wounds had made them think he'd been killed by the blast, but he wasn't dead and had now regained consciousness.

He saw the door cave in. He heard the two of them talking. And despite the ringing in his ears and a general state of confusion, he knew what he had to do.

He stood awkwardly and began walking toward them. He pulled a hunting knife from the sheath in his boot, gripped it tightly, testing and retesting the strength of his hand as he got closer. With his anger fueling him, he charged forward.

Gamay heard the footsteps coming and turned to see the man racing toward them. "Paul."

The man crashed into both of them, sending her tumbling into the trench and taking Paul to the ground.

Gamay watched in horror as the attacker straddled Paul, raising the knife above his head for the kill shot.

Just as the man's arm reached its maximum extension, his back arched suddenly and the point of a spear burst from his chest. His mouth opened but no sound came forth, only blood. He toppled over onto his side, dropped the knife and lay in the snow not moving.

Gamay ran to Paul as a snowmobile slid to a stop beside them. Kurt was at the controls. Joe had thrown the spear from the spot behind him.

Paul squirmed out from under the dead man, pushing and sliding backward. "Never thought I'd be happy to see someone harpooned."

Gamay checked the man with the spear poking through his chest. He was definitely dead now.

Stepping away from him, she turned to Kurt and Joe. "We thought we'd lost you. We heard the avalanche."

"You almost lost me," Joe said. "Kurt took his sweet time digging me out. I think he even stopped for a coffee break halfway through."

Kurt laughed and explained the search and rescue effort. Then he explained why they'd created the avalanche and what happened after.

"Are Yvonne and her people gone?" Gamay asked.

"Yvonne is buried and frozen," Kurt said. "But something else was unearthed, or perhaps *uncovered* would be a better choice of word."

"And what might that be?" Gamay asked suspiciously.

"The Dornier flying boat that Captain Jurgenson crash-landed. It was up there on the ridge. When Joe set off the explosives, the avalanche cleared eighty years of snow, revealing the plane's last resting place."

"And the spear?" Paul asked.

"It's one of the Nazi markers from the expedition," Joe replied. "We found several of them lying around back there."

"That's amazing," Gamay said.

Kurt agreed. "Assuming we can put a stop to all of this, it might be fun to come back and excavate the old aircraft."

"As long as we come in the summer," Gamay said.

"Then let's make sure there's going to be a summer," Kurt replied. "What's the story here?"

Gamay explained how they'd fought their way to the front door and had finally smashed it in. "We were about to go inside. Care to join us?"

Kurt grinned. Right on time. "Wouldn't miss it for the world."

53

With weapons drawn, Kurt, Joe and Gamay entered the bunker. The roof, walls and floor were plated with steel. The walls sloped inward at the top, a design that helped support the weight of the ice and snow above it.

While the three of them moved inside, Paul remained on guard near the entrance where he could be warmed by the heat escaping the station.

As soon as they were out of earshot, Kurt turned to Gamay. "How bad is Paul's leg?"

"Worse than he's letting on," Gamay said. "But the bleeding has mostly stopped."

Paul would need help soon. The loss of blood would magnify the effects of the cold. His body would struggle to compensate. Falling into shock was a distinct possibility.

"As soon as this is done, we'll break into the habitat," Kurt said. "We can shelter there, wait out the storm and dig around for medical supplies."

Gamay nodded. "Do you think we'll face any more resistance?"

Kurt shook his head. "No one bothered Joe and me after we got out of the snow. No one showed up to rescue Yvonne. If there's any resistance left, we're going to find it in here."

"Or more likely," Joe said, "down there."

They'd come to a gap in the metal floor. It was a portal to a vertical shaft that dropped straight down.

While the bunker was steel, the shaft had been carved, or more likely melted, from the solid ice of the glacier. The walls were smooth and the hole was almost fifteen feet in diameter. A sturdy pair of steel beams stretched across the gap. Several cables hung from a pulley system connected to counterweights and a heavy-duty winch. They dropped down into the darkness, connected to something that could not be clearly seen.

"Lifting cable and counterweights," Joe said.

"But no elevator," Gamay said. "There's never one around when you need it."

"I think it's down there," Kurt said.

"You want to bring it up?" Joe said, pointing to the controls.

"And let them know we're coming?" Kurt said. "No thanks."

He swung his weapon over his shoulder and climbed

onto the beam, stepping carefully until he reached the central cable.

"You shouldn't go alone," Gamay said.

"We only have two explosive charges," Kurt said. "There's no sense in all of us risking our lives to set them. Besides, I might need the two of you to pull me back up if anything goes wrong."

Dropping down, he swung his leg out and hooked the cable with his foot. Easing off the beam, he wrapped his hands around the cable and began a controlled slide.

Picking up a little too much speed, he gripped the cable tighter, allowing the friction to bite into his gloves and slow him down. He reached the bottom, touched down almost silently and pulled the MP5 from his shoulder.

Crouching near the wall, he glanced around. The shaft had brought him to the intersection of two tunnels—or galleries, as miners sometimes called them. One went off to the left, but it was narrow and short, and as he shone a light into it he could see the far end. It had either been abandoned early or excavated for some other purpose. He saw tools and gear stored in there, but nothing important.

The other tunnel was far more impressive. Twice as wide and deeper, it had electrical cables running along the wall and was an off color, to a degree. Stepping closer, Kurt found the walls to be translucent to a depth of several inches. He could see metallic mesh hidden inside. Its appearance reminded him of the submersible that had rammed the *Grishka*.

Touching the walls, he found them to be cold and wet yet oddly granular instead of slick. They were made of ice, but some strange form of ice he'd never seen before. Despite the heat in the complex, he saw little evidence of melting.

He wondered if Ryland and Yvonne had used their algae to shore up the walls or if they'd found some other way to manipulate the formation of ice crystals. Deciding that was something to ponder later, Kurt began exploring this larger tunnel. He could hear and feel a machine-like hum coming from the far end.

He moved cautiously, noticing that the floor led slightly downslope and was marred by parallel grooves where something heavy had been dragged along it.

Kurt hugged the wall and moved deeper. The humming grew more pronounced, a definite high-speed vibration. It had to be the turbine.

The tunnel widened at the far end. An opening yawned directly ahead of Kurt, while on the right he saw a large machine with a circular, convex front. It sat motionless on a pair of Caterpillar tracks. It reminded him of a drilling machine without the bit on the end.

After a cursory exam, he bypassed it and arrived at the opening to a large cavern.

The interior looked like the floor of a power plant or a factory left over from the early days of the Industrial Revolution. Pipes of all sizes crisscrossed the ceiling and floors. A makeshift boiler and steam engine were connected to reduction gears that were linked, in turn, to the turbine system brought in by Tunstall Industries.

The turbine was connected to a pair of large-diameter pipes that entered from one side of the room and pierced the wall on the far side, heading toward the sea. The operation buzzed and hummed like the engine room of a great ship, but Kurt saw no one at the controls.

He took a step forward and saw movement. A man with a shotgun appeared from behind the steam engine. Kurt pulled back as the man fired. The spread of buckshot tore into the wall, showering Kurt with chips of ice.

"I won't let you stop us," the man shouted. "Not now."

Kurt glanced into the room and saw an older man with stevedore arms hiding behind part of the steam engine. He pumped the shotgun and fired again.

Kurt spun backward and pressed himself against the wall. The man seemed to be handy with the shotgun. Even if he hadn't been, the twelve-gauge wasn't the type of weapon that required a marksman.

"Yvonne and the others are dead," Kurt shouted. "You don't have to die with them."

The man started laughing. "I was willing to sacrifice myself the moment I got involved. You think I'm going to change my mind now? Trust me, you're going to be the one who dies here. Not me."

Kurt dropped to the floor, peeked around the corner and fired back. Sparks flew from the steel frame of the large piston, but it kept churning. The man stepped behind it, firing blindly around the corner without looking.

Pulling back once more, Kurt considered the dilemma. There was little chance of getting into the room without getting cut down by the shotgun, but, like Paul and Gamay had realized earlier, a stalemate was a win for the other side.

He shrugged off the backpack and pulled out the charges. He wanted to save them for destroying the pumps yet was willing to bet that one, in just the right place, could do the job.

He took out a charge, set it to sequence 1 and armed it. Pressing his back against the wall, he readied himself to throw it. "Sorry, old man," he said to himself. "I need you out of the way."

With a swing of his arm, Kurt hurled the twelve-pounder around the corner. It flew in the general direction of the cave's lone defender.

A pair of shotgun blasts rang out in quick succession, but Kurt was safely back behind the wall. He dropped to one knee and pressed the detonator button.

Nothing happened.

He reset it, double-checked that the selector was turned to sequence 1 and pressed it again.

Still nothing.

"What the . . ."

Kurt risked a glance around the corner and instantly saw the problem. The explosive charge lay on the ground in pieces. The guy had literally shot it out of the air like a clay pigeon.

"Crafty old codger," he said.

Kurt reached into the pack for the last of the explosives. This one he'd detonate midair, rushing in behind it and using the explosion for cover like a flashbang grenade.

Before he could arm the charge, the machine beside him cranked to life.

"Now it's my turn," the man shouted from the cavern beyond.

Spinning around on its tracks, the van-sized machine surged toward Kurt, attempting to crush him against the wall.

Kurt dove out of the way and rolled to the side, but it surged toward him again.

Backing down the tunnel, Kurt leveled the MP5 and opened fire. Bullets hit and ricocheted off its bulbous nose. Dents appeared, along with several punctures, yet the machine kept coming. A second burst was similarly ineffective.

Without warning, the nose began to spin. Superheated jets of water blasted out around the rim, scouring the walls and instantly filling the tunnel with steam. In seconds, the visibility dropped to mere feet. Still, Kurt could hear the machine grinding forward.

He had no choice but to retreat as the monster emerged from the fog. He fired again and again and all he managed to do was punch a few more holes in the high-pressure dome. As a result, new blasts of steam shot forward, nearly scalding him.

Kurt ducked and backed up farther. He had no desire to set off the last of the explosives, especially not in a tunnel with a thousand tons of ice hanging over his head, but could see no way around the machine and no way to stop it.

Backing up to the vertical shaft, Kurt armed the last charge and slid it down the icy hall. It went right down the middle. "So glad I watched all that curling during the last Olympics."

Ducking around the corner of the shaft for cover, Kurt pressed the detonator switch.

This time, the bomb went off.

The blast traveled upward, through the heart of the relentless machine. Deflected by the ceiling, the pressure wave surged along the hall in both directions. It swept into the vertical shaft, slamming Kurt against the wall in the process.

When the echo receded, Kurt looked around. He saw nothing but fog.

"You okay down there?" Joe shouted.

Kurt's ears were ringing from the gunfire and the explosion. He could barely make out what Joe was saying.

"Never better," he shouted back.

Stepping back into the tunnel, he found the visibility was no more than two or three feet. He moved forward, listening to the sounds of water dripping and steam hissing but not the squeaking of the tank-like tracks under the machine or the grinding of its rotary nose. A thin layer of boiling water trickled down the center of the hall.

Easing forward, Kurt came upon the shattered aggressor. The tracks had been blown off to either side and much of the machinery bent and mangled. Water was leaking from its tanks while steam vented upward into the ceiling above.

Kurt moved toward the less damaged side, easing past the wreckage, careful not to get scalded. He reached the far end and stopped.

The explosion had literally brought the house down. An impassable jumble of ice filled the tunnel beyond. It had buried the back half of the machine and was blocking all access to the cave. More ominously, small chunks of ice were still shifting and falling while jets of steam sprayed upward from cracks in the machine's boiler. Even now Kurt could see that the steam was cutting into the weakened ceiling.

As Kurt stood there, contemplating how long it might take to dig through to the other side, the sound of cracking slithered through the hallway above him. Looking up, he saw a section of the reinforced ice shift and fall.

"Time to go," he said to himself.

He slipped past the wreck and ran for the escape shaft. Reaching it, he jumped onto the platform and flipped the control lever to the rise position.

The platform lurched upward, but the pace felt painfully slow to Kurt. He held on as the cavern shook and the platform swayed.

A new explosion of steam surged upward as more of the tunnel below collapsed. Unfortunately, the imploding tunnel and shifting ice were destabilizing the vertical shaft. Cracks snaked up the side while sheets of curved ice broke loose and fell toward him.

A small chunk hit one of the cables and started the platform rocking. A larger piece dropped from the wall fifty feet above and could have crushed him. Kurt dodged it, but it slammed into the platform, tilting the platform precariously to one side.

Higher up, Joe and Gamay released the counterweights. The platform rose quickly, banging to a stop as it reached the top.

As Kurt leapt off it, the ground beneath their feet shook and a large section of the shaft gave way.

Kurt glanced back down into the well, the bottom third was plugged with ice and debris. There would be no getting through that. Nor was it safe to stay any longer.

"We should probably get out of here," Gamay said.

The three of them ran for the exit, moving out into the frigid night and stopping only when they'd cleared the exploded doorway.

"What happened down there?" Paul asked. "Did you blow the turbine?"

Joe and Gamay looked at Kurt.

Kurt looked off into the distance. The plumes of steam were still blasting from the exhaust pipes without any sign of the pressure waning.

He looked back at the others and shook his head. "No," he said. "Not yet."

54

Ryland Lloyd sat in a compartment that was a combination of luxurious and spartan appointments. An expensive Persian rug covered the floor. A crystal chandelier hung from the vaulted ceiling. Sleek furniture, bolted in place, occupied each corner of the suite.

The walls, on the other hand, were gunmetal in color, cold and dim, made even duller by a layer of frost clinging to the surface. Pipes ran along the ceiling while insulated electrical lines, held in place with heavy-duty fasteners, snaked along the walls.

The room temperature hovered in the mid-forties and Ryland wore a winter coat and ski pants while sitting at his desk. There were no portholes or skylights, but a false impression of the outside world was granted by a trio of high-definition screens set vertically in one wall.

The screens were connected to the vessel's camera system and often showed views directly outside the ship. At the moment, they displayed the image of a tropical island fronted by sandy beaches and turquoise seas.

Ryland had taken the photo himself several years before while traveling the Indian Ocean aboard his yacht. The families that lived on the island had been in the process of moving to a larger and dryer island a hundred miles away.

They left reluctantly and only because their island flooded more dangerously year after year. With climate change raising the seas and intensifying the storms, the place had become uninhabitable. But once Ryland's efforts bore fruit, the situation would reverse itself. Ryland expected that island to double in size over the next ten years, growing as the sea level fell. It would become another sanctuary.

Switching the image off, Ryland stood up, walked to the door and pulled it open. Stepping out into the corridor, he turned to the left, heading forward to the ship's command center.

This corridor was even colder than Ryland's suite, but it had a different look. Instead of steel, the walls of the corridor were made of the gray-white ice. It was also covered with a cooling mesh, which kept things cold enough that it wouldn't melt.

Here and there, refrigeration coils could be seen looping in and out of the walls. They ran through the deeper parts of the structure, ensuring that the interior supports remained well below freezing, which was important since the vast majority of the ship he called the *Goliath* was made out of reinforced ice.

Moving to the end of the corridor, Ryland stepped through a door into the ship's bridge and control room. This was one of the few compartments in the vessel that allowed direct viewing of the exterior world. A bank of short but wide windows, covered with multiple layers of non-glare film, looked out over the bow of the vessel.

All that could be seen were snow and ice. No funnels, no decks, no anchors or lifeboats. Just ice piled on top of ice and now covered with fresh snow.

Seen from the outside, the ship appeared to be a small iceberg. All the lines were irregular. One side was mostly flat while an oddly shaped section on the port side cantilevered over the sea. A small hill of ice near the bow hid a bank of cameras and several satellite receivers. A larger mound on the stern hid the ship's helicopter bay. Insulated doors painted white and made to look like snow and ice would have been the envy of any Hollywood set designer. They could be opened at the touch of a button, while the helicopter moved in and out of launch position on a conveyor belt.

The ship's electrical power came from an array of well-disguised solar cells. But to move the ship's massive bulk required power and torque. A pair of monstrous diesel engines, each the size of a city bus, took care of that. They drove four large screws hidden under the hull, while a trio of heavyweight thruster pods mounted directly under the center of the keel provided stability, ballast and maneuverability in tight quarters.

Since hot exhaust was an infrared signal that could give them away, the engines were shut down when not in use. And when running, they vented their heat through a complex system that mixed it with supercooled air pumped in through openings located all around the vessel.

Ryland knew his system wasn't perfect. If the military of any major country started looking for him, they would find him eventually. And once that happened, he had no illusions about the *Goliath*'s ability to fight back. Aside from two batteries of anti-aircraft missiles, purchased on the black market in Angola, the ship had no war-making capability.

But, then, it wouldn't really need it. The *Goliath*'s "hull" was thirty feet thick, made from the reinforced ice, which was stronger than hardened concrete. Tomahawk missiles would splatter against its surface like spitballs. Thousand-pound bombs would bounce off the upper deck like acorns hitting the roof of a car. Ryland's ship would shrug off any attack short of a nuclear weapon and keep plowing forward.

They would get him, of course, but their nearest ships were half a world away at the moment. To win, all Ryland needed to do was get the *Goliath* into the West Wind Drift, where he could dump the algae now being pumped into the cavernous interior of the ship.

Once he'd accomplished that, any furious bombardments would be for nothing. The new ice age would be seeded and inevitable.

"What's our status?" Ryland asked the ship's captain.

The captain deferred to Ober, who stood beside him.

Ober had transferred from the oil platform to take charge of loading of the *Goliath*. It was a tricky operation. The vessel was longer, wider and larger in every respect than Liang's supertankers.

"Base Zero signaled the commencement of pumping two hours ago," Ober replied.

"And?"

"It's eighty miles from here," Ober reminded him. "Even at the maximum flow rate, we won't receive the first trickles of water for another hour."

"Are they pumping full out?"

"That was the indication."

"Was the indication?" Ryland didn't like sloppy behavior. "Why don't you check with them to make sure?"

"We've tried," Ober said. "No response."

A warning went off. "What do you mean?"

"We've tried shortwave and satellite," the captain explained. "No response on the radio and no handshake from Yvonne's satellite phone. It's not linking up. Most likely the storm is interfering."

"I've used a satellite phone in a hurricane," Ryland insisted.

"A commercial one," the captain reminded him. "We built our own system so no one could track us. It's jury-rigged to a data platform from a single satellite. It's not as robust as the commercial networks."

The captain's reasoning was sound, but Ryland sensed danger. "Keep trying," he said. "I want a report every thirty minutes until you reach them." He turned back to

Ober. "I want you to do anything you can to accelerate the loading process."

"We already are," Ober said. "We're drawing down the pressure on our end of the conduit. With negative pressure on our side and positive pressure on theirs, the water will flow that much faster. We should begin filling the tanks within the hour. Still, we're looking at five or six hours to take on the full cargo."

Ryland understood that. It took a while to move a hundred million gallons of water. He looked at the pipeline indicators on a screen. Sensors placed upstream showed the first drops of lake water only twenty miles away. The flow rate and volume were both increasing steadily.

He continued to feel uneasy, yet if anything had gone terribly wrong the pipeline would have been shut down. "Do everything you can to speed that timetable up," he ordered. "And let me know when you've reached my sister."

55

Kurt and Joe stood in the dimly lit habitat module that had once been Yvonne's command station. A few feet away, Paul lay on a makeshift bed with his leg elevated as Gamay dressed his wound with the medical supplies she'd found.

With Paul in the best possible care they could provide, Kurt turned his attention to Yvonne's laptop computer, which remained where she'd left it on the desk in the main habitat module. Its screen displayed a schematic of the pipeline's route, complete with indicators relaying pressures, temperatures and flow rates.

A secondary display showed the status of the turbine in the cavern beneath the surface of the glacier. It was operating with aggravating efficiency and the pipeline was shipping massive volumes of water.

"We've done everything but shut this pipeline down," Kurt said.

"Bad luck that the collapse didn't extend to the cavern," Gamay said, still taping up Paul's leg.

"Luck had nothing to do with it," Kurt said. "From my brief glimpse inside, it was pretty clear they'd shored up the roof and walls."

"Can you do anything with that computer?" Paul asked.

Both Kurt and Joe had been trying. It wasn't helping. "The system is locked out. It's just a mirror of what the guy down in the cave is looking at. In other words, we can see what's happening but we can't do anything about it."

"What if we had the last pack of explosives?" Joe suggested. "The pack we lost in the avalanche."

"No telling where the pack would be," Kurt said. "You started off next to the snowmobile and wound up a hundred yards away. Even if we did find it, four small charges won't get us through that collapsed tunnel."

"And blowing it from the top isn't feasible," Gamay added. "Paul and I already determined that."

"Ah . . . ah, ouch," Paul said, pushing Gamay's hand away from his wound. "Easy with the antiseptic."

"At least you're still feeling something," she replied. "That's good."

Kurt looked their way. Paul was no longer bleeding, but he looked pale.

"What if we shut off the power?" Joe asked.

"Believe it or not, they're using a steam engine to spin that turbine," Kurt said. "I was admiring it right before the old guy started shooting at me. I'm assuming it's run off the same geothermal strike that they used to burn a hole through the glacier. Which means there's no power to turn off, the whole thing is self-contained."

Kurt leaned closer to the computer screen, tracking the progress of the fluid through the pipes. Studying the numbers, he saw that the flow rate was picking up speed and increasing in volume while the pressure at the far end of the line was falling.

"What do you make of that?" he asked Joe.

"Has to be a vacuum system," Joe said. "Like the hyper-loop idea. They're lowering the pressure on the far end to reduce resistance and increase the flow. I'd say they're using two pumps. One up here applies pressure and pushes the water forward, a second down there sucks it through the tunnel like a giant straw."

"Makes sense," Kurt said. "Tunstall was shipping a pair of turbines and I only saw one down below."

"You seem happy about that," Joe said. "What are you thinking?"

"It's simple," Kurt said. "If we can't turn off this pump, maybe we can get to the end of the pipeline and turn off the other one. Or switch it into reverse and blow the whole system."

"Is that possible?" Gamay asked.

"It's worth a shot," Kurt said. "Especially if both setups have the same turbines at their heart. That would make them equal in strength. And if the pressure inside the pipeline goes sky-high, we might even be able to collapse it from the inside."

"Sounds like a plan," Joe said, standing up and stretching. "Or the beginning of one, anyway. But the end of that pipeline is eighty miles from here. How are we going to get there? Our snowmobile is barely holding a charge and the other one needs a new front end before it goes anywhere."

"Our sled will get us to the Jayhawk," Kurt said.

"Which is out of fuel," Joe said.

"True," Kurt replied. "While we may not have fuel or batteries, we have wind. And once this storm completes its turn, it'll be a downwind run from here directly to the coast."

"We'll never beat the algae to the coast," Joe said.

"Nope," Kurt admitted. "But with a little luck, we'll get there before too much of it goes into the water."

56

The ride to the helicopter was uneventful. The snow-mobile performed flawlessly and its battery held. It was still showing a twelve percent charge as they pulled up to the snow-covered Jayhawk.

"I'm surprised you remembered where we parked," Kurt said, the headlights of the snowmobile shining on the helicopter.

After brushing the snow away, they opened the heli-copter door and retrieved the plastic case protecting the snow racer. Kurt opened the case and pulled out sections of the carbon fiber frame. Simple twists linked them to-gether while levers that were easy to turn tightened and locked them in place.

They mounted the frame on a tripod made from wide

skis. While Kurt tightened everything down, Joe attached the hammock-style seats made of ballistic nylon.

"Not exactly built for lumbar support," he said.

"I'd be happy if they included seat warmers," Kurt said.

Joe tossed the extra cold-weather gear they'd taken from Yvonne's compound on the nylon seats. "Seat warmers," he said. "As requested."

While Kurt installed the mast and rigged the sail, Joe placed their weapons, ammunition and every piece of equipment he thought might be useful into a cargo compartment. That done, he climbed into his seat.

When Kurt was satisfied, he took his own seat and unfurled a bit of the sail. The wind caught it immediately and they moved off, heading for the glacier and out toward the coast.

"Are we forgetting anything?" Kurt asked.

"Only our sanity," Joe said.

With Joe navigating and Kurt following his directions, they moved off toward the glacier and turned toward the coast. They traveled mostly on soft snow laid down overnight or blown in by the storm. The ride was astonishingly smooth, though Kurt was constantly fighting the wind and adjusting the sail.

For the most part, he used only half the available sail. It made for a more stable adventure and easier maneuvering. An hour into the journey, they'd covered thirty miles, their heated jackets, boots and gloves keeping them toasty warm. Hunger was an issue, but Joe had an answer for that. He broke out two bottles of a specialized beverage.

"What is this stuff?" Kurt asked suspiciously.

"A combination of protein powder, electrolytes and a high-calorie mix of lard and easily digestible carbs." As Joe spoke, he shook up his own bottle, opened the top and took a sip. "Only one problem. We're going to need a spoon."

Kurt gave Joe the reins, lowered the scarf and the balaclava and tipped his own bottle back.

The mixture flowed like mud, but he was able to squeeze a portion into his mouth. "First beverage I ever had to chew," he said. "It tastes like sawdust mixed with toothpaste and castor oil."

"Castor oil would improve it," Joe said, then added, "It's thirty-five hundred calories per bottle."

Kurt squished the bottle tighter and choked down more of the pasty mush. "A thousand calories' worth is all I can take."

With the sky brightening, Kurt unfurled a little more of the sail and the snow racer stretched its legs. They were on the smoothest part of the journey, cruising atop the unbroken heart of the glacier on piles of deep, packed snow. With the wind directly behind them, they were traveling fifty miles an hour.

Without much to do, Joe began studying the road ahead on the screen of the tablet. The route of the pipeline was superimposed over a satellite image of the terrain. Joe studied it, section by section, all the way down the coast to where the pipeline ended in Fimbul Bay.

Despite the reconnaissance flight by the Navy P-8 and

an imaging pass by one of NUMA's satellites prior to the storm hitting, Joe found nothing near the end of the pipeline that could be construed as another pumping station. Stranger still, he found a problem. Not for NUMA but for Ryland.

"Tell me about the Fast Ice plan again," he asked Kurt. "Not the part with the iceberg. The second part. Drafting Jurgenson and the search for the 'magic liquid' he found."

"They were going to release the algae into the bay and freeze the Russians in their port," Kurt said.

"That's what I thought." He held up the tablet for Kurt. "Take a look at Fimbul Bay. What do you see?"

Kurt glanced over quickly before turning his attention back to the task at hand. "I see a deep bay with a hook of sea ice where it reaches the ocean. What am I missing?"

"Nothing," Joe said. "That's what I see. But based on the contours alone, I can tell it's a stagnant backwater without much circulation. Now, what do you think happens if Ryland starts pumping that algae into the bay?"

"A quick freeze," Kurt said. "The fast ice would grow out from the edges toward the middle, sealing the bay shut, just like the Nazis intended when they came up with the plan to begin with."

Joe nodded. "And the rest of the algae would be trapped in a pool behind it. Which is part of the reason the normal ice age process takes thousands of years. Because the algae tends to trap itself, only leaking out into the ocean in very small quantities over a period of centuries."

"An issue Ryland is trying to circumvent by filling tankers with the stuff and dumping it on the other side of the ocean," Kurt replied.

"And if he's smart enough to do that," Joe said, "he's smart enough to do something similar down here. He's not going to be content with letting the algae trickle into the bay and inch its way to the ocean fifty miles beyond."

"Could he have built a physical pipeline from the end of the ice tunnel out to the bay?" Kurt asked.

"That depends," Joe said. "How large would you say the conduit is?"

"From what I saw in the cavern, the outgoing pipe was about four feet in diameter."

"That would match the estimate Hiram's computer came up with for the underground tunnel," Joe said. "How long do you think it would take to build a fifty-mile pipeline four feet in diameter?"

Kurt continued to guide the craft while doing some mental calculations. "It took about three years to build the Alaska Pipeline," he said. "It's about eight hundred miles long, so that's about twenty to thirty miles a month. And there were fifty thousand people working on it."

"And it was aboveground," Joe said.

"Good point," Kurt said. "Even if Ryland had a thousand people for the job, which I doubt, he couldn't possibly build more than a couple miles' pipe per month in an ice-filled bay. Not even with multiple submarines."

"It's slow work," Joe said. "I've done some of it in the Gulf of Mexico and we had nice weather."

Kurt understood what Joe was getting at. "Ryland has a ship down there."

"That would be my guess," Joe said. "A tanker. Or several of them."

Kurt tightened his grip on the tiller and leaned back. He repositioned the sail to keep the snow racer running in a broad reach. It whipped across the open field of white, picking up even more speed. A tanker meant the algae was being stored and contained. It meant the genie was still in the bottle and he and Joe had the chance to keep it there.

"You're a genius," he told Joe. "Now, get on the satellite phone and give Rudi an update. Tell him to look for a ship in the bay and let him know if we stop the ship, we stop Ryland's plan."

57

Joe's satellite call reached the NUMA tactical room in Washington, where Rudi had gathered with Hiram and Lee Garland.

As Joe's voice faded in and out, it became impossible to parse the words from the distortion and gaps in the signal. Rudi turned to the satellite wrangler. "Why is it so broken up?"

"The storm is wreaking havoc with communications," Garland said. "I'm amazed the call came through as well as it did."

"We need to hear what Joe's saying," Rudi replied. "Can you clear it up?"

Garland shook his head. "We can boost our signal and get a message through to them, but the handheld unit isn't going to suddenly double in transmission power and be able to cut through the storm. I suggest we tell them to use the datalink. It's like texting. It uses far less bandwidth than voice communications and will be more likely to get through."

"Do it," Rudi said.

Garland tapped out a message explaining the difficulty they were having and the procedure for using the datalink. A minute went by before they got a response. The text appeared on a big screen at the front of the room. It read like a message from Tarzan.

Pumps still in operation. Pipeline intact. Both out of reach. Ryland's plan unaffected.

Rudi read the message stoically.

"Two strikes," Hiram said from beside him, "but at least we're still at bat."

A second message followed.

Be advised saboteurs ready on Liang's ships. Must take by surprise or will scuttle.

Rudi nodded to Garland. "Signal them 'Understood.' And get the saboteur information over to the Navy, they're tracking down Liang's ships."

"Are they close?" Yaeger asked.

"Last I heard," Rudi said. "As I understand it, SEAL teams are ready to pounce on three of the tankers, with

British SAS units taking the other two. The plan is to hit them simultaneously."

As Garland typed the reply, a third message from Joe arrived.

Paul and Gamay still at pumping station. Paul injured but stable. Suggest evac ASAP. We are heading to the coast. Ryland must have ship. Large ship. Find it in Fimbul Bay. We will disable. Somehow.

For a second Rudi was baffled. "A ship?" he turned to Hiram. "Could they be right?"

"I don't see how," Hiram said. "We had multiple satellite passes over that bay before the weather closed in. We would have seen a heat plume if there was a ship operating in the area. Especially a large one."

Rudi looked at Garland. "What do you think?"

Garland offered a quick shake of the head. "The infrared detectors on our satellites are incredibly sensitive. A large ship operating in a cold ocean is the easiest thing in the world to spot. Don't see how we could have missed a vessel operating in that area."

"What if it was a submarine?" Rudi asked.

Hiram's eyebrows went up. "That's a possibility."

Rudi turned back to Garland. "Tell them we've seen nothing to indicate a ship but we're considering the possibility of a submarine."

Garland sent the message out and everyone waited. The return text was adamant.

Not a submarine. Has to be larger. Look for a
supertanker or LNG or several. Ryland needs to get
algae out of bay in large volume.

Rudi now understood. He looked to Garland once
more. "Can we run another pass?"

"It won't do any good," Garland said. "The area is
under a thick layer of cloud. We can't see through it on
a visible wavelength and infrared will be scattered and
absorbed as well."

Rudi glanced at the weather screen, where the storm
appeared as a swirling mass of clouds hiding everything
underneath it in the fog of war.

"What else do we have?" Rudi asked. "There has to
be something."

"Radar might do it," Garland said. "We have a long-
wavelength system designed to give us land contours, but
the image isn't going to look like a photograph. More
like an X-ray."

"Will it be able to distinguish a ship from the surroundings?"

Garland nodded. "We should get a much stronger reflection off a steel-hulled vessel than from ice and snow
or water."

Rudi was satisfied. "Get that satellite in place as fast as
possible. We need to see through those clouds."

58

The radar scan proved disappointing, showing no sign of a ship in the bay. Just ice, snow and water. Even when Hiram ran the data through a program that sharpened the details, there was nothing to see.

"What are we overlooking?" Rudi asked.

Hiram rubbed the stubble on his chin. "If a ship were hidden under a massive shelter, like the German submarine pens at Saint-Nazaire and Lorient, we wouldn't pick it up."

That seemed unlikely to Rudi. "The largest U-boat pens were a few hundred feet in length. Ryland would have to construct a shelter ten times larger. It would have to be wider and higher. And he'd have to carve it out of unstable ice at the crumbling end of a glacier. Perhaps they've installed a man-made covering along the shoreline," he mused. "White fabric coated with snow."

Hiram shook his head. "I'm not sure fabric could stand up to the punishing winds and weather there."

Garland chimed in. "The radar beam would pass through the fabric and light up the ship. We'd see it on the return like the image on an X-ray. Like a gun hidden in a suitcase."

Rudi acquiesced. "This is like searching for Harvey, the rabbit."

Hiram thought a moment. "Maybe not Harvey, but Habakkuk."

"Habakkuk the rabbit?" Rudi asked.

"Habakkuk the prophet," Hiram replied, retrieving a report from a folder in front of him. *"Behold ye among the heathen, and regard, and wonder marvelously,"* he quoted, *"for I will work a work in your days, which ye will not believe, though it be told to you.* Habakkuk, Chapter 1, Verse 5."

"Is that from the Old Testament?" Garland asked.

"It is," Hiram said. "Written by a Jewish prophet in the seventh century B.C. He was speaking to his people about God's coming wrath. He was about to remake their world. And was going to do it violently."

"Sounds like something our apocalyptic friend Ryland would agree with," Rudi said. "Why do you bring it up?"

"Because Kurt saw the name on the model in Ryland's office. He put them in his report, but he was more focused on the George Bernard Shaw quote about the value of the 'unreasonable man.' I pulled some research on both. Like everything else we've learned about Ryland, what's presented up front is one thing, what's hidden is something else."

Rudi wrinkled his brow. "I fail to see how a religious quotation from twenty-seven hundred years ago will help us now."

"Because it's not just a scriptural quotation," Hiram said. "It's also the code name of a secret plan the Allies considered during World War Two. The Nazis had their secret plans involving ice and we had ours. In this case, Project Habakkuk."

"Go on," Rudi said.

"The idea was simple. During the early part of the war, German U-boats were hitting Allied convoys in the middle of the Atlantic with impunity. They remained stubbornly out of the Allies' reach as even the longest-range aircraft, operating from the east coast of the U.S., the southern tip of Greenland and the west of England were unable to close that gap. A sprawling area a thousand miles across remained unpatrolled. And that's where the wolf packs did their hunting.

"To close that gap, a man named Geoffrey Pyke came up with an idea. He wanted to build a massive aircraft carrier and place it in the center of the ocean. His initial proposal suggested it be nearly three thousand feet in length, others proposed an even bigger structure the size of a land-based airfield. This aircraft carrier/base would allow anti-submarine planes to cover every inch of the Atlantic, putting an end to the wolf pack's ability to hunt freely."

"Sounds far-fetched," Garland said.

"It was. Because such a ship would use as much steel as an entire fleet and the high command was not interested in diverting that much material for what they considered a long shot. But then Pyke suggested the massive ship could be built out of ice. He and his team even came up with a formulation of frozen water mixed with sawdust and wood pulp that proved much stronger than regular ice and more resistant to melting. He called it Pykrete and insisted it could be manufactured on blocks and then shaped and stacked as easily as bricks and mortar."

Rudi was silent. He'd heard of Pykrete and the Habakkuk idea long ago. "You think Ryland built a ship out of ice?"

Hiram shrugged. "It's the only explanation that fits all the facts. He needs a ship, it must be massive, as Joe told us, and it must be invisible to a radar scan looking for steel."

Rudi considered the idea. "Ryland and his friends do seem to be experts in the manipulation of frozen water. But as I recall, tests of the Pykrete idea for use in shipping failed miserably."

"I can't say how they did it. Kurt's description of the submarine that hit them is a possible clue," Hiram replied. "He said the hull appeared almost translucent when the light hit it at a certain angle. More importantly, there's Joe's report of dirty ice all over the deck of the *Grishka*. It was piled up on the side where the ship had obviously been in a collision. Joe described this ice as gray-yellow in color and containing a mesh-like network of fibrous material and a residue of dry powder. That's about what Pykrete would look like if you used fiberglass instead of wood pulp."

Rudi tried to recall the details of Joe's report. "It certainly does sound like Pykrete. Or a new and improved version."

"The Antarctic would be the place to build a ship out of ice," Hiram said. "Aside from the fibers or resin you'd have to bring in, all your raw materials are right there at hand. It would be like building a giant igloo."

Garland added to the consensus. "A ship of ice would explain why we're not getting a radar return. And by that I mean we're getting one, it's just indistinguishable from the surroundings."

"All right, let's run with this," Rudi said. "Compare the radar image with the visual and infrared images from twenty-four hours ago. And any older images you can find. Anything in the new image that wasn't in the old one— that's our ship of ice. And once we find it, we can sink it."

"That might prove easier said than done," Hiram said. "The whole point of the Habakkuk project was to build a ship that was indestructible. In such a vessel, thick ice is necessary for strength and stability, but it also results in a hull that is impervious to bombs, mines and missiles. Even the original design for the *Habakkuk* was intended to be invulnerable to German torpedoes of the day—and those carried six-hundred-pound warheads designed to break the spine of a battleship. If Ryland has built his own *Habakkuk*, we could pound it for hours with everything in our arsenal and do nothing but deafen the people inside."

Rudi knew enough about engineering and ship construction to know that everything was a trade-off. Even a ship of great size and strength would have a weakness somewhere. "First things first," he said. "Let's find that ship and make sure we're not guessing ourselves right out of the ballpark."

59

Gamay sat at the table Yvonne had once occupied. She stared at the same computer, monitoring the same flow of water through the tunnel bored in the ice.

She turned to Paul, who remained on the bedroll with his injured leg elevated. "The water in the tunnel has gone past the final sensor. If this is accurate, it's already pouring into the sea."

Paul had the satellite phone with him. He'd been trying to reach Rudi through the storm but to no avail. "Either Kurt and Joe didn't get there or they've made it and haven't been able to do anything about it. Odds are that station is going to be as well defended as this one."

Gamay knew that but there was little she could do about it. She had a more immediate concern. Paul's voice was strained. He didn't sound like himself. Gamay came over to check on him. The new gauze was bloody but not soaked. Still, he'd lost a fair amount of blood. "We need to get you to a hospital."

"Good luck finding one," Paul said. "Even if we could reach Rudi, there's no way to get a helicopter through this storm."

The sun had risen on a whiteout in the making. Wind-driven snow had cut visibility to a hundred feet or less. And it wasn't just the snow coming down from the sky, it was being whipped up off the surface like dust and streaming in places like smoke. Already the changing direction of the wind was scouring away drifts that had formed overnight.

"We don't have to get you back to the mainland," Gamay said. "A ship or a manned scientific station where they have a medical officer would do just fine."

"I already looked," Paul said. "The nearest outpost is an Indian science station two hundred miles to the west of us with a mountain range in between. That's too far to walk."

She knew he was right, but she hated feeling powerless. "You know I'd rather be the one who got shot, right?"

"So I could worry?" Paul said. "No thank you. Relax, I'm going to be fine. Our real concern should be helping Kurt and Joe if we can."

"They're eighty miles away, Paul. It's out of our hands now."

"I'm not so sure about that," he said. "I've been

thinking. We should make another attempt to disable that pumping station. Kurt and Joe may not make it to the coast or they may get there and find a platoon of Ryland's people guarding whatever they find there. We can't count on them pulling this off, which means we have to try again, back here."

"What can we do?" Gamay said. "Our explosives are all used up, the shaft to the pumping station is sealed off by a hundred tons of ice and we have nothing we can use to cut through that."

"We need nothing," he said. "Yvonne and her people left plenty of equipment lying around. There's a drilling rig out there with a half mile of pipe stacked up beside it. There are cutting tools and welding torches in storage, where we found these mats. There are hammers, shovels and everything else they used to set up these modules."

"That drilling rig looks like an ice sculpture," she reminded him. "It's frozen solid."

He propped himself up on his elbows. "The pipe isn't."

"And what, exactly, are we going to do with it?"

"We could capture the heat and steam pouring from the exhaust ports and use it to tunnel through the ice the way Yvonne and her people did."

Gamay raised a finger, primed to shut down any idea that would put her husband at risk, especially as it all seemed pointless. Yet before the words left her mouth, she realized the idea had merit. "You forget that pipe is big and heavy."

"What about those pipes," he said, nodding toward the ceiling.

Gamay looked up. Running along the ceiling were thick PVC pipes. She'd seen lengths of it stacked vertically in another room. Yvonne and her people had used it for water and warm air circulation. While the PVC would get brittle in the cold, the heat from the steam would keep it from cracking.

"If we funnel the steam from all four exhaust ports into one pipe and then angle that pipe downward," he said, "that would give us a high-temperature knife that would slowly cut through the glacier, melting its way through to the pumping station down below."

Ten thousand miles away, Rudi was staring at the large screen in the front of the room. It displayed two satellite photos side by side. One was crystal clear, the other blurred by fog or clouds.

Garland pointed at the images. "The first one is from a NASA glacier study done ten weeks ago. The second is our satellite pass made just before the storm came through. Hiram has normalized the photos so they're of the exact same scale and angle."

Yaeger nodded. "I've pulled out the cloud layer and had the computer scan for discrepancies. Here's the result."

He touched a button and the photos synced up as the clouds were stripped away.

"Zoom in on the end of the pipeline," Rudi ordered.

"Stand by," Yaeger said.

The frame tightened and compressed, zooming in closer and closer to the target zone.

The truth was easy to see. In the NASA photo, the terminal moraine of the glacier stretched across the screen, from one side to the other, with only the tiniest icebergs and growlers appearing in the dark water beyond. In the NUMA photo, an irregular diamond-shaped iceberg sat at the very end of the glacier.

The radar return had painted it as ice, which it was. Its absence in the earlier photograph gave it away.

"It doesn't look much like a ship," Rudi said. "If the point is to disguise it—"

"The computer thinks it's an iceberg calved from the glacier," Yaeger said. "If something that large broke off the glacier, it would leave a mark. There's no mark."

"That's our ship," Rudi said. He had no doubt. Its position matched up too closely with the far end of the pipeline for it to be anything else.

"If it is, it's a huge one," Garland said. "Eighteen hundred feet in length, three hundred feet wide amidships."

Yaeger agreed. "Joe said 'aircraft carrier size or larger.' He was right on target. Now, what do we do about it?"

Rudi's euphoria gave way to reality. He'd already spoken to the Secretary of the Navy and the Chief of Naval Operations. While they had ships, submarines and planes scouring the seas for Liang's tankers, there were no combat units within six thousand miles of the Antarctic coast.

The nearest surface vessels were in the Indian Ocean. Any of those ships would take five days at flank speed to reach an intercept position. That would be five days too late.

"We send the information to Kurt and Joe," he said. "And hope they can stop this thing from ever leaving port."

60

Kurt and Joe crouched down and gazed over the edge of the glacier. Ahead of them lay what appeared to be a large iceberg. It was covered with ridges and swales and jagged peaks, just like every iceberg Kurt had ever seen. It appeared to be crumbling on top and eroding on the near side where the sea lapped against it. With the snow still falling, the visibility was such that he couldn't even see the far end of the vessel.

"So, that's a ship?" Kurt asked, studying the contours through a pair of binoculars.

"According to Rudi," Joe said. "Do you think they've started filling their tanks?"

Kurt glanced at his watch and nodded. Despite the snow racer running downwind, the trip had taken three hours. Terrain, and caution, had slowed them. The flow of water had almost certainly beat them to the finish line, but it couldn't have been by much. "How long does a supertanker need to top off?"

"Eight to ten hours," Joe said. "With crude oil, you have to go slow. You have to stop and vent the tanks from time to time to avoid buildup of explosive gases. You have viscosity issues, too. Even light crude is relatively thick. Ryland is filling this thing with lake water and he's using a larger pump, at higher pressure. Even if this vessel is as big as Rudi says it is, back-of-envelope calculations say four or five hours to fill it."

Kurt would put Joe's back-of-envelope calculations up against a computer from MIT any day. "That means he's at least a third of the way home."

"What do you want to do?"

"Stop the pumps like we planned," Kurt said. "And keep this ship from leaving port. If it's stranded in the bay, it can't spread the algae beyond it."

"In that case, we're going to need a way to get aboard," Joe said. He pointed downslope and to the left. "How about the mooring lines?"

Kurt raised the binoculars again and aimed them in the direction Joe had pointed. The lines were hard to see through the blowing snow, but once Kurt spotted them they couldn't be missed. A half-dozen heavy lines, stretching from the ice ship to a forest of large bollards that had been drilled into the glacier in various places.

Even though the lines were frozen over with ice and snow and pulled taut, they held against the wind, which was blowing out to sea.

Scanning back in the other direction, Kurt found a second collection of four lines. Farther on, he spied a third that looked like another six-pack.

"They've docked her Mediterranean-style," Kurt said, referring to the method of mooring a ship with its stern against the dock and its bow outward.

"They must want to make a quick getaway," Joe said.

Kurt slid the binoculars back into an outside pocket of his jacket. "Let's make sure that doesn't happen."

They backtracked to the snow racer and traded their expedition jackets for the cold-weather gear they'd taken from the Base Zero locker.

"Glad you brought these," Kurt said.

"Might as well look like we belong," Joe said.

Dressed this way, they made their way downslope and took cover behind an outcropping of ice near the first mooring lines.

The lines, three inches in diameter, were thick and heavy. They were attached to the sturdy bollards that had been drilled into the ice. The bollards were as thick as telephone poles, but much shorter, and topped with mushroom-shaped caps that would keep lines from slipping off.

As Kurt and Joe watched, several crewmen from the ice ship came across a gangplank and approached the closest bollard. These men checked the lines and, after a brief discussion, made a radio call to someone before moving off toward the second bollard farther on.

Kurt watched until they vanished in the snowstorm. "Now's our chance. Follow me."

Kurt picked his way down to the very edge of the glacier. An eighty-foot drop into freezing water awaited if he took one wrong step.

By now, they were below what Kurt would have called the ship's main deck. It loomed above them, jutting out across the water with a large overhang from what was the lower hull of the ship.

"Impressive freeboard," Joe said. "You'd need a monster wave to splash that deck."

Kurt was looking up. The overhang was at least thirty feet above their heads. The flight deck of an American aircraft carrier cleared the water by about sixty feet. The main deck of the ice ship rose nearly twice that height. "It'll be a lot lower once they've filled their tanks to the stops."

"True," Joe said. "Now, about your plan to get on board. I assume we're sneaking aboard like rats."

Kurt nodded.

The mooring lines stretched from the bollards on the glacier across the water and down to the ice ship. They vanished through a wide gap, secured inside to hidden cleats and anchors.

Studying the opening, Kurt saw nothing to suggest anyone was standing inside. "No one home."

He ducked under the first two lines and then climbed up toward a third line that had been attached at a higher point on the ice. Pulling the MP5 from under his coat, he disconnected its strap and then stuffed the weapon back into his jacket. He took the strap, looped it over the mooring line and then twisted the two ends around his wrists. Gripping the strap tightly, Kurt pushed forward, leaping off the end of the glacier and sliding down the angled line to the vessel.

He picked up speed as he went, the icy synthetic cable proving almost frictionless. It took only seconds to cross the gap, with Kurt raising his legs as he approached the ship, using them as shock absorbers to cushion the impact when he reached the hull.

Hanging suspended just below the opening where the mooring line went in, Kurt dug the spiked tread of his boots into the hull, pulled himself up, and clawed his way into the gap. To get to the compartment beyond required him to crawl across ten feet of ice, which acted as the outer hull of the ship. It was impressive and strange all at the same time.

Reaching the inner hull, Kurt dropped to the deck and glanced around. He was alone in the compartment, which was the size of a five-car garage. Heavy gearing connected to a powerful winch system gripped the outgoing lines.

Turning back to the outside, he saw Joe come down the mooring line and climb inside.

"That was easy enough," Joe said. "Do you think anyone saw us?"

"I don't see any windows for people to watch from," Kurt said. "Even if there were, someone would have had to have been looking at exactly the right place at exactly the right time. Add in the blowing snow and the monotony of staring at a blank white canvas and I like our odds. Now all we have to do is find our way to the pump room."

"Lead on," Joe said.

Kurt got up out of his crouch and made his way to the inner wall, which was made of steel. A hatchway in the wall awaited. Kurt leaned on the handle and was able to pull it open. Inside stretched a gloomy hallway lit only every thirty feet by a few LEDs.

"Someone forgot to pay the electric bill," Joe said.

Kurt stepped into the corridor, happy to be in semi-darkness. "They must be conserving power, trying to keep the ship cold or save all the juice for the pumps. Either way, this plays to our advantage."

"Which way do we go?" Joe asked.

"Inward and down," Kurt said. "Pumps are heavy machinery. They'll be on the bottom deck."

"In that case," Joe said, "let's find a ladder to take us there."

61

Gamay leaned into the wind, dragging a sled through the snow like a plow horse. She stopped only as she neared the ruined entryway to the pumping station.

The bodies of the men who'd been killed there were now buried under mounds of snow. But the four exhaust ports continued blasting heated vapor into the air.

Throwing off the strap, Gamay found herself sweating from the effort. She backtracked to the sled and lifted the first section of pipe she and Paul had cut and melted together. She dragged it to the nearest vent and then laid it down. Three more sections were given similar treatment.

As the last one landed, Gamay rested, breathing hard and waiting for Paul, who was limping toward her on the snowy surface.

As he came within earshot, Gamay announced a unilateral decision. "When we get back to civilization, you're in charge of throwing the garbage out," she said. "For the rest of our lives."

"Gladly," Paul said, moving up awkwardly next to her. "Let's link this up and get back inside. I'm freezing."

With the blood he'd lost, Paul shouldn't have been out in the elements, but he'd refused to remain in the shelter. He had insisted it would take both of them working together to fit the network of pipes together and lower them into place. Even if she did most of the heavy lifting, a second pair of hands and arms would be crucial.

Girding herself for the effort, Gamay took several deep breaths and dragged the largest section of pipe over into position. It was made up of a curved section that would fit over the exhaust port and a long length of PVC pipe that would channel the superheated steam to a new destination. Each of the exhaust pipes would get a similar section fitted over the top and they would then all meet in the middle, where a makeshift connector in the shape of an X would link all four exhaust streams together and direct the boiling vapor downward.

Despite being made of plastic and only five inches in diameter, each section of PVC pipe weighed more than a hundred pounds. Lifting and moving it without breaking the improvised connections took leverage and patience. Gamay knew the seams would never pass inspection, but she felt they would hold as long as needed here.

With Paul's help, she fitted the PVC pipe into the X, then they lifted the first curved section over the nearest exhaust stack. It was awkward and strenuous work because of the length and weight of the now interlocked contraption, but they had to do it in this order or otherwise they'd be trying to connect the X while scalding steam was blasting out of the pipes onto their hands.

The second curved section went on easier. The third was more difficult and the fourth a serious problem.

Gamay heaved and pulled, trying to get the plastic pipe to cover the steel exhaust stack. No matter how hard she tried, it wouldn't line up.

"It's no good," she said, looking over at Paul, who was now shaking.

"I'll help you," Paul said, limping her way. "I'll heave, you pull."

If Paul could have seen her face through the balaclava, he would have known instantly what she thought of that plan.

He got into position and pushed upward. Gamay pulled with all her might, but they could move the section only so far. The two ends still would not slot together.

Paul slipped when the weight became too much. As he got back up off the ground, Gamay noticed a bright stain of blood on the snow.

"Paul."

"I know," he replied. "Let's just hurry."

"Three is enough," she replied, pointing to the steam surging out from underneath the X. A vast curtain of fog was forming, the ice already melting beneath it.

"If we don't do all of them, there's no point," he replied. "There won't be enough heat."

"Paul Trout," she snapped. "You are so damned stubborn. You know I'm right."

"The sooner we get this done," he said, "the sooner we go back to the lodge and get a hot toddy."

"Fine," she said. "One more try."

Paul dropped down and put his shoulder to the bottom of the pipe, forcing it upward and toward Gamay. Gamay grasped the connector and pulled, leaning back into it. It covered but wouldn't slide into place.

"A little more," she urged.

Paul shoved harder and Gamay put her weight against the top of the contraption, shoving it downward. This time, it locked into place.

She stepped back, breathing hard but ecstatic. She turned to Paul, who offered a weak thumbs-up before he staggered backward and fell over into the snow.

She raced to his side and dropped down next to him. His arms were limp and she could see through his goggles that his eyes had rolled back.

"No, no, no," she insisted. "Don't you do this to me."

She had to get him inside. She stood up and dragged him unceremoniously by the arms. Reaching the sled that they'd used to bring out the sections of pipe, she rolled him onto it and crossed his arms over his chest.

"Don't you die on me," she said, taking up the strap reins. "Don't you dare die."

With the strap diagonally across her chest, she leaned

forward and began dragging Paul toward the habitat. She dug in with each step, working her legs like pistons.

Her heart was pounding, her chest heaving, as she breathed the frigid air. She pushed forward, oblivious to the wind and the snow and the cold. Even though the whiteout made it almost impossible to see the habitat and the danger of getting lost was very real, she kept the trench in sight and plowed her way forward.

After what felt like an eternity, the silhouette of the habitat finally appeared in the distance. Gamay kept moving, as even now it seemed so desperately far away.

62

Navigating the corridors of the ice ship was nothing like moving around in a regular vessel. To begin with, the spaces were vast. So vast, it was hard to tell if one was near the bow, stern or amidships. Or even if such terms mattered.

The halls were long and angled. Every fifty feet, they turned slightly. The effect was such that one could look down a corridor in either direction and never see the end. Between the strange layout and dim lighting, it began to seem like a maze.

Finally, Kurt and Joe reached an intersection. It led to a ship's ladder that dropped them down another deck. They rounded a turn and continued dropping. Eight levels down, they heard footfalls.

"Someone's coming up," Joe said.

They stepped away from the stairwell and hid behind the nearest wall. Voices and boots on the metal steps' rungs told them the men climbing upward were nearing their floor.

Kurt poked his head out just as the two men made the turn to go up to the next level. Lunging forward, he grabbed both men from behind by their coveralls and heaved backward.

The men tumbled off the stairs, landing on the metal deck. They popped up, cursing, only to see Joe holding the submachine gun on them.

"Who are you?" one of the men asked. He had a mane of strawberry blond hair, a thin brown beard and a Norwegian accent. The coveralls had no rank or insignia on them, but they were stained with ball bearing grease.

"I'm from the health department," Kurt said. "I need to see the pump room. Care to show us where it is?"

The two men set their jaws but stared at the weapons.

"They're not going to talk," Kurt said. "Might as well kill them."

Joe raised the MP5.

"Wait," the Norwegian said. "We'll show you."

With his hands raised above his head, he got to his feet. His partner followed suit and they turned back down the stairwell in the direction they'd just come.

Kurt and Joe followed and the four of them descended another six levels.

On the bottom deck, the Norwegian pointed down the corridor.

"Go on," Kurt said.

The crewmen continued down the hall, with Kurt and Joe a few paces behind.

"How many crew in the pump room?" Kurt asked their prisoner.

"Five or six."

"Is it automated?"

"Most of it."

Like any other ship, especially one this vast, there were markers and numbers to help the crew understand where they were. They stepped off the stairs and onto E-15—Deck 15, Section E. Unlike cruise ships, most merchant and military vessels were numbered from the main deck, up and down, so one deck above the main would be 1 A. Kurt, Joe and their prisoners were now fifteen decks below the main.

"We're underwater here," Joe said.

Kurt nodded. He estimated they'd been below the waterline for the last seven decks.

Section E led to F and then to G.

They passed multiple compartments and storage areas, finally arriving at a hatchway that read *Pump Room*.

"After you," Kurt said, nudging their prisoners forward with the barrel of the gun.

The Norwegian pulled the door open and stepped inside. He'd just gone three paces when he shouted something and broke into a run. His friend lunged for Joe's weapon but got a knee to the gut instead and fell to the floor.

Kurt charged into the pump room, firing in the air and shouting at the top of his lungs, "Everyone on the floor. Facedown."

He triggered off several shots for emphasis. Activity ceased. The Norwegian man stopped running. One by one, the crew sat down in front of him.

Joe dragged the other engineer into the room, tossed him to the ground and then dogged the hatch down tight. "We're secure."

Kurt studied the captives. The six of them were from all over the world. Random selection or part of Ryland's plan, Kurt didn't know. One look told Kurt none of them were gunmen or killers. Not one had tried to fight. Even the Norwegian had run. It didn't matter at this point. Kurt did wonder if any of them really knew what they'd become a part of.

Joe tied them up using electrical tape and ropes they found. He even gagged them to keep them quiet.

With the threat of resistance quelled, Kurt pulled off his coat. "Hot in here," he said. "Unlike the rest of the ship."

"Steel all around," Joe said, pointing out the walls. "Did you see how thick that hatch was? They've isolated this singular compartment from the rest of the ship. Probably dropped into the middle of the vessel as they built up the ice. Interesting way to construct a ship."

"Save it for your after report," Kurt said. "What are we looking at?"

Joe pointed to a bank of analog gauges, just beyond which stood huge levers and circular wheels designed to open and close various valves. To their right were several computer terminals.

"These are all tied into the system," Joe told Kurt.

"Like the guy said, it's all automated. The levers and manual valves and all the analog gauges are just here for backup. In case the computers go down."

Kurt moved to the computer terminal while keeping an eye on their prisoners. He motioned to Joe. "Can you see how much lake water they've taken on?"

Joe tapped into the first terminal and began to click through various screens. He found a schematic showing the diamond-shaped vessel and the vast areas of the ship given over to storage.

"The tanks are at forty-nine percent and rising," Joe said. "They're halfway to the top. Even if we shut this down now, Ryland has fifty million gallons of lake water on board. That's five times what the *Exxon Valdez* spilled when it ran aground off the coast of Alaska."

Kurt took the grim news without reaction. Twenty million gallons, sixty million gallons—it didn't really matter. It was enough to wreak havoc on the world's climate. That being the case, Kurt couldn't allow it to leave the bay.

63

Yvonne's foreman had done his job well. He'd sent the members of her security team up to the surface and used the time to prepare a final line of defense in the subterranean station.

In a way, Yvonne had prepared them for this. She'd warned them from day one that they'd be attacked. She'd instilled in all those who followed her the idea that the wealthy and the powerful nations of the world would do everything they could to prevent the change she and Ryland were trying to bring about. And she'd steeled everyone to the sobering truth that they might very well have to sacrifice their lives to bring about this change.

The foreman had no doubt that Yvonne and her team had done just that. And, soon enough, it would be his turn. There was no way out for him now. No way back to the surface short of someone digging him out and that would mean capture or death.

He would die at his post, he decided. *But not until my job is done.*

He continued monitoring the flow of lake water, unnerved only slightly by the sound of cracking and shifting ice around him. He figured it was settling just in the collapsed hallway. But with each additional rumble, that certainty fell away.

Having checked the passageway and, finding it utterly impassable, he came back to the control room, where the hum of the turbine and the soft heartbeat of the steam engine comforted him. Checking the computer panel, he saw that the backflow pressure had risen in the steam pipes, but not to a level that was dangerous.

He looked for a problem in the steam engine setup and found nothing.

Perplexed, he continued to stare at the screen until a large drop of water splattered on it from above. He looked up.

The ceiling was weeping. It had water clinging to it that had begun dripping here and there. Pear-shaped dollops fell next to him while other drops hissed as they came in contact with the hot machinery.

Another drop hit the computer. A third landed on his shoulder. He caught a fourth drop in his outstretched palm. To his surprise, it was warm, not cold.

Turning back to his computer, he wiped the screen and checked the temperature. Heat in the cavern was a problem—and it always had been—but the cooling mesh attached to the walls and ceiling was supposed to whisk it away. The resin applied to the layer of ice was supposed to insulate it to prevent the heat from being given off.

Clicking through a dozen temperature readings, he saw that the situation was contained. The cavern was the same temperature it had been for hours, a fact that would have assuaged his fears had not the dripping become more steady and grown louder.

"This makes no sense," the foreman said, double-checking the refrigeration system only to find it working at maximum capacity.

Without warning, a crack opened up above him and a chunk of ice fell from the ceiling. It shattered as it hit the floor while water began to pour in a constant stream through the opening it left behind.

The foreman moved out of the way, dragging the workstation with him and desperately seeking an answer. He tapped away at the computer as more cracks appeared and the existing one widened.

Another crack slithered across the ceiling. A desk-sized chunk of ice broke away, again crashing to the floor, and pulled half the cooling mesh down with it. The mesh collapsed like a net, piling up in a heap on the floor, as a waterfall cascaded through the ice.

Now steam began filling the room, some of it from water hitting the hot machinery, the rest bursting through fissures above him.

More ice fell, coming down here and there like boulders dropped from the sky. The workstation was smashed, the turbine housing and other equipment dented and damaged.

The foreman dove to avoid being laid out by a hundred-pound chunk that seemed to take aim at his head.

He hit the floor and slid face-first, as the ice was now slick under an inch of water. Getting to his feet, he heard the largest displacement yet. He looked up. The center of the ceiling was bulging. Jagged fractures were spreading around it in all directions. "No," he shouted. "This can't be."

All at once, the ceiling gave way.

Tons of ice and snow dropped straight down. A thousand gallons of meltwater surged into the cavern along with it. The turbine was knocked from its cradle, the pipework mangled and wrenched apart. The foreman was swept aside by the wave of water and ice and snow.

It threw him against a wall just as the rest of the ice fell—a thousand tons of it—crushing and burying everything in its path.

Eighty miles away, on the bridge of the *Goliath*, Ryland and Ober noticed the pressure drop immediately.

"Sensors going green to yellow up the line from us," Ober said. "All the way back to the pumping station at Base Zero."

Ryland stared at the monitor. Virtual, real-time gauges that measured the pressure along the way showed water velocity and volume dropping. Tension ripped across Ryland's body. "Can we compensate for the drop on our end?"

Ober checked the status of their own turbine. He shook his head. "We're already at full power."

He turned to the *Goliath*'s captain. "Have you been able to reach anyone at Base Zero?"

The captain shook his head. "No response. Nothing from Yvonne."

Ryland found himself gripping the edge of the monitor in frustration. His knuckles were turning white. The pressure distorting the edge of the screen. "It has to be NUMA," he whispered. "Damn them."

The captain offered a suggestion. "We could send a team to—"

Ryland cut him off. "There's no point. It's too far. And remaining here is now too dangerous."

"But Yvonne—"

"Is dead," Ryland snapped. "Or in NUMA's hands, which would be far worse."

"It could be anything," Ober said calmly. "These turbines are temperamental. They may have had to shut down to reset. Give us a few minutes to see if they come back online."

"No," Ryland said. "Look at the screen. Water volume is zero. We're sucking on an empty straw. It's not the turbine. They've cut off the supply somehow."

Ober turned back toward the monitor, his face a shade paler. Ryland waited for him. Finally, Ober nodded. "You're right. The line has either been blocked or cut off. But it's not a problem in the tunnel. It's back at Base Zero."

"NUMA," Ryland said under his breath. "It has to be." He turned to the captain. "Fire up the engines and cut the lines. Don't even bother to bring them back in. I want this ship under way as soon as possible."

The rumbling of the massive diesel engines could be felt throughout the ship, especially belowdecks in the pump room, which was only two compartments over from the engine room.

"We've run out of time," Kurt said.

"The tanks are at fifty-one percent," Joe said. "They can't be leaving now."

The ship's intercom began to squawk. "Departure imminent," a voice said. "Shut off acquisition pump and detach umbilical."

Kurt looked at Joe, who nodded. He could do it. He pressed the talk button. "Understood," he said in a clipped voice. "Pump room out."

Joe found the controls. "We could leave acquisition lines attached?"

"It would just bring them running down here to find out what went wrong," Kurt said. "Cut it loose."

Joe disconnected the umbilical cord tying the ship to the mouth of the tunnel. He closed the valves one by one and shut off the pumps. "Can't imagine why they're leaving early," he said. "Once this ship gets under way, it's going to be impossible to stop."

Kurt knew that. He was considering the options. They ran the whole gamut, from long shot to impossible.

The obvious option was breaking into the engine room and sabotaging the ship's propulsion system. But they wouldn't be able to hold it for long. And large diesel engines were notoriously robust. Any damage he and Joe might cause would be easy to fix once Ryland's private soldiers had stormed in and taken the compartment back.

At best, they'd get themselves killed in exchange for a brief delay in the ship's departure. Not exactly a fair trade.

He needed a better idea. "This ship is made of thick ice," he said, thinking aloud. "Not thin steel. That ice makes it all but impervious from the outside yet also gives it odd sailing properties. It's naturally top-heavy. Worse than the *Grishka* with all that frost on the superstructure."

"Sure," Joe said. "But it's got a wide hull with a lot of stability. It's drawing eighty feet of water. That's going to make it more stable."

"Except unlike a ship made of steel plates that would sink if disconnected from the hull, every portion of this ship would float on its own. Every slab of ice making up the hull is lighter and less dense than the water around it. From a physical standpoint, every part of the underside of this ship would prefer to be on the surface. That makes the ship unstable dynamically."

A gleam appeared in Joe's eye. He could see where Kurt was going. "Icebergs roll over all the time," he said. "Once enough of the underside is worn away, they capsize like eggs trying to stand on the pointy end. But you're forgetting one thing. Sixty million gallons of lake water. Those half-filled tanks are enough to weigh the ship down and stabilize it."

"Not if you transfer all of them to one side."

Joe's eyebrows went up and a grin appeared on his face. "Now you're making sense."

"Can you do it from here?"

"And nowhere else but here," Joe said confidently. "We've got cross-feed lines and high-pressure pumps. If I use the manual override, they won't be able to turn them off from the bridge. Or anywhere else. But if they notice, they might come down to investigate."

Kurt had a plan to prevent that. "I'll go topside to give them something else to worry about. The longer I distract them, the more weight you can shift to one side."

"If you happen to wander by the bridge," Joe said, "a sharp turn would do nicely."

"I'll see what I can arrange."

With the plan decided upon, Kurt looked over the schematics of the ship to plot out a route to the bridge. That done, he checked his weapon, jammed the magazine back into place and hid it under his heavy winter coat. Double-checking that his radio and headset were in another pocket, he turned for the door.

Joe grabbed his arm before he could walk away. "We can't leave these people down here when it happens."

Kurt looked at their prisoners. They were Ryland's followers, but there wasn't a violent one among the bunch. "Cut them loose before we go over. Give them a chance, just don't get yourself killed in the process."

As Joe nodded, Kurt opened the hatch and stepped into the corridor beyond.

64

Kurt cut across to the ship's outer passageway and then back up toward the main deck, passing two men coming the other way.

Resisting the urge to salute or act official in any way, he offered a slight nod and continued on. Neither of the men even bothered to return the gesture.

Kurt continued forward, walking at a brisk pace. The ship was so lengthy, it took five full minutes to get to the forward stairs. He began climbing again, eight more flights before he reached the bridge deck.

"No need for a gym on this ship," he whispered under his breath.

Passing a navigation room, he reached the doorway to the ship's bridge. He could hear voices through the steel door. Three or four men.

He unzipped his coat and pulled out the MP5. Safety off, he put his hand on the door. It began to move before he applied any pressure.

Kurt stepped back. The door swung open. Ryland Lloyd appeared in the entrance.

He stopped at the sight of someone in his way. Recognition didn't happen instantly. He stared for a split second, flummoxed at the impertinence of someone blocking his path, before realizing just who it was.

Kurt saw that realization hit him. He saw Ryland's eyes go wide and his body tense. He tried to step back and slam the hatch shut, but Kurt knocked Ryland's hand free and then barged forward, knocking Ryland over onto the deck.

When he landed on the plating with a hearty grunt, the eyes of the other two men in the room swung to the source of the commotion.

Kurt saw one of the men reach for a weapon. "Don't."

The man drew his pistol anyway. Kurt pulled the trigger, firing a two-shot burst. The first bullet hit the man in the gut, the second hit his shoulder.

The gun flew from the man's grasp as he fell backward, clutching his stomach. But as he landed, the ship's captain charged from the other direction, rushing Kurt from behind.

Kurt had sensed him coming. He ducked and spun, rolling his shoulders and flipping the captain over, sending him flying into a large, bearded man who'd drawn a knife and was getting ready to charge.

The two of them went down like bowling pins. Kurt

turned back to Ryland, who was scrambling across the deck, grasping for the loose pistol.

Ryland managed to get his fingers on it but never raised it off the deck as Kurt stepped on his hand, crushing a few of the smaller bones and drawing blood with the spikes on his ice shoes.

Ryland pulled his hand back and Kurt kicked the pistol away. He then shoved Ryland toward the other three men and leveled the submachine gun in their direction.

Ryland slid backward and raised his hands. The others did likewise.

"You'll never get off this ship," Ryland said.

"When I'm done," Kurt replied, "we'll all be looking for a way off this ship."

Back in the pump room, Joe stood beside an intersection of valves and pipes. He had a large box wrench in his hand. This one was specialized, like those used to open fire hydrants. It had a long handle, which allowed the user to get much more leverage, and a closed end with five sides that could fit over the large bolt on the top of the hydrant.

Joe placed it over one of the cross-feed valves and leaned into it. The first shove moved the bolt a fraction of a turn, the second moved it an inch or two and the third effort opened the valve wide. He performed the same task on three other valves and then returned to the control panel.

With the cross-feeds locked in the open position, he activated the pumps at the center of the room. They clanked to life one by one and began to build up pressure. A hiss of air whistled through the pipes, followed by the sound of rushing water. The pipes were large-bore, each one a foot in diameter. They would transfer thousands of gallons a second, once the pressure built to full, but it would still be a long, drawn-out process.

From the bridge of the ship, it was easy to feel the *Goliath* picking up speed. The diesels were running at full power, the twin screws at the aft end of the ship biting firmly and pushing the vessel forward. The fact that it was half filled and riding high made the ship lighter and allowed it to run with less drag from the water. The wind off the glacier was helping as well, pushing on the hull like a sail.

"You're too late," Ryland said with pride. "We're already under way. My men will be suspicious if you try to stop the ship now or order us to turn back. Especially without word from me or the captain. They'll storm the bridge and you'll run out of bullets trying to fight them off."

"I'll save the last bullet for you," Kurt promised.

"That won't help you," Ryland replied. "My life or death is irrelevant at this point. My people believe in what we're doing. Killing me will just make me into a martyr. It will fire their spirits to see the job through."

"And what job is that?" Kurt asked. "Destroying the world? Burying it in ice?"

"I'm simply accelerating what nature will begin in another thirty years or so," Ryland insisted.

"If that's true, why not let nature take its course?" Kurt asked. "Let humanity reap what it sows?"

"Because the planet will be weaker and worse off in thirty years," Ryland insisted. "Humans are destroying the biodiversity of the Earth as fast as they're destroying the climate and environment. You know it to be true. I've read your work on saving the reefs from ocean acidification and the effects of overfishing. I heard you thundering at me in my own home, when you thought I was a man who might burn up the world if there was a profit to be had."

Kurt stared at Ryland. "What difference does it make if the Earth dies in fire or in ice? It still dies. You've offered no solution."

"The Earth will survive," Ryland said. "Humanity will as well. But its gross overreaching will be checked. It will emerge again, newer and wiser."

Kurt turned briefly back to the computer screen and then spoke again, addressing the others. "Is this what he promised you? A part of the new world he'd create for you?"

Neither the bearded man nor the captain responded.

Kurt refocused on Ryland. "Either you haven't run the simulations correctly or you haven't shared them with your followers. But there's a chance your ice age becomes a runaway train. A vicious cycle, colder air creating more ice that cools the air further. In the end, the whole Earth is iced over and locked in a frozen state. What happens to your little sanctuaries at that point? I'll tell you. The forests, the animals, the people—everything dies. And doesn't come back."

"Exaggeration," Ryland said dismissively. "A fantasy created from false data."

"Your sister's data, taken straight from a paper she wrote years ago."

Ryland went mute for a moment, his jaw clenched and his teeth grinding. "And what would you do about it?" he asked finally. "If the warming isn't checked, half of the tropics will be unfit for human life within thirty years. Half of the world's coastlines will be flooded."

"I'd work for a solution," Kurt said. "I'd trust in human nature to ultimately be rational. Even if it takes a long time to get there. I'd trust in science to figure out methods to prevent the worst-case scenario. And I'd fight for a compromise that brings people together instead of setting them against one another."

"You're a fool," Ryland said.

"No," Kurt said. "Just unreasonable enough to ignore the madmen on either side."

Kurt turned away from the conversation and back to the computer screen. He'd found what he needed—a detailed chart of the bay made by Ryland's people so they could get the huge ice ship in and out of the area safely. It showed plenty of submerged obstructions, including an underwater ridge three miles away.

The ridge angled sharply outward, jutting into the bay from the shoreline and running at a depth of fifty feet on average. Deep water in front made it particularly dangerous, especially as the *Goliath* was drawing seventy or eighty feet.

Kurt stepped over to the command terminal, from

which the captain would guide the ship. It was a modern system but fairly standard, like those in any large merchant ship.

The engines were already set to full ahead. The ship was doing ten knots and building toward sixteen. Not a speed demon by any means. But once something this size got moving, it would take forever to stop.

Using a control knob, Kurt adjusted the course a few degrees. The helm answered. The rudder swung off center. The huge ship of ice began a slow and shallow turn.

Even then, Kurt felt it lean. The vessel was top-heavy and unstable.

With the straightening up on its new course, Kurt kept his eyes moving. A quick glance at the screen was followed by a quick glance at the prisoners and then the hatch to make sure the handles were still locked down tight.

Operating this way, Kurt saw the whole room. What he didn't see was the captain keying the mic of a handheld radio behind his back. The man was clicking the transmit button on and off, sending a call for help to anyone who might be listening.

Two miles from the ridge, Kurt made a second small adjustment to the ship's course and then a third, more significant change. This put the *Goliath* on a line to intercept the submerged ledge.

He peered through the bridge windows, searching for any sign of the shoreline, but could barely see past the bow of the ship. A camera system gave a better view. Black water beneath a gray sky, low-lying cliffs just visible in the distance.

The speed reached thirteen knots and was rising. An alarm began flashing on the navigation screen. Blinking yellow accompanied by chirping.

It was a first-level hazard warning. The system had determined that Kurt's course would take them over the rocks.

The captain stirred first, sitting up taller. "What are you doing?"

"What is that?" Ryland asked.

"Hazard warning," the captain said. "He's running us aground."

Ryland shifted his position, getting ready to attack. Kurt turned toward him, prepared to fire if any of them got up off the floor.

As he looked their way, the latch handle on the hatchway swung up and the door flew open. A pair of Ryland's men burst in with guns in their hands.

Kurt opened fire, cutting one of them down and forcing the other one back into the passageway.

The man ducked out of sight and then aimed his weapon through the opening, pulling the trigger and spraying lead around the bridge. Kurt threw himself against the bulkhead and kicked the hatch door, slamming it on the man's arm.

The door rebounded after a sickening crack and the man bailed, falling backward and grunting in pain.

With nothing blocking the hatchway, Kurt forced it closed and slammed the handle down. As he sealed it tight, Ryland and Ober lunged for him.

They caught him at the waist, knocking into him

and taking him down. He landed on his back as Ober climbed on him.

Unable to bring the submachine gun to bear, Kurt smashed its stock into Ober's bearded face. Ober rolled away, grabbing his mouth.

Ryland reached up and gripped the barrel of the MP5 before Kurt could give him the same treatment.

The two of them fought for the weapon. Ryland got a second hand on the stock. Kurt tried to yank it free, but Ryland had reached the grip and ended up forcing Kurt's finger to compress and hold down the trigger.

The gun erupted, firing on full auto. Bullets drilled into the ceiling and ricocheted off the walls. The captain, who'd rushed to the navigation panel to try to change the ship's course, took a hit in the knee and went down.

Ober and Kurt were both hit by ricochets, while a line of bullets stitched its way across the windows fronting the bridge. One of them shattered and caved in. Cold wind began howling through the gap.

Kurt headbutted Ryland, stunning him just long enough to pull the weapon free and get his finger off the trigger. He then threw Ryland off, slid himself backward and fired at Ober as the man charged once more, bloody teeth and all.

Ober dropped to his knees and fell sideways.

With the odds back in his favor, Kurt jumped up and spun the knob on the navigation panel, turning the ship more sharply toward the cliffs.

As the *Goliath* rolled into the turn, the hatchway

swung open once again and Kurt fired his last rounds of ammunition.

The intruders ducked back once more. But with the bolt on the MP5 locked in the open position and no ammo, Kurt's ability to fight was suddenly curtailed.

With nowhere else to go, he climbed up onto the navigation terminal and dove through the shattered window.

Still in the pump room, Joe felt the *Goliath* turn once and then more sharply a second time. He sensed the ship's list increase as the starboard side grew heavier and the port side grew ever lighter.

He'd transferred five million gallons of lake water so far and the pumps were still humming. By choosing the outermost tanks to empty and fill, he'd magnified the change in list to the greatest extent possible.

The ship's outer right-hand side was now carrying forty thousand tons more than the outer left side. The ship was leaning ten degrees already and the angle was growing by the minute.

Finding some chains and a padlock, Joe rigged the setup to hold tight and then took the key with him. Moving back to the prisoners, he lowered the Norwegian sailor's gag.

"What's your name?" Joe asked.

"I'm called Björn."

"Well, Björn, you seem like a smart man," Joe said. "I assume you know what I'm trying to do here?"

"You're making the ship unstable," Björn replied. "You're going to roll us over."

"That's the general idea," Joe said. "Now, you can either be down here when it happens or watching it from a lifeboat at a safe distance."

"We have no lifeboats," the man said.

"There has to be something."

"We have runabouts," he said. "And inflatables."

Joe pulled out a knife and brandished it. "If I were you," he said, "I'd make my way to one of those." He tossed the knife a short distance from where Björn sat. "Don't waste your time trying to reverse what I've done. I've rigged it so that you'll never be able to undo it. Just get off this ship before it goes over."

With that, Joe walked to the hatch, opened it and ducked through.

Björn sat in shock for a second, staring at the watertight door. Only when one of his hog-tied comrades began grunting and nodding toward the knife did Björn spring into action.

Dropping onto his side, he inchwormed his way to the knife and then turned so he could get his hands on it.

Gripping it awkwardly, he got the blade onto the thin rope that bound his hands. He began sawing back and forth, happy to find that the knife was both serrated and extremely sharp. In ten seconds, he'd cut the rope and freed his hands. His feet took no more than a second.

Free of the bindings, he rushed back to his comrades and went to work on theirs.

The first man he cut loose was his assistant. "Free the others," Björn said, handing over the knife.

As the assistant went to work, Björn rushed to the controls Joe had tampered with. The valves were chained in the open position. The pumps running full out.

Looking for some way to reverse what Joe had done, Björn found a length of pipe and tried to use the leverage from it to break the lock.

Leaning back, he put all his weight into it. But the lock held. And the pipe slipped. It flew out of his hands and landed on the deck, clanking loudly as it struck the metal plating and then began rolling away.

"Forget about it," his assistant shouted. "We have to go."

Björn took another look and gave up. Turning away from the pumps, he made his way across the tilted deck and joined his friends at the hatch. They pulled it open, stepped through and took off down the passageway.

As they moved away, a figure stepped out of the shadows.

Joe watched them for several seconds and then began to follow. If human nature held sway, they would run to the nearest boat. Joe would follow. Where there was one boat there was bound to be another.

65

Kurt dove through the forward bridge window onto a slope designed to make the superstructure look like nothing more than a raised part of the iceberg. He slid uncontrollably for seventy feet, careening downward like a skier who'd wiped out on a particularly steep slope.

Reaching the roof of the third deck, he slid forward, came to a stop and then jumped to his feet as quickly as possible. Bullets struck the ice around him, but dressed in white, running across the snow-covered hull in the middle of a storm, Kurt made an elusive target.

Reaching the edge of the third deck, he dropped over the side and landed on the roof of deck two. Pressing his back against the ice, he was now effectively out of sight.

With a second to breathe, Kurt rummaged in his

pocket for the radio headset. Pulling it out, he placed it over his ears and switched it on. Swinging the mic close to his mouth, he switched the transmitter to the voice-activated setting.

"Joe, do you read?"

A few seconds went by.

"Come on, buddy," Kurt said. "Pick up."

Joe was following the men and women from the pump room as they raced down the passageway and charged up the stairs. They climbed five flights, gathered up a stray crewman they encountered and turned toward the stern.

Joe checked the corridor and followed.

By now, the *Goliath* was listing twenty degrees. Joe wondered how Kurt was faring and then remembered the headset.

He pulled it from his pocket and put it on.

Kurt's voice came through almost immediately. *"Don't know if you can hear me, amigo. This ship is about to meet a rock ledge in the worst possible way. Get topside, if you haven't already."*

"I'm heading aft," Joe said. "Hoping they haven't run out of boats at the local marina. Got my reservation in a little late."

"I'm trapped on the low side near the bow," Kurt replied. *"If the rental line isn't too long, come get me."*

"Will do."

The group ahead of Joe had pushed through a hatchway. Joe eased up to it and cracked it open. Inside lay a vast compartment, half filled with water. Several tenders were tied up in there along with a couple ribbed inflatables.

The scene was oddly jumbled, as the list had caused the water to flow to the low side and the boats were all bunched up.

As the others climbed aboard one of the tenders, Björn forced a lever on the wall from the closed position to open. Machinery cranked to life and the doors at the far end of the compartment began to open.

A wave of water surged in, jostling the boats and banging them against one another. The self-leveling dock rose and the boats along with it. Joe raced up the steps as Björn and his mates cut the mooring line and shoved off, pushing toward the gap.

Joe jumped into a ribbed inflatable, which he chose for its speed, maneuverability and overall toughness.

He released the line, started the outboard motor and spun the boat around.

As he finished the turn, he saw the tender lifted on a swell that had surged into the compartment. The wave pinned it against a low-hanging section of the ceiling, its roof snagging on a bundle of pipes and cables.

"You've got to be kidding me," Joe said.

Whoever was manning the tender's controls gunned the throttle. The engine revved and the prop churned the water, but the tender was caught like a truck that had gone under too low of an overpass.

Joe was considering how he might give them a push,

or otherwise free them, when the swell outside the ship turned into a trough. The water surged toward the exit, dropping rapidly and sweeping the tender out of the compartment and into the bay.

Joe had no desire to get pinned up against the overhanging pipes and cables, especially as the inflatable lacked a roof to protect his head.

He spun the inflatable in a circle as the next wave rushed in and then pointed the bow toward the exit as it pressed him up near the ceiling.

Joe raced out of the ship and turned toward the bow. "I'm on my way," he shouted into the radio. "Get as close to the edge as you can."

Bloodied and beaten, Ryland heaved the captain up to his feet. "Get control of this ship," he demanded. "We're heading for the cliffs."

"It's not the cliffs that are the problem," the captain said. "It's the rocks."

Grunting with pain, he slammed the engines into full reverse and grabbed the rudder control, pushing it as far to the left as possible.

The *Goliath* began to shudder as the rudders deflected to their stops. The nose of the ship began to swing away from the cliffs, but the turn transferred all the ship's weight and momentum to the low side of the hull.

The list worsened to thirty degrees and then forty. The ship continued toward the submerged outcropping of rock.

"Why aren't we slowing?" Ryland demanded.

The *Goliath*'s captain just stared at the screen. "We're too heavy," he said. "I'm sorry."

The ice ship ran across the submerged shelf at fifteen knots. Boulders the size of railcars were blasted loose, while similar-sized chunks of ice were carved from the bottom of the ship. The deepest part of *Goliath*'s V-shaped keel ground into the ridge and broke through it. And at a terrible cost. The heavy thruster pods and thousands of tons of ballast were scraped from the hull.

The massive weight and momentum of the huge ship allowed it to continue forward as if it were merely shrugging off the blow. The captain knew better, as he stared apoplectically out the bridge window at the tilting horizon.

Kurt felt the ship's rudder go hard over. He knew this would mean the end. The ship simply could not turn away from the danger and not capsize. Not with all its weight on one side.

The outer edge of the main deck dipped into the water. Kurt dug the spikes of his boots in and leaned back, trying to keep from sliding. His perch grew steeper and more precarious as the big ship rolled. Soon, he was back on his haunches like a man shingling a steeply pitched roof.

From the corner of his eye, he spotted an inflatable with an outboard racing toward him. It rode up on the water that was engulfing the *Goliath*'s hull.

Kurt's left foot slipped, then his right. He slid down

FAST ICE 455

the angled deck toward the water, digging his boots in at the last second and jumping for the inflatable. He landed in the bow, crashing awkwardly and staying down as Joe gunned the throttle and turned away.

Looking up, he saw the *Goliath* standing on its side, stretching upward and then leaning over like a skyscraper about to fall. It picked up speed as it sank down. Joe cut away, racing to escape the pending collapse.

B ack on the bridge, Ryland shook with rage and panic. He grabbed a pipe overhead to keep from falling. The ship was rolling.

"Do something," he shouted.

The captain didn't even respond. He just kept staring out the window.

The ship rolled past fifty degrees and then past sixty. The bulkhead wall became the floor.

The dark sea appeared through the windows. Ryland stared as it surged upward toward them and smashed home like a tsunami.

The surviving windows imploded and the seawater blasted in. The swirling water was frigid and unmerciful. It filled the compartment, battering everyone inside and forcing the air out of their lungs.

Ryland felt himself tumbling uncontrollably. He crashed into the wall and the floor and then ended up on the ceiling as the furious motion subsided. His lungs were filled with water, his eyes wide open, as his body went limp and still.

66

The storm would continue to blow for the next three days. By the time it waned, the *Providence* had arrived at the mouth of Fimbul Bay. It came upon the *Goliath*, floating, inverted, like a giant dead whale. The only thing that made it look like a ship were the red-painted propeller shafts and the broken stub of one rudder.

Kurt and Joe had set up shelter nearby, surviving the storm and guarding twenty-six members of Ryland's crew, most of whom were too cold and hungry to walk by the time they were rescued.

Kurt called in to Rudi as soon as they were on board the ship. He found that the SEAL teams and the British SAS units had done their jobs flawlessly. Liang's tankers had all been captured. All the boardings had gone without incident except one, where the captain of the ship had shot the saboteur after realizing what the man intended to do.

With Kurt and Joe safely aboard the *Providence*, a C-130 equipped with skis took off from McMurdo Station, crossing Antarctica toward Ryland's Base Zero.

Touching down on the glacier, the aircraft rumbled to a stop but kept its engines running. Three figures got off and rushed toward the habitat. Rudi Gunn led the charge, having flown from Washington in the aftermath of the operation only to be forced to wait out the storm.

He found the structure just as Kurt had described it, though now it was almost completely buried in snow.

Pushing his way inside the first module of Ryland's former base, Rudi saw no sign of life. He feared the worst. They hadn't heard from Paul or Gamay even as conditions cleared and satellite communications were restored.

"Split up," he ordered, sending the two Navy medics with him in different directions.

Each of them entered a different module, with Rudi following his nose. He smelled smoke and followed it through the building.

Pulling open an inner door, he spotted two figures lying on the floor, covered in blankets. A small fire crackled in front of them. A makeshift chimney constructed of PVC pipe evacuated the smoke through a hole in the roof above.

Neither of the figures stirred upon his arrival and Rudi stepped closer without saying a word. He touched

Gamay on the shoulder and called her name. Her eyes opened slowly. She looked pale and seemed dazed.

"Rudi," she said. "What are you doing here?"

"We came to get you," he replied. He looked to Paul, who still hadn't stirred. "Is he—"

"It's okay," Gamay said. "He's still with us."

She pulled back the blanket and revealed a line connecting her arm to Paul's. "I gave him a transfusion. I'm a universal donor. Lucky for my husband, whose blood type I should really know."

Paul opened his eyes, looked briefly at Rudi and then drifted back into unconsciousness.

"You're a miracle worker," Rudi said as the medics joined them and began to undo her work. "Now, let's get both of you out of here."

67

The Antarctic winter was beginning to set in as a small fleet finished up the salvage job around the *Goliath*.

Kurt, Joe and Rudi led the team. There were also a dozen ships on-site from various countries.

The initial effort had kept any algae that might be leaking from the ice ship from reaching the open ocean. For that reason, long floating barriers, known as booms, similar to those used to contain oil spills, were stretched around the ship in concentric rings.

Other ships housed crews that had cut into the ice, eventually allowing access to the storage tanks, which were then pumped full of sterilizing algicide. Another salvage vessel was on hand to off-load the diesel oil and other contaminants lest the ship break up and start leaking.

Ryland's body had been recovered the first week. Eighty-four others had been recovered since. According to the survivors, including Björn, the toll accounted for the entire crew.

On a short day, when the sun barely made it off the horizon, the operation was deemed complete. The salvage ships and oceangoing tugs that had come to participate in the cleanup left the bay one at a time. Soon only NUMA's *Providence* remained.

Kurt was busy breaking down the last vestiges of equipment on the shore when Rudi and Joe arrived to pick him up in an orange-hulled tender.

The bow of the small craft slid up onto the stony beach and Rudi stepped forward. "Time for us to go."

"So soon," Kurt said. He was joking of course. The frigid days and long, dark nights had made three weeks feel like an eternity.

"I have a date with Leandra," Joe said. "I'd like to make it back to Johannesburg before she forgets who I am. And if I remember rightly, you owe Lieutenant Zama and his crew a round of drinks in Cape Town."

"That's true," Kurt admitted.

"And I," Rudi said, "have to figure out how to pay for Paul and Gamay's month in the Seychelles along with a shopping spree in Milan."

Kurt gave him a sideways look.

Rudi shook his head. "Don't ask."

"Well, that should help Paul heal up at any rate," Kurt said.

"It better," Rudi told him. "In the meantime, this

ship will remain frozen in the solid ice. Six months from now we'll come back down and finish up. And when we do, I'll make sure there's something in the budget for the excavation and salvage of a certain aircraft left over from 1939."

"So the Trouts get sunshine and golden sand, and we get to dig in the ice and snow, is that it?" Kurt laughed. "I must have been born under a lucky star."

"Don't try to kid me," Rudi said. "If I didn't send you two back down here, you'd probably take all your vacation time and come south on your own. This way at least I get to keep an eye on you."

Kurt laughed again and carried the final crate of equipment to the tender. With everything packed and ready to go, he took a moment to look around. He noticed his boots firmly planted on a thin section of ice that had formed between the rocks where the water was shallow. It cracked under his feet but remained in place.

As the nights grew longer and colder, the fast ice was stretching across the bay from both shores. At the same time, sea ice was filling the sound in from the middle. He pointed out the one thing they couldn't account for. "You know, we can't be certain we've contained all the algae."

Rudi disagreed. "A hundred samples of water say otherwise. We've tested, tested and retested. No sign of algae in the bay."

"And the *Goliath*?"

"We've pumped everything out of it, surrounded the hull with rings of containment booms and used sixty thousand gallons of algicide to sterilize the tanks inside. I doubt anything has gotten past us."

Kurt nodded. He figured that was as much as they could do. "What about the samples we sent back to Washington?"

"A team of experts are studying them now," Rudi said. "It was Cora's idea that we might use the algae as a bandage to keep some of the world's glaciers from melting, at least until humanity can create a future where the environment is more stable. It'll be up to the nations of the world to decide if that's possible . . . or if it's wise. But at least we've averted one disaster."

Kurt climbed into the boat and took a seat. "Cora would have liked that," he said. "Who knows, with a little luck, she might have changed the world after all."

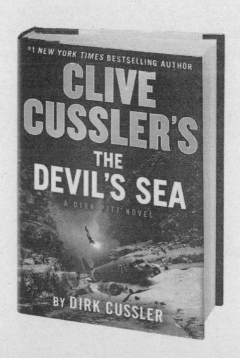

The Pratt & Whitney radial engines rasped and hunted as they struggled to inhale the high-altitude air. A pair of the venerable Twin Wasp fourteen-cylinder aircraft motors, produced by the thousands during the war, powered the unmarked C-47 transport as it buffeted through a stormy night. Absent any cargo in the rear fuselage, the plane, known as the Skytrain, was particularly susceptible to the fickle air drafts it battled above the top of the world.

"Scraping twenty-two thousand feet in altitude," Delbert Baker drawled from the copilot's seat, a toothpick dangling from his lips. Disheveled and moon-faced, he had the droopy-eyed gaze of a man who would yawn if a space alien tapped him on the shoulder. "Engines ain't too happy."

"We're well under our ceiling, even if the motors don't seem to think so," the pilot said crisply. The antithesis of his copilot, James Worthington sat upright in a clean, pressed flight suit, his grip tight on the plane's yoke. Yet he was equally impervious to the bumps and creaks of the empty cargo plane as it was knocked around the violent sky. Though unseen mountaintops passed just beneath the plane's belly, Worthington remained as calm as a man playing checkers.

Like Baker, Worthington had plenty of experience flying over the Himalayas in transports. Both had regularly flown the Hump during World War II, when the U.S. Army Air Force supplied arms and supplies to the Nationalist Chinese from bases in India. Now they flew for the CIA, but the dangers of crossing the towering mountain range in marginal weather had not lessened.

Worthington tapped a pair of red-knobbed handles protruding between their seats, assuring they were pulled fully back. The throttle quadrant controlled the engine fuel mixture. They were set to their leanest settings for the crossing of the world's tallest mountain range.

Their headsets crackled with the voice of their navigator, seated in a compartment behind them. "About twenty minutes to Lhasa. Maintain current heading."

The airplane suddenly bounced like a roller coaster flying off the rails. Baker glanced out his side window at a steady snowfall pelting the wings. "Hope our boys turn the lights on."

Worthington nodded. "They'll be hiking across the Himalayas on their own if they don't."

The plane soldiered on through the night, the pilots fighting sudden drafts that would send the craft hurtling upward. Less frequent, but more precarious, were the sharp downdrafts that struck without warning.

Soon they approached their target, and Worthington began descending, knowing the highest peaks were now behind them. Through the cold black night, a handful of lights appeared on the ground, glowing like distant candles.

"This must be the place," Baker said.

The navigator provided a new heading, and Worthington adjusted their flight path, turning over the scattered lights of Lhasa. Tibet's historic capital, it was a colorful but dusty city that stretched along the narrow Kyichu River Valley at an imposing elevation of twelve thousand feet. The country's one and only official airport lay eighty miles to the northeast, but Worthington had no intention of making a formal arrival in the Chinese-occupied territory. Instead, he guided the C-47 toward an ad hoc landing strip created for the mission by friendly locals, who had secretly cleared rocks from an open plain on the town's west side.

The snow diminished, then ceased altogether, as Worthington flew low over the city, both aviators scanning the ground through the broken cloud cover.

"There, ahead, to the right." Baker pointed out the windscreen. The toothpick in his mouth suddenly twirled, the first indication of tension.

Worthington saw it, too. A pair of faint blue lights, lined up perfectly east to west, with a long black patch between them.

Baker squinted at the distance and lowered the landing gear. "Not sure they gave us the two thousand feet we asked for."

Worthington shook his head. "Too late to argue now." He aligned the nose of the Skytrain with the nearest light and reduced speed. A brisk headwind seemed to bring the plane to a standstill, while rocking the wings. Worthington waited until the blue light disappeared beneath the nose, then called to Baker. "Landing lights."

Baker flicked on the plane's lights as the craft descended. With the skilled hand of a surgeon, Worthington countered the angry winds and eased the plane lower.

The landing lights showed a flat, dusty field as the tires kissed the ground a yard past the blue light. The C-47 bounded over the uneven surface as it slowed under Worthington's hard braking, its tail wheel licking the dust. The pilot guided the aircraft to a stop shy of the second blue light, then spun around and jostled it across the field to the first light. He turned the plane into the wind for takeoff and cut the engines.

Baker opened his side window and looked across the field. To the south were lights from several houses, but otherwise all was dark. There was no one waiting for them. "Either we're early," he said, "or our passengers are late."

"Or not arriving at all," Worthington said. "At least there was no welcoming committee waiting." He cocked an ear, then slid open his own side window. He turned to Baker with a grimace and shook his head.

Over the murmur of the gusting winds came the unmistakable popping of gunfire in the distance.

Ramapurah Chodron listened to that same gunfire arising from the city's center and cringed. If the mission had gone as planned, there'd have been no shooting. Just a quick extraction and a quiet flight out of town before the Chinese knew what happened. But the gunfire from the vicinity of Potala Palace said otherwise.

Ram, as his CIA trainers had called him, pressed his palm tight against a silenced Colt .38 and peered around a low stone wall. The Nechung Monastery a dozen yards beyond had the look of a morgue, dark and silent. But the distant shooting meant their cover had been blown and they no longer had the luxury of a patient entry.

He squinted through the darkness, but saw no movement around the structure. One of a dozen Tibetan guerrillas parachuted into a wide valley northwest of Lhasa two days earlier, Ram had been assigned to lead the easier of their missions. He guided a four-man squad to capture the Nechung Oracle, the Dalai Lama's most important spiritual advisor, and whisk him to the airfield for a flight to safety.

The more difficult task lay in the center of town. There, the remaining eight men were to sneak into the Potala Palace and extract none other than the Dalai Lama himself.

While Chinese troops had occupied Tibet since 1950,

things had heated up with the Lhasa Uprising. Emboldened insurgent attacks and rebellions around the country had culminated with demonstrations in Tibet's capital for independence. Those actions had brought swift retribution. A large contingent of Chinese armed forces had filtered into Lhasa a few days earlier, heightening tensions.

Rumors were rampant that the Chinese were about to seize the Dalai Lama, remove him from Tibet, and throw him in prison. Exiled Tibetan government leaders in India responded by consulting with their primary source of support, the CIA.

For years, the Central Intelligence Agency had been supporting exiled Tibetan leaders and providing arms to guerrillas as a means of gathering information on China's atomic bomb program. Now, with local resources hurried into action, the agency agreed that attempting to extract the Dalai Lama was worth the risk.

The Tibetans selected for the mission had a long history with the CIA. They had been flown across the globe to Colorado, where they trained in the Rocky Mountains and became paratroopers. Chodron was one of the earliest graduates, rising through the ranks due to his aptitude with field radios.

As he gripped his pistol tightly, Ram heard rumblings from an old yak wandering a field beside the monastery. It reminded him of the Hereford cattle he'd seen grazing in the mountain pastures of Colorado. He recalled with fondness his first taste of beefsteak, served at a roadside café near Vail.

He shook off that image as a fellow militant in dark camo crawled alongside and nudged his elbow.

"Looks clear in back," the man whispered.

"Okay, let's move in. Have Raj and Tagri hold position outside the entrance while we search inside."

The guerrilla nodded and relayed the message to a pair of gunmen in the shadows behind them. He followed as Ram rose to a crouch and moved to the monastery entrance.

No one knew how long the site had been deemed sacred, but the current monastery had been standing there for close to four hundred years. It was a modest structure, built at the base of the city's northern hills. Ram entered through open blood-red doors to find a large courtyard. Steps at the back led to chapels on either side, while an upper floor housed the resident monks.

A fire glowed yellow next to the left chapel, and the aroma of incense wafted through the air. Ram hugged the side wall and made his way toward the back steps. He detected a rustling from within and froze. A figure emerged onto the steps, unsteady on his feet.

It was a Chinese soldier, carrying a bolt-action rifle, which he waved in Ram's general direction. "Who's there?" he called in slurred Mandarin.

It was too dark for Ram to see the soldier's bloodshot eyes, but he was close enough to smell the alcohol on his breath. The .38 in his hand tilted upward, then spat two muffled bursts. The soldier's head snapped back, and he slumped to the ground, his rifle clattering onto the stone paving.

"Hide him," Ram whispered to his partner, who had hurried to his side.

Ram stepped toward the chapel and approached the small fire burning in a makeshift ring to keep the soldier warm. Its flames cast dancing shadows on the far end of the chapel, where an elevated altar was decorated with candles. The room appeared empty. Then a sliver of light appeared from a side stall. Ram raised his pistol and slipped behind a stone pillar as a figure approached. Ram waited until the man passed him, then jumped from behind and pressed his pistol into the intruder's back.

"Is there trouble?" the captive asked. He turned and faced Ram.

The light from his small candle revealed an elderly man with a shaved head, dressed in the red robe of a monk. Unusually broad-shouldered, he stared at Ram with calm, unblinking eyes.

Ram lowered his pistol and dropped his head in a slight bow of apology. "I seek the Nechung Oracle," he said in the monk's native Tibetan tongue.

"The Oracle is not here," the monk replied. "He went to the Potala Palace two days ago to meet with the Dalai Lama. He has not returned." The monk eyed the guerrilla's dark uniform. "You are here to help him?"

Ram nodded. "It is believed the Chinese intend to imprison the Dalai Lama and his advisors. We are here to help them escape."

The monk nodded. "The Oracle foretold of imminent danger."

A walkie-talkie on Ram's hip buzzed with a static-filled voice. "Red Deer, this is Snow Leopard. The target has departed ahead of our arrival. We are under fire. Heading to the elevator. I repeat, heading to the elevator."

"Red Deer reads affirmative," Ram replied. "We will be on our way."

Ram gritted his teeth. They were to have met up with an advance team that had parachuted in a day earlier, but they hadn't appeared at the rendezvous point.

It made sense now. Something had gone wrong. Maybe the Chinese were tipped off. The advance team had either been captured or had already shuttled the Dalai Lama out of Lhasa on foot. Ram glanced at the smoldering fire and prayed it was the latter. Either way, their own mission was now for naught.

Ram replaced the walkie-talkie and looked at the monk. "Have the Dalai Lama and the Oracle already fled Lhasa?"

The monk nodded. "I believe that to be a possibility."

"Who are you?"

"My name is Thupten Gungtsen. I am the *khenpo* for the monastery and assistant to the Oracle."

As the monastery's abbot and chief administrator, Gungtsen was a man at risk.

"You will not be safe once the Chinese discover the Dalai Lama has fled. You must come with us."

The monk gave him a contemplative gaze. "I am not important, but the Nechung Idol is."

He motioned over his shoulder to the altar. Positioned in a niche above it was a dark statue. Ram recognized it as Pehar, a Tibetan deity known also as Nechung and the namesake of the monastery. "The Oracle cannot properly perform his duties without it. The statue must be taken to him."

Ram gazed across the temple and nodded. "Quickly."

"I will need your help." Gungtsen turned on his heels. He crossed the chapel at a measured pace and halted in front of the niche. Inside, the thick stone carving stood, surrounded by an assortment of smaller statues of the same color.

Ram had visited the temple as a boy, but had never been so close to the ancient artifact. Two feet high, it was hewn from a glistening black stone. The monk knelt before the statue and started to mumble a prayer, but Ram stepped over and pulled him up. "There is no time."

The monk nodded and gathered the smaller deities together. He wrapped them in a gold cloth from the altar and passed the bundle to Ram. The guerrilla stuffed the bundle in his jacket, surprised at its heavy weight, and urged the monk to hurry.

Gungtsen wound another cloth around the Nechung Idol, then hoisted it onto his shoulder. "I am ready."

They exited the chapel, joining the second guerrilla in the courtyard. As they exited the monastery's front entrance, a single gunshot sounded from a few feet away. Across the wide dirt street, an armed man in green staggered from the shadows and slumped to the ground.

The guerrilla named Tagri poked his head from behind a shrub, clutching an M1 carbine. "He was a point man for a patrol coming this way."

His words were confirmed when a deep yell echoed down the street, followed by the crunching of boots on gravel.

"The Oracle is not here," Ram said. "We must evacuate to the airfield."

"What about the enemy patrol?" Tagri asked.

"We take care of them here."

Ram grabbed the monk by the arm and pulled him behind a pillar. He thrust his pistol around the curved stonework and aimed the Colt at the far end of the street. Behind him, the monk crouched low and began whispering a chant.

The Chinese patrol was small, just three young men clutching Russian-made rifles. Their lack of training showed when they all rushed to their fallen comrade, encircling him with their guns aimed high.

Ram didn't pause for their foolishness. He aimed his .38 at the soldier nearest him and squeezed off three rounds. The first struck the man in the shoulder, while the second two missed.

But it didn't matter. The other Tibetans opened up with their carbines, cutting down all three Chinese soldiers in a flurry.

Ram tugged on the sleeve of the monk. "Come this way."

He waited for the monk to retrieve the Idol. Stepping from the monastery, Ram led them past the bodies as the other guerrillas took up a loose perimeter around them.

Nechung Monastery stood on a low rise in the northwest edge of Lhasa. The improvised airfield was just about due east, beyond a range of open hills. While a direct line would have been shorter, Ram didn't want to get caught by a superior force out in the open. Intelligence had told them that in the past few days, a full battalion of Chinese People's Liberation Army soldiers had been transported to Lhasa.

Following the dirt road, he led the group down the hillside to the cover of the city landscape on the lower flats. To the southeast, where the large Potala Palace stood on a rocky rise, heavy gunfire sounded. Ram hoped the battle there would draw any Chinese away from their path.

Reaching a side street lined with shops and dwellings, they turned and followed it east. At that late hour, the street was dark and empty. The group moved at a fast clip, ever on the lookout for enemy soldiers. The monk, ignoring the heavy burden on his shoulder, moved with quiet urgency.

At the sound of an approaching vehicle, the group ducked for cover in the closest doorways. A Chinese military truck approached at high speed with a half dozen soldiers clinging to the fenced sides of its bed.

Ram felt the monk squeeze next to him in the doorway of a fabric shop and noted the man's rugged frame beneath his robe. "You are not from Lhasa," Ram whispered.

"No, a small village in Amdo."

"You are Golok?"

The monk nodded.

Ram knew the area and the tribal inhabitants who lived there. The Golok were known as the toughest people in Tibet, and Ram could see why.

The truck rumbled past them in a hurry elsewhere. Ram glanced at his watch as the dust raised by the vehicle's thick tires settled to the ground. The guerrilla team was late for their rendezvous.

"Let's go," he said. "We need to pick up the pace."

The team moved at a run, crossing several blocks. The buildings fell away on their left, exposing open fields that extended to the foot of the neighboring mountains. Gunfire still sounded from the distance, but it had moved from the southwest to directly ahead of them.

Ram turned to exit the streets and make for the open hills to his left. He led his team up a rocky rise, each man breathing hard. Gungtsen struggled at the rear with his cargo, but managed to keep apace. Clearing the crest of a rocky rise, they reached a flat plain. Ahead, Ram spotted a blue light.

They heard the grinding of an aircraft motor turning over and whirring to life, followed by a second one. Several muzzle flashes and accompanying pops from beyond the light told him it would be a race for their lives.

A second blue light came into sight as they hustled over the barren mound, then a faint light appeared in the aircraft's interior. The gunfire grew louder as they approached the C-47.

"Can you make it?" Ram asked the monk.

The statue weighed heavily on the old man, but the quiet monk replied in a strong voice. "Yes."

As the group reached the long plain used as an airfield, the wind blew light sleet that needled their backs. Near the distant blue light, they could both see and hear the C-47. Wisps of smoke streamed from the engines' nacelles as Worthington and Baker readied the plane for takeoff. A small group of men crowded around the open fuselage door and climbed in as the plane began to move.

Ram's walkie-talkie crackled. "Red Deer. We're at the departure point. We must leave now. Where are you?"

"Approaching now," Ram shouted. "Hold the plane." He turned to his team. "Run for it."

The guerrillas broke formation and sprinted for the plane. Ram held back to accompany the monk a few yards behind. Despite his burden, Gungtsen showed surprising fleetness, just about holding his own with the other men.

As they drew closer to the plane, muzzle flashes burst through the darkness from the far end of the field. A half dozen Chinese soldiers had crested the end of the field and begun firing at the plane. No one had to tell Ram's men to run faster, as bullets peppered the ground around them.

The last guerrilla from the other team, waiting his turn to climb aboard, dropped beneath the wing and provided covering fire, silencing several of the Chinese guns. It was enough to allow the three men from Ram's team to approach the doorway and scamper aboard.

Ram and Gungtsen were almost to the plane's tail

when the monk tripped and fell, the Nechung Idol bounding off his shoulder ahead of him.

"Are you hit?" Ram yelled over the roar of the engines. He stopped and pulled Gungtsen up by his arm.

"No, I fell."

"Get on the plane. I'll get the statue."

He pushed the monk ahead, then reached to retrieve the temple artifact. The C-47's Twin Wasps howled as Worthington throttled up for takeoff. A blaze of dust and snow blew onto Ram as he shouldered the Idol. As he rose to his feet, the plane began pulling away. The monk had just reached the doorway and was yanked inside as the plane accelerated.

Ram ran after the aircraft, struggling with the Idol's weight. He couldn't believe the old monk had carried it all the way from the monastery without complaint. It was heavy, much heavier than it appeared. Its weight crushed the movement of Ram's legs as if he were mired in a pool of molasses.

But he had to move, and fast, as the C-47 was accelerating away from him. He squinted through the blowing dust, but could still see the flicker of muzzle flashes from the end of the airfield. The plane's engines roared in his ears as Ram summoned all his strength to run. With a labored effort, he sprinted alongside the fuselage. As he approached the open door, he flung the statue through the opening.

He nearly tripped at the effort, but regained his footing as the plane outpaced him.

Tagri appeared in the doorway. "Come on, Rama-purah, you can do it," he yelled.

Ram felt like collapsing, yet summoned a last burst of energy and flung himself at the door as the plane's tail bounded from the ground. His fingers grasped the sill and he started to slip, but Tagri and another guerrilla grabbed his sleeves and pulled him inside.

CLIVE
CUSSLER

"Clive Cussler is just about the best
storyteller in the business."
—*New York Post*

For a complete list of titles and to sign up for our
newsletter, please visit prh.com/CliveCussler